Kane's eyebrows rose. "Hangar."

"Where the Mother Ship is kept." Jonny frowned again slightly, this time in obvious perplexity instead of disapproval for Kane's coldhearted interrogation technique.

"Except he keeps throwing in the word for blimp. Airship, anyway. Now what on Earth d'you think he means by that?"

It was a giant delta, matte-black, was what he meant. Giant, as in its rounded wings were as easily broad as an old-style American football field from wingtip to blunt wingtip. Although it did not possess discrete wings so much as it seemed to *be* a wing. A vast, fat, bloated wing, mounding to impressive height in the center before tapering away both sides. It rested in a cradle like the keel and spars for Noah's Ark done up in gleaming alloy, held in place by what appeared to be hinged clamps.

"It's a *mother* ship," Tyree said. "That's for dinkum sure."

Other titles in this series:

James Axler
Outlanders

ULURU
DESTINY

A GOLD EAGLE BOOK FROM
W💥RLDWIDE®

TORONTO • NEW YORK • LONDON
AMSTERDAM • PARIS • SYDNEY • HAMBURG
STOCKHOLM • ATHENS • TOKYO • MILAN
MADRID • WARSAW • BUDAPEST • AUCKLAND

To Mike and Karly. I'm back and you helped. Thanks.

First edition November 2004

ISBN 0-373-63844-2

ULURU DESTINY

Special thanks and acknowledgment to Victor Milán
for his contribution to this work.

We all carry within us seeds of the Transcendent which,
the good no less than the ill, 'twere fatal to suspect.
—Z. Rickard Jondemeer, Eleusis, 1843

The Road to Outlands—
From Secret Government Files to the Future

Almost two hundred years after the global holocaust, Kane, a former Magistrate of Cobaltville, often thought the world had been lucky to survive at all after a nuclear device detonated in the Russian embassy in Washington, D.C. The aftermath—forever known as skydark—reshaped continents and turned civilization into ashes.

Nearly depopulated, America became the Deathlands—poisoned by radiation, home to chaos and mutated life forms. Feudal rule reappeared in the form of baronies, while remote outposts clung to a brutish existence.

What eventually helped shape this wasteland were the redoubts, the secret preholocaust military installations with stores of weapons, and the home of gateways, the locational matter-transfer facilities. Some of the redoubts hid clues that had once fed wild theories of government cover-ups and alien visitations.

Rearmed from redoubt stockpiles, the barons consolidated their power and reclaimed technology for the villes. Their power, supported by some invisible authority, extended beyond their fortified walls to what was now called the Outlands. It was here that the rootstock of humanity survived, living with hellzones and chemical storms, hounded by Magistrates.

In the villes, rigid laws were enforced—to atone for the sins of the past and prepare the way for a better future. That was the barons' public credo and their right-to-rule.

Kane, along with friend and fellow Magistrate Grant, had upheld that claim until a fateful Outlands expedition. A displaced piece of technology…a question to a keeper of the archives…a vague clue about alien masters—and their world shifted radically. Suddenly, Brigid Baptiste, the archivist, faced summary execution, and Grant a quick termination. For Kane there was forgiveness if he pledged his unquestioning allegiance to Baron Cobalt and his unknown masters and abandoned his friends.

But that allegiance would make him support a mysterious and alien power and deny loyalty and friends. Then what else was there?

Kane had been brought up solely to serve the ville. Brigid's only link with her family was her mother's red-gold hair, green eyes and supple form. Grant's clues to his lineage were his ebony skin and powerful physique. But Domi, she of the white hair, was an Outlander pressed into sexual servitude in Cobaltville. She at least knew her roots and was a reminder to the exiles that the outcasts belonged in the human family.

Parents, friends, community—the very rootedness of humanity was denied. With no continuity, there was no forward momentum to the future. And that was the crux—when Kane began to wonder if there *was* a future.

For Kane, it wouldn't do. So the only way was out—way, way out.

After their escape, they found shelter at the forgotten Cerberus redoubt headed by Lakesh, a scientist, Cobaltville's head archivist, and secret opponent of the barons.

With their past turned into a lie, their future threatened, only one thing was left to give meaning to the outcasts. The hunger for freedom, the will to resist the hostile influences. And perhaps, by opposing, end them.

Prologue

As the desert world of the great landmass beneath the Southern Cross held its breath in anticipation of the dawn, the little girl waited patiently.

To all appearances she appeared an unexceptional little girl. Perhaps seven years old, squatting on a flat, slightly tilted rock slab, her elbows braced on skinny brown thighs. She wore a ragged smock that had long ago taken on the color of the sere reddish brown land that stretched around her. She held a small, vaguely humanoid effigy, twisted together of rags so old and grease-impregnated they had virtually fused together, clamped beneath one tiny arm. Her constant companion, the effigy had little knot-nubs for ears on either side of its round, featureless head.

Beneath a mad mass of ropy curls, dark brown with a hint of auburn, the girl's little face was a study in serene concentration as she watched the space, darker within darkness, beneath a tumble of flat boulders. Most humans would call her pretty, even those whose beauty image did not fit well with the strong features characteristic of her folk, which she herself possessed, albeit in child form. But she wasn't giving that, or them, any thought.

Perhaps she was extraordinary in her stillness. But she was concentrating. It had a purpose.

A band of yellow silhouetted ridges to the east. The dark

star-scattered sky above, the tortured land below, seemed to undergo a subtle but sudden phase transition. All was about to change, and something already had.

Something, more, had sensed that change.

First she felt it stir, through her bare feet pressed to the rock with toes splayed. Then she heard it, a dry rustling and scraping.

And then she saw it as it emerged into the night, which had not long to live.

It moved by slapping the rock before it with its huge splayed claws and dragging its dry belly and great wide tail along behind, pushing with clawed hind limbs as if swimming across the rock instead of walking. It blinked great sunflower eyes and sampled the suddenly freshening wind with a flicking forked tongue.

The vast head turned toward her, trailing flags of pale wattle from the bottom of its lower jaw. It sensed her, right enough. Its eyes made out the hump of vague lightness against a sky that had not yet begun to lighten except along its lower eastern seam. Its restless tongue brought particles of mammal scent to receptors within its mouth.

It was *megalania,* a monitor lizard, more than five meters long from blunt snout to the dagger tip of its tail, and weighing more than a metric ton.

After the nuclear devastation of roughly two hundred sun cycles before, certain types of animal had grown to enormous sizes. *Megalania* was not one. It had always been this large—this one, a male with a missing toe on its right hind foot, had taken fifty years to grow this large and would grow larger as it continued to live and feed. Its kind had ruled this desert island continent, vying for meat with giant flightless predatory birds and carnivorous kangaroos. Those rivals had vanished, long before the nukecaust.

Megalania had vanished, too—but only from the eyes of humankind. Its numbers had dwindled, had begun to dwindle millennia ago when the upstart hairless apes arrived to compete with it and the hunting birds and killer marsupials. But it had never died completely away. It had simply stayed sheltered, as this one had against the night, hidden among the rocks.

For a moment it watched the small mammalian creature watching it. It hungered. And this creature fit the profile of prey.

The creature knew the hairless apes could kill it. But this one was too small.

Yet the lizard didn't stir. It was sluggish, its metabolism running off the last of the heat it had stored during the sun's reign the previous day. Its bulk held heat well, shed it slowly, especially with earth and rock around to insulate it. But its size could also be a lethal disadvantage: if it stayed too long under the direct eye of the sun, now that the hot time of year was beginning, its blood could literally begin to boil where it ran near the surface of its thick yet fine-scaled skin. Its daytime life was a dance of sun and shade. And hunting, of course.

Sensing dawn's advent perhaps in the shifting of the wind—or perhaps, within, simply *knowing*—it had issued forth despite what to it was life-sapping chill. For the very first rays of dawn, feeble and slanting, would begin to reenergize it, restore mobility to its limbs and keenness to its senses with little risk of lethal overheating. This, then, was prime hunting time: the beginning of day.

Still, it was sluggish with chill and sleep. The little prey was near, and showed no fear. Yet the monster lizard did not launch itself with the last of the energy stored within its vast body—and there was enough, if little more. Nor did it slash with giant jaws, rimmed with teeth like shards of broken glass, and moreover toxic to warmbloods by reason of the by-products of the microorganisms that dwelled in its mouth, feeding off the rotting shreds and sinews of its former meals. And then clamp, and hold, and wait, should the prey be slow to cease its struggles.

Beyond the boulder jumble and its guardian monster, beyond the red desert and the purple-blue-black mountains, rose a brilliant point of light, blue-white. This was Lilga, in the language of the people who dwelled here: the Morning Star.

The little girl smiled to greet it. She was also Lilga.

The huge reptile stared at her a moment more. Then it turned away its vast and ominous face and dragged itself laboriously off, skin hissing on sandstone, to seek elsewhere for its breakfast.

Lilga watched, happily fascinated, until the immense beast vanished with a final flourish of its sharp-tipped tail. Then she stood and stretched, and ran back toward where her people were gathered. Because little girls, like big lizards, got powerfully hungry of a morning.

A mile before her the great rock Uluru caught the sun's first direct rays and took crimson fire to start another day.

Chapter 1

For the first time since the Program of Unification's final victory, intrusion-alert Klaxons blared within the sterile confines of the Palladiumville Monolith's upper levels. Men encased in shiny black-beetle armor carapaces began to move purposefully, guns gripped in polycarbonate-gauntleted hands.

Elsewhere confusion ruled. Within the disciplined ambit of baronial ville life, periodic drills were regularly scheduled for every conceivable emergency up to and including evacuation of the upper levels. No such plans were considered necessary for the population of the Tartarus Pits below each ville. The Pit dwellers were considered thoroughly expendable assets, to the extent they were considered "assets" at all. However, over the decades adherence to that schedule had slipped slightly. The prospect of someone unauthorized actually finding his or her way into the upper stories of the gleaming white Administrative Monolith seemed remote at best.

Yet now it was happening.

And not just within one of the four subsidiary Enclave towers in which most of the privileged few actual citizens lived, but within the gleaming white stone phallus of the monolith itself, thrusting three hundred feet into a hot blue summer sky feathered with clouds by the winds off Lake Erie. Indeed, according to the light blinking in the command center of the Magistrate Division on Cappa Level, the intrusion was taking place in a storage area of the Historical Division, one floor above.

Just one floor beneath the sacrosanct aerie of Baron Palladium himself.

"Quit your bitching, Hendrix," snarled the commander of the Magistrate ready squad as he headed down a Cappa Level corridor with alarms blaring from the walls. He slammed home the bolt of his Copperhead on a gleaming silver 4.85 mm cartridge.

"But this is bogus, Senior Magistrate," Hendrix said. He carried his black hard-contact helmet in the crook of his arm. His tow hair was a thatch at just the limit of regulation length. "This is supposed to be an easy pull."

It was. Palladiumville Mags were no softer than the men of any other barony's Magistrate Division. But they had limits that even their unsympathetic superiors had recognized. The half-dozen men on the internal-alert response team had spent too long on high-stress hard-contact details, either patrolling the Tartarus Pits, named for the caverns below Hell, where Zeus imprisoned the overthrown Titans, or the Outlands beyond the barony's high walls.

Which were worse than Hell.

Palladiumville's environs were especially brutal: the Great Lakes region had taken a pounding during the nukecaust. While it hadn't received the same degree of thermonuclear scourging as the east coast, it still boasted plenty of lethal hot zones. Much of the rest of the area was a nightmare of urban and industrial wreckage, a jungle of concrete and structural steel that provided a fertile environment and excellent cover for the nastiest kind of Outlands scum: Dregs, Roamers, taints and the very nastiest kinds of mutants, scabbies and stickies and even more exotic horrors. The trashed cities and industrial zones had provided a wonderland of hiding places from the genocidal campaign the nine barons had waged against muties following the Program of Unification.

Despite the fact that the Mags were, by design, the baddest boys on the block, with the best armor, the heaviest firepower and lethal, well-protected support vehicles like Deathbird attack choppers and Sandcat FAVs to lay serious and immediately lethal hurt upon all who challenged the authority of their baronial masters, the desperate hell-scum swarming in the Pits were dangerous. Even to Mags cased in their distinctive, near indestructible, black hard-contact armor.

And the stonehearts and literal monsters in the Outlands were a hundred times worse. Service in either environment took a brutal toll on even the most case-hardened Magistrates. They had to be rotated regularly to lower-intensity assignments, even if for short periods of time.

Not that the barons and their administrative subordinates were tempted to allow their human pit bulls too much downtime. So what better way to give them a break than by keeping them ready to answer an alarm that, in over three generations, had never sounded?

"Fuck the luck, anyway," Hendrix grumbled.

"Clamp the chow-lock and put your damn hat on," Senior Mag Laydon snarled.

"What've we got, boss?" asked Creedy, a wiry light-skinned black who was the tallest man in the Palladium Mag Division. His helmet was secured and he spoke over the trans-comm channel.

His mouth, visible below the sweep of his visor, twitched periodically. Ten days before something resembling a four-foot-wide blend of pitcher plant and Venus flytrap had suddenly clamped down on the upper half of his partner,

Montañez, while they hunted Roamers in the trashed-out sub-
urb of Shaker Heights, almost in view of the monolith. The
plant had drawn Creedy's partner into itself. Creedy had
promptly pulled his buddy out of the giant tangle of green and
bilious vegetation, but all he got back was Montañez's hips
and legs.

Mag life's a bitch, Hendrix thought, and then you get dissolved by some fucking acid-generating plant.

"Intel has an unauthorized database access from a computer terminal in Archival Storage 23-Bravo," Laydon said.
Pointing to Marchetta and Dorsey to cover with their blasters, he led the way up the stairs to the level above, Copperhead in hand. Whatever else he was, Laydon was no coward.

"Who'd be triple stupe enough to get vidded waltzing down
the hall and busting into a damn storage room?" asked Hendrix, who had his helmet on now and was on the net, too.

At the door to Bravo Level, Laydon turned. He showed a
nasty grin beneath the dark-tinted visor of his helmet. "Nobody," he said.

"What do you mean?" Nguyen asked.

"I mean the vid pickups show no one entered the room."

"Then who the hell's inside?" Hendrix asked.

"Who the fuck knows? Nobody ever put a cam in the storeroom itself. Why waste Mag time watching a bunch of crap
dug out of the rubble moldering on shelves, when we could
be kicking doors and busting heads?"

The Klaxons died as he held his forearm so a scanner beside the landing's blast- and fireproof door could read the identichip planted beneath his skin. Hendrix was glad; that
merciless rhythmic racket was giving him a migraine and just
generally getting on his tits. The door swung open with the
slight hiss of an airtight seal losing integrity. Bullpup Cop-

perhead ready in both hands, Laydon stepped through and to one side, quickly clearing the doorway's so-called fatal funnel.

Laydon was a twenty-year Mag and hadn't gotten that way by taking shit for granted. Somebody *had* gotten into the Historical Division storage compartment. The only way in was through the corridor. Therefore the best bet was that the cams in the corridor had been jobbed, probably by a tech—and if that had been done by anybody but the perp or perps now doing the deed, Laydon would be more than happy to personally bang on as many technicians as needful to get the true ungarbled word. And if the corridor surveillance had been compromised, there might just be bad guys awaiting them outside the storeroom.

There weren't. As Nguyen and Creedy burst through and took up kneeling positions, Nguyen in front of Laydon and the beanpole Mag on the other side of the door, the senior Magistrate could clearly see the corridor was empty, the door to 23-B shut.

Laydon gestured. Taitt and Hendrix, his posture and the whole way he moved eloquent of resentment, trotted down to secure the corridor from the far side of 23-B down. Marchetta and Dorsey took up positions flanking the door, their Copperheads tipped toward the sound-deadening acoustic-tile ceiling. Creedy and the dubious Hendrix stationed themselves at the door proper.

Laydon strode after them, as tall and ominous as an avenging god, the sound-sucking properties of ceiling and wall material absorbing the heavy falls of his polycarbonate-armored boots. He took up position behind the two Mags waiting to go in.

"Now let's see who the smart-asses are," he rumbled. Once again he used his identichip to activate the door-opening mechanism.

The door slid aside with a swish. A scent of dust and age wafted out to the Mags, quivering with something they hoped Laydon would take for eagerness. Inside stood ranks of racks of stamped metal shelves. They bowed under the weight of a myriad assortment of objects, some encased in plastic, others just in dust, pieces of equipment, unidentifiable junk, old tools covered with cancerous growths of rust; weird embryos, some human, some vaguely so, some not even, floating in murky fluid in fat glass vessels; a head, a skull rather, that came to a weird point high and in back and then slanted down to where the neck used to be, with tufts of mouse-colored hair still straggling from parts of it, and a humanlike arrangement of staring-empty eye sockets and nostril holes crowded way down on the front.

"Shit," murmured Marchetta, who had slipped through and taken up a standing position flanking the door to the left. His partner, Dorsey, knelt to the right. "Place creeps me out."

"Can the chatter on the net," Laydon snarled. He stood contemptuously framed in the doorway, ignoring procedure and sense, as if daring the intruders to try to shoot it out with him.

Fused-out fuck, thought Hendrix. The tow-headed Mag gave his back a hate look.

The far wall had display cases filled with more weird, inexplicable crap running along the base. From a quick briefing as they suited up in the ready room Hendrix knew the workstation in unauthorized use was on that wall to the left, out of sight behind the silent shelves of relics from the two centuries of misery and desolation that followed the nukecaust—and beyond, rumor said, maybe tens of thousands of years, speaking voicelessly of secrets it was death to know.

The Archivist Division types all went around as if they had corncobs stuck up their butts. But behind their prissy exteriors, Hendrix knew, they were all fused solid. In the locker rooms and commissary of the Palladiumville Mag Division it was said that everybody born into Archives got a termination warrant filed along with the birth certificate. They either went crazy or reached a point at which they just knew too much. In either case the boys in black paid them a visit, sooner or later. Life in Archives sucked almost as bad as life as a Mag.

Yet Hendrix knew full well either life was better than being a crawling subservient tech, and that in turn was worlds ahead of being one of the human rats and maggots pullulating in the Pits below their booted feet. And it would be insulting vermin to compare the Outlands scum to them: they were more like the black crud that grew in toilets that weren't cleaned often enough—something else that seemed to be happening around the ville more these days, or so Hendrix perceived.

In sum, life sucked if you were Magistrate Hendrix, but it sucked worse for most everybody else. This had led him to the conclusion that life sucked. It was the nearest he had ever come to philosophy.

The top Mag took a couple of slow steps into the room, clearing the way for the rest of the squad to enter. Creedy and Hendrix looked at each other. Hendrix suspected the lean, looming black man was as glad as he was their hard-contact visors hid almost all of his expression.

"You first," Creedy's visible lips said soundlessly.

"No, you," Hendrix shot back the same way.

"You!"

"No, *you!*"

"Fucking *move,* ladies," Laydon snarled, "or I'll start handing out some extra assholes—"

A young woman walked around the corner from between shelves into the main aisle that ran from the open door to the display cases at the rear. She was short, dark skinned, dressed in blue jeans and a dark pullover, with a knit cap pulled down over a mass of brown curls. Her features were odd, emphatic, blunt with a broad nose. She had them tipped down toward a clipboard she was carrying.

Laydon shot her.

She just glanced up from her pad. Her eyes were big and tawny gold. She saw the Mags before her in their gleaming armor and her jaw dropped. Then muzzle flame jetted yellow from the muzzle brake of Laydon's Copperhead with a shattering noise.

As if by magic a handful of red holes dotted the front of the young woman's woolly-looking blouse. She staggered back as the tiny slugs lanced through her. The clipboard fell with a winging of white sheets to clatter on the floor. Then she collapsed as if melting in fast motion, flinging out an arm and knocking a rack of shelves.

Loud sounds crashed out like gunshot echoes as nameless objects fell off the shelves. "Yow, shit!" Nguyen exclaimed, jumping at the noise.

"Didn't we want to question her, Senior Magistrate?" Nguyen asked.

For a moment Hendrix thought Laydon would blast him, too. He was on the edge, like the rest of the ready squad.

"We got a vermin infestation," the senior Mag snarled. "We clear it out. Later we ask questions. Okay, now—"

At the far end of the aisle an eerie blue glow sprang into existence. It grew brighter.

"What the fuck?" Laydon asked.

A man stepped into view. He was indistinct, surrounded by a globe of blue radiance. Rings of pale yellow light rippled through the glow.

Even Senior Magistrate Laydon had allowed his blaster to fall offline as he stared at the extraordinary spectacle. Now with an inarticulate snarl he tried to snap it up for a burst.

Too late. From an object in the figure's hand a white line lanced out of the center of the blue glow. It struck almost dead center of the contoured polycarbonate breastplate of Laydon's armor.

It smashed the man backward into Creedy, who had gotten jammed up in the doorway with Hendrix when Laydon chilled the woman. The senior Mag's breastplate shattered like a clay pot struck with a hammer. His rib cage unfolded outward like two halves of a gate, gouting reeking steam. It seemed as if a miniature blue sun burned momentarily within his opened chest.

The white line went out. Laydon's big body, what was left of it, sagged. Creedy was dragged downward with him. Laydon's armor had been flash-welded to the front of Creedy's own breastplate. Staring down at his stricken superior in uncomprehending horror, Hendrix saw that the ends of the dead man's splayed ribs were glowing white, cooling to yellow before his eyes.

Bent half over, Creedy looked up. His mouth was so far open it looked as if his chin might just rip its way out of his face and flee floorward at any second. "Uh," he said. *"Uhhhh!"*

A second beam, surrounded by blue nimbus, reached out and touched the center of Creedy's visor with a sound like thunder. Hendrix felt his hair stand on end.

Creedy's helmet and head exploded.

Hendrix threw himself to the side. Nobody had yet shot back. The blond Mag went right across the sights of Dorsey's blaster.

Marchetta fired. The blue globe was already collapsing onto the man as he stepped back into the shelter of the crowded shelves. The kneeling Mag blasted through his whole 15-round box without easing off the trigger as Dorsey screamed curses at Hendrix for fouling his own shot.

Whether from fear of hitting any of the putatively valuable doodads stacked on the shelves—not knowing what kind of relics Baron Palladium might treasure more than a mere human life, even the life of one of his elite Magistrates—or out of sheer brain-fused panic, Marchetta did not so much as twitch the blaster's barrel left to follow the man with the weird energy blaster. Instead he blew the display cases against the far wall into a blizzard of glass fragments and knocked the objects therein to pieces.

Hendrix was huddling between a row of shelves and the front wall of the storeroom. His nut sac contracted as he saw the horrid blue glow appear again. Then Dorsey's left shoulder vanished to another blinding-white stab and lesser globe of blue. Dorsey bellowed and toppled to his right, firing his Copperhead mindlessly into the ceiling as another thunderclap assailed Hendrix's ears.

Marchetta was torn apart in the process of trying to fumble a fresh magazine into the well behind his blaster's pistol grip.

Hendrix heard voices in his ears—presumably Taitt and Nguyen, still out in the corridor, demanding to know what the hell was going on. Hendrix's mind wouldn't process the inputs his ears delivered. He was nearly catatonic from panic.

Artifacts danced and sparked and toppled or shattered in place as both the Mags in the hall stuck their blasters one-handed around the door frame from either side and cut loose, firing blind.

Dropping his own Copperhead, Hendrix clapped both

gauntlets to the sides of his head as if to shield his ears and screamed.

For the roar of mindless panic in his ears he could hear nothing. Not even himself. But he saw even through jammed-shut lids the horrible blue glow, twined with writhing serpents of light, and the hell beams that stabbed out, burning through the storeroom's metal walls as if they were plastic sheets, reaching out to touch Taitt and Nguyen where they fired from what they thought was cover. He felt the thunder rattle in his bones.

And then the glow was gone, and the terrifying God's-hammer crash of the mystery blaster. Hendrix crouched, howling and cowering, waiting for the horrible intruder to come and finish him.

But he didn't come.

Hendrix was still screaming voicelessly when Mag Division reinforcements arrived.

Chapter 2

Heavy-machine-gun fire smashed khaki chips and dust from the boulder next to Brigid's left calf. Tiny fragments stung her cheek. A ricocheting copperjacket round from a USMG-73 tugged at her flame-colored hair as it moaned past.

She dropped prone. "Are you all right, Baptiste?" demanded her companion from a cleft in the sand-colored boulders a few yards up ahead.

She glared at him. A strand of hair had come free from the bun she had tied it in—possibly plucked loose by the bullet—and was sweat-glued to her high forehead. "I'm fine, Kane," she snarled. "Why shouldn't I be fine?"

He showed her a wolf's grin through a couple days' salt-and-pepper stubble that fuzzed his handsome scarred face. "You volunteered."

"Not originally," she reminded him grimly. Like him—like most of the Cerberus complement except the Moonies from Manitius Base—she had been manipulated by the redoubt's director, Dr. Mohandas Lakesh Singh. Set up, not to put too fine an edge on it, so that she had no choice but leave her not exactly comfortable but prestigious position as senior archivist in the barony of Cobaltville for the exciting and diverting life of a renegade, rebel, outlander scum. "But when did you ever know me to hang back?"

"Never once, Baptiste," he said with frank appreciation. "Never once. Now haul it or lose it."

He glanced down at the smaller, slimmer woman hunkered down in cover by his booted feet. She had round spectacles and graying blond hair cut close to bone. "It's okay," he said encouragingly. "We always talk to each other like this."

Another burst of heavy-machine-gun fire snarled. This one sounded different. It originated from the Sandcat that had brought them here and now lay at the base of the cliff, immobilized by a shattered track.

"Grant," Kane said for the benefit of his trans-comm, "get the hell out of there."

"You claim point man's right to lead off," his partner's voice came back. "So let me bring up the rear."

"You're going to be bringing up wildflowers in a shallow grave if you don't get your rear out of there."

"Then don't let my sacrifice be in vain. Haul."

Kane frowned. It would be out of character for Grant to throw his life away on a rat's-ass mission like this, even if it had turned, true to form, into what the two privately termed a "classic one-percenter."

Of course, Grant was a man who did what was necessary, like Kane himself, and both of them knew violence had a way of striking you down when you least expected it. Neither man expected death in bed, nor ever had, but each understood, without much appreciating the fact, that he might not go down in a blaze of glory fighting some grand noble battle, but chilled in some sordid little skirmish for nothing much, or even by accident....

No, Kane told himself. You're thinking too much again. His longtime partner had been acting strange lately. But not so strange that he had lost his dry, if infrequent, brand of humor.

The big man had a plan, Kane decided...and Baptiste was being a bad influence on Kane.

A machine-gun burst crashed like thunder over his head. He ducked into a crouch beside the woman they had come to these western isles of the Cific Coast to rescue. "Regretting signing on to this fused-out outfit yet?"

Her eyes were as watery pale as the sky above, and huge behind the thick round lenses of her glasses. Two round spots of pink shone high up on thin, otherwise colorless cheeks. "You'll probably think I'm crazy myself, Mr. Kane," she said in a small voice. "But no. I'm having the time of my life, however this turns out."

He shook his head. His shaggy hair was dark but brushed lightly with strands of gray. "You are crazy, and it's just Kane. But I will say you definitely have balls."

He was going to say more. But there was a sharp heaven-splitting crack from the desert below, and his heart leaped into his throat as he turned to see the unmistakable black smoke of a burning fighting vehicle rolling into a cloudless sky.

SALLY WRIGHT WAS, as Brigid Baptiste had once been, an archivist in one of the nine baronies—in this case Snakefish-ville, on the Cific Coast. She had called the attention of Dr. Lakesh to herself by the simple expedient of sending him an encrypted e-mail.

It had provoked quite the stir in Cerberus, not least within the two-hundred-plus-year-old breast of Lakesh himself. For a long time after his unfreezing he had played a double role: that for which he had been removed from cryogenic suspension, serving as science and technical adviser to the barons in the interests of the shadowy Archon Directorate on the one hand. But, atoning for the limitless evil he had helped them unleash on suffering humanity, he secretly created and headed a resistance to those barons—and to the Archons.

Toward that latter end, now his true purpose in life, he had recommissioned Cerberus redoubt, hidden away among the peaks of the Bitterroots. For years he had lived and worked a double life, carefully cloaking his public persona—that known to the barons—in mystery, so that his protracted absences would attract small notice. So he had contrived to route messages sent to him covertly and untraceably to Bravo redoubt, the once and future Cerberus, which so far as the barons and their minions knew was lost and derelict, forgotten.

Even though the barons had discovered Lakesh's perfidy, as they saw it, the intel departments of their Magistrate Divisions had never tumbled to his secret communications. Nor could their magic Mnemosyne cipher-busting devices have enabled them to read his mail if they had: Lakesh had written the Syne himself, and like any prudent programmer had not neglected to write in back doors and loopholes he, and only he, could take advantage of.

His crypt, anyway, was still safe: the message he had received from Sally Wright was in a special baronial cipher, also immune to Syne. Deciphering the message had been trivial. The message itself, in a few text bytes, had rocked his world. He had in fact declined to reveal its actual contents to his operators.

Although Lakesh was no longer the unquestioning dictator of Cerberus redoubt and the resistance, he still pretty much ran things. No one else wanted the job, with the exception of Brewster Philboyd of the lunar-refugee contingent, who had hinted he might be available if Lakesh wanted to slough off the weight of responsibility from his no-longer rejuvenated shoulders anytime soon. The trouble with that, other than the fact Philboyd was a dick, was that none of the old-line Cerberus people would work for him. And while a certain degree of polarization remained and had in ways deepened between the small, original Cerberus contingent and the much more numerous Moonies, even some of the latter had confided to the originals that they were none too eager to have the astrophysicist put in charge.

So while Kane and Grant, particularly, chafed at Lakesh's high-handed ways, they had to put up with them or take over themselves. And both erstwhile Mags would rather nail splintery prenukecaust railroad ties to their feet with big spikes and take up tap-dancing in chem storms than try to run Cerberus, which with the addition of the fugitives from Manitius Moonbase was now more than ever a task akin to herding cats, so they had to indulge Lakesh's quirks to some degree.

While suggesting—not ordering, but strongly suggesting—that Kane, Grant and Brigid should go forth and retrieve Lakesh's mystery correspondent after she released herself from Snakefishville on her own recognizance, Lakesh had let slip a few details. Their objective was female, an archivist and from the westernmost barony. She had deduced that the Preservationists, long the bête noire of the nine Magistrate Divisions, were a hoax, a straw enemy created by the mastermind of the real resistance to divert and drain the attentions of his enemies; had deduced that the chief of that resistance was the missing Lakesh—not in itself a big leap, since the barons knew that all too well by now, although they hadn't exactly announced it on the Enclave public-address systems; had deduced that Lakesh, now fugitive, was running his show from Cerberus.

So she had written to Lakesh to let him know she wanted in. "Why don't we just ice her?" Grant had asked at the briefing in the Cerberus cafeteria, his voice a characteristic rumble from deep within his huge chest.

"You're thinking like a Mag again," Brigid pointed out.

Grant made noises like a pile of granite boulders settling. Not long ago his reflex answer would have been that he *was* a Mag, dammit. For a long time after his own flight from Cobaltville with Kane, Brigid Baptiste and Domi the little albino outlander girl, Grant had considered himself a Magistrate. He had been the maximum Mag, in personality and demeanor if not administrative authority, his whole adult life. Even more than Kane, who even as Baron Cobalt's most single-mindedly lethal agent had always harbored something of a rebel streak, Grant had bought into the mission and mind-set of the Magistrates: to protect and serve his baron and the Program of Unification, and the order-out-of-chaos edict for which that stood. And even after he had become like Kane an outlaw beyond hope of redemption, for whom the carrying-out of a termination warrant would be the nicest thing the baronies or their servitors would ever possibly do for him, he had kept a lot of the attitudes and thought patterns.

In recent months that had begun to change. For Kane the real moment when everything changed had probably been when he found his long-vanished father, what was left of him, as a gene-machine in the hybrid base beneath Archuleta Mesa outside Dulce in what was once New Mexico. Grant's road to Damascus had been longer and twistier, and instead of a lightning bolt he had gotten more of a trickle current. But he had begun to entertain more than a few doubts about himself, his life and even his involvement with the resistance. It had drawn a dark curtain between him and Kane, to both men's distress—which neither would ever acknowledge—although it had not yet managed to sever the bond between them.

"Because she is obviously a person of extraordinary ability," Lakesh told the big black operator. "We have need of such ability."

"And then again," Kane pointed out, "if it turns out she's running a game on us, we can always put one behind her ear and dump her in a canyon for the vultures."

"You don't mean that, Kane," Brigid had told him.

He offered a slow grin. "Sure, I do."

BULLETS WHANGED off the ceramic-armaglass laminate armor plate of Grant's crippled Sandcat like a giant wearing iron gauntlets hammering to be let in. Firing from the topside blaster turret beneath its clear armaglass bubble, Grant grinned beneath the downward sweeps of his gunfighter's mustache. It was a standoff: the two vehicles were virtually identical, which made sense since Grant and his friends had swiped their wag from the little Snakefishville garrison situated on the island's shore. One weakness, although one seldom uncovered in operational terms, of Magistrate Division armament was that it was not meant to defeat itself. It was deliberately designed for one-sided combat, indeed to insure any necessary combat would be as one-sided as possible.

A lucky burst from the pursuing wag's heavy MGs had clipped the starboard tread of the fugitive Sandcat. It was the irreducible Achilles' heel of any track-laying vehicle: the tracks themselves are the component most vulnerable to damage from outside, and like a chopper's rotor, cannot be made much less than very vulnerable indeed.

Unfortunately the crippled Cat lay upslope from its pursuer. Firing at a downward angle kept Grant from getting a clear shot at the enemy's treads. Not that even the heavy USMG-73s were a good bet to cut them.

But the big ex-Mag didn't care. He'd gotten a bungee cord from his wag's stowage—they always carried them, standard gear, because you never knew when you'd need one—and was busily wrapping it around the triggers of the twin blasters in the bubble mount. Firing machine guns continuously wasn't good technique: aside from the fact it wasted bullets, it practically guaranteed either a rock-hard failure-to-feed jam or a slagged barrel.

But this wasn't Grant's wag, and he wasn't planning to come back to it.

He finished up. His big twin blasters continued to chug away, cycling through the rounds stored in huge armored bins within the boxy hull. He went out the back hatch, low, rolling behind a rock.

The bad guys were on the ball. That was one of the huge advantages to the Cat's bubble dome: on a sunny day like today, it was a real greenhouse, hotter than hell, but it kept the high-velocity particulate pollution pretty much off the gunner, while affording him a wonderful view of his target and surrounding terrain. Or, if you were in Grant's state—on the receiving end—a huge disadvantage; the Mag gunner spotted him and stitched a line of dust geysers behind the soles of his shadowsuit as he made his escape.

Grant got up to a crouch. "Dammit," he muttered, "this was supposed to be a pure snoop-and-poop." It was why they'd worn the shadow armor instead of their own Mag hard-contact suits, this mission's prime requisite was supposed to be stealth, not gunplay. And while the shadowsuit gave the wearer unparalleled flexibility with a high degree of protection, it didn't prevent incoming rounds from transferring energy right into you the way the hard polycarbonate shell of Magistrate combat armor did. A heavy slug from a USMG-73 might be stopped by a hard-contact breastplate, or it might not. It would poke the tough weave of spider silk, Monocrys and Spectra fabrics in an icicle all the way through you, doing your internal organage no good at all.

Ducking back down, Grant took a three-second look around the side of the boulder. The pursuing Sandcat, he noted, was nearing a spot where a washout had cut the dirt track, such as it was, leading up into the rocks with a currently dry arroyo floored with soft sand. The Cat driver churned toward it without evident concern; soft sand meant nothing to its treads. Soft footing was one of the very terrain features track-laying vehicles laid track to overcome: naked wheels would sink to the hubs, so they carried their own pavement around with them.

The gunner in the bubble was reasonably on the ball. A raucous rip of heavy fire chipped big chunks off the rosy granite boulder behind which Grant had already ducked once more.

Whistling soundlessly to himself, he raised a little hand unit. The hand unit looked vaguely like an ancient preskydark television remote. The resemblance wasn't entirely happenstance, although one significant difference was that this device didn't require line-of-sight the way an old infrared channel-switcher did. Nice rock-penetrating microwaves were the way to go, baby.

The big ex-Mag considered popping a final squint at his foe. He decided against it. No point copping a giant slug in the face when he could finesse it. He could read the land wag's speed as well as any man, and because he'd heard neither a change in the rumble of its 750-horsepower engine nor the clunk 'n chunk of its automatic transmission, and because the grade it was on was pretty constant, he had childlike faith its speed had not changed significantly.

Kane would tell him he was rationalizing a round of show-boating. His old point man and partner, he reflected, was too much under the influence of Brigid these days. Not altogether a bad thing, but it made him think more than was called for.

"Screw Kane," he murmured and held up his remote control.

"What's that?" Kane's voice demanded instantly.

"Watch."

AT HIS FRIEND'S laconic syllable Kane stopped just shy of the crest of the boulder-broken slope, half straightened to look back. Following closely and cautiously, both Brigid and Sally Wright popped their heads up, too.

Just in time to see the Snakefishville Sandcat rise a full five yards in the air atop a gusher of sand. It tipped with amazing slowness to one side and dropped back earthward on its back as debris continued to rocket skyward.

"Down," Kane said, and dropped as if shot.

"But we're so far, I don't see—" Sally Wright began, adjusting her round rimless spectacles on her narrow nose.

Brigid grabbed her wrist and with a strength Sally was not expecting, even from a woman of her height and breadth of shoulders, yanked her down into the weeds and pebbly dirt behind the outcrop.

A boom, surprisingly flat but big, rolled over them like surf. Sally felt wind on her cheeks and pressure on her eardrums as dynamic overpressure eddied down over the top of the rock. She even felt a slight caress of heat, no more than warmth really, on her exposed narrow cheek.

Then fist- to head-sized chunks of rock began to clatter and bounce among the rocks around them like giant irregular marbles pitched out of a bucket.

"Now I see," she finished sheepishly. "Thanks, Dr. Baptiste."

"Show-off," Kane muttered.

Down by the foot of the hill Grant stood up and bowed sardonically. Then he hustled to follow them toward the mattrans gateway concealed just down the hilltop's far side.

Chapter 3

"What did you say?" Baron Mande of Mandeville asked sharply. His words echoed off bare vanadium-steel walls curving to a vaulted ceiling overhead. He was a tall man, and built more sturdily than most hybrids. His dark hair had a reddish cast. His eyes were a strange, almost luminous topaz yellow. "I cannot hear you for that ridiculous contrivance over your face."

"I said," Baron Thulia said, his words muffled by the respirator mask with two lobes like blank goggles that covered the lower half of his ivory-toned ascetic's face, "that these are most unsanitary surroundings into which Lady Erica has chosen to summon us. There might be rats." Even with the mask there was no mistaking the slightly contemptuous inflection he gave the word *Lady*.

Erica van Sloan, after all, was a mere human—apekin, as the hybrids called them, when they didn't call them something worse. Yet she was also mother of Sam, who, although fallen or rather pushed from his lofty self-proclaimed perch of imperator, was still a force to be reckoned with.

She had called this conclave in a redoubt buried not far from the overgrown ruins of Muskogee—neutral ground, although nominally part of Mandeville. Her own pet pair of Baronial Guards stood behind her. By hastily initiated prearrangement, each baron was likewise backed by a pair of his personal, gene-enhanced bodyguards.

"Do you forget, Baron Thulia," the tall, striking woman said, her own violet-flecked eyes giving him back contempt for contempt, "that your carefully selected genes render you resistant if not immune to most of the diseases to which we mere humans are prey?"

"All manner of unforeseen mishaps have been befalling my brother barons of late," Thulia said as the others tried not to show sign of straining to catch his muffled words. "I prefer to take nothing for granted."

The truth was Baron Thulia was something of an obsessive-compulsive, a fact of which his brother barons were uncomfortably aware. Uncomfortably because, despite—or perhaps because of—the fact that they had intelligences far vaster than did humans, which some of their whitecoats had estimated would extrapolate into four-figure IQs had the ancient measuring system extended so far, they seemed unusually prone to mental disorder and psychic malaise. Of the barons surviving, and present, Thulia showed the most overt signs of personality disorder.

"Perhaps he just fears Lady Erica plans to gas us all and have done," another baron said dryly.

"That remark was in poor taste at best, my esteemed Baron Samarium," Erica rapped, eyes flashing.

Baron Samarium smiled and shrugged. His own features were a trifle broader, less sharply chiseled than the other baronial-class hybrids', which still would have scarcely sufficed to distinguish their elfin, almost ethereal beauty from human eyes less attuned to the hybrids than Erica van Sloan's. His manner was more languid, his speech slower and easier than that of any other baron, almost any other hybrid. Among other things the unification program had intended to eradicate all regional variations among the human cattle who had survived the megacull, thirty years of nuclear winter and a century of desolation. Yet the rhythms of the south Louisiana bayou country off Vermilion Bay, which surrounded his baronial ville, seemed to have infected him nonetheless, to the eyes and ears of the twentieth-century-born Erica.

It made it easy for her to underestimate him, given the prejudice against rural Southern whites that she, like most mid-Americans of her epoch, had been raised with. She suspected it was the same with his fellow barons, who tended to speak as fast as they thought fast. She also suspected he intended precisely that effect.

Undervaluing themselves in relation to others, even their nominal peers, was not a common failing among the baronial hybrids. Playing upon that arrogance was one of the ways she, mere apekin that she was, managed to stay a consistent jump ahead of them without invoking her progeny's tenebrous powers.

"Erica van Sloan has summoned us here as if we were drudges from our own Tartarus Pits," Baron Palladium snapped. "I demand to know why at once."

"And yet you came," Mande said. "As did I. As did we all. Obviously, brother, we have a common problem far more substantial than our dear Thulia's phantom rats and contagions."

Thulia glared at him over his mask, which he was holding to his face with one inhumanly slender hand as if afraid the seal might not otherwise hold. Mande ignored him, which made him glare the more fiercely.

"Intruders, I'd warrant, were I the gambling kind," Samarium drawled.

Erica nodded briskly, causing her vast mane of raven hair to bob around her shoulders. "Intruders. We have all received a recent rash of reports of peculiar intruders in our domains.

I have reason to know more than one of us has suffered penetration of baronial monoliths—by intruders whose means of ingress and egress remain likewise mysterious."

She turned to look at Palladium. His expression remained disdainful. His hair was almost white, his eyebrows invisibly pale and fine, like glass fibers.

"One of us, at least," she said, "is in possession of the body of at least one intruder."

"I resent the implication that you are spying on me, Erica van Sloan!" he flared.

"We all spy on one another," Mande said acerbically. "Deal with it."

"Suffice it to say I have my means," Erica said unflinchingly. "Perhaps you should be glad of the fact, Baron, since if it weren't for my learning of the fact of the widespread nature of these incursions, we might never learn just what kind of threat they might pose, given the atmosphere of mutual distrust that prevails among us."

"Or civil war, to call a thing what it is," Samarium said, as if to himself.

"Just what kind of threat do they pose, Lady Erica?" Thulia asked.

Erica looked at Palladium. "I fear it might be substantial," he admitted sulkily. "Six men of my Magistrate Division were destroyed in instants by an unfamiliar beam weapon of extraordinary potency."

The other barons exchanged looks. "My own Magistrates have encountered similar devices," Mandeville said.

"As have Cobaltville's," Erica acknowledged. The other two barons said nothing.

"My men did, however, recover the body of one of the interlopers," Palladium acknowledged.

"Was it human?" Thulia asked.

"In a manner of speaking," Palladium said. "It was that of a woman in her late twenties. She appears to have been an Australian aboriginal, purebred or nearly so."

"An inferior breed of an inferior species," Thulia said, sneering.

"How impertinent of them to equip themselves with weaponry we ourselves cannot match, eh?" Samarium said. Thulia glared at him.

"And what do you make of that fact, Baron Palladium?" Erica asked.

He hesitated. His lips moved slightly, as if to unvoiced words. "I am not sure," he said at length. "We have received similar reports of unaccounted persons in various areas of my domain. The physical descriptions all appear to be roughly similar—generally medium height or below, brown skin, dark shaggy hair."

A peculiar light gleamed in Erica's steely eyes. "Dressed how?" she inquired.

The baron shrugged. "In the same manner as all outlander scum. My patrols did report they seemed cleaner and neater than the average Roamer."

"They weren't wearing loincloths?" Erica demanded. "What about paint?"

Palladium's perfect brow knit. He wasn't accustomed to being interrogated, especially by a mere human female. "No, no…loincloths. Nor did anyone remark paint on their clothing."

"Not on their clothes! What about their faces, their bodies?"

Now the baron of the Great Lakes region looked mostly perplexed. "No, nothing like that at all. At least not that my men reported."

"It appears that the imperator's reverend mother has first-hand experience of these savages," Samarium said.

"I do." Her somewhat wild expression and clipped delivery did not invite further exploration, even from barons.

"I fail to understand," Thulia said peevishly. "If they are mere savages, why are we troubling ourselves with them?"

"Perhaps because they're apparently cropping up all over the continent and disappearing as inexplicably?" Mande said. "And let us not overlook their distressing propensity for walking through solid walls. Those things certainly get my interest."

"But what can it all mean?" Palladium asked.

"For millennia our progenitors have eyed the aborigines with suspicion," Mande said. He turned to fix Erica with a wide-eyed but piercing gaze. "Apparently our associate Lady Erica has had her own dealings with them."

"I have," Erica said. "Why did the Archons suspect the aborigines?"

"That I do not know. They never seemed able to educe anything concrete against them. Yet there was something about those creatures that gave rise to distinct unease."

"What could they possibly want?" Thulia asked.

Erica swept the table with her eyes. "They have been repeatedly sighted in archives, in old libraries, even old machine shops," she said. "I will make no attempt to dictate to you. I do submit that we are all of us faced by a joint and possibly grave danger. We need to lay aside our differences—as I myself have, for example, in agreeing to treat amicably with Baron Mande despite recent severe armed clashes between our forces—and address it."

"Obviously there's only one thing to do," Samarium said, sprawling in his chair as if unconcerned. Only an almost metallic glitter in his sky-colored eyes betrayed the intensity of his interest. "Send an expedition to Australia to get to the bottom of it."

"There is a problem," Mande said dryly, sitting up and allowing his own blasé mask to slip, momentarily giving way to a look of reptilian dislike in Erica's direction. She could almost see the Annunaki in him, and she shivered, remembering what she had glimpsed in her son.

"What might that be?" Palladium demanded.

"We cannot."

"AUSTRALIA," Dr. Mohandas Lakesh Singh said, standing with one fist on his hip and gazing up at the wall-sized digital map display in the Cerberus redoubt command center.

"Not again," the tall woman with hair like a flow of Hawaiian lava said. Like the others she appeared at least somewhat restored from the rigors of the jaunt to Snakefishville by a shower and a night's sleep.

"How's that?" Lakesh turned and adjusted his heavy-framed glasses, whose use he had been forced to resume as Sam rejuvenation treatment wore off. "My dear Brigid, how can you say that? The valiant combined efforts of Domi, Shizuka and yourself on your recent sojourn there were crowned with nothing but success."

"Too damn weird," the slim but shapely little albino Domi said, chewing a chunk of pemmican traded for from Skydog's Lakota band, the redoubt's neighbors to the east. Her T-shirt had been cut off well above her navel and sported some fairly substantial holes, through one of which her left nipple kept threatening to peek. She also wore faded jean shorts cut off so high an apple-wedge cheek of shapely alabaster ass showed either side, husky steel-toed hiking boots and in between thigh-high red stand-ups. They were something of a trademark, and her closer comrades all counted themselves lucky when she bothered to wear something *with* them.

"Domi's right," Brigid said.

"Surely you were not unsettled by your encounter with apparently paranormal forces?" Lakesh asked.

"Surely I was. I do not know whether they were paranormal forces—that would require my notion of what 'normal' means to be very much stronger than it has grown over the time I have spent here in Cerberus—but they were inexplicable to me. And enormous."

"Strong enough to help us kick the asses of that old witch Erica and the fused-out girl baron," Domi said, "but not strong enough to do the job themselves. How does that add up, huh?"

Lakesh sighed deeply. "I wish I could answer your question, dear child," he said.

Turning back to his big, beloved blinky-light board he added, "Now indeed more than ever."

The companions had answered one of Lakesh's peremptory summons to the command center. A mix of old redoubt hands and Moonies held down the seats at the various consoles, commanding everything from environmental conditions within Cerberus to displays of the views garnered from still-operational satellites such as the Vela and Keyhole signature birds. The stocky, grizzled astrophysicist Neukirk hunched down at the swivel chair at the main board, a knot of resentment with an almost visible dark aura emanating from him.

Sally Wright stood to one side, eyes wide behind the thick lenses of her eyeglasses, an almost apologetic smile on her face, her hands clasped behind her back. A standard-issue white Cerberus jumpsuit hung on her gaunt frame.

"So you're sending us to Oz," Grant said. "And this time Kane and I don't have a doctor's note to get out of it."

Kane folded his arms and leaned against the wall by the

entryway. A cold lopsided smile showed through his beard. "We could sit this one out anyway. The ladies did such a squared-away job cleaning up down there last time."

The two ladies in question looked death beams at him.

"There will be ample employment for you all, I assure you," Lakesh said. "But not, at least for the moment, in Australia."

Kane raised an eyebrow. "Why not?"

Lakesh smiled thinly. "Because, my very good friend, the very phenomena that now command our attention render it impossible to get there."

Chapter 4

"How's that play out?" Grant asked.

Lakesh nodded to Neukirk. The physicist's jaw tightened beneath his close-cropped beard. His blunt finger stabbed a key on his board. A red dot appeared on the projection of Australia, in almost the center of the kidney-bean-shaped island continent.

"Uluru," Brigid said glumly.

"Why am I not surprised?" Domi said.

"World's biggest rock," Kane added. "You've shown us this before. What, is it getting up to tricks?"

"Evidently so," Lakesh said.

The scientist was unable entirely to conceal his smile of pleasure at the others' expressions. "It has begun radiating energy. Copious amounts of it, although not within the conventional electromagnetic spectrum."

"It's doing something to interfere with matter transmission." Despite the fact that her archivist training militated against offering speculation unless it was solicited, Brigid did not ask a question. Rather she stated a fact.

Which Lakesh's answering nod duly acknowledged. "Emitting signals so strong they register, faintly, on the instruments monitoring our own mat-trans gateway here in the redoubt. These interfere with any attempt at matter transmission onto the entire continent, making it impossible to heterodyne the signals in order to complete materialization. Several of the baronies have attempted transmissions to Australian gateways. These have simply failed—they find themselves unable even to initiate transmission sequence."

"Too bad the bastards don't just materialize inside the damn boulder," Kane said.

Grant's massive frame shuddered. "Don't even say that."

Kane cocked a brow toward him. "I thought your soft spot for Mags had hardened over," he said.

"Mebbe so," Grant said. "But I wouldn't wish any kind of jump screwup on anybody. Even a baron."

"Why do we need to involve ourselves in this?" Kane demanded. "Okay, it's another weird phenomenon. World's full of them, haven't you noticed?"

"We tend to pay special attention to those phenomena that indicate unusual influences on, perhaps even manipulation of, the space-time continuum," Brigid said.

"Now, here I thought you were the lady showing signs of reluctance to pay Uluru a return visit. Just trying to help out here."

Brigid gave an irritated toss of her head.

"We have, in addition to the excellent reason adduced by Brigid, even more pressing cause to take immediate interest in the phenomena that appear to be emanating from what once was known as Ayers Rock," Lakesh said.

"Such as?" Grant said.

"The barons recently held a meeting at a secret location— a redoubt in what once was the state of Oklahoma and is now nominally within the barony of Mandeville."

"Pardon me, Dr. Lakesh," Sally Wright said timidly, actually raising her hand. "I don't mean to intrude, but how can the meeting place be secret if you know it?"

Lakesh smirked.

"Gotcha," Domi murmured around a chunk of pemmican.

The new arrival blinked around, confusion plain on her face. Her eyes were greatly magnified behind the thick lenses of her glasses, turning her into a caricature of a big-eyed waif.

"You've gratified his ego by allowing him to show off," Brigid amplified.

"Quite so, dear Brigid," Lakesh said, beaming fatuously. "Of course the meeting place was supposed to be secret. But I have resources of my own, as evidenced by the fact of your presence here."

"She wrote us, remember?" Grant said.

"Be that as it may," Lakesh said, totally unfazed, "I have my sources, as I said—one, Archivist Wright, being an ability to monitor use of known mat-trans gateways. Jumps were made from Mandeville, Palladiumville, Thuliaville, Samariumville, and Cobaltville."

Leaning back against a console with his arms folded across his chest, Kane elevated his eyebrows. "Cobaltville?"

"Sounds like Erica called a meeting of the clans," Grant said.

"And they responded despite the fact several of those baronies are fighting a fairly hot undeclared war with one another," Kane said. "Interesting."

"I knew you would find it so, friend Kane. My intelligence sources do not extend to providing me minutes of that meeting, although I do not doubt it was entirely fascinating."

"Wouldn't've minded being a fly on that wall myself," Kane murmured, "although watching through a vidcam attached to a remotely detonated, low-yield thermonuclear device concealed *in* the wall would've been better still."

"You got that right," Grant said with quiet fervency.

"Sadly we were denied such simple gratifications." Lakesh forged ahead, a hint of asperity evident at having some of his thunder stolen by badinage. "But I have learned that the barons are quite concerned about recent apparitions of Australian aboriginals within their domains."

Brigid frowned. "'Apparitions'?"

"It seems the appropriate word. Magistrate patrols from almost all the nine baronies have reported contacts with groups of mysterious scavengers, usually in the ruins of urban areas, and showing a curious propensity for museums and machine shops. They tend to vanish instantly and tracelessly, although there are reports of them using some kind of unknown handheld beam weapon against the Magistrates."

Brigid's brow furrowed farther. "That hardly squares with what we encountered at Uluru."

"Yeah," Domi agreed. "Buncha naked mystic hunter-gatherer types, they looked like."

"That description would differ from you how?" Kane asked.

"I'm not mystic."

"Be that as it may," Lakesh said, "the reports are widespread, and becoming more frequent."

"What makes you so sure they're aborigines?" Grant asked. "When I was a Magistrate cadet, anyway, they didn't burn a lot of time teaching us comparative ethnography."

"We were taught to bash heads," Kane agreed, "not measure cranial indices."

"The Palladiumville Magistrates recovered a body," Lakesh said. "They killed an intruder. Apparently that intruder or others worked remarkable execution on the Magistrates in turn with the energy weapon before vanishing."

Kane and Grant exchanged glances.

"That in itself is not the most extraordinary part of it all," Lakesh said. "What is, is the place the intruders were discovered, and where the brief gun battle took place."

"Enough suspense," Kane said. "Give."

"On Bravo Level of the Palladiumville Monolith. Inside a Historical Division storage room."

"That's impossible," Grant said flatly.

Lakesh smiled again. "Precisely," he said, nodding. "And that, my very good friends, is why you will soon be paying a visit to Palladiumville itself."

"IT'S COME TO THIS," Grant grumbled beneath his breath. They walked through the boisterous, bad-smelling crush of the Palladiumville Pits. Or, in Grant's case, limped. Wrapped in stained, khaki-colored in rags like a particularly down-on-his-luck Roamer—or an ambulatory mummy—the huge ex-Mag carried his right leg stiff. "I'm masquerading as a Pitter now. I can sink no lower."

"Outland scum on a day pass," Kane corrected. He was more colorfully dressed in shabby, dusty scavvie clothes, with a faded bandanna tied around his head and a patch over his left eye.

"Look on the bright side," Brigid said. "If you are worried about what your old comrades would think if they saw you, remember the only one not dead or sworn to shoot you on sight is right here beside you doing the same thing."

She herself was got up like a gaudy slut. Unless she wanted to wear an old cement bag head-to-foot with two eye holes poked in it, she was going to attract attention. So her distinctive fireworks-colored hair was dyed black and wrapped in a loud kerchief to boot, dark contacts turned her emerald eyes to brown, and the top she was wearing, if it could be called that, was designed to lift and press together a pair of breasts that frankly needed no such help.

The idea, candidly, was to insure nobody looked much of

anywhere else. From the ways eyes tracked as the unlikely trio passed, it was working even better than anticipated. Nobody was paying any attention to her male companions, either.

The harshness of the artificial lights hanging from the streaked and stained concrete ceiling not so high overhead accentuated both the grime and the washed-out quality of the streets. And those who moved along them.

"If our briefing was right," Kane said quietly, "this alley coming up to our left leads to the gaudy we're looking for."

"We know what a big 'if' that is," Grant said sourly.

They had considered going in as Mags. Few people would dare look at them closely enough to make them for strangers. Looking too close at a passing Magistrate was a good way to get a mouthful of busted teeth or worse. Openly, at least—but they would be subject to minute inspections through cracks between boards and from behind stained second-story windows. Neither Grant nor Kane felt enough faith in his acting ability to try to pass himself off as a cherry Mag on his first Pit detail. Not that two rookies would normally be paired up anyway. PPP, or Pit Pedestrian Patrol, was commonly a first-year gig, but at least one of any pair would have logged some time in the barrel. The local denizens, at least a hard core of them, would know all the veteran ville Magistrates cold. So, needless to say, would any real Palladiumville Mags they encountered.

"Lakesh indicated very strongly he had a solid contact inside the Leaping Weasel," Brigid said somewhat crisply as she deftly eluded a drunken beggar sprawled against the front of a tinker shop, who had made a grab at her translucent skirt with a three-fingered hand. Although she sparred with Lakesh as much as any, she had been his protégée. Sometimes she felt a perverse urge to defend him, especially against the aspersions of the rough-and-tumble types.

"Did he happen to share any of his corroborative sources with you?" Grant rumbled.

"Well, no—"

"Uh-huh," Grant grunted. "And who do we know with a strong tendency to outsmart himself, Brigid? Remember that time he had Bry pretend to defect, and you went hunting him and almost chilled him? Plus he got tortured into the bargain."

"Well—"

"He's got you, Baptiste," Kane said with a ragged grin. "Lose gracefully."

She glared death at him. Brown rather than green. "When do you lose gracefully?"

"Never," he said, halting at the entrance to the noisome alley to bow. "Touché." He made a sweep with his right hand. "And also *après vous.*"

"Where'd you learn to speak French?"

"In the torture chamber of the Duke of Burgundy. Delightful spot. Now step lively, wench, lest I smack your rump."

"You wouldn't dare—"

"Wrong answer," Grant murmured, as Kane, grinning so widely the top of his head seemed in peril of toppling off, slapped her across the buttocks with a sound like a handblaster lighting off. She jumped and squalled in outrage.

"It's the Pits, remember?" Kane said through his grin, sotto voce without unclenching his teeth.

Giving him a harpoon look, she gathered her skirts and swept haughtily past him. The louts and idlers on the street nearby burst into spontaneous applause.

"LOOK AT THIS!"

Brigid knelt before the sign painted alongside the saloon's filthy bat-wing doors. It showed a cartoon mustelid jumping straight into the air from a bipedal pose, with big startled eyes. The sounds of boisterous conversation and insipid rock music spilled out over tops and bottom of the doors.

"So?" Grant demanded. "It's a picture of a weasel leaping. What'd you expect, the archangel Gabriel?"

"But this is a Scooter Trash original!" the tarted-up archivist said.

Kane peered over her shoulder, frowning in curiosity, more at her behavior than what she was looking at. " 'Scooter Trash'?"

Brigid pointed to a small sharp-angled signature to the lower left of the cartoon animal. "The most famous graffiti artist of the Outlands," she explained. "Except perhaps for Skids Rodey."

Kane looked at Grant. Grant shrugged a huge shoulder. "I didn't know they had famous graffiti artists in the Outlands."

"Who knew they had artists?" Kane asked.

"He's very famous," Brigid insisted. "I've heard of him, so he must be."

Grant scowled more deeply than usual. "You've been hanging out with Domi way too much," he growled. "That's Domi logic if ever I heard it."

THEY WERE TOSSING the dwarf inside the saloon.

Though half the height of a normal man, the human projectile had the chest and shoulders of one more than average sized. His head, proportional to his torso, showed none of the distortion some dwarfs' did. It made his stubby arms and legs see the more cruel a joke genetics had played upon him.

Inside the Leaping Weasel was, if anything, worse than outside. It smelled worse, or maybe it was just that air circulation was bad, so that the smells had a chance to congregate.

And it was dark, stumbling dark at first to eyes accustomed to the harsh artificial glare without.

"But then again," Kane said softly, "maybe we don't want to see our surroundings too clearly."

A few yards to the right a black man even taller and wider than Grant was holding a slagger with a blond mullet by his shirtfront with one hand and methodically punching his face with the other.

"I told you," he grunted in time to the blows, "what'd happen if you played Loverboy on the damn box."

Against one wall stood a CD-playing jukebox. Its yellow, red, amber and green lights were the brightest illumination in the joint. It was pinching off the strains of "Everybody's Working for the Weekend."

"Loverboy," Brigid confirmed. "A pop-rock group of the eighties. Extremely popular but blessedly short-lived."

"How do you know this stuff?" Grant demanded.

Ignoring the byplay, Kane peered around the dim, low-ceilinged room. It was packed asshole to elbow. "No empty damn tables," he said under his breath. "Popular armpit we got here."

"I specialized in late-twentieth-century politics and culture, remember?" Brigid told Grant. She nodded at the other hulking black man, who was still pummeling his unresisting victim. "He should count himself lucky it's not Flock of Seagulls."

Kane's single visible wolf-gray eye lit upon a round corner table occupied by a pair of slight, furtive men, who didn't look the sort to pack shivs beneath their grimy rags. He smiled, looked to his companions and jerked his head toward the pair. "Come on. Table's about to open up."

He met Grant's eye. His partner nodded once. Deliberately they strolled to the table so that each came to stand behind an occupied chair.

"Thanks for holding the table for us, gents," Kane announced.

The two looked up with glittering timid eyes. "What? What's that?"

"Man says, you two were both leaving," Grant said in a voice like approaching thunder. He grabbed his man under the elbows, picked him up out of the chair, pivoted and set him down. The man only just got his well-holed athletic shoes planted on the gooey floor in time.

His friend popped a single squint at Kane's pale eye and scrambled to his feet. The pair bolted out the door, caroming off bodies heedlessly as they went.

"And that didn't risk calling unwanted attention to us?" Brigid asked, watching them depart. Nobody else paid the slightest attention, not even the people they bounced off.

"Couple slaggers with phony chips in their arms, sure as shit," Grant said as they settled themselves. "Don't dare raise a stir that might bring Mags. You still got an eye, partner."

Kane grinned bleakly. "It's like riding a bicycle. You never really lose it."

"When did you ever ride a bicycle, Kane?" Brigid demanded.

"Never. But I read about them."

A solemn nine-year-old girl in an apron appeared to take their order for three mugs of Orion Pale Ale, the local Pit boss's microbrew, famed the length and breadth of the former Midwest and beyond. The unofficial and unchallenged queen of the depths below Palladiumville was famous as a flamboyant, larger-than-life figure whose sheer talent for survival was evidenced by the fact that she continued to do so in a ville lorded over by such a noted tight-ass as Baron Palladium.

"Are you sure this is safe, Kane?" Brigid asked as the child left.

The song ended. The burly black man quit pounding the

smaller slagger, started to let him go. The music machine clunked as it replaced the disk just played with another from its selection of scavenged ancient treasures.

The box emitted the opening strains of Loverboy's "Turn Me Loose."

The beaten man looked up at his tormentor and grinned weakly.

"I'm sure it's not safe," Kane said.

"No such thing as safe," Grant added. "Not in the Outlands. Not in the Pits. And not anywhere for three renegades like us."

"You're the one who was defending Lakesh sending us on this wild-rat chase a moment ago," Kane told Brigid. "Getting windy now?"

"I am not exactly comfortable—let me put it that way."

"Appropriate response to the surroundings," Grant said.

But Kane leaned forward and put his elbows on the little round table. "Getting a warning from your gut, Baptiste?"

"She's not a doomie, Kane," Grant said.

"That's an indelicate question to put to a lady, even in a place like this," Brigid said.

"But you've been in the field a long time now," Kane said. "You're a veteran operator. Is this a bad feeling, or just not liking the company and the decor?"

"I honestly don't know."

She paused as the little girl returned bearing a tray with three dirty glass mugs filled with sickly yellow fluid. Kane tossed a scatter of early-twentieth-century silver dimes, obverses and reverses worn to amorphous lumps, on the table for payment. They had started turning up and becoming a popular means of exchange in the Outlands in the past year or so, especially east of the Rocks; somebody had to have hit a major cache of the things. The little girl scooped them into a pocket of her immaculate blue-and-white apron and went wordlessly away.

"Cute kid," Kane said. "Wonder what she's doing in a cesspit like this."

"Same as everybody," Grant said.

He held his mug up as if the faint shine from a strand of anemic lights might help him see it better. "This stuff better taste less like piss than it looks."

"It's quite good, actually," said Brigid, taking a second sip.

Cautiously Kane tasted the brew. It didn't make him heave. To his surprise.

The dwarf-tossing game was still going on, two knots of about half a dozen work-stained roustabouts tossing him across a ten-foot stretch of sawdust-covered floor, his hank of coarse black hair flying. Brigid's lips compressed in distaste.

"I'd think that would be against the law," she sniffed.

Kane knocked back a bigger slug of beer. Baptiste was right. It was good.

"It is," he said, wiping his mouth with the back of his hand in true Pitter style.

Brigid's camouflaged eyes darted left and right. "Doesn't that mean the Magistrates are likely to descend at any moment."

"Ease off the trigger, Brigid," Grant said, hunching forward over his mug as if determined to enjoy it in defiance of the world, if need be. "Shows the kind of pull this Orion has. No reason to fear the Mags."

"Is that such a good thing?" Brigid asked.

Kane shrugged. "If he's got the goods Lakesh sent us for, she's got heavy connections upstairs. Speaking of which, I wonder where our contact is?"

A shadow loomed up in Kane's peripheral vision, a darker dimness against the barroom murk. A spike of alarm went through him as he looked around. He carefully did not form the fingers of his right hand into a half fist. Neither he nor Grant had been willing to come here without their Sin Eaters strapped in their accustomed power holsters beneath loose tear-away sleeves on their right forearms. But if they revealed the trademark side arm blaster of the feared and hated Magistrates, it would give the game away for true. And to be taken for infiltrating Mags in a setting such as this would be no less immediately lethal than to be identified correctly as renegades. The blasters were present frankly as a form of reassurance—and a very last resort.

A woman stood there, a tall, sinuous and beautiful young black woman with a certainly false ruby in her right nostril. She wore garments similar to Brigid's and if possible even more revealing in front, although she had less to work with. Her smell made Kane's eyes water; the stale scent of her body, her hygiene not being much better than Pit standard, was largely masked by what appeared to be crown-to-sole drenching in perfume. Scavenged perfume, its original aroma long since warped and transmuted by two centuries of mixing, evaporation of volatile esters and other forms of dark chemical decay. Its actual smell, and effect, was of tear gas, with hints of musk and candy.

"Here's some handsome strangers," she purred in a thrilling low contralto. "Traders in on a day pass?"

"You got it, sister," Grant said in a neutral voice.

"That means you had something valuable to trade, for them to let you in," she purred. "And that means you have jack."

She started to sit sideways onto Kane's lap. "They're mine," Brigid snapped. Her brown eyes, flashing, looked scarcely less formidable than when laser green. "Find your own damn johns."

The black gaudy slut smiled crookedly. She had decent teeth, anyway—only one visible gap, up near the upper-right corner of her smile. "Ah, but these are clearly gentlemen of taste," she murmured. "Perhaps they're in the mood for something a little younger and slimmer."

She sat on Kane before he could stop her. The smell of her now was making his head spin. He half wondered if this might be some sort of concealed chem attack.

Brigid had gone paler even than usual beneath her troweled-on makeup. "Clear out!" she barked.

The black woman laid her delicate right hand on the back of Kane's scarred one. "Clearly he prefers me," she said.

She began to caress her fingers upward along his forearm—toward his Sin Eater. He tensed.

"You lose, you bleached old slut," the woman said.

Brigid nailed her with an overhead right and knocked her sprawling into the middle of the carousing throng.

The saloon erupted in mayhem.

Chapter 5

A wide man smelling hard of mechanic's grease dived over an overturned table at Grant in a flying head-high tackle. Grant reached out for him, touched him with his big hard hands and then, pivoting about his body's centerline, simply steered the hurtling body past. The tech flew into a knot of men bashing ineffectually at each other with beer bottles. The whole bunch toppled together over a table.

"That stuff Sifu Chen taught me in New Edo is the real deal," he said meditatively.

Kane blocked a blow from a cudgel that might have been a wrenched-off table leg with his right forearm. His assailant, a gap-toothed man with a deep scar crossing one milky dead eye, looked surprised when his makeshift club made a distinct clacking sound. Instead of striking unprotected bone, the stick had hit the metal-reinforced power holster holding Kane's concealed Sin Eater.

As the dead-eyed man gaped, Kane whipped his shin up into his groin. Foul breath oofed over Kane, and spittle sprayed his face. The attacker doubled. Kane straightened him back up with an uppercutting elbow beneath the chin. The man went over backward in a boneless flail of limbs, stunned senseless.

Kane wiped his face.

Brigid crouched at his side. Clutched in her fist was a

nasty little knife with a single-edged triangular blade, no more than four inches long. Her own erstwhile opponent still lay stunned and stretched out herself in the sawdust on the floor.

Brigid's punching her had catalyzed a volatile reaction. Resentment and anger never lay far from the surface in the Tartarus Pits. It took very little to trigger explosive violence.

The outbreak's sudden fury was consequently random, not directed against the undercover trio except incidentally. Indeed for a moment they found themselves as it were in the eye of the storm that raged about them.

"Way to keep a low profile," Kane murmured out the side of his mouth to Brigid.

She turned a stricken face back toward him. "I thought I had to do that! To maintain credibility."

"And that was the only reason?"

Before she could answer a weight landed on Kane's shoulders from behind.

It was the dwarf with the hank of wild black hair. He clamped his legs to Kane's ribs beneath the arms and began belaboring him with his own stubby arms.

Kane whacked at him. The half-sized man ducked with surprising alacrity. Kane was operating under severe constraints: it wasn't that he felt any qualms about bashing a dwarf—he'd done lots worse things even after leaving the service of Baron Cobalt and his Trust, and not felt particularly bad about it. But the angle was bad and Kane determined not to commit the low-comedy error of punching himself in the head.

The dwarf grabbed handfuls of Kane's cheeks and brought his mouth close to Kane's right ear.

"Fall down, schmuck!" the dwarf hissed.

"In your dreams."

"You want to see Orion or don't you? Your call, Daddy Longlegs."

Kane let himself fall to his knees as quickly as he could without banging them on the mostly smooth-worn planking. Then he tugged the sleeve of Brigid, who was already staring at him as if he'd sprouted antlers.

"Who are you?" Kane asked over his shoulder as Brigid hunkered at his side.

"Call me Hanratty," the dwarf said. "I'm supposed to take you to the boss. Since you blew the covert approach all to fuck and gone, our best bet is to shag ass out of here while this fracas is going on to cover for us."

The black man-mountain who had been pounding the Loverboy devotee was engaged with Grant. He didn't seem near as happy. Grant had his left hand twisted around and back upon itself, which had had the effect of straightening his arm and locking out the elbow, leaving the larger man helpless and bereft of options.

"Kane? What the hell are you doing?" Grant demanded, glancing down to see his partner, the covert redhead and a dwarf all staring at him from the vicinity of the floor.

"Get down," Kane mouthed.

Grant shrugged, put his free palm on the other man's locked elbow and spun, running his victim headfirst into the wall. Hard. The man's eyes rolled up in his head and his knees buckled.

Keeping a weather eye on him in case he was faking, Grant crouched beside his partners. The trio, now a quartet, was more or less sheltered from the chaos in the lee of their corner table.

"What's the joke, here, Kane?"

"You're enjoying that *qin na* stuff way too much."

"Works. Adds some spice to the old Mag rough-and-tum-

ble style we're both used to. You got down here with the projectile midget to tell me that?"

"I'm a dwarf, schmuck, not a midget," Hanratty said.
"Midgets are proportioned same as you big pukes."

"Whatever."

"Now what?" Brigid asked.

"You walk around back behind the bar. Go through the
beaded curtain."

"What about you?" Kane asked.

"I'll catch up with you. Right now I'm going to stir the pot
a little, make sure it keeps turning over long enough for you
three to scram."

He slid off Kane's back, waddled out among the forest of
legs. The brawl seemed to be settling down of its own accord.
Hanratty made for the biggest man still standing, a redhead
with an HVAC technician's badge on his stained jumpsuit.

"All right," the dwarf bellowed in his startling deep voice.
"Who wants some?"

He punched the tall tech right in the nuts.

"I CAN'T BELIEVE you of all people started a bar brawl, Brigid,"
Grant said as they hurried down the slimy-walled passageway.
Hanratty, who had emerged from the renewed ruction miraculously unscathed—obviously a well-tuned talent—led the
way bearing a pine-knot torch that streamed orange flame and
a thin black drool of smoke and stank vigorously of kerosene.

"I had to stay in character. As Kane kept reminding me."
Brigid glared at the other man. "I still owe you for that crack
on the backside, mister. Don't think I've forgotten."

"We never ever forget you've got an eidetic memory, Baptiste," Kane said, "because you never tire of reminding us."

"Can the chatter," Hanratty called over his shoulder. "We

don't exactly want to advertise the presence of this secret passage. Notice that word 'secret'?"

The passage continued down and down. The walls sweated. Grant gave them a jaundiced look.

"I don't like seeing all this moisture," he said in a low rumble. "We're pretty far down, and not so far from the lake that a little tremor might not make it want to come in and visit us."

"Hasn't so far," Hanratty said. He himself made no effort to subdue his foghorn honk.

"I'm curious, Hanratty," Brigid said. "You appear to be accepted, yet generally throughout the Outlands little people are suspected of being muties."

"Little people? Little people? Jesus, what's wrong with you? I'm a dwarf, not a friggin' leprechaun. Are you trying to make me feel better? You figure, well, the world got blown up and turned to shit, everything's run by a bunch of fascist megalomaniacs in these dippy castles, but I'll feel all better if you avoid calling attention to my affliction?"

"I'll hold him still if you want to hit him, Baptiste," Kane offered helpfully.

Brigid swallowed. "I apologize if I have offended you."

He waved a hand on a stumpy arm. "Never mind. I'm Orion's factotum, you might say. The Pit boss's strong but sneaky left hand. People don't fuck with me for the good and sufficient reason that if they do, they get fucked back harder. That enough answer for you, Red?"

Reflexively Brigid raised a hand to her bandanna, from concern a lock of hair might have slipped its surly bonds. Then she realized she'd dyed it anyway.

Grant stopped his gimpy progress down the tunnel. "Not so fast, there, shorty," he called. "Why'd you call her 'Red'?"

"What else would I call the famous Brigid Baptiste, Grant? Or should I say 'notorious'?"

"SO THIS IS what your modern-day baron blasters look like," the immense woman said. "Suitably disguised, of course."

It was a little half bubble of concrete deep below the earth. Its walls were covered with bizarre machine-made tapestries of snarling tigers and dogs playing cards. Kane guessed it was part of an ancient fallout shelter, the private miniredoubts that enjoyed a certain popularity in the late 1950s and early 1960s. Unfortunately they had gone out of fashion, with the result that most of them were filled in or just lost by the time the nukecaust came, when they might have done some good.

Maureen Orion dominated the little chamber by sheer bulk alone. She had to have stood well over six feet tall and weighed well over four hundred pounds, much of it fat. It was stuffed into black velvet pantaloons and a stained white blouse with puffy sleeves; her bodice was tight, although it would have been hard for it not to be, given what it had to contend with, and it was cut away too low for Kane's peace of mind. The face on the front of her beer-keg head was so heavily painted that it didn't actually have to have any physical features at all, although she did seem to possess the normal ones in relatively standard arrangement. Hair of a red so startling it was almost a metallic magenta was piled high atop her head. The color owed more to chemistry than genes, unless she had more than a bit of taint to her.

"How did you happen to recognize us?" Brigid asked.

The four of them sat around a large round table topped with worn and stained green baize. The Pit boss had been playing what looked like a game of solitaire with a tarot deck when Hanratty, who now stood back against the wall, escorted the visitors within. Basically Orion occupied half the table, the three outsiders the other, and all three felt themselves collectively outmassed.

"Your boss Lakesh got word to me he wanted to make talk-talk. Our channels aren't the sort to allow exchange of much information, not safely or reliably. Which meant he'd be sending agents for a face-to-face. Even the barons, who're a lot smarter than they actually have any notion what to do with, and consequently, as I'm sure you're well aware, generally display about the sense of a four-week-old kitten, know that the three top operators for the resistance on this continent are three renegades from Cobaltville. So when a tall drink of water with a wolf's eyes—eye—an even bigger black cold-heart and a prissy librarian type with a truly outstanding rack turn up in my dive, what conclusion am I supposed to draw?"

Only Kane managed to maintain a poker face, not without superhuman effort. Grant, who had started to build up major thunderheads at hearing Lakesh termed their boss, dropped his jaw. Brigid turned a red as bright but of different value than the Pit boss's unearthly hair, her expostulations at being characterized as a prissy librarian type remained unvoiced behind carplike motions of her mouth.

Orion roared with laughter.

On the basis of sheer size alone she invited comparison to the late and markedly unlamented boss of the Cobaltville Pit, Guana Teague. Making much—anything—of that would be a grave mistake, Kane judged. The Palladiumville boss was if anything bigger than Teague had been. She also struck him far smarter, and was definitely more...*aware*. That was the best word he could put to it.

Consequently he judged her far more dangerous.

"I won't blow smoke up your butts." She did, however,

blow smoke out of her heavily painted lips, toward the low ceiling of her headquarters deep below the Palladiumville Pit. "I deal with those above, as well as those below."

She stuck the end of her carved-ebony cigarette holder back in her mouth and toked deeply of her ditchweed joint. "But ease the hands away from the blasters, there, boys—or, rather, don't go forming up your fists to summon forth the Sin Eaters you undoubtedly have strapped beneath those loose sleeves of yours."

"If we're who you say we are," Kane asked in conversational tones, sitting back in his chair and crossing his long legs, "why shouldn't we?"

She shrugged a bare mountainous shoulder. "I guess it depends on how badly you want to waste all the trouble you took getting here. Not to mention your chances of getting back into our Midwestern winter sunshine, such as it is, alive. If I was going to shop you or scrag you, would I have gone to this much trouble?"

"Would you?" Grant asked. "Never known a Pit boss who wouldn't sell his mother, if the price was right."

Again Maureen Orion laughed uproariously.

"Maybe if we asked her directly what she meant," Brigid said stiffly, "she might actually tell us."

"Forgive my mirth," the huge woman said, dabbing at the corners of her paint-outlined eyes with a hankie plucked from the crevasse of her bodice. Her laughter subsided. Seismic flesh waves flowed through her cheeks and overexposed bosom. She leaned forward across the table. "It's just that my dear mother sold *me,* to Outlands slavers, when I was four. She was Pit boss of Tartarus before I was. And I came back to supplant her. But I didn't sell her. No, indeed. No, although she would have much preferred that, I suspect."

She fixed Brigid with a gimlet eye. "As for your question, sweetie, the answer is simple. Corruption. That's how I know everything that goes on up there—" She jerked her head to indicate the ville and its great white monolith thrusting like a rockcrete phallus high above the lakeshore.

"Or rather," she continued, "business as usual."

She sucked down some smoke and leaned forward. Her small eyes glittered like polished obsidian in the rolls of fat that were her cheeks. "That's another trap, that word 'corruption.' It doesn't mean what most people think it means. The barons and their little scam are no worse than any government throughout history in that they're all about enslaving the human race, and always have been. The kind of corruption that gets rulers' panties in a wad is when one of 'em gets a little too greedy, risks giving the whole game away by grabbing at too much. Makes it too obvious what's really going on. Alternately, it's when their greed leads them to make deals with us marks, to cut us some slack. This has the effect of cutting into the pies of the rest of the power structure, a definite no-no."

"I admit I am a bit confused here Ms. Orion," Brigid said slowly. "Which kind of corruption led to your discovering our identities—our existence?"

The woman shrugged, and laughed again. "You pick. You wondered earlier, and probably still, what my price was. Fair enough, but you'd get a lot more out of wondering what *their* price is. Anybody in government is always on the take for power and wealth—that's the only reason they're in government, the only reason *for* government. Only reason there's ever been. And like any thieves, there's no loyalty among them. No government is ever anybody's friend. Nobody in government is, either."

Kane tipped his head to the side. "That seems kind of like a sweeping statement," he said.

She fixed him with a stare like a couple of carbide drills. "You were in government," she said huskily, deep down in her vast throat, "all three. Right?"

"Right," Grant agreed. "And it was just exactly Kane's damn-fool notions of friendship that—"

He stopped and scowled more deeply.

"Exactly," Orion trumpeted. "When feelings of authentic friendship cropped up, what choice did you have to make?"

Grant lowered his head in a bull-like manner and thrust his head forward.

"She's got you, partner," Kane said. "Might as well yield gracefully, no matter how badly against the grain it goes."

He turned his icy gray gaze at Orion. He had shifted his patch up to his forehead to return binocular vision to his eyes. Not, he reflected, that he needed a lot of depth perception in viewing the mountainous Pit boss.

"How do we know we can trust you?"

"You can't. You trust me or you don't. Evidently your friend Lakesh trusted me enough to send you here."

Grant made a rumbling deep in his throat.

"Which is to say," Kane said, "that Lakesh trusted our ability to get out of here alive. At least we hope so."

"What is your price, then?" Brigid asked.

"So the cloistered senior archivist has learned practicality in her years as a renegade and refugee? It shouldn't surprise me, I suppose. You must have been a quick study for Lakesh to make you his protégée. Don't look so surprised—despite the growing friction among the baronies, Cobaltville's Magistrate Division shared substantial intel on the three of you with the other eight. And so it came to me."

Kane glanced at Grant. Unless she actually was blowing maryjane smoke up their butts—and so far she did show the goods—the rot within the Palladiumville Mag Division, and possibly its Trust, ran far wider and deeper than it ever had within Cobaltville. There had been covert dealings between the Magistrates and Guana Teague, to be sure, but they were more in the nature of the dealings between a puppet master and his marionette.

"And the price for telling us what we want to know?" Brigid persisted.

"You know, Red, I like you. I like you all. You each and every one of you have that go-to-hell look in your eyes, even if they're all of different shades. Mebbe the price should be a turn in the rack with all three of you at once."

Fortunately Grant's scowl was already at maximum depth. If it got any deeper his head would implode. Kane felt his own face turn to steel, although his stomach did some turning of a different kind. Brigid paled.

Maureen Orion laughed again. Huge and loud, ringing off the bedizened concrete walls. There didn't seem to be a lot this double-size woman did by half measure.

"I can tell by the looks on your faces you're none too thrilled by that offer. Too bad—I'd rock your worlds. I know some tricks—ah, but never mind."

She leaned forward again. Her imposing frontage got caught up on the edge of the decayed card table, and the billow of white flesh exposed by the plunge of her neckline swelled ominously. "I'll tell you what you can do for me," she said in a low, intense voice that was almost a hiss. "You can destroy the bastards!"

Even Kane recoiled from her sudden vehemence.

"Who?" Brigid asked.

"The barons. Their goons and toadies. And whoever it is behind them, who helped set them up and who props them up today. I want them pulled down. Smashed. Completely and utterly chilled. And I want to watch it happen before I die!"

Grant shook his head. "I don't quite see what you want from *us*."

"That you continue doing what you're doing. Until you win."

She sat back and trailed smoke out of her extravagantly painted lips. "So you see, I'm asking a very high price indeed."

"Oh, we'll pay," Kane said with a sidelong glance at Grant, who periodically made noises about running off to join the circus—or rather running off to playing shotgun with his squeeze Shizuka. "It's not as if we have much choice."

She nodded briskly, causing the pile of brilliant hair atop her head to wobble dangerously. In a few succinct words she recounted what had happened upstairs in the monolith: the intrusion, the fatal battle between Mags and intruders armed with wonder blasters, the literal postmortem and its still tentative conclusions.

She plunged two fingers into the tight crack between her ponderous breasts and brought forth a pearl-shiny disk. "Here's a copy of the files on the incident, all the reports and intel analysis."

She tossed it onto the faded and worn green baize as if dealing a card. Kane eyed it with distaste he found hard to conceal.

Favoring him with a "men are such babies" glare, Brigid leaned forward, picked it up and stuffed it into her own bodice.

"What we really came to find out," Grant said, "was how your mystery intruders got in and out."

Orion breathed smoke. "Easy. They didn't."

"I beg your pardon?" Brigid said.

"I don't see everything that goes on inside the whole ville. The maggots don't see everything that goes on inside the ville. Put us together, though, and you've got pretty complete coverage. If you look on the disk tucked away between your pretty titties, girlie, you will learn that the Mags' own vidcams showed no movement or activity in the corridors leading to the storeroom. Nobody was detected approaching any of the spaces bordering the room's six sides. Nor was there any sign of entry being forced through wall, floor or ceiling, as well as the door. As you're well aware, the HVAC ducting in the monolith and Enclaves is too small to pass anybody larger than a human child—even Hanratty wouldn't fit, with that chest of his. Vents weren't tampered with, no signs of motion picked up by the sensors in the ducts themselves. Fine layers of dust on the floors of all ducts leading to the storage space, meaning no one as large as the woman they chilled had passed through by any means including levitation."

"But somebody got in," Grant said.

"And out. Unless dust bunnies came to life, chilled a bag of Mags and left an altogether human corpse behind."

"Then how?" Kane asked.

The Pit boss shrugged. "You'd know more about that than I would, wouldn't you? Some variation of those jump gateways you use."

Once again Kane found the limits of his poker face being tested.

"How do you know about that?" Brigid asked.

"I got the official internal report on the incident upstairs, sweetie," Orion said. "You think I have that kind of access without knowing the maggots have a way of hopping instantaneously among their castles? And other places. Besides, everybody knows there's such a thing—the legends talk about the amazing ability to be, irrefutably, in far-apart locations without time to travel the intervening distance."

Kane looked at his companions. They were looking at him. He shrugged. His best guess was that the intruders had their own form of portable quantum interphase matter-transmission inducer, just as they did. But he was damned if he was going to let on to that in front of this woman. Even if she was as friendly as she acted, what she didn't know, she couldn't tell the Magistrates. Willingly or under duress.

Orion spread her tarot deck face up on the table. "That's all I got, honeys," she said.

Kane nodded. "This isn't part of our business, mebbe," he said in a measured way. "Mebbe none of our business at all. But I long ago learned to be wary of dealing with people when I didn't know what they stood to gain from it—or thought they did, which isn't always the same thing."

"I told you, hard man. To bring down those above. The ones who squat on our backs. Make us live like rats. Tell us it's all our fault. Like it was us pressed the buttons made the nuke-caust happen. Instead of the powerful—the ones they took over from."

She took a furious hit off her stogie. "Or mebbe not. Mebbe it was them all along. Either way, I wanna watch 'em fall."

"Perhaps Kane was wondering what actions you're taking to attain those ends," Brigid said. "Corruption, you said. But to be candid I'd like to know, too—how?"

Maureen Orion laughed. A quiet little laugh for her. It only made the curved walls of the concrete cocoon seem to bulge a little bit.

She leaned back and brandished her smoldering cigar. "Easy. Wonder where the cigars come from? They're not scavvy. People down in Beausoleil grow the weed in secret patches. Mags can't find 'em, not all. Not that they necessarily try that hard. Everybody wants something, my friend, and it's not always what the ones in power want you to want. As you three demonstrate in your own ways, don't you, now?

"If they're not interested in jack, sure as shit rolls downhill they're interested in something jack can buy—that price thing again. The profit from growing, chopping, curing and rolling those smokes is enough to make people run risks— and enough to make sure they can provide whatever it is the Magistrates in their area *do* want.

"The cigars come here in trader caravans. I swap 'em various things—my brew, mostly. Do they haul it all the way back down to the Carolinas? Generally not. They sell it off to thirsty scavvies, say, who found things in the ruins of Chi-town that the tobacco choppers down south want. Whatever.

"All I do is trade."

She smiled at them.

"That's it?" Kane finally asked.

"Nothing more subversive. And believe me, I specialize in finding out what those above—" once again a shoulder hunch and eye roll, which somehow emphasized the colossal weight of the monolith looming unseen over their heads "—want that they're not supposed to get. And supplying it to them. In exchange for favors, goods and services and, of course, selective vision problems."

"But isn't that dangerous?" Brigid asked.

Again the woman shook and roared with laughter. "You ask that question? The combat librarian?" She shook her head. "Anyways, I got a fatal disease. One nobody ever walks away from."

"What's that?" Grant asked. He had an edge in his voice. People weren't susceptible to contagion these days, by and large—most of those who were had turned to dust without passing on their genes, during skydark and the years of struggle afterward. Most sickness today was caused by postnatal exposure to rads or toxins. But infectious diseases still did stalk the land, and those who caught them could be triple-red danger zones. "What disease do you have?"

"Life," the vast woman said.

Grant frowned. Kane surprised himself by bursting into his own brief fit of laughter. "She's got us there, partner. No one here gets out alive."

"Dunno," Grant said, spinning the word out long. "We've known some people lived an awful long time—from that fused-out Nazi Skorzeny to our very own Lakesh." He didn't mention they'd known beings other than human who had lived longer still—by orders of magnitude.

"Which only means they've succeeded in cheating death so far," Brigid observed. "It's like gaming at a gaudy house—even if the tables are honest, if you play long enough, the house always wins."

"That's the spirit!" Orion exclaimed. "Spoken like a true gaudy slut. You know how to throw yourself into your role, Brigid Baptiste."

"Not too well, I hope."

The wooden door behind Orion jumped forward off its hinges with a crash and a squeal of tormented metal giving up the ghost.

Two Magistrates in full black hard-contact armor burst into the little room brandishing Sin Eaters.

Chapter 6

"Hands on heads, scumbags. Do it *now!*"

Kane, Grant and Brigid passed a look around. The Pit boss sat as if suddenly turned to a statue. Did Orion set us up? Kane wondered.

Slowly the Cerberus trio rose, hands obediently clamped to the sides of their heads. Faceless behind their red-tinted, slightly concave visors, the two Palladiumville Mags tracked them with their handblasters.

When the three were almost upright, two things happened simultaneously. Without so much as twitching a muscle beforehand Orion sloshed the pint of homebrew over her right shoulder, into the faceplate of the Magistrate on that side. And although no signal had passed between them, Hanratty the dwarf—despite his earlier outspokenness, had stood throughout the whole meeting so quietly against the wall that Kane forgot he was there—hurled himself at the legs of the other ville enforcer.

Grant dropped his big right hand, driving it into his pocket. Then he brought it up and forward.

The front of his raggedy pant leg gave way as if it had only been tacked by a few weak threads—as it had. A big gray Franchi SPAS combat shotgun came with it.

The Mag who'd taken the brew to his visor had just slammed the faceplate up: evidently they had orders to take prisoners, since the easiest thing in the world would have been to haul back on the guardless trigger of his Sin Eater and wave it back and forth until everybody was down and kicking or trending toward room temperature. Although his face was now vulnerable, Grant shot him in the chest.

The noise of the big 12-gauge scattergun going off was mind crushing. Under most circumstances the thick, curved polycarbonate breastplate of full Magistrate armor would shed either a full charge of buck or a rifled slug, even from a mighty 12-gauge, even close enough to get scorch marks from the muzzle flame. But Grant had loaded his scattergun specifically for Mag armor: it carried depleted-uranium penetrators sleeved in plastic sabots that fell away when the projectile left the barrel. There was nothing ferrous in the Magistrate carapace to activate the heat-flash chemical reaction of a DU round, and the projectile's velocity was way too low anyway.

But the pointed slug was incredibly dense and hard. It punched through the polycarb breastplate as if it were a pre-dark soft-drink cup. It began to yaw slightly as it smashed a rib in two, carrying fragments through the Mag's left lung and ripping a huge tear in the pericardium as it nicked the heart's left ventricle. It passed on through the fringe of the lung, fully sideways, knocked a rib clear loose from its mooring as it passed out the man's back, just missing the left scapula.

It didn't penetrate the backplate of the Magistrate armor. Instead it bounced back into the man's body cavity, now spinning like a slow, blunt, but supremely massive circular saw, and did it all over again.

The Magistrate folded without ever triggering his blaster.

The other fired a triburst as the dwarf flew at him. The little man struck him at the armored crotch, and his weight slammed the Mag back against the wall.

Blood squirted from Maureen Orion's pale bare skin as a round punched through her left shoulder just beneath the joint. Her vast mass sagged in her plush chair.

Kane was already in motion, throwing Brigid toward the floor as he lunged for the Magistrate.

Off balance, with the dwarf's dead weight sprawled on his legs keeping him tipped back against the wall beside the door, the Mag triggered another triburst. Two rounds missed. They bounced off the far walls and went whining and keening through the cramped space, miraculously intersecting no live meat, though one whanged off the fallen Mag's carapace. The third slammed into Kane's ribs three inches down and out from his left nipple.

"Fuck!" he exclaimed, losing a step. "That really hurts."

He closed with the Magistrate. As tall as Kane and bulkier in his black armor suit, the man seemed stunned to find that his attacker had just copped a solid hit from a nine-ball and was still coming. Kane grabbed the Sin Eater's perforated barrel shroud with both hands and put his whole weight into torquing it inward. It slipped from the Mag's fingers, pivoted off the base of his thumb, came away in Kane's hand.

The Magistrate lashed out with the hand from which the blaster had just been twisted. He caught his assailant across the bearded face and sent him reeling face first against the wall. Unfortunately for him Kane kept a firm grip on the Sin Eater, ripping it loose from the rig strapped to the Magistrate's forearm armor.

The big black man was swinging a shotgun to bear on the standing Magistrate and pumping the slide. Kicking aside the limp but bulky dwarf, the Mag lunged toward the man he'd slugged, intending to use him as a shield and try to reestablish control. The Outlands scum looked stunned, and a thin line of blood drooled from the slack side of his mouth into his unlikely blond beard.

The Mag grabbed Kane's left arm and tried to crank it up in a hammerlock behind his back. Kane bent quickly forward, dropping his purloined blaster. He grabbed the smooth slick armor behind the Mag's right calf with his own right hand, then straightened quickly, yanking the man's leg straight up between his own.

The Magistrate fell with a resounding crash. The thin rug, now sodden with blood, did little to cushion his fall. He let go his semicaptive's arm on the way down.

Kane spun. He curled the fingers of his right hand. His own Sin Eater ripped free of the sleeve of his shirt and slammed into his hand. As the fallen Mag struggled to rise, Kane dropped astride his chest, thrust the muzzle of his blaster up under the red visor and squeezed off a single shot.

Blood squirted over his hand and torn sleeve.

He felt the Mag's body spasm once and then go still with utter finality. He stood. The Sin Eater hissed back into its holster, and he turned to take stock of the situation.

His companions were unscathed. The same couldn't be said for their hosts. Maureen Orion emitted a croak of alarm and knelt in a tectonic movement at the side of Hanratty the dwarf, who still lay facedown, doing a lot of not moving. The back of his big head, where it curved in to met the neck, was a red crater.

"Hanratty!" Ignoring her own wounds, which were pumping fresh scarlet out into air with each pulse of her adrenaline-charged heart, she turned the dwarf over. Where his right eye had been was a pit filled with blood.

Maureen Orion looked up. Tears bubbled over the painted shelves of her lower lids and cut tracks through the makeup on her great cheeks as she cradled his ruptured head on her lap. "Those bastards. That's one more to pay them for!"

Grant had moved to secure the entry through which the Mags had entered with his shotgun at the ready, having reached wordlessly down to give Brigid a hand back to her feet. "You okay, Kane?"

Kane was bent over rubbing his chest where the bullet had hit. "Yeah. It just hurts like a son of a bitch."

No blood showed on his shirt. The shadow armor he wore beneath his clothes had kept the bullet from piercing his flesh. Unfortunately it hadn't absorbed the whole impact. "Probably cracked a rib," Kane said. "Feels like a knife stabbing me every time I breathe. *Damn.*"

"We likely to have more company?" Grant asked.

"No," Orion said. She sat up with the lifeless Hanratty sprawled across her lap. "If there were more, they'd have landed on us already. Somebody found Harrington and Ruiz here out on PPP and dropped a bug in their ears."

She had a pudgy hand pressed to her shoulder. Red worms crawled out between her clutching fingers and down. Her capacious face had a greenish tint visible even through its layer of makeup. Brigid came to her side but the huge woman waved her off.

"Go," she said in a pain-taut voice. "I'll be fine. It's just a flesh wound."

She laughed bitterly, pain turning her husky contralto to near baritone. "And I've got a lot of flesh to spare."

She laid Hanratty tenderly back down on the rug, stood with effort, moved to her desk, where she pressed a hidden button.

"Somebody'll come in a moment to guide you out. We can get you clear outside the walls without ever getting above the ground. This hellhole was built on top of the ruins of a pre-dark ville, like most of them. Us Pitters have spent generations making a tunnel system out of sewers and basements."

Grant jerked his head at the dead Mags cooling down and leaking into the threadbare throw rug. "What about them?"

"Leave them. My people will make them disappear. And then I'll make some Mag bastards pay—starting with telling me who shopped me to these dung beetles. Now clear out of here. I can explain two dead maggots better than I can the live three of you!"

As Maureen Orion's wound was bound, she told one of her lieutenants to guide them to the surface.

It was the slim black gaudy slut Brigid had decked, currently sporting quite a mouse beneath one puffed-out eye. She grinned at Brigid and said, "That's quite a punch you got there." Then she hefted a kerosene lantern and led off without further palaver.

Their route took them through an up-and-down path like a mad angular inchworm. As promised it encompassed stairways, ramps, tunnels, basements, buried rooms and ancient sewers. Some not so ancient, to judge by the smell.

Where a dark stairway from above debouched onto the damp tamped-earth floor of a large basement lay the sprawled body of what appeared to be a middle-aged male Pitter. More than that was hard to tell, since it had been beaten and stabbed almost shapeless. Recently, from the rich stench of fresh-voided bowels.

Their guide nodded grimly at the sacklike corpse. "Brought the Mags."

"Pit justice," Grant grunted.

"Swift and certain," Kane agreed.

"Got to be," said their guide.

"LAKESH HAS BEEN KIDNAPPED," Domi announced as soon as they returned to Cerberus redoubt.

"Kidnapped?" Brigid repeated incredulously.

"Yes. By Aborigines," the albino girl said. "I wasn't even there in the command center when it happened."

"Who was?" Brigid asked. They were gathered in the commissary in lieu of the giant main briefing chamber. The returned travelers had not yet even changed out of their disguises, although Kane had his shirt off and the top half of his shadowsuit skinned down around his waist so that a grim-faced Reba DeFore could bind his chest. The impact site still pained him when he breathed.

Domi hesitated, then nodded at the lanky bespectacled man sitting on the other side of the table from Kane. "Philboyd."

Kane looked at Grant and rolled his eyes.

The astrophysicist, one of the refugees from Manitius Moonbase, nodded his large narrow head sagely. "We were monitoring your vital signs signals from your biolinks. Dr. Lakesh was just remarking that from the sudden spike in respiration and heartbeat it appeared you three had managed to embroil yourself in another brawl."

"A bar fight," Kane said with a certain relish.

Philboyd didn't actually sniff, but looked as if he came *that* close. "We were so engrossed that we had no inkling anything might be amiss here until the door burst open and a trio of men with wild hair and watch caps burst in. They shouted at us in harshly accented English not to move. I was, however, so outraged by the invasion that I was, quite by reflex, in the process of standing up already. My unpreventable action appeared to provoke the invaders. One of them discharged some sort of hand weapon that surrounded him with a bluish nimbus and emitted an intolerably bright beam that shattered the environmental-ops station. Poor Neukirk had duty at that console, and he was scorched by the discharge and sustained facial cuts from flying glass—an unexpected consequence of consigning a man of Dr. Neukirk's attainments to menial tasks better suited to a common technician."

Kane winced as DeFore snugged the wrapping tight with perhaps a touch more emphasis than necessary. She disapproved of him and Grant, from habit if nothing else. It had not quite gone far enough that she sympathized to any visible degree with the hostility some of the recent arrivals showed the main Cerberus operators. The refugees tended to treat her as superciliously as everybody else from the original redoubt contingent. She just seemed to like to get her digs in on her own hook.

"Everybody takes their turns doing different jobs," Kane rasped.

"Except you, Grant, Domi and Brigid," Philboyd said.

"Anytime you want my job, tough guy," Grant said, "you got it."

The gash scar on Philboyd's prominent forehead turned scarlet.

"Gentlemen," Brigid said, "this is not helping to get Lakesh back."

Kane lolled his head back and around and looked at his partner. "Do we want him back? That seems like a question worth addressing."

"Of course we want him back!" Brigid flared. "What kind of question is that?"

"Perfectly reasonable one by me," Grant said. "But let's hear the rest of the story. If people are popping up inexplicably inside Cerberus, that's…interesting."

Both his companions on the just-ended Palladiumville mission glanced his way. Evidently he didn't feel like sharing what they learned there with the semi-outsider Philboyd.

"Done," DeFore said crisply, snapping shut her medikit. "Try to take a breather on getting bunged up for a while, will you, Kane?"

"No. I'm just totally addicted to the feeling of getting smacked in the ribs by fucking bullets. It's such a rush."

The stocky blond-dreadlocked woman glared at him and marched out.

Kane pulled the top half of his shadowsuit back on. "Okay, Philboyd, let's hear the thrilling climax."

"There's little enough to tell," the astrophysicist said. "We offered no resistance under the circumstances. We had little choice—even such a man as yourself can clearly see that. Can't you? We really could not possibly have acted—"

"Save the elaborate self-justifications for your pillow and get on with it," Grant growled.

The astrophysicist moistened his lips and fluttered his eyelids. "The intruders seized Dr. Lakesh and hustled him out the door. And then—"

"Let me guess," Kane said. "They vanished."

Philboyd's pitted cheeks tautened at the interruption. "Into skinny air," Domi agreed. "With Lakesh."

"Do you believe his captors were Australian aborigines, Dr. Philboyd?" Brigid inquired. She had taken to treating the Moonie physicist, who had made it repeatedly apparent that he had a more than passing interest in her, with all the cool correctness of a senior archivist.

He shrugged. "I'm no ethnologist," he said. "But my impression, as well as that of the other technicians on duty at the time, was that they resembled Aboriginals. If only because we'd seen features on them on the Discovery channel, back in the day."

"What about their speech?" Brigid asked. "Did they have Australian accents?"

"Would they?" Kane asked. "When you, Domi and Shizuka got back you mentioned that the vision they showed you had the whites getting pretty well wiped out during the nukecaust."

"It did," the archivist said. "It has occurred to me subsequently that, like much of the vision, it may have been intended more as allegory than a portrayal of literal truth. For example I doubt strongly that any Annunaki were literally transformed into outcroppings."

"I dunno," Grant said. "That punishment process Megaera had for sinners turned you into something a whole lot like a black rock statue."

"Be that as it may."

"Did the guy you spoke to have an Australian accent?" Kane asked. He looked to Domi, who shrugged; the diminutive albino woman, Outlands born and bred, had no referents for what such an accent might sound like.

"He did," Brigid said. "It stands to reason—even if the European-descended Australians were totally or substantially exterminated by the nukecaust and its aftermath, if English were still spoken by the aborigines—as Yindi spoke to us— it would presumably be descended from that dialect."

"If you'll permit me to answer," said Philboyd with a trace of irritation, "inasmuch as I was present for the incident in question, yes, the kidnappers did speak with Australian accents, and yes, I am familiar with such accents."

"I still don't see what use Australian aborigines would have for Lakesh," Grant said. "But if they do, they're welcome to him, as far as I'm concerned."

"You don't mean that," Brigid said.

"Sure, I do."

"You're the one who keeps talking about retiring from the game," Brigid said. "Does this mean you're willing to take over direction of operations against the hybrids?"

Grant looked sour. "Baptiste's got you there, partner," Kane said. "Don't feel bad. I can never put anything over on her, either."

He sighed and touched himself gingerly over the wrapping DeFore had placed on his ribs, now concealed beneath his shadow armor. "Still hurts like fire," he commented. "But it looks as if I'm going to Australia anyway."

"Have you looked at the map recently?" Philboyd said with a barely concealed sneer. "Australia is a largish sort of place."

"Uluru good place to start, no?" Domi said around a mouthful of a PBJ sandwich she'd just made herself.

"Makes sense," Kane said. "That's where this new quantum-space interference originates from, and if I remember correctly from your earlier jaunt, it's the big holy place for the aborigines. Isn't that likely where they'd have taken him?"

"You go," Domi stated flatly. "I stay home."

Everybody looked at her. "But you've been there before," Kane said.

"Sure have." Something was clearly distressing her; she was reverting to the clipped speech of her Outlands upbringing. "Aborigines got some spooky powers, them. They pissed at us, want no part of them. Big time."

"She has a point, Kane," Brigid said reluctantly. "They did indeed display remarkable abilities to us—including ample evidence that they might be able to exert such mastery over the space-time continuum as to account for the intrusions into the baronies and Cerberus."

She frowned. "I find myself disturbed, as well as perplexed. The aborigines are doing things that seem to run counter to the way they dealt with us before. While they did not leave us abundant choice as to whether to help them against Erica van Sloan and Baron Beausoleil, they seemed well-disposed toward us for doing so, even though it was, after all, what we had gone to Australia to do. But they seemed to have completely restored their traditional culture, including language and dress. The descriptions of the intruders, including ours, all portray them wearing contemporary Western clothes and speaking English. And these mysterious energy-beam weapons—" She shook her head.

"Mebbe this is some other faction of aborigines," Grant suggested.

"They didn't seem too prone to factionalization when we were there," Brigid said.

"Everybody's got factions, Baptiste," Kane said, looking pointedly at Philboyd.

The astrophysicist's pitted cheeks colored. "If you are insinuating—"

Everybody jumped as the intercom interrupted. "This is Bry in the command center," it said. "You all better get up here right away. We've got a communication coming in from Dr. Lakesh."

Chapter 7

"It is customary," the strange baron said, "to abase oneself when addressing the living god."

Sprawled on a throne of silken cushions and marble, the god-king may have chosen for unfathomable reasons to present himself in a setting barbaric even by apekin standards, but he still had Baronial Guards, these naked to the waist, wearing scarlet turbans wrapped tightly about their heads, and with extravagant curved swords thrust through the scarlet sashes they wore over spotless white pantaloons. A pair closed in on either side as if to lay hands upon the guest who stood before him.

If only the other barons could see what is befalling me! Baron Thulia thought. His cheeks burned with humiliated anger and more than a touch of fear. Then, as he dropped hastily to his knees—at least there was a gilt-edged crimson carpet laid on the steps up the dais to ease his frail knees—it occurred to him that this might have been precisely what his brother barons, and that presumptuous apekin she-devil Erica van Sloan, might have had in mind.

At the very least he knew to a bitter certainty, lowering his head like a common human in obeisance to the Dewa Raja of Tanimbar, that their prime reaction would be, *Better you than us.*

"Better," the baron murmured, sipping from a vessel that looked like a gilded skull.

Thulia sneezed as a calico cat walked before him, swaying its rump like an apewoman gaudy slut. Its tail trickled loathsomely across his face.

It was like a steam room within the secret throne chamber. A shaved-headed male slave, small, brown, gnarled and naked but for a loincloth, worked a silken cord that led to the ceiling, over a pulley and thence to a complicated but decidedly low-tech reciprocating drive that worked a ceiling fan. The fan itself, a giant kitelike assembly of bamboo and what appeared to be faded colored paper, did stir the air in the fashion of a paddle churning dense muddy water.

Dense, muddy, hot water.

"You may arise and be welcome, Baron Thulia," the god-king said. His voice had a peculiar piping quality, and seemed compound, as if comprising various flutes.

With difficulty, Thulia stood. His mouth was filled with sourness, and his nose ran with snot in a most undignified manner. The capital city of this bizarre and bizarrely unlooked-for baron—a hybrid of his own class, whose existence he had never so much suspected until the despicable van Sloan creature briefed him prior to his jump—was called Kuching, which meant "cat." And cats there were in mad profusion: cat frescoes staring from the walls, cat tapestries, carved cinnabar cats taller than Thulia himself flanking the throne. And of course the actual, repulsive, incessantly shedding beasts themselves. To which the baron was violently allergic.

The Baronial Guards had resumed their posts near marble columns twined with apparently living vines. Thulia felt a prickling, slightly stinging flush in his thin cheeks that had nothing to do with the temperature within the room, histamine reaction and possibly not even with his fury at being treated in such manner. Have I already contracted some beastly con-

tagion in this egregious pesthole? I've barely been here half
an hour!

"Your Majesty," he said tentatively, sniffling and angry all
over again at being forced into choosing his words like one
of his own human underlings, "I have come to—"

"You have come to Tanimbar to direct our efforts to insure
that they are conducted according to the liking of your fellows
in North America," the god-king said. His English was without accent. "We are quite aware."

He gestured languidly. "You may draw nearer, cousin."

Clamping down a scowl, Thulia did. As he came closer,
mounting the wide low base of the dais itself, he felt cool air
wafting from the direction of the throne itself. The duplici-
tous bastard! He's got a refrigeration unit built into the thing!

His small mouth sphinctered into near invisibility as a pair
of human servants brought forth a chair for him. Glancing
around, he momentarily froze with something more like horror than he thought himself capable of.

The servants were small, stocky, dark skinned and black
haired, like most of the admittedly few apekin he had encountered since jumping into the palace of the god-king. But they
differed in one terrifying respect: instead of eyes they had concave membranes over obviously empty sockets. Nor was there
any sign of surgical alteration such as sewing the lid closed.
To all appearances, the skin of their faces had grown that
way, stretched over cavities, like blind cave fish. He realized
the servant plying the fan was the same.

They placed the chair precisely, then withdrew, their bare
soles making only the slightest wisps of sound upon the polished
cinnabar of the floors and the carpets laid down upon them.

"Yes," the god-king said. "All my body servants are that
way. A simple genetic alteration. I make use of many biofacts

as servitors—these sightless ones, gilled fish-men to patrol my harbors, seven-foot-tall man-slayers with four arms and red skin."

He leaned forward. "The key—beyond my own convenience—is *awe*. You of North America rely upon your gleaming white castles and your black-armored legions with their firearms, fighting vehicles and helicopters to instill awe into your subjects. Despite your access to an overall higher level of technology than my modest kingdom, it derives, with only minor if key enhancements, from that of late-twentieth-century America. It is of course because you have but limited resources of the higher art at your disposal."

A smell of incense, alien, sweet, incisive, was carving its way through thick air and nasal mucus and into Baron Thulia's sensorium like a subtle scalpel. The light of tropical morning sun, which Thulia was grateful he had not yet had to confront directly, slanted in through angled slots in the ceiling, producing a soft luminance in the chamber that was almost liquid itself. He became gradually aware of music playing faintly, as if from a distance, yet sourceless and seemingly all around, with just persistent haunts and hints of melody to separate it from the random tinkling of wind chimes, although chimes there were, and a whistle of flutes, and an almost subliminal percussive beat.

He felt his head nodding, blinked rapidly to clear the fog from his brain. Is the bastard trying to hypnotize me?

"When we journeyed to these islands almost a century ago," the god-king continued, "we likewise possessed some advanced tools and much advanced knowledge. But unlike you we did not have the mighty North American industrial base to draw upon. Even after the devastation of the megacull and two centuries of aftermath, great and even relatively accessible resources remained for you to salvage during the building of your baronies."

He smiled thinly. "Not so for us exiles. The empire to which these islands belonged, the so-called Republic of Indonesia, had industrial technology only slightly behind that of your North American antecedents. But it was more centralized, and accordingly more easily neutralized. Indeed, most of it was wiped out of existence, a far greater proportion than North America lost.

"Whereas you suffered catastrophic damage to the western extreme of your continent, these islands received the effects of the Soviet earth-shaker devices salted along the Pacific Rim far more directly. The eruptions, the quakes, the tsunami they engendered—especially the explosion of a supervolcano beneath what was once the island of Rabaul—simply scoured most of the islands bare not only of life but of most of even the most enduring of industrial works. Whereas many shops and factories remained for your exploitation even a century after the nukecaust, most of what base these islands had was simply eradicated. Even the foundations were swept away as if they had never been."

He paused to sip from his golden skull. Thulia could definitely see condensation on its contoured surface now; it was doubtless self-chilled, as well. The low-tech appearance of this semi-inner sanctum was just that, appearance, down to the stultifying heat and humidity that would only affect visitors.

Beyond that the only words Thulia could summon to describe it were "barbaric splendor." The throne of polished marble, the lustrous deep red floor, the vine-twined pillars of marbles, the great fleshy-fronded plants flanking the throne, the rich carpets, the censers smoldering on their skinny stands, the omnipresent cats: all could have belonged to a throne room centuries or even millennia before. Nothing visible or even perceptible clashed with that impression—unless one were close enough, and as perceptive as Baron Thulia.

It's not just to evoke awe, he realized with a sudden insight flash. He enjoys this.

Somehow that realization made him as uneasy at the sense of being altogether at the mercy of another being, a being whom everything he had known throughout his life argued should not exist.

THE HYBRIDS AS A WHOLE made much of their incapacity to feel. Emotion was a messy, chaotic thing. Emotion was what made it impossible for the apekin ever to rise above the level of savages, of animals. Hybrids were creatures of the intellect, their minds far more powerful than those of mere humans, their feelings subjugated both by their innate qualities and by disciplined thought. The barons, as the highest form of hybrid, were supposed to be the most rational and unemotional of all.

Baron Thulia, on the other hand, was high-strung. Positively skittish.

He had originally thought himself a freak, had desperately feared—itself an emotion supposedly holding little sway over hybrids, far less barons—discovery that he was tainted, and so would be expunged by his fellows. Over the years he had come to harbor ever less furtive suspicions that all was not as he himself believed it ought to be. He gradually became aware of quirks within his fellows' psyches. It was nothing overt: a comment made during their regular rejuvenation sessions in the base beneath Archuleta Mesa, odd tidbits of demeanor or reaction during councils, gossip concerning peculiar behavior.

In the past few years what had been hints became blazingly

obvious. It all seemed to have sprung from, or at least been catalyzed by, Baron Cobalt losing control over his own minions, with the result that three key underlings went rogue. Since then, everything had gone to pieces—including quite literally the Archuleta Mesa facility itself, destroyed when the wretched Cobaltville renegades crashed an Aurora craft into it.

Since then outright baronial eccentricities had been driven into the open: the megalomania of Baron Cobalt, the odd obsession with enjoying carnal knowledge of apekin women that consumed Baron Ragnar, Baron Sharpe's delusion of immortality.

Yet while Thulia now knew he was not unique in being subject to certain mental weaknesses, he could not combat the dread that he was the most afflicted among the survivors and that those weaker than him had already succumbed.

Doing the opposite of allaying those fears was the fact that his was the smallest and frankly least consequential barony of the nine. Consisting of what had been considered New England, his domain had once contained one of the greatest concentrations of population and wealth in the United States, which meant of the entire globe. Unfortunately that had made it a prime Soviet target in the nukecaust. So Thulia ruled over a tiny territory with a minute population that was, however, rich in ruins—mostly still lethal hotzones, quite beyond useful exploitation.

Smallest and weakest though his barony unmistakably was, one advantage had come into play since the breakdown of unity: Thuliaville alone was not surrounded by rivals potential or actual. His domain adjoined only Sharpeville, plus regions of what had been eastern Canada reclaimed by wilderness, which so far as Thulia and the other barons were concerned, was welcome to them. If he lacked the buffer around his baronial ville provided the other barons by the enormous territories they ruled, he also lacked the enormous problems entailed in ruling such sprawls. A fact that the other barons had pressed upon him as the prime reason he should be the one to undertake the mission to the South Seas to cut out the heart of whatever evil was infiltrating the very fastnesses of the barons: he, simply, had less to risk by his absence, since his small territory was, almost paradoxically, least vulnerable, either to attack from without or internal disorder.

He might have played one final card: that the most suitable emissary would be the mere human Erica van Sloan, de facto baron of Cobaltville or not. In part he had not done so because of his dread of his own inadequacies. Despite the fact van Sloan was a mere human, even if of greatly superior gifts, and consequently inferior to any hybrid, much less that crowning glory of assisted evolutionary progress known as a baron, he was flat afraid of her. She intimidated him.

He knew he was not alone in that. And van Sloan enjoyed after all the patronage of her son, Sam, who, if temporarily thwarted in his quest to make himself imperator first of North America and then Earth, was still a force of unknown nature and unplumbed but horrific potency. All barons feared her cunning and her malevolence, human or not—and even more, they feared Sam.

That, finally, had been what prevented Thulia from pressing a case that Erica, not himself, should be dispatched like a servant to dance attendance upon this barbarian baron in the southern hemisphere; he didn't trust her. At least when she was at home in Cobaltville she was more or less contained, as contained as anybody could be who could jump at will to a hundred locations on Earth's surface and beyond, including to the fallen imperator's sulking spot by the great pyramid outside the ruins of Xian in China. Whereas who knew what mischief she might get up to unleashed far beyond the boundaries of North America and any sensible ability of her fellow barons to keep tabs on her?

Especially inasmuch as she alone—but for, presumably, her demon offspring—had known of the very existence, not just of other colonies of hybrids upon Earth, but of other baronies. Such as this savage satrapy in the South Pacific islands.

"YOU HAVE the advantage of me, O God-King," Baron Thulia said. He sneezed again. "Evidently you have long been aware of the existence of the nine baronies of North America. Yet until the last few days I and most of my fellow North American barons were entirely unaware of yours."

"Perhaps the information you and your fellow barons of North America have been given has been as carefully managed and measured as what you yourselves choose to tell your own human cattle."

Thulia felt his cheeks burn. He had subconsciously resisted acknowledging what was an all but self-evident fact. Irrationally, he hated the strange baron for forcing him to confront it.

"You believed you were quite alone, did you not? That you were the only hybrids on Earth. Yet there are other colonies of us scattered across the planet. Perhaps all were founded by fugitives such as myself. Perhaps some were seeded as part of a deliberate policy, and the knowledge of one another's existence just as deliberately kept from them. Who knows? We exist. We are not as powerful as you of North America—even as I have said, our technological base is not so wide and deep as yours. For that reason if no other, we have been assiduous in keeping our existence secret from you. But now with the onset of troubling events in Australia, we have allowed you to learn of our existence."

"But why? Why not deal with the situation yourselves, or simply lie low and allow us to confront the problem without revealing yourselves?"

The god-king nodded smilingly. "Wise questions. The answer is simple—we fear." .

Thulia blinked his exceptionally large and limpid blue-green eyes. He knew fear too well. He knew also what the other hybrids feared, even other barons: they feared loss of power, feared loss of access to the technologies that kept them alive, feared most of all, the brutish lusts and unthinking passions of the apemen. Yet it was rare for one to admit it so baldly. He moistened his lips with his tiny pale pink tongue.

"Fear what, Your Majesty?"

The strange baron leaned forward and spoke one word: "Uluru."

"Uluru?" Thulia blinked. It took him a moment to recall that van Sloan had spoken of the thing. An immense boulder, sacred to the peculiar subspecies who had been manifesting themselves so mysteriously in the baronial strongholds. "I don't understand."

"You will. It is a threat potentially so great as to endanger the dominion of our people over the ape-kind. Therefore I have chosen that we should work together to put an end to it."

The Dewa Raja leaned back in his throne. "By my command an invasion force and a fleet to carry it assemble upon the island of Tanimbar, to the south and east of here. Tomorrow I sail to join that fleet, finalize my preparations and then put paid to the savages and their magical rock for good and all. And to possess myself of the powers of Uluru itself—a task at which even Erica van Sloan and Baron Beausoleil failed."

Thulia blinked his eyes more rapidly. The creature was either deluded, lying to him or knew something else Thulia himself had no inkling of.

"But I shall not fail," the god-king continued. "And because you have come to assist me, I shall graciously share the bounty of our conquest with you."

For some reason a jocular vulgarism from his own ville's Tartarus Pits tolled like a bell within Baron Thulia's mind: *When pigs grow wings.*

Chapter 8

"Lakesh!" Brigid exclaimed, staring at the large communicator screen. "You're alive."

Seated within what appeared to be a tent, Lakesh frowned. "Why would I not be alive? I was abducted, not assassinated." He turned to an aged Aboriginal man with a short furze of snow-white hair covering his round head, who sat across a small camp table from him. He wore a khaki shirt. "Yes, thank you, I would like more tea, if you please," Lakesh said. The elderly man smiled benignly and nodded to a young man standing by, who refilled Lakesh's cup from a brass teapot.

"They're giving you a break from the whips and chains, is that it?" Kane demanded.

"Don't be more obtuse than necessary, Kane. The aborigines have no whips and chains. Surely the account of our female friends showed you they're not like that at all."

"I also know that every culture has its subgroups and factions, some of them outlaws who do not follow the same rules as the overculture," Brigid observed dryly.

"These are indeed the same people you dealt with before—the Anangu branch of the Arrernte group. Uluru lies just beyond the flap of this very tent." He waved appropriately.

"Where's Yindi?" Domi demanded, referring to the middle-aged aborigine who had escorted the three women through a personalized presentation of Tjukurpa, the Dreamtime, as

well as debriefed them for their attack to free the pregnant
Quavell from Erica, Baron Beausoleil and their henchmen.

"He is busy about his affairs. I can ask Old Man to summon him if it would make you more comfortable."

"I'd also observe that kidnapping you wasn't altogether
consistent with the impression we received of Yindi and his
people," Brigid said.

The Cerberus director seemed in an unusually waspish
frame of mind. Perhaps he was not expecting to be greeted
by a barrage of questions. "Why not? He kidnapped you ini-
tially, didn't he? Diverting you on a jump, no less. In any
event, I am not a prisoner at all, as you can clearly see. That
was all a misunderstanding."

"Yeah, a bunch of these dudes accidentally happened to
materialize out of thin air and zap our environmental-ops
workstation," Kane said, gesturing at the slagged console.
"Then when they realized where they were and what they'd
done they hightailed it home, equally accidentally dragging
you with them. Imagine their surprise. Hell, it could happen
to anybody."

Lakesh's blue eyes blazed furiously either side of his thin
nose. His companion leaned farther into the picture.

"Perhaps you could introduce me to your charming friends,
Doctor," the Aboriginal said in a lilting accent.

"Um. Ahem. Yes, of course. Old Man, these are my associates, Dr. Brigid Baptiste, Dr. Brewster Philboyd. The tiny,
exquisitely pale creature with the ruby eyes is Domi. The hulking, surly one is Grant, the lean, sarcastic one is Kane. Ladies,
gentlemen—I use the terms advisedly—this is the Old Man."

"'Old Man'?" Kane echoed. "Is that a name or a title?"

"It is whatever you wish it to be, friend Kane," the elder
said in a burbling bass voice. "Old Man, Old Guy, Old Abo,

the Elder—call me anything you like, only don't call me late for supper."

He beamed immoderately. Kane crossed his arms and leaned against his friend. "Great," he said. "Another pushy old guy."

"Who thinks he's a comedian," Grant added.

"Ignore their badinage, Old Man," Lakesh said. "It's their way of covering for their insecurities."

"Watch that," Grant rumbled. "Or the next time we happen to be together in the same room—the same continent, anyway—I might just get to feeling so insecure I'll turn your head around backward on your neck for you."

Lakesh glowered. "Do not try my patience, Grant—"

Domi stamped her foot. Even in her waffle-stomper hiking boots it didn't make much noise on the resilient tile floor of the command center. But everybody shut up and turned to stare at her.

"I've read about people stamping their feet when angered," Sally Wright said, "but I don't think I've ever actually seen anybody do it before."

"Will you men stop wagging your weenies at each other and get the damn hell to the story?" the albino woman yelled furiously.

Lakesh blinked. "Why, certainly, Domi, my sweet. I am so sorry to have distressed you. In short, Old Man directed his associates to abduct me because of sheer misunderstanding."

That produced nothing but silence among the listeners in Cerberus. This made Lakesh smile.

"For some time Old Man has been monitoring electronic communications worldwide, including North America. Apparently some of his capabilities are quite sophisticated, because his people have eavesdropped on baronial traffic and even some of our own."

"Impossible." In the background, Donald Bry tried without success to restrain his exclamation.

"I would have thought so, too, Donald, dear boy," Lakesh said. "I also thought it impossible for normal human beings to teleport themselves without the use of any external equipment whatsoever. Be that as it may, listen in they did. But their penetration of our communications was less than perfect. Among other things, they derived the impression that I was still working for the benefit of the so-called Archon Directorate."

"He posed a possible threat to us," Old Man said, still entirely jovial. "But he knew more about the Totality Concept and the Archon Directorate and its schemes than any human alive. And also because his unparalleled knowledge of physics might prove of use to us in our current endeavor."

Kane felt his eyes narrow at the way Old Man said "human." Unquestionably he knew more than a little about the true nature of Earth's self-appointed masters—including the fact that the Archon Directorate itself was a scam. He turned to the red-haired archivist.

"These are the same people you and Domi and Shizuka saw dancing around campfires wearing mostly red-and-yellow paint, Baptiste?" Kane asked.

Brigid could only shrug helplessly. "What we told you was what we experienced. You can ask Domi or Shizuka if you doubt me."

"Perhaps they use different technologies for different applications," suggested Sally Wright. "The traditional practice including Dreamtime when it works best, modern science when that seems called for."

She cringed her head into the collar of her jumpsuit as everybody turned to look at her. "Sorry for speaking out of place. I know I'm a newcomer here...."

"Makes as much sense as anything else I've heard so far," Kane said.

"Sally has hit upon the gist of it," Lakesh said. "You must understand, my friends, what is happening is nothing less than that the Australian aborigines are recovering racial memories lost for millennia."

"Tens of millennia," Old Man said, smiling through his short snowy beard as at some private joke.

Irritation barely flickered across Lakesh's face. "At least we'll get some entertainment out of watching these two try to upstage each other," Grant said sotto voce. Domi sniggered.

"I beg your pardon, Grant?" Lakesh said. "Did you have some comment you wished to share?"

"Just clearing my throat."

Lakesh's desire to hold forth won a quick victory over any inclination he may have had to press issues. "What is happening is tremendously exciting. Not even I can grasp the full ramifications of it all. I can tell you that Old Man has utterly convinced me to throw the whole weight of Cerberus and its resources behind him and his people."

"That's big of you," Kane said in a thin voice, "to commit all our time and energy and lives and little things like that."

"I understand your resentment, friend Kane, of what must seem from your perspective to be even more than my customary high-handedness," the whitecoat said with more than customary charity. "But you must also realize there is a terrible threat hanging over our heads, and all of humanity. The hybrids even now assemble an invasion force in the Cific islands north of Australia to capture Uluru. Should they come into possession of its secrets the consequences would be disastrous. They would give an untold boost to their goal of subjugating humankind without hope of redemption."

"Secrets?" Brigid frowned. "Secrets not even Erica van Sloan found in weeks of work inside Uluru?"

"The very secrets she sought, Dr. Baptiste," Old Man said. He smiled even more widely. "But they were not available then, when my new friend Yindi called upon your help, and which you and your friends so generously gave."

"What secrets are those?" Domi demanded. Kane judged she didn't understand what was going on here and it was making her peevish.

Lakesh assumed a look of ineffable smugness. "Think, dearest Domi—if we told you, they wouldn't be secrets any longer."

She turned and stamped out of the room.

GRANT'S BIG, STRONG FACE crinkled. "What's that smell? Roses?"

They appeared on a vacant patch of armory floor. One moment there was nothing except the light strips shining from the low ceiling on an open expanse of concrete stained with spilled lubricants and painted with broad red-and-yellow bands and markings of lost significance, the shelves and racks and piles of crates dark silent masses around.

Then they were there: eight humans. Two women and six men. Unmistakably aborigines, although two of the men were unusually large, as tall as Kane.

Aside from the floral smell, which Kane also distinctly noted even as Grant was mentioning it, there was no other manifestation. No shimmer, no fall of glittering motes, no sound, no fury, no nothing. Just—they were there.

Dressed not as Brigid, Domi and Shizuka had described the aborigines they encountered in Australia not long before, in loincloths and paint. But rather in what appeared standard Western dress.

They stepped forward grinning. "G'day," said one, an exceptionally dark-skinned young man, a little shorter and wirier than the other men. He was dressed in loose red trousers and athletic shoes, a light windbreaker over a white shirt pinstriped pale blue. He had a whole jungle of hair grown into thick dreadlocks and more or less confined within a big, saggy red, yellow, white and black mushroom of a knit cap. Like several of the others he had swirls and spirals painted on his cheeks in white. "Fair dinkum pleasure to be among you."

He stopped and looked around him with the total self-assurance of a terrier confronting a mastiff convention. "To whom ought I of politeness present myself to first, then? Don't want to ruffle any feathers."

Stone-faced, Grant nudged Kane in the ribs.

"Hey!" Kane said. "Since when am I the leader of this mob?"

"Didn't say you were the leader," Grant said. "But you are the point man."

"Oh." Kane stood and straightened his own faded denim shirt. "Right. I'm Kane." He stepped forth and stuck out his hard scarred hand.

The teak-colored hand that gripped it in return was as unmarked as an infant's, oddly slim and graceful, in some ways almost reminiscent of a hybrid's. But there was nothing hybridlike in its firmness. It felt like steel wire wound around a vanadium-alloy armature. Kane sensed that if he gave in to the old, old Mag impulse—which he had to admit to himself he had felt, stirred by the almost feminine delicacy of the hand's appearance—and tried the old metacarpal-crushing game, he might be lucky to reel his own digits back unmangled.

"A pleasure, Kane," the aborigine said earnestly. Except it came out "Kine," like what Baptiste told him once was an old word for cattle, and stretched out more than a little. He had a clipped way of speaking, almost staccato. "I'm Jonny Corroboree, and this here's my mob."

He turned. "We brought a couple teams with, just the way our Old Man worked it out with yours. This here's War Boom Ben, my tech boy." He indicated a gangly youth with a narrow knobby face and a dark green ball cap turned backward atop a shag of curly brown hair. He wore a dark green T-shirt with a few narrow sinuous stripes of black and others of gray that seemed to be intended as camouflage. He wore pants of a different camou pattern, basically desert beige, so grandly wide they seemed to be wearing him. The copious cargo pouches were bulging with stuff. He stepped forward nodding shyly.

"Next is my far walker, who answers to Mary Alice," Jonny said. "She conveys us all about this broad blue globe of ours."

Mary Alice smiled and said, "Hi," also shy. She was tall for this group, though shorter than Brigid, slim. Her skin was lighter, almost olive, and her features were finer than those of the others. Her hair streaming down from beneath a slate-gray beret was darkest, almost blue-black, pin-dreaded. She wore a lightweight dusty-pink blouse and faded dungarees.

Next Jonny indicated a man of Kane's height, incredibly wide, squared-off shoulders and a chem-drum chest balanced atop a pair of almost comically skinny bowed legs. He had an incredible scarred badlands for a face, and little perceptible neck, so that his long bearded chin seemed to rest on his clavicle. His eyes were striking yellow. "This is Tyree, my bull boy."

"Pleased to meetcha," Tyree told Kane in a sonorous voice, shaking his hand with a huge meat hook.

Jonny put his arm around the shoulders of the next, a man not much taller than he, with dark dusty-red dreads and characteristic Aboriginal features: broad nose, prominent brow ridges. He wore khaki cargo shorts and a tan shirt with loops on the shoulder. "And this here's my cobber Billy Handsome," Jonny said. "You'll not want for a finer mate, even among this fine lot. In his case the handsome goes straight down to bone."

"A pleasure," Billy said, grinning, and when he grinned Kane could see he was very handsome indeed, even if his appearance was unorthodox by the standards Kane was used to. "I'm talker for our other team, even though Jonny has a tendency to do the talking for us all, and a good number besides. Allow me to present my friends—Nobby, Rita and Bush Baby Bob. They're my tech boy, far walker and bull boy respectively."

Nobby was a small, round-faced youth with his brown eyes swimming behind a pair of giant dark-rimmed glasses. What looked like a magnifier attachment was folded away along one wing. Rita was a pretty, sturdy woman with dark blond dreads reminiscent of Reba DeFore's. Bush Baby Bob was huge, almost as tall as Grant, and wider. Kane, who'd encountered a few Samoans knocking around the Cific islands, wondered if he had one or two of those for ancestors.

Kane shook hands with all in turn, and then introduced his own companions, including Sally Wright, who seemed a natural appendage to the core group, and Philboyd, who emphatically was not but had tagged along because he didn't want to miss anything. The newcomers, even the painfully shy War Boom Ben and the scarcely less Mary Alice were nothing but smiles.

"Were they all like this when you were down there, Brigid?" Grant asked quietly out the side of his mouth.

"They were cordial, or at least Yindi was, he being the only one we spoke with at length."

"And even he was pretty stern," Domi added. "Don't know why they're all so happy all of a sudden."

"If you don't mind my asking," Sally Wright said tentatively, "how is it you're able to appear here in the middle of the redoubt as you did?"

Jonny Corroboree grinned his infectious grin. "Like I told you, it's our far walkers do the trick."

"How do they do it?" Kane asked.

Mary Alice and Rita looked at each other. Rita laughed. She had an easy way with laughter. A very handsome woman, if not so quietly striking as Mary Alice, Kane couldn't help noticing.

"It's something of a genetic predisposition," she said, "and then again, something of a skill. Not easy to describe in words—especially not English, if you'll pardon my saying so."

"You mean you really do just walk through walls?" Domi exclaimed.

"Oh, yes."

"It's not fair," Grant burst out.

Kane gave him a cynical look. "When did you start expecting life to be fair, partner? In case you've forgotten, that was the whole point of Mags—to make sure life never did become fair. Not that we ever saw much danger it might happen."

"But look, Kane. We jump and it turns us inside out. We come out puking up our guts. Them, they traipse through time and space without turning a hair, and come out literally smelling like roses!"

Kane cocked a brow. "Since you put it that way—" he turned to Jonny Corroboree "—can you teach us that trick?"

"No chance, cobber." The apparent Aboriginal leader flashed his toothpaste-ad smile. "Sorry."

The others were conversing in a fluid alien speech. Listening to them, Brigid's brow slowly furrowed deeper and deeper.

"Is that your Anangu language?" Brigid asked. "I can't pretend I learned more than a smattering, but this sounds different from what I heard spoken when we…when we were in Australia before."

The newcomers shared a secret glance. "It is now," Billy Handsome said. "It's crew talk."

"And whatever might that be?" Sally Wright asked.

"The original language all us folk you call *aborigines* spoke," Jonny said, "seventy-five thousand years ago."

Chapter 9

"How come everywhere we go recently is overrun with these damn mutant-freak survivals?" Kane demanded, whacking with his machete at an enormous snake that dropped its horse-sized head at him from a dead fallen tree that arched over their path. It regarded him with a baleful orange eye as big around as a Krugerrand. It was a true monster, brown with brown lozenges outlined in black running up a body that, where Kane could now see it coiled around the trunk of the fallen tree, was not much smaller around than Kane's own. It successfully dodged his cut and recoiled hissing out of harm's way.

A small voice behind him said something. "What's that?" he demanded, edging under the tree, menacing the serpent with his heavy-bladed knife.

"I said, it's not a mutant, sir."

Kane looked around. The speaker was War Boom Ben, the team's tech boy. How he got a name like that being so damned diffident was anybody's guess. Mebbe it was some kind of ritual thing.

Kane waved at the monster. "Got to be. Look at the size on that thing. Got to be twenty feet long at least."

Ben smiled shyly. "Might be even bigger, sir," he said in a voice soft but heavily weighted with what Baptiste assured him was an Australian accent. "They were known to grow to ten meters even before the nukecaust."

"I'm going around the tree, myself," Domi announced. She had on a khaki shirt, khaki bush shorts, steel-toed boots and of all the damned things a pith helmet. Hell knew where she'd found the thing in the Cerberus armory. She carried in her hands, not slung, a .308 NATO M-14 battle rifle about as long as she was. If you asked Kane, she was taking this jungle girl thing way too far. But of course nobody asked him.

"Not a mutie?" he asked, staring at the snake and feeling fresh waves of sweat cascade down his face to join the many layers exertion in the brutal heat and humidity had already laid there. The snake gave back an unwinking orange gaze.

"Not at all, sir."

He uttered a little laugh, unconvincing even to himself, and straightened from the unconscious crouch he'd assumed. "Well, then. Nothing to worry about, Domi. Big guy's probably as scared of us as we are of him."

Jonny Corroboree strode beneath the python without so much as glancing up to slap Kane on the shoulder. "Naw," he said. "That lot ate people even before the nukecaust. Since that time we're like a major food group for these blokes. Good job this lad wasn't hungry, eh?"

"City boys," Domi said. "You can put that silly chopper away, too. The brush here isn't anywhere near thick enough we have to hack a path through it."

"Not on your life," he assured her. "Not after coming face-to-face with that thing."

By this time Ben, Mary Alice and Tyree had all strolled beneath the vast serpent with equal unconcern. So far their blue-beam wonder blasters had been nowhere in appearance. Bringing up the rear, Tyree was toting an altogether conventional AKM assault rifle borrowed from the redoubt's seemingly endless supply.

The snake raised its head and laid it onto its twined body, as if the humans were too puny to bother with anyway.

"Tell me again," Kane suggested as they tramped into a clearing, "why we couldn't just land in downtown Tanimbar City?"

"Spies," Jonny said with his indestructible cheerfulness. "The Dewa Raja's spies. They lie thick on the ground in Tanimbar. Not so unusual for a major port city."

"Dewa Raja?" Kane asked. "What's that mean?"

" 'God-king,' " Mary Alice said, smiling shyly at him.

He didn't find particularly appealing the heavy features of most of the aborigine contingent, including those of Rita, the other far walker who was back in North America with Baptiste, Grant and her three teammates searching for some kind of mystery artifact. He didn't think they were ugly, just somewhat strange looking. Which admittedly was something of an obstacle to acceptance for a man conditioned since birth to regard as suspicious any deviance from what he had been taught to consider standard human appearance. The group's relentless friendliness has begun to eat away at that reservation even as it had ground on Kane's nerves.

But Mary Alice was pretty by Kane's standards. Very pretty. Definitely easy on the eyes. Her presence might go a long way to lighten the load on this fool's mission.

He showed her his grin. She paled just a little, and her step faltered briefly. Damn, he thought. Am I that scary?

Probably, he admitted. And these folks don't have lots of reason to trust white people, even after all these years.

"So how do you know so much about what's going on in Tanimbar City?" he called after Jonny, who was leading the way with a confoundedly springy step as if taking a Boy Scout troop for an afternoon hike through the world's tamest nature preserve.

"Our spies are thick on the ground, too," he said. "Thank Old Man for that. And cheer up—the coast is just ahead over this next ridge."

They had jumped—or far walked, as the aborigines called it—onto the island a couple of miles back, beside a giant tumble of granite boulders atop a hill rising out of the forest. Kane suspected the rocks served somehow as roadmarks or anchors for Mary Alice, although quite obviously the far walkers didn't require special geomagnetic nodes to function the way Lakesh's interphasers did. But they had offered no explanation, and Kane harbored a suspicion that if either he or Domi asked, they'd get a figurative pat on the head and a smiling, "Hard luck, mate, but you wouldn't understand."

Although lush and tropical, the woods weren't exactly jungle. Or maybe they were: Kane was anything but clear on the niceties of what exactly constituted a jungle. It certainly wasn't swamp, like the boggy bayous of the Mississippi delta in south Samariumville. Although the general lushness and profusion of the foliage indicated they obviously didn't stint on rainfall hereabouts, the drainage was evidently pretty good. Their elevation had been steadily if subtly declining since they left the rock clump and made their way between alternating stands of trees and undergrowth-choked clearings.

"So, why you people so different, anyway?" Domi asked. Obviously she was somewhat weirded out by the whole experience, despite her carefully maintained air of jaunty unconcern; she was lapsing sporadically back toward the elliptic outlander speech she'd grown up with. "When Brigid and I went to Uluru before, everybody was dancing, naked except paint and loincloths, mostly paint. Dancing and doing *aunquiltha.*"

Kane grinned at the way the Anangu word for *magic* slipped effortlessly from her tongue. She and her companions had had some knowledge of the language inserted directly in their minds via the strange Dreamtime by the shaman Yindi. He also grinned at the way Shizuka's name didn't cross the albino woman's tongue at all. Although sharing danger had reconciled them somewhat from mortal-enemy status, they had apparently not progressed to the inviting-each-other-for-sleepovers stage.

"We woke up," Tyree said with an air of finality. His long, craggy face, even more scarred than Kane's own, smiled. But the expression didn't touch his lynx-yellow eyes.

"Why couldn't we at least have come out on the beach, then?" Kane asked, as much to change the subject as anything else.

"Got to be careful how we approach the people hereabouts. Touchy blokes."

"And who might they be?"

"Sea Dayaks."

"And what are they, headhunters?" Kane asked flippantly.

Something whirred past his right elbow to thunk and stand quivering in the squat pineapple-like bole of a cycad. Kane had to stare at it for a couple of heartbeats before the optic center of his brain made sense of it: yes, a dart, carved of pale yellow wood or even middling-fresh bone with a twist of white plant fiber for a flight.

"Why, yes," Jonny said, as small dark-skinned men with white skull faces painted over their own features rose from the undergrowth all around them. "Now, how'd you guess that, mate?"

"IT'S A TURTLE," Nobby said.

"What?" Grant demanded.

The round-faced tech boy cringed. "Don't let his lack of manners intimidate you," Brigid said. "He's just gruff by nature."

"*Do* let my manners intimidate you, if you know what's good for you," Grant growled. "You didn't just tell us we came all the way out here to look·for a turtle, did you?"

Nobby blinked behind his dense specs. "Yes."

Flashlight beams crisscrossed ahead of them, illuminating floating motes, some with wings. They were in the death-dark corridor of the storage area of a derelict museum beneath the mounded rubble of the erstwhile University of Wisconsin at Madison, and being ultracautious. Their own monitoring of traffic within and among the nine baronies had turned up reports from Palladiumville's Mag Division indicating a nasty bunch of cannie scavengers claimed the turf as their own. Maybe, maybe not—Brigid didn't doubt there were nasty things about, probably lurking right around that next turn in the corridor, or in one of the empty doorways. There always were in the Outlands, she had learned.

She swept the corridor with a Magistrate-issue Nighthawk microlight. Grant used the light-gathering visor on his hard-contact armor. Instant escape was available if Rita had even a second to concentrate on her mystic ability, but in case of trouble fight would be more important than flight; they didn't want to have to go back to anyplace they'd been. So if trouble found them, they'd hang and bang as long as they could; speed and firepower were their tools more than stealth. More than a little mindful of Kane's adventure getting shot while wearing shadow armor in the Palladiumville Pits, Grant had opted to go the hard-shell route. He cradled a Copperhead in his polycarbonate-gauntleted hands.

Brigid carried a 9 mm Heckler & Koch Universal Service Pistol, true double action and holstered with one round loaded and fifteen more in the double-stack magazine. Her Kevlar vest, with a steel-ceramic-laminate trauma plate in the middle of it, was stiff and chafed a bit under her arms. But under the circumstances—such as not having to hump the damn thing over miles of Outlands to get to a gateway and back to the relative safety of Cerberus redoubt—she was glad of the protection it offered. If extremely conscious of the fact that its coverage was far from complete.

"Okay," Grant said, "I'll go along with the gag. We're looking for a turtle. What kind of a turtle? Does it bite? Or is that information classified, too?"

Billy laughed. "Sorry, mate. Don't mean to play things too close to our vests. It's a figurine of a turtle, too right. Rita, can you be a love and show our friends?"

"No worries." Rita, though far less outgoing than Billy, was less reticent than her fellow far walker, Mary Alice. She stopped in midhallway, half turned, raised a hand palm up and partially cupped.

Golden light streamed upward from the pale skin of her palm, illuminating spidery metal braces holding up the high ceiling. In the light funnel an image took form: a stylized figurine of a turtle, as advertised, about three inches long and two wide, head up and rotating slowly like the 3-D display of a computer-assisted drafting program. It appeared to be made of rich green stone, smooth and lustrous, veined with hints of black and dark yellow or lighter green.

"Damn," Grant muttered under his breath.

"The Mackenzie Turtle," Rita said. "Here's what we're looking for."

"A ritual artifact?" Brigid leaned close to peer at the image carefully. "It appears to be of malachite."

"So it does," Billy agreed. "It's the most important thing on Earth to us right about now."

"If the evil ones you call barons get their hands on it,"

Rita said, "the results could be disastrous for your people and ours."

"We'll do anything to find it and get it back as soon as possible to Lilga," Billy Handsome said.

"Lilga?" Grant echoed.

"It means 'morning star,'" Brigid said.

"It's a little girl," Nobby said, poking his glasses back true on his nose.

"Our national treasure," Rita said.

"Can we move this along?" Grant asked, sidling over beside Brigid with the muzzle brake of his Copperhead tipped toward the low, water-stained, acoustic-tile ceiling. "This is all real interesting, but we don't know how long we got down here before we attract company."

"Don't you think we might spend less time searching," Brigid snapped, "if we had a better idea what we were searching *for?*"

Grant grunted, nodded.

Nobby stuck his head out a side door. "Might be worth checking in here," he said in a tone of voice that suggested he feared somebody might hit him.

"Let's you and me just hang here outside the door and keep an eye out," Grant said to Billy.

"Too right," Billy said.

"Snap it up in there," Grant added. "Hairs on the back of my neck are starting to rise."

"It'll take as long as it takes," Rita said with an apologetic smile. Her face was a black-and-white nightmare mask in Grant's light-enhancing visor. "Tough roads, eh?"

INSIDE THE STOREROOM it was even mustier than the corridor outside, as well as seeming darker. Brigid could just imagine herself inhaling clouds of mildew spores with each intake of air. It was like trying to breathe soup.

She tried to track Rita's gaze with her microlight beam. There was some disorder, inevitably a few shelves toppled, objects displaced onto the floor and now obscured by cobwebs and drifting dust. But nothing not likely explainable by war and earth tremors; there was no sign of the systematic scavenging that had struck so many other preskydark sites. There had to be nothing here to attract looters or ten whole generations of scavvies and Roamers.

Either that or the museum basement was too well guarded.

"If I knew a bit more about the turtle's history, maybe I could be of some actual use," Brigid said, watching the two pore over the shelves.

Nobby sneezed. He just got his hand before his face in time. "Whoo! Almost lost a piece of my soul, there. And only just after getting it put back to rights, too."

Brigid cocked her head quizzically. Rita answered her question in a way that seemed hurried. "The Mackenzie Turtle is one of the very few examples of Aboriginal sculpture the Euros ever found."

She said something to Nobby then, in the tongue Jonny claimed was his people's original one. The tech boy answered in a subdued tone, head tipped forward, eyes down.

"A Scots naturalist named Angus Mackenzie discovered it on the Kimberley Plateau in western Australia in 1843," Rita continued. "As no doubt you know was common in those days, he promptly made off with it."

She cleared a mass of cobwebs from a small object on a shelf at about her own eye level. It proved to be a fragment of pottery. In the bad light Brigid could tell no more about it.

"The turtle found its way to North America by the latter

half of the nineteenth century, as part of an ethnographic collection. Unfortunately even that knowledge is incomplete—we don't know which collection or where. And we lose track of it altogether right after. Nothing to go on but hints—none of which's panned out so far."

"Is there any chance it might have been destroyed?"

Rita shook her golden-dreadlocked head. "None. Old Man feels it's still in this world, and Yindi concurs. But sadly not even their doings are enough to pin it down."

Brigid was frowning thoughtfully. "I'm sure you know your affairs best. But has it occurred to you that rummaging through museum shelves might not be your optimal search mode? What about records?"

Rita shrugged. "Computerized records are pretty much beyond our reach, what with the nukecaust and salvaging and all. We go through paper records when we find them. It's a bloody task, as well, I'm afraid."

"But computerized records aren't beyond our reach! The baronies have made a concerted effort to collect everything they can of digitized records. I was an archivist. It was my job to collate such data. Which definitely did include things like records of museum collections."

She shook her head. "At this stage where we should be is back in Cerberus, scanning through what's available there. Over the years Lakesh managed to siphon a great deal of information out of Historical Division storage."

Rita stared at her with wide eyes. Then her face broke into a smile. "See? Old Man was right when he said we needed you lot. Come on, then, let's collect the others and—"

And suddenly the sibilant threatening whispers were all around them like a cloud of disturbed moths.

Chapter 10

"He says the god-king's hiring mercenaries to attack Oz," Jonny Corroboree told Kane, who stood with one boot up on the sprit of the sailing ship hobbyhorsing along across a bright blue-green sea. "They're using that as cover, that they're going there to enlist, same as we are."

"What they do when we get there?" Domi asked, standing on the foredeck behind Kane.

Jonny shrugged. "Probably sign on as mercenaries."

Kane turned a scowl back at him. "I thought they hated the god-king and his minions."

"Oh, they do, too right. But he pays in good gold. And they can always desert. Besides—" he turned and shouted something, grinning, at the tribesmen, tattooed, painted and nearly naked, lining the red decks of the ship "—they seldom shy away from a good scrape, these lads. Just the opposite in fact."

Next to Jonny stood a roguish-looking young man wearing a red-and-yellow turban, scarlet pantaloons and a yellow sash with an alarming weapon like a saber with a bifurcated tip thrust through it. His chest was covered with scrolled tattoos of a tree with outspread wings above it and palm fronds flanking it. A narrow beard and mustache fringed his somewhat sensual-lipped mouth and square jaw.

Like most of his men, who were mostly gawking at Domi's

bare milk-white legs, in addition to the sword he also wore a dagger with a curved hilt and a nasty wavy, straight-tipped blade.

He gestured off to sea, at the red triangular sail billowing and booming overhead in the crisp salt-scented breeze, and then at the green furred landmasses humping up like a convention of mossy-backed sea serpents inland past the blinding white beaches.

"Bendera Merah says if the wind stays in this quarter we should raise Tanimbar City by midafternoon," Jonny said.

"Bendera Merah?" Kane asked.

"He's the captain. Name means 'red flag.'" Jonny flicked his dark eyes upward to the long forked pennon snapping at the jackstaff. "Taken from his personal banner."

"These people like red," Domi commented.

She turned to survey the crew. They returned the favor with an intensity that did not make Kane altogether comfortable. He reminded himself that the Iban, as the Sea Dayaks called themselves, had no body armor, and *he* had his Sin Eater tucked away out of sight. As well as the aborigine quartet for backup, who, with the exception of Tyree, as obvious a coldheart as Kane would ever care to lay eyes on, admittedly did not seem too formidable. Yet a team much like this one had blasted a passel of Palladiumville Mags to smoking carcasses.

"Tough bunch bastards," Domi said, her tone entirely appreciative and almost a purr. "Good-looking, too."

Kane turned to her in alarm. "For hell's sake don't go screwing any of them," he said.

"It's not like you're interested," she said pointedly. "Why hell you care?"

"We don't know what the damn ramifications might be."

He glanced at Jonny Corroboree, who appeared to be silently laughing his fool head off at them. I probably would be, too, Kane reckoned, under the circumstances.

That didn't soften his spike of irritation that much. "What?" he demanded.

The young aborigine shrugged. "Don't rightly know, truth to tell. You could well be right."

Domi sulked. She still had her jungle explorer regalia on. Her M-14 was slung over her shoulder, indicating she felt relatively secure but wisely did not wish to let it out of her reach. Aside from being unwieldy for one of her small stature, it was a heavy piece of ironmongery, originally designed to fire high-powered .308 cartridges full-auto—which hers could not do, since it had proved near impossible for men the size and strength of Grant to control the blasters on full rock-and-roll, and they had been converted to pure semiauto long before sky-dark. Yet she bore it, as she bore the astounding heat and humidity, without the slightest sign of wilting. Just as her gamine beauty and frankly slutty affect made it easy to underestimate her intelligence, her slight size made it easy to forget that she had been born and raised in the rawest Outlands hell, where the weak never got a first chance, never mind a second.

For his part Kane wore dark blue pantaloons, a loose yellow blouse with his Sin Eater in its power holster strapped out of sight within one voluminous sleeve, a blue head rag, loose-topped boots of soft yellow leather. He had no idea how the Sea Dayaks had come up with the garments, since he stood a good head above the tallest of them. Given what he'd learned of them, he was none too sure he wanted to find out.

Tyree came swaggering up, wearing nothing but a loincloth and a good coating of sweat. He'd been practicing grappling with Iban warriors on the high poop deck. "Not bad folk," he said, "if you can get past the beheadings."

"Beheadings?" Kane asked. Even Domi's scarlet eyes widened beneath the brim of her pith helmet.

"They're really headhunters, mate."

"These're our allies?" Kane asked dubiously.

"Like you haven't chilled a few hundred people," Domi pointed out.

"Never cut their heads off," he said. "Well, not after they were dead. Except mebbe once or twice…but I don't take trophies, okay?"

Domi shrugged. "Think about some of the things the people you used to work for do."

His eyes narrowed. "Back off it, Domi," he said in a low voice. "You win the point. Now clamp it shut." An image of his father, bound in unending servitude in the nightmare caverns of Area 51, flashed through his mind. He knew the albino woman hadn't meant to prod—no, that was wrong; she most certainly did. It was her way. But she hadn't meant any harm, and didn't quite grasp how exposed that nerve still was. Somebody once told him ferrets were that way: always probing, looking to get a rise out of you—Does that bug you?—but never meaning hurt.

To their friends. To prey and enemies they were, gram for gram, among the most efficient chilling machines Earth had ever seen.

Again a lot like Domi.

Possibly sensing something of the conversation's drift, Red Flag spoke earnestly to Jonny. "He wants to reassure you his people aren't cannibals."

Kane stared at him. "The fact he feels compelled to do so isn't real reassuring in itself."

Jonny shrugged. "Well, truth to tell, there are some that are. Some just ritually, some because, well, you know—they rather got the taste when times were tough."

Kane looked out to sea as if expecting to see the bloodred triangular sail of a cannibal ship rise like a shark fin above the horizon. Their ship had scarlet sails; why shouldn't the cannibals'?

Domi elbowed Kane's ribs. "What?" she demanded. "Don't fuse. We got cannies back home."

"Yeah. And they're not my favorite play pals, either."

"All this talk makes me hungry," Domi said. "What do they got to eat on board here?"

"Jesus," Kane said.

"What?" She blinked up at him so convincingly he bought it. Halfway, anyway.

"Never mind."

A fresh crowd of Iban wandered forward. They had been watching the wrestling match between the aborigine bull boy and their own champions. From the way Tyree held himself and the way the homeboys were acting, Kane gathered the aborigine had got the better of it, but only slightly. He also suspected really strongly that that outcome was just exactly what the scarred, almost yellow-skinned man intended: to display dominance without humiliating the locals on whom their mission, not to mention their lives, currently depended.

The Australians acted like nothing so much as a bunch of happy puppies. Yet at the same time Kane sensed that beneath that bouncy exterior lay bones as hard and durable as the vanadium steel of a redoubt. They had already displayed quick wits and unswerving determination, not to mention the odd unnerving power. And, of course, the still unseen miracle blasters they'd used to torch the Palladiumville Mags.

Unfortunately this new lot of pirate spectators had got a good testosterone dump into their systems watching all the macho horseplay aft. They started crowding around the bare-armed and legged Domi, jostling one another and tossing jocular comments at each other in Malay. Kane thought he caught an edge to their banter, and it was getting sharper, like a blade held sparking to a spinning wheel.

"Jonny," he said out the side of his mouth, "we may have a situation developing here."

"They've never seen a woman quite like her," Jonny said. "It's got their interest running high, I won't lie to you."

"It's not as if they haven't seen female skin before," Kane said. They had passed the night in the Sea Dayak village, where many of the women wore little more than skirts and occasional tattoos. Some of the younger ones, Kane had noticed with a certain discomfort, were definitely easy even on his North American eyes.

"Mebbe they think I'm a goddess 'cause of my white skin and red eyes," Domi said in chipper tones.

Kane's eyes narrowed in suspicion. "What kind of vids have you been watching back at the redoubt?"

"Old Republic serials from midtwentieth century."

"Shit. Baptiste needs to rein in on you."

The red eyes flared like embers to a bellows. "Like to see her try!"

Kane turned to Jonny. "Don't they notice she's wearing a longblaster bigger than she is? They know blasters, don't they?"

Jonny shrugged. His perpetual smile seemed to be getting a mite taut and glassy. "Too well, mate. And they respect their power, believe you me. What they tend not to respect is people who depend on 'em to do their fighting for them."

"Mebbe you should head belowdecks and see what Mary Alice is doing," Kane suggested.

"Mite too late for that," Jonny murmured. The all but imperceptible edge to his voice was as loud an alarm as any Kane had heard in his life.

"What they do respect is edged weapons," Tyree said. The big aborigine was toweling his scarred hide dry with a startlingly fluffy and clean white towel. His manner was relaxed, and his mouth smiled, but his tiger's eyes were open wide and he swiveled his head constantly from side to side. Kane knew instinctively the bull boy's eyes were in soft-focus mode, to take in the widest possible field of vision, probably well past 180 degrees. Magistrates were trained to it, too: you couldn't see detail for shit, but any movement whatever—especially what was known and loved in the ancient vernacular as a false move—stood out like a railway flare.

A bell rang in the back of his brain. "Edged weps—" he said.

Domi showed him a distinctly feral grin. "On it, Kane."

Suddenly metal glinted in her little bone-white fist: nine inches of nasty serrated knife blade. As always, she had been carrying it out of sight, which she could do seemingly when clad in nothing but her pet red stand-ups—another one of those mysteries Kane had decided he really didn't want to solve. The encroaching mob of head-hunting pirates stopped, gave back a collective step, uttering an appreciative ooh.

She twirled the blade expertly and stuck it deftly through the belt of her shorts.

The Iban applauded. The crowd began to break up, chattering a lot more relaxedly to itself.

"Well," Kane said, letting his own tension out in a long exhalation, "that looks like one more massacre averted. Good move, Domi."

"Of course."

"That's something about you, Domi—no false modesty. Nor real modesty, either."

She grinned wider.

Kane turned. "What's the story, here, Jonny?" Kane

asked the good-looking mahogany-skinned talker. "I thought the nukecaust pretty much wiped out this part of the globe."

"Right you are, mate," Jonny said. He nodded toward War Boom Ben, who stood with his back to the rail and his dark eyes lemur large; nerd or no, he wasn't too otherworldly to smell the potential bloodbath that had passed them by. "Ben's the man to hear from here. Come on, lad, give us a story, then."

The tech boy stepped forward tentatively. "Nobody suffered so much devastation from the nukecaust and its aftermath, probably, as the folk of the South Seas," he said, flicking his eyes to Jonny. The talker nodded encouragingly. "What with the tsunami and the great volcano blasts and all. Especially the Rabaul one. Whole islands, whole archipelagos, were just scoured clean like *that*." He snapped his fingers.

Domi gestured to the land they sailed along. Beyond a broad strip of beach gleaming so white it pained the eyes rose tall palms, and beyond them lush green undergrowth cut off deeper penetration of vision. "Like here, you mean?"

The tech boy bobbed his knobby head. "Right. It was bad here, even though they had the mass of New Guinea to soak up the worst of it. But this is a good place for life, a fertile environment. It came back even where it had departed completely, don't you see? By wind and water, by seeds dropped in bird shit if nothing else."

He had an unusually strong grasp of the humanistic realm of history for a gear-head, Kane thought. He kept it to himself. It was dawning on him that these people perceived, and compartmented, for lack of a better word, *reality* in a way much different than he did.

Which should not surprise him, given what Baptiste had told of her experiences with Uluru and Dreamtime. Except their behavior didn't match up with what she had seen and learned, and he knew that bothered her.

It didn't seem to impinge upon their survival. Not so far as he could see, anyway. So he was content to let things flow as they would.

For now.

"Same way with the people," Ben was saying. "The Malay, the Polynesians—they sprang from the greatest seafarers this planet ever saw. And even when the balloon went up in what you called your twentieth century, a great many of them still lived in close harmony with the great mother ocean. So, although a hundred million died in a day, an instant, a large proportion of the survivors took to the sea and rode the storm out there. Then they came back, and even despite the darkening of the skies began to reestablish themselves right away."

"How you know all this?" Domi seemed to be semistuck in her Outlands speech patterns. Mebbe it was the company.

Ben shrugged. "Old Man, mostly. Old Man, he knows most everything that goes on in the world. He watched."

"How come the women didn't meet this Old Man when they went to Uluru before?" Kane demanded.

War Boom Ben blinked and sucked his head down between his shoulders. Kane realized he had no referents to the question, that though he probably understood the words he could make little sense of them—and that made the tech boy acutely uncomfortable.

"Because he didn't choose to show himself to them, like enough," Jonny said quickly.

From above drifted a seagull-like cry. Kane didn't understand the words, but there was no mistaking its crackling urgency.

The assembled Sea Dayaks reacted as if lightning had just struck the mainmast. They scattered in all directions like a covey of purposeful quail. Swords and polearms of a bewildering variety of sizes and shapes appeared in hard brown hands, and round curved shields were strapped on forearms. Great saggy nets were unfurled from the gunwales up the lines guying the mast.

"What?" Kane asked, looking around at the frantic activity. "Pirates?"

"Thought we were the pirates," Domi said, munching a green plantain.

"Even sharks fear bigger sharks," Tyree said, grinning all over his long ugly face. This smile seemed heartfelt.

"For now," Jonny said cheerfully, "it's nothing but a sail poking over the horizon off the starboard bow."

"Which means?" Kane prompted.

The talker shrugged. "Anything from sweet damn-all to enslavement or torturous death," he said.

"What we do?" Domi asked in alarm.

Jonny Corroboree laughed. To Kane it sounded as if that laugh were not snatched away like a stray scrap of cloth by the unremitting wind, but echoed instead down corridors big as the cosmos. He seemed to find this the grandest joke of all. "We roll the bones, lass," he said. "That's life all over, isn't it? We roll the bones."

Chapter 11

"What's that smell?" Baptiste asked as the chanting swirled around them like mist.

"Shit," Nobby said succinctly.

"Human," Rita added.

The whispering was solidifying, acquiring cadence. Chanting, Brigid thought.

Then coalescing into words, low, slurred, barely intelligible—perhaps learned by ancient rote and repeated, liturgy-like, with no real knowledge of what the words themselves once meant:

"Not acceptable!"

"Abusive tolerance!"

"Diversity, diversity."

"Incorrect! Incorrect!"

"Exploiters."

"Slay them!"

The three were turning circles amid the dusty shelves, looking all around and up at the dropped-tile ceiling, trying to figure out where the voices were coming from. "I don't half fancy the trend this talk is taking," Rita said, eyes wide.

"Grant," Brigid subvocalized for the benefit of her Commtact chip implanted beneath the skin over her larynx.

"I hear it," his voice said behind her ear. "What's it mean?"

"Divisive! Exclusionary! Slay!"

"Trouble," Brigid said aloud. "Rita, I think we should get out of here now. We can work more efficiently back at Cerberus anyway. Ask Jonny—"

"The call is mine, my friend," the far walker said softly but firmly. "He knows my choice. So does Bob—he comes now. But we must all be together before—"

The grille over a ventilation duct blew in as if dynamited, practically over her beret-clad head. She ducked.

Brigid caught a flash of a pallid animalistic form, of gaping toothy jaws and outstretched talons, already in flight for her face. By reflex she pushed her microlight and her USP out to an isosceles position, inner wrists crossed, and squeezed off two shots, the quickest controlled fire possible.

Then she sidestepped, remembering another nuance of handblaster combat drilled into her by Kane and Grant and reinforced by experience: the bullets wouldn't stop a body in rapid motion. The white figure crashed against a rack of metal shelving and toppled it, setting off a domino chain as it took down three more sets of shelves with it, artifacts bouncing or smashing on the floor in a tumult of noise and dust.

The creature itself thrashed on the floor, spraying blood everywhere in a wild arterial fan, snarling and snapping at itself like a dog hit by a truck. It was the size of a large human child or very small adult. It appeared to be nude, although Brigid couldn't tell, with the bad light and its convulsive movement, what gender it was.

Nobby raised his right hand, which proved to contain an altogether ordinary .40-caliber "Baby" Glock 27. He fired a single shot and blew the narrow snouted skull apart.

Techie he might be, and reticent when not discussing his specialty. Yet he chilled the thing with the aplomb of the most seasoned stoneheart.

Brigid had no time to mull apparent contradictions in the young man's character. The creatures were pouring out of the gaping vent shaft as if a tap had been opened, leaping, capering, scrambling over shelves fallen or still upright, circling them.

And all were chanting, "Death! Death to the hate criminals!"

THEY CAME in sight of Tanimbar City instants after the swollen sun dissolved in an ocean like a pool of blood.

The sail sighted had been white, belonging to a merchantman, whose consuming interest, once her lookouts had in turn spotted the Sea Dayaks' scarlet sail, had been to get as far and fast away as possible from the oncoming pirate vessel. There were more than a few no more than semijocular curses and dark-eyed glances of disappointment cast after the sail as it vanished back below the horizon, cutting as close to the wind as its lateen-rigged mainsail would permit.

The swords and bucklers and polearms had been reluctantly racked or thrust back through sashes. Kane had observed the blowpipes the Iban had first used to announce their presence to the party had not been in evidence.

"They use poison," Tyree had explained. "It acts slowly, and a single dart won't carry enough to kill a grown man, at least not with any consistency."

"What good is it, then?" Domi demanded.

Tyree grinned. "Put yourself in the boots of an invader crashing through their bush. Dart comes out of nowhere, hits your mate. You and the rest of your party go all mad minute, bust caps in every conceivable direction. Does no good, of course—even if you hit the bloke with the blowgun you'll never likely find him. If he can he'll crawl into deeper brush to die.

"Meanwhile your mate knows right off he's poisoned, fancies he can feel it burning in his veins, even if the poison doesn't really work that way, catch me? So he's thrashing about and hollering his head off and in general taking on. Not uncommonly he'll work himself into such a state he'll see himself off with a self-induced coronary. If he doesn't, so much the worse for you, because you've now got to tend him and carry him while the poison really does act on him. Another strike will finish him, like as not—and meanwhile, as you tramp through the bush, you're waiting every second for the little invisible whisper of breath and the sting of the dart with your name on it."

"Very poetic," Kane said. "What he's telling us is, the pipes aren't much use in a standup gunfight."

"I got that," Domi had said snippily, then stamped off in search of more to eat.

Now, with the night gathering about them like a heavy black cloak, the horizon still a line of fire underlighting a squall line of clouds colored like a bruise, yellow and purple and green and black, they passed a spit of land crusted with dark palm trees and the city appeared. The fairyland of twinkling yellow and orange and crimson lights, dark ramparts and towers and minarets seemed to float upon the waters of the bay.

"It's beautiful!" exclaimed Domi, who had come up to stand at Kane's side in the bow.

Then she gagged as the smell hit her like a befouled cricket bat.

Kane craned over the rail to see a bottle bob past, shouldered aside by the felucca's wake, in the midst of a brownish-seeming stain on the dark-wine water.

"Sewage bloom," he commented. "Guess the hybrids haven't installed the same sort of environment regs they have back home. If they really run the show here."

"Oh, they do, cobber," said Jonny, who had come forward with his three companions to look as word ran through the little vessel that their goal had hove into sight. "No worries there. They surely do."

THE MUFFLED RAPPING of Brigid's 9 mm double-tap was echoed by a boom from along the darkened corridor in the direction they'd come. Then a second and a third, echoing out of the stairwell.

"Bush Baby Bob's sore beset," Billy Handsome said, frowning for once. His tone was as if he actually saw what was befalling his comrade, not making an inference—if a blazingly obvious one—from the aural evidence of the shotgun blasts.

Grant was swiveling his whole body side to side from the waist, Copperhead held muzzle up, keeping face and eyes locked rigidly ahead, as if he were a solid slab from hips up. He was trained to shoot by reflex in the direction he was looking. Staying connected, as the itinerant Chinese internal martial artist Master Chen put it, kept his body indexed properly to make shots fast and make them count.

"He need help?" Grant asked.

"He can take care of himself," Billy said, "that being his line of country. I reckon the question's more—"

Up and down the corridor of them the grilles went flying off vent shafts on either wall. White shapes began to slop forth from them and lope toward the two men, hissing their half-intelligible speech and waving clawed hands like apes. At the same time a white tide of distorted bipedal figures, moon-white, washed toward them from the shadow-lost depths of the corridor's far end.

"—whether it's us in need of saving," Billy finished. He

shrugged, and the two micro-Uzi machine pistols he wore in shoulder holsters beneath each armpit appeared in his hands. "What say you take right?"

As he spoke he pivoted left. Twin ruby beams sprang from the blasters in his fists. The shambling horde of humanoid figures paused in momentary bewilderment.

"You got it." Grant's own laser aiming beam stabbed out as he turned clockwise.

He had already switched his fire selector from safe past single and triburst to full-on rock and roll. This was your basic target-rich environment—close targets. He could smell not just human shit but a scent at once sweeter and far more repellent, not to mention unsettling: the heavy, cloying stench of rotting human flesh.

The Copperhead erupted dancing fire and hammering noise. The pale figures shrieked in terror and anguish as needle-like 4.85 mm bullets tore through their naked filthy bodies. They fell slashing at the air with long black-nailed hands, scarlet pennons of blood unfurling from their bodies. Ropy strands of pink bloodshot saliva trailed from their inhumanly long, fanged jaws.

Grant let his whole magazine go in one shuddering volley, sweeping the blazing blaster in an infinity sign in the dense air before him. Even over the racket it made chilling, and the noises its victims made dying, Grant could hear the slightly out-of-phase yammer of Billy's twin autoblasters at his back.

The talker had his arms stretched out to just short of elbow-lock, wrists crossed and the backs of his hands pressed against each other for mutual support against the recoil of the short-barreled blasters. Though the rounds they fired were substantially less potent than the bottlenecked high-power cartridges Grant's blaster digested, by themselves each made even more noise. The energy of rapidly expanding gases the Copperhead used to ram bullets down the grooves of its much longer barrel, came bellowing out the muzzles of the handblaster-sized micro-Uzis in the form of pure blast.

For a moment, noise and carnage ruled the subterranean corridor, then slammed down a silence that throbbed in the ears and very temples like high-blood-pressure pulse. The groans and involuntary gurgles of the torn and dying hardly scratched the surface of that silence: they were as sounds heard through thick glass.

Even with hearing protectors built into his hard-contact helmet Grant was all but deafened. He heard a distinct metallic snick behind him and half turned; Billy Handsome had holstered his left-hand blaster and dropped the empty box out the butt of the other for a rapid reload from a mag carrier at his waist. He grinned over his shoulder at Grant.

"Not much stomach for a fair fight, eh?" The white figures that hadn't fallen to the multiple barrages had vanished, ducking into side passages or scrambling in noisy terror back into the open vents. The reek of death and burned propellant and lubricants was enough to turn the stomach of a Mag inured to years of PPP.

"Nothing fair about it," Grant said in satisfaction. He snicked home his own replacement mag in the well behind the pistol grip of his Copperhead. "Just the way I like it."

A fresh burst of fire sounded from inside the storeroom. "Brigid!" Grant exclaimed. He spun, trying not to wince; if the people inside fired in panic, these walls wouldn't stop a bullet. His hard-contact armor would protect him probably. But Billy had no armor Grant could see, and warm, fuzzy sentiments aside, Grant enthusiastically did not want to lose the firepower of those twin handblasters. As far as he was concerned, the cannie creatures weren't through with them. They were only hunkering down and waiting for their chance. One he fervently hoped they never got.

But no stray shots punched through the cinder block, painted maroon to the height of Grant's sternum and what had probably once been dingy yellow above. Instead Rita burst through the door, reloading her own handblaster, which to Grant's quick but expert glance looked like a Makarov. It was a decent piece but underpowered for serious social work, maybe midway between .380 and standard 9 mm Parabellum. A moment later and Brigid burst out, hair unbound like a flame halo, holding her still-lit Nighthawk and her H&K out before her like the blazing torch and sword of righteousness. Nobby backed out last, aiming back into the storeroom a piece that Grant at first thought might be the famed mystery blaster. A longer look told him that, no, it was a Vektor, a late-twentieth-century South African design that, while it had a definite Buck Rogers look to it—and, if he recalled right, a weird triangular front sight—was a thoroughly conventional 9 mm semiauto handblaster.

"What the hell," he demanded, "were those things?"

"Glad to see you're intact, too, Grant," Brigid said, flashing an uncharacteristic sardonic grin. Conceivably she was getting into chilling more than she wanted to admit to herself. "Degenerate humans, is my best guess." Then she stopped and stared in wide-eyed shock at the corridor, its floor littered with torn-open corpses and greasy unreeled guts, the walls hosed with black-looking blood, trails of runny excrement drooling down from the yawning vents.

"We did a little redecorating," Grant said. "Can you get us the hell out of here, Rita?"

"Where's Bob?" she asked. "Can't leave without him."

The chanting began again, an indistinct murmur. It held an edge of rage that had not been audible before.

"Are you sure about that?" Grant said, looking around for the source of the sound. It seemed to come from everywhere at once.

"I won't leave him," Rita said. "And we all have to be in contact to walk far."

More echoing blasts erupted from the stairwell they had descended, now accompanied by brief yellow flashes. Bush Baby Bob backed down the stairs jacking shots from his bulky SPAS riot gun with machinelike speed.

Rita cried something in her own language. She flung an arm out, angled up toward the exposed ducts and girders snaking above their heads.

Ghost faces peered down at them. Sinuous tongues licked yellow fangs.

"They're above us!" Rita screamed.

Chapter 12

The harbor was packed so tightly that the ships riding to anchor within the shelter of a long mole—made, so War Boom Ben claimed, from basketsful of the rubble of preskydark cities carried on the backs of conscript laborers during the first days of the god-king's reign—that their hulls looked like one solid landmass and their masts a dense forest. Red lights glowed from the tops of lofty structures, perilous looking even in pitch dark, that truly put the "castle" in "sterncastle." Flames danced pale blue and gold above firepots full of hot coals, providing the illusion of an army encamped in that imaginary forest. Although not wholly illusion, since if they weren't the fires of an invading army, they were the fires of a mighty invasion fleet.

To Kane it made no kind of sense to burn open fires on craft made of kindling, with immense sheets of readily flammable cloth slung in webs of equally ready-to-burn ropes right above them. But every tub bigger than a dinghy sported its cheery blaze, and larger vessels more than one.

Threads of tinkling music and nasal song wove through the heavy night air. They vied with the sounds of drunken revelry. The mingled smoke of all the fires, plus undoubtedly many of the lights visible mounting in tiers up a hillside in the city beyond, hung like a fog bank down to just about the level of Kane's head if he stood well forward in the reared-up bow.

Which contributed mightily to his standing somewhat back. Jostling for room in the crowded air were likewise the smell of curry and spices less identifiable; roasting meat; tobacco and bhang, the cinnamon and hot alcohol of mulled wine.

"Why anybody would drink hot wine in this sauna is way beyond me," Kane remarked, trying not to flinch as the pirate prau ran so close under one skyward-tumbling stern its bowsprit nearly poked gilt from one of the demons wielding huge scimitars carved among the fancy scrollwork ocean waves. With the anchorage too crowded for sailing, and the wind blocked by hundreds of hulls besides, the Sea Dayaks had furled the sails and unshipped the sweeps, and now rowed the craft at the pace of a brisk walk. It seemed recklessly fast to Kane, especially since they had only a bull's-eye lantern hung from the sprit to light their way, which cast its jaundiced beam a good four feet at least.

Jonny shrugged. *De gustibus non disputandum est.*

Kane gave him a narrow eye. "What the hell's that mean?"

" 'Of taste and sense there's no arguing.' Latin, mate."

A hundred yards or so across the water a tongue of yellow fire spurted up as a drunken carouser kicked over a firepot. Laughter and merry catcalls turned to cries of distress as flames ran up a slanting line like phosphorescent rats. Somebody hurled a bucket of water onto the coals, which had the effect of distributing them wider across the deck without necessarily extinguishing them. A huge cloud of steam obscured the area where the coals were scattered, although they gave it an interesting orange underlighting. Outraged choking cries from the afflicted vessel and wild caws of laughter from neighboring decks suggested to Kane that some idiot in the grip of fire-zone panic had hit the coals with the contents of a honey bucket, not a water vessel.

"What's to keep a blaze from sweeping this whole anchorage like, well, wildfire?" Kane asked.

Jonny clapped him jovially on the shoulder. "Sweet bugger all, mate."

Kane looked around for Domi. Normally she'd be even twitchier than he was. From the sound of her laughter falling like rain from above, she was up in the crow's nest with some of the crew. Kane thought he'd seen War Boom Ben scrambling up the precarious rope ladder with her, which allayed his fears somewhat. He suspected, possibly on the basis of wishful thinking, that the shy tech boy would tend to act as chaperone.

Jonny lightly touched his forearm—the left one, without the Sin Eater—with two fingers. With his other hand he pointed off across the harbor.

Kane's first thought was that his worst fancies had come true and the biggest ship in the whole damn harbor was fully involved in flames. Then he realized it was with the lights of lanterns that the giant multidecked vessel was ablaze. Yes, and something more.

"Tell me that's not electric light shining through those windows or portholes or whatever the hell you call them," Kane said.

"I cannot tell a lie, cobber. That they are. Yonder lies the mighty *Varuna*, stately pleasure barge to the god-king his very self—and covert hydrofoil. She does have masts, but under all plain sail would be pressed to keep up with a glacier."

"Looks more like a floating gaudy house to me," Kane said.

Since he had never seen a predark wedding cake, nor a nineteenth-century Mississippi river paddlewheel steamboat, "gaudy house" was a fairly close call. All gleaming white hull with multiple decks outlined in gilt, and yellowish white artificial light spilling out myriad openings, the ship did resemble a gaudy house. An exceptionally large and prosperous one. It dwarfed even the largest war junk.

"If we could just put a good volley of Shrikes into the son of a bitch," Kane said wistfully, "we could all go home to the land of climate-controlled air and hygiene. Plus all of Cerberus won't burn down every time some triple-stupe drunk waltzes into a charcoal grill."

He shook his head. "Never thought I'd be nostalgic for that gloomy hole in the planet."

"No joy," Jonny said. "His Nibs has no doubt shifted to his palace-away-from-home away up the hill there."

"That'd be the great big place that looks like a gaudy house overlooking the whole city?"

"Right."

"I don't suppose Mary Alice could pop us back for a few man-pack missile launchers—"

Sadly but firmly the talker shook his dreads. "Not and live. The god-king has some special defenses, of a kind I'm sure you're well aware of—and possibly some you're not. There's no easy way out of this one, I fear."

"Is there ever?"

"DEATH TO BLUE EYES!" they screeched. "Death to white males!"

"White *males?*" Grant roared, blasting a pale figure springing for his eyes. "There aren't any white males here, you stupes!"

He gazed down as the figure he had shot slammed into a wall and rolled bubbling onto its back. Its sharp-featured, almost muzzled face was the white of sun-bleached bone—the same shade as Domi's face. But unlike Domi the eyes staring through the tracery of blood that covered the face like a veil were the blue of spring sky.

"Except you," Grant said in a subdued voice.

"I doubt they even know what they're saying," Brigid said, putting her back to his and slamming a new mag home in the butt of her USP. She had already cycled through the old one, winnowing ghouls from their bracework perches overhead.

At corridor's end Bush Baby Bob had run out of shells. Creatures piled onto him. He reached back, grabbed a gibbering form clinging to his shoulders by its naked nape. He flung it against the wall, then reversing his grip on the longblaster, he swung it as if it were an ax, stoving in a narrow skull stranded with hair like wisps of optic fiber.

Grant's Copperhead ran dry as another creature hit the floor ahead of him and bounced straight at his throat. He let it fall by the long sling looped around his neck and met the ghoul with an overhand right. With a most satisfying crunch of bone and teeth the thing's face imploded. Blood squirted black around Grant's armored fist.

"Rita!" he yelled without looking around. "We can't hold them!" He managed to stave off another leaping horror with a hand to its sternum. It hissed and gnashed at the slick armor of his forearm, leaving trails of slobber.

The butt of Bob's shotgun was clotted with blood and spilled brains. It flung trails of gore and tissue bits across the walls as he flailed at his attackers. He laid them waste in serious profusion, but they were too many, too fired by fury at the intrusion and the lust to sink their fangs into sweet human meat. They swarmed him over like giant maggots, biting, clawing, clubbing with misshapen fists, doing as much damage to one another and themselves as the huge aborigine.

He sank to his knees.

"Nobby!" Rita screamed. *"Help him!"*

The tech boy stood with his back to the wall, eyes round

in his round face. Then his jaw set and his right hand dived into the black fanny pack strapped around his waist.

The hallway filled with uncanny blue radiance. Grant saw it on the walls to either side, saw it splash the ceiling high overhead, saw it cast his more-than-man-size shadow across suddenly cringing ranks of attackers. "Brigid," he roared, launching himself in a dive for the floor without regard to landing on blood muck or bodies, dead or otherwise. *"Down!"*

Brigid simply dropped. A pale beast leaping at her sailed fortuitously over her head to slam into the wall with a crunch of finality. She and her companions, she saw, were surrounded by a sphere of subtly pulsating blue light, veined with thin, undulating circles.

A rod of brilliant blue lanced forth. Thunder louder than all the blasters going off together threatened to split Brigid's eardrums. The back of the white beast at the top of the writhing mound hiding Bush Baby Bob from view blossomed like a horrible fast-motion flower, red and white around a globe of white brilliance.

She looked over her shoulder. Nobby held a blaster that looked like a cross between a handblaster and the hilt of a seventeenth-century rapier, a central mass surrounded by loops of curved rods whose convolutions her eyes refused to follow with any degree of closeness. Although the ring of the muzzle itself was a circle of actinic glare, the blue glow seemed to emanate from the blaster as a whole.

Bracing firing hand with his other, Nobby discharged the weapon once more. Again a blinding bolt; and again a crack like lightning striking right at Brigid's side. The blue glow flared. Nobby took a step back as if from recoil.

The pale-skinned creatures shrank back, covering their

snouted faces and squalling in ecstasies of terror. They piled off Bob as if the vid of them overwhelming him were being run backward at unnatural speed. Some fled back into side rooms or vents or leaped back to the girders with inhuman strength. Others merely cowered against the walls, as if not even terror of the awesome light-that-killed was enough to drive them off, with the smell of their fellows' spilled blood filling their distended nostrils.

Nobby raised his blaster toward the shadowed ceiling. The blue glow died. "Bob?" he called, as if afraid he'd get no answer from the large black shadow sprawled on the floor.

It stirred. Using the Franchi scattergun as a crutch, it began painfully to lever itself to its feet. Rita started to run forward to the injured bull boy's aid.

Billy caught her wrist and hauled her back urgently. "Sorry, lass," he said, not omitting a flash of apologetic grin. "I can be spared—you can't."

He dashed to Bob's side. Several of the creatures, emboldened by the vanishing of the blue hell glow, moved forward. He raised a micro-Uzi in his left hand and the ruby pencil stabbed out. They squealed and jumped back.

Then he was returning, the torn and bleeding bulk of Bob draped over his shoulders. The bull boy moved his powerful legs as purposefully as he could, but it was apparent the much smaller talker was doing the real locomotion for both.

Sensing somehow they were about to be cheated, the white beasts screamed and began to charge. "Close in, close in!" Rita urged, making gathering sweeps with her arms. Grant with his Sin Eater in his right fist and his Copperhead in his left, and Brigid holding Nobby's discarded Vektor as well as her USP, backed toward the common center, covering as best they could.

Billy Handsome and Bob practically fell into the others. "Arms around," Rita shouted. "Grab each other tight."

"Great," Grant said. "Facing danger with a group hug."

A tidal wave of white skin and fangs and howling malice rushed in upon them....

"YOU SURE you know where we're going?" Kane asked.

Tyree gave him a quizzical look. "I've seen a map," he said flatly, as if that explained all.

The nighttime streets of Tanimbar were if possible more thronged than the harbor. Kane, Domi and the four aborigines had taken a boisterous farewell from their Iban friends on the docks. The Sea Dayaks had been loudly disappointed when the outsiders had declined to join them for a headlong assault on the stews and a glorious night of gambling, drinking, serial whoring and with any luck the slitting of a few gullets. But they hadn't pressed the issue. Apparently they were well acquainted with the eccentric ways of Old Man's people.

The three aborigine men had packed their Western-style clothes into rolls slung over their shoulders and donned flowing local garb. Jonny Corroboree and Tyree had their dreads tied up with big swatches of cloth, so that they looked as if they had masses of tentacles sprouting from the tops of their heads. As far as Kane could tell—the streets of the district they were in were so narrow and dark that the occasional light spilling from the odd tavern or late-night money-changing kiosk only served to make the stretches in between seem the blacker—they weren't the only ones abroad sporting such hairstyles. Kane would have been hard-pressed to name a style, sartorial or tonsorial, that wasn't in evidence just in the klick or so they'd covered. Nor would he have sworn some of the shadowy figures they brushed up against didn't have tentacles sprouting from their heads.

Kane himself still wore his pirate togs. There was one addition: he had a wavy-bladed dagger, which Red Flag had told him was called a kris when he presented it to him with great solemnity, thrust through his sash. In return, Kane had presented the Sea Dayak chieftain with something called a "hobo tool," a sort of multitool composed of a folding knife, fork and spoon set, along with sundries such as a corkscrew. They had boxes of the things stashed away in the Cerberus armory, quite possibly for the very purpose Kane put this one to: trade goods.

In any event, it may have been unnecessary. Despite their obvious obsessive fondness for cutlery, the Iban seemed to have a serious surplus of daggers. Kane chose not to delve too deeply into what that might imply.

Nobody, it seemed, took you seriously if you weren't displaying some kind of serious shank. Jonny now sported a Bowie-type knife with a nine-inch blade, War Boom Ben a similarly sized weapon with a leaf-shaped chopping blade called a parang, which a lot of the Iban also carried. Tyree had thrust through his belt a pair of weps like outsized forks with round, hyperthyroid center tines, which Kane would have called *sai* but which were known as *tjabang* hereabouts.

The two women were got up in loose but somewhat heavy head-to-toe garments, including trousers, brocaded blouses and veils; the Iban had been Muslims before skydark but had back slid, but the women—who went happily naked, or near enough so as to satisfy even Domi's exhibitionistic urges, back home—covered themselves on trips to town to avoid inciting the perverted lusts of degenerate city dwellers. Domi, who never gladly put on *more* clothes, had balked at first. But Mary Alice, giggling and glowing with a vivacity she hadn't shown before, got her to think of it all as a game of dress-up.

At an intersection where five winding ways met, Tyree

paused a moment in the fitful glow of a lantern in the form of a blue paper fish. Then he nodded and led them off down the narrowest and twistiest path of all. Also, of course, the most ripely feculent.

"City smells worse than the damn bay," Kane said.

"Look on the bright side," Domi said. "Less chance of drowning here."

The ground was slimy underfoot. No light showed at all except little amber slivers extruding between tight-drawn shutters on upper floors. Bats fluttered just over the outsiders' heads.

"Now I know what it feels like inside an intestine," Kane said. "Except for the bats, that is."

"You mean," Domi said, "you never—"

Kane suspected he was just as glad when Domi's query was interrupted by Tyree halting before a low arched door set a foot back in a stone doorway, hunching down and rapping sharply three-two-three backhanded.

A moment. A squeal and then a dim yellow shaft of light made a break for it as a brass Judas gate was opened. The light was momentarily blocked, sprang forth again, and then the door opened on hinges that protested far more loudly than the little vision port had.

Only to reveal the business end of a Kalashnikov leveled straight at Kane's navel.

Chapter 13

"I wonder," Brigid said, cradling her coffee cup in both hands with her elbows on the table in the main Cerberus commissary, "just how much Orion knew?"

Grant sat peering down into the opaque blackness of his own coffee as if he suspected something might be swimming beneath its surface. "Why do you say that?"

"She knew a great deal about what goes on in the baronies. A disconcerting amount, frankly, although she certainly seemed to back up her professions of sympathy to our cause with genuine actions, not to mention risks. But I can't help wondering how much of the real truth she knows."

"You mean like about the hybrids?"

Brigid nodded.

Grant sighed deeply. "Listen, Brigid," he said heavily, "I'm not sure *we* know anything like the real truth. I'm dead sure we don't know anywhere near the whole story."

"No doubt you're right."

"Once we think we got the truth nailed down, everything gets turned on its head or inside out. Seems every few months we find out everything we knew for sure was wrong." He arched a brow at her. "But that's not what's really eating at you."

"So you're a trained psychologist now?" she flared.

"Mebbe," he answered evenly. "Us Mags were mostly

trained up as door kickers—blunt instruments, just the way you always seem to think Kane and I are."

"I don't think of either of you as *blunt*," Brigid said crisply.

"Whatever. But we did do some investigative work. And you do know Kane and I were good at what we did—we made a point of it, and we were on the job for a lot of years. So I learned a little about reading people. Enough to know that your getting pissy with me was another stab at getting around answering my question, so I'm not offended or anything."

Brigid scowled briefly, then her face relaxed and she emitted a brief, brittle laugh. "Very well. It's the aborigines."

"They're nothing like the people you told us about. Nor Domi or Shizuka. Well, not much, anyway."

"There are similarities. The way they move, the way they carry themselves. And of course we didn't interact closely with any except Yindi, who is no doubt not exactly typical. But still—"

She shook her head. Her unbound hair, gleaming red-gold from a recent shower, swept back and forth across her shoulders like a horse's tail. "They seemed to be typical preliterates—what were called 'primitive' long ago. Now part of the time they act the same way, very tribal. Other times, it's as if *we're* primitives, and they're trying their best to humor us."

"They're good sports about it, though," Grant said.

"So you see it, too?"

He nodded.

Upon their eerily painless jump back to the Cerberus armory, Grant and Brigid had headed for their quarters to get changed and cleaned up. Though Bush Baby Bob had grumpily insisted he was all right but for a few "cuts and bruises," and a quick but thorough examination by Rita had established he had suffered no visible major damage, his three fellows had insisted on accompanying him to the infirmary. Subsequently Reba DeFore had called Brigid on the intercom, just as the archivist stepped out of the shower, to tell her that she had put Bush Baby Bob under sedation to get him to rest, and that his friends had asked her to arrange a meeting between them and Brigid and Grant to discuss their new search strategy.

Sally Wright, whom Brigid had called, still naked and rubbery-skinned from her shower, right after speaking to DeFore, turned up just ahead of the three aborigines. Brigid suspected that in some abstract way she ought to feel threatened by the new arrival, who after all was supposed to be a wizard archivist in her own way. Yet what Brigid mostly felt was relief: she would be somebody to share the burdens Lakesh placed upon his longtime protégée. Many of the Moonies were highly intelligent and excruciatingly educated—a fact they seldom let anybody forget—but they also tended to be resentful, refractory. Nor did Brigid altogether trust them.

Whereas the escapee from Snakefishville Historical Division was diffident, eager and, yes, grateful for her deliverance. So much so that Brigid found it impossible to resent her.

It didn't occur to Brigid Baptiste that perhaps she was by nature ill-suited to resentment. She was also ill-suited to that kind of self-examination.

Smiling and nodding a shy greeting, Sally went to draw tea, asking first if either Brigid or Grant needed anything. Which made Grant's head snap up and his eyes regard her narrowly, as if suspecting a trap, before he declined.

The three aborigines came in, got their own refreshments and joined the others at their corner table. Grant sat with his back to the wall. The aborigines had recovered some of their ebullience.

"The wildest jaunt we've been on yet," Billy Handsome remarked, slipping into a chair beside Brigid.

She gave him a quick, sharp look. She wasn't exactly over-used to receiving sexual attention, despite the fact that she had been assured over and over by a frankly bizarre assortment of people, since fleeing Cobaltville, that she was highly attractive. Which had made Philboyd's clumsy persistence so trying for her.

But while she would be first to admit she was anything but expert in scoping out signs of sexual scrutiny, she was as sure that the talker had no more sexual interest in her than if she were a log or a dog. She hadn't glimpsed anything false lurking behind the trio's almost wearying affability. But she did get the feeling, from Billy's grin and nod of greeting—quick firm eye contact, then his attention marched away forthrightly elsewhere—that something lay behind it. Not contempt; certainly not disdain. Perhaps...condescension.

Rita and Nobby agreed heartily. "I'm happy we all made it out intact," Rita said, "leaving aside a few patches of Bush Baby Bob's hide. Which'll grow back, right as rain."

She was looking at Grant when she spoke, and there was nothing covert about her interest in the big man. At first touch that puzzled Brigid, since it was Billy Handsome who was, after all, professionally friendly and charismatic. Then, primarily by force of intellect, Brigid made herself realize that there was no intrinsic identity between job or team role and personal inclinations; whatever reservations Billy may have had about their North American comrades-of-convenience, Rita clearly didn't share. When it came to Grant, anyway.

To her own surprise, Brigid had to hide a quick grin behind her coffee cup. *I wonder what she'd make of Shizuka.*

"I don't understand what those people were about," Nobby remarked, perplexity clearly overcoming his natural nerd reserve. "How they came about, if you know what I mean."

Grant studied him from under lowered brows. "Don't have much experience of the Outlands, do you?"

"Don't have the like back in Oz," Billy said. He and Nobby had gotten hot tea. "A few scattered settlements descended from the colonists, who, granted, aren't what you'd call well off. Nothing like that, though."

Brigid looked at him. "The vision Yindi showed us indicated that the Piranypa had been wiped out by the nukecaust and its aftermath."

Billy Handsome's reddish-brown eyes widened ever so slightly. He started to answer, then looked pointedly at Rita.

The blond-dreaded young woman was gazing frankly at Grant, who was ignoring her. Possibly he wondered what she'd make of Shizuka, too. Or perhaps more to the point, what New Edo's de facto lady shogun would make of her. But the far walker instantly picked up her talker's nonverbal clue. So quickly, in fact, that Brigid suspected some sense in play beyond the customary five.

"Yindi showed you a glimpse of the Dreamtime—what he called Tjukurpa, right?"

Brigid nodded.

"Tjukurpa is…" She held up her hands, surprisingly large and strong looking for a woman's hands—enough to give Brigid, really looking at them for the first time, a twinge of inadequacy—as if trying to draw the words out of air. The archivist in Brigid was instantly fascinated by what that evidenced about the aborigines' roles: far walker Rita had the most extensive lore, where her people were concerned, but didn't always have the talker's fluency in putting it into words.

Or at least words, Brigid thought ruefully, sipping her strong black drink and feeling its warmth suffuse her tongue, we can understand.

"…true," Rita continued. "It's our core truth, y'might say. Yet you can't take it necessarily as literal truth. Especially if you're…an outsider. So you might consider what you saw, the waves sweeping the land clean of the, ah, the Piranypa—"

"Tsunami never got near that high, even with the Rabaul eruption," Nobby broke in, "especially what with New Guinea to take the brunt and all."

"You might consider that allegory. Metaphorically true, in that the nukecaust did break the back of the colonial domination."

"So, anyway," Nobby said, "you were about to explain your theory about those curious blokes in the basement, there, Dr. Baptiste?"

"Brigid, please." She shrugged. "It strikes me that the Madison campus of the University of Wisconsin offered plenty of underground space, relatively safe. Groundwater level is high—we encountered plenty enough seeping in. The faculty members, I suspect, naturally felt reluctant to leave the familiar, comforting confines of academia. Especially once the world blew up."

"What'd they do for food?" Grant demanded.

"I guess they were already accustomed to living off the student body," Sally said.

It was her turn to experience his slit-eyed look. To her credit—and Brigid's surprise—she didn't quail. "You're joking, right?" the former Mag demanded.

"No. I don't think so. It makes a twisted sort of sense."

Grant subsided grumbling into his seat. "No wonder I never decide to up and leave this crazy outfit," he muttered at last. "I'd still be in this crazy world."

"Would you leave it if you could, Grant?" Rita asked.

He snorted a bitter laugh. "Eventually I will. Feet first. Just like everybody."

She smiled. "Perhaps," she said, "not everybody."

"AT LEAST THERE ARE no cats," Baron Thulia said to the screen.

Erica van Sloan stared at him with dark eyes hard as tungsten-carbide drills. "What?" All that was visible on the communicator was her face and mane of black hair.

"In this palace," Thulia said, waving a soft fine hand around the bedchamber he had been assigned by the Dewa Raja's chamberlain. "The god-king's palace at Kuching was overrun with cats. I developed a most intense allergy to the filthy, skulking little beasts."

"Your ineffectuality continues to expand my appreciation of the possible, Thulia," Erica said. "All that your vaunted hybrid intelligence has served to accomplish thus far is the discovery cats make you sneeze?"

He bridled. "How dare you speak to me in that tone, you—*human.*"

She laughed. "You know how I dare. What makes you think *you* dare to talk back to me? Remember, for instance, who it was who knew of the existence of a barony of your cousins in the South Pacific."

His cheeks burned so hot he feared again he might have contracted fever. It wouldn't be surprising. Barons paid for their enormous superiority with compromised immune systems: they all knew and understood that. And this humid hothouse was nothing but a greenhouse for pestilence. It was a miracle even the apekin with their brutish animal vitality didn't succumb in droves.

At least the god-king had seen fit to give him a spacious and suitably appointed chamber, one set high up in the palace, which itself sat atop a hill overlooking city and harbor. While it made for an inconvenient amount of climbing—Thulia was fairly certain the Dewa Raja could move between floors without deigning to tramp up and down stairs, but if he possessed such means, he hadn't revealed them to Thulia—it also meant he was well up out of the concentrated odors of mere humanity. Which to Thulia's mind, and nose, were sweat, rancid body oils and, of course, shit.

With the wind in off the sea and the windows opened—with even fine-mesh metal screens to keep out the most pernicious insects—the breeze blowing through the chamber with its whitewashed walls and silk-caparisoned bed was cool and fresh. Or almost so.

"Do you have any purpose in this call other than to abuse me?" Thulia demanded.

Erica laughed again. "So! A show of defiance, however token. Perhaps the tropical climate has stimulated your production of testosterone—I note the god-king can actually manage something of a fringe of beard. Perhaps you'll grow a real cock, rather than that shriveled vestigiality that now dangles between—or is it ever so slightly protrudes above?—your thighs."

He lowered his face. Fury burned within him like the sun. His hatred of this polluted slut of an ape-woman was matched only by his hatred of the very ineffectuality she had cast like a bucket of man-slops in his face.

"But perhaps we ask too much of you, Thulia," Erica almost purred. "Therefore I have decided to help you."

His head snapped up. "You mean the barons have agreed to recall me?"

"Not at all. I am dispatching the best operator from my Magistrate Division—one Vladek. One of the few surviving contemporaries of the hated renegade Kane. He will be at your entire disposal."

Meaning, Thulia knew, the vat-bastard apekin will follow

my command so far as they do not conflict with your secret instructions to him, you bitch.

"This will allow you to employ your vaunted intellect to full effect," Erica said, not even bothering to taunt with her tone, "while Vladek supplies all necessary spine—and balls. Erica van Sloan, speaking for the nine, out!"

Her image dissolved into a whorl of colored fog. Then emptiness.

SMILING GENTLY, almost sadly, Billy Handsome came back from replenishing his tea and up from behind and laid a hand over one of his far walker's. He spoke quietly to her in their language. His normally boisterous affect was subdued. Rita nodded matter-of-factly.

"The ghouls specialized right quick," Nobby said. "Two centuries is not very long for those kinds of physical divergences to take hold." As always when he had something technical to discuss he came alive, came out of himself; he held his head up and looked you in the eye, if briefly, when he spoke. But Brigid noted that his conception of what was technical was different from hers and most of her peers'.

For instance, general history seemed to lie in his area of specialization along with physical, scientific theory and knowledge of gadgets. The specific history of the people—the crew, as they had referred to themselves once or twice, which apparently covered all aborigines of whatever tribe or lineage—was Rita's province. So was more esoteric theory.

Yet when the far walker discussed details of what it was she did, the limiting factor was Brigid's limited capacity to understand, a difficulty, she had been assured, that would be not noticeably less severe were Rita talking to Lakesh himself. Brigid couldn't restrain herself from a private smile, now, over the rim of her cup as she raised the fragrant fluid toward her lips and felt its heat shine on her mouth, envisioning anybody, even Old Man, trying to tell *that* to Dr. Mohandas Lakesh Singh.

Nobby for his part seemed to enjoy a frankly mystical communion with machines—an almost empathic sense of how to make them work, what was wrong with them when they did not.

It's almost as if the left brain/right brain divisions we're used to don't operate in them, she thought. Or perhaps they operate differently.

She came out of her reverie. Sally Wright was talking about limited gene pools and a kind of high-energy natural selection. "They had their own evolving culture—and from what you've said, it evolved into something more than a little strange—which applied selection pressures of its own."

She noticed Brigid looking at her, stopped, blushed, fluttered and then looked hard at the table with her gray-blue eyes. "I'm sorry if I'm speaking out of place. I got carried away, I guess—"

"It only looks to me," Brigid said, "as if you're doing the very thing you were brought here for. No need to apologize for that." She made herself break through her own carefully programmed reserve to smile reassuringly.

"All this is quite fascinating," Billy Handsome said, "but I trust you'll all forgive me if I none so subtly steer us back to the issue at hand. Which is, Brigid tells us she has a suggestion as to how to proceed that doesn't involve mucking about in places like that ghastly basement. Which I for one am all in favor of."

"Too right," Rita said.

"Simply," Brigid said, "I believe it is more efficient to search records than shelves."

"Great idea," Billy said, bobbing his head. "You'll have to forgive us—we're new to this looting-cultural-relics game. All we know is what we've learned from having it done to us."

"But we've been looking through records in the places we've been—all our teams, that is," Nobby said.

"But they're fragmentary when you find them at all. Isn't that right?" The tech boy nodded. "The ones you find have suffered all manner of damage—looting, vandalism, fires, paper decaying to nothing through simple age. You probably find water damage has rendered a lot of the records you locate illegible."

"All true," Rita said.

"And the computer records aren't much better. I suspect you have your own portable power supplies, but I doubt that you find many working computer systems with uncrashed hard disks. And very little by way of backups such as tapes and CDs."

Nobby reared back in his seat blinking through his bottle-bottom lenses. "But that's exactly right. Find bugger-all most places. Um, pardon the language, ma'am."

Not least of the mysteries about these people was not that they spoke the language of their colonial oppressors, but they spoke it with the very accent of their oppressors—not to mention the idioms that had been current in the years before the nukecaust. Perhaps that was just the form in which their only common tongue survived.

She nodded to Billy Handsome. "You spoke of looting cultural relics not long ago. The people I used to work for were in the business of doing precisely that—to the remnants of our own North American culture. Since unification the baronies have combed the continent for all the records and stored data on prenukecaust America they could get their hands on. Most of the places you've visited have probably been cleaned out already seventy years ago."

"Crikey," Billy Handsome said, running a hand through his dusky red dreads.

"We have been looking in the baronies, though, remember?" Rita pointed out.

"Sure. Their storerooms. Same problems of inefficiency, if a great deal neater setting. And the risks, if anything, greater."

"As we know to our sorrow," Billy said.

"But we've searched the databases in the monoliths when we've gotten in," Nobby objected.

Brigid smiled thinly. "And found not much, I suspect."

Nobby hunched his head down on his neck and tipped it to the side. "Well…more than you might expect. We've got our own software, good as your Mnemosyne. Courtesy of Old Man!"

Still smiling, Billy said something in their language. Nobby blinked and let his shoulders slump. Brigid surmised it amounted to, "Quit showing off."

Billy looked back to Brigid. "So what is it you're proposing, then?"

"We have our own copies of virtually every byte the baronies got their hands on," Brigid said, "in our mass storage right here in Cerberus. And we can search it without having to play whose-is-biggest games with encryption and decryption software."

Nobby blushed a bright red Brigid hadn't suspected he was capable of. Rita laughed out loud.

"Nor, for that matter, to worry about Magistrates kicking in the door to serve termination warrants on you. Or us. Sally Wright, if she's willing—"

"Oh, yes, by all means." The thin-faced woman seemed flattered at being included.

"—and I will search for mention of the turtle. You're welcome to help, as long as you're willing to undertake not to try to probe too deeply into *our* secrets. Our own encryption was written to defeat even the Syne—and please don't take that as a challenge, Nobby."

"He won't," Billy said with cheery certitude.

He pushed back from the table. "Well, I'm up to start the search, especially since it seems to entail a marked lack of cannibal interlopers. Who's with me?"

Brigid looked to Sally. The Snakefishville fugitive's cheeks shone pink, and her eyes were actually bright. "I think we're good."

All rose except for Grant. "Question," he said in the direction of Billy Handsome.

"Ask freely, mate."

"Why're you sneaking around machine shops if what you're looking for's an ancient statue of a turtle? Or is all that just Mag Division intel with their heads wedged up their butts again?"

"Oh, no, mate, they got that right," Billy Handsome said. "We've been whipping up kit, you see—"

"'Kit'?"

"Gear. The rough and ready. *Équipage,* as the French might say."

"How do you know what the French might say?"

"He knows every language," Nobby said.

For just an instant Billy Handsome's well-named face hardened. Then he flashed a smile again. "Now, Nobby, don't go exaggeratin' the way you do. As to your question, cobber, we're remembering, as you might say, how to build all kinds of wizard stuff from out our own dim, dark past. But I daresay you've seen the photos of roundabout Uluru. The center of our existence, yes, the cradle of our being to be bloody sure. But bugger all in terms of halfway modern fabrication facilities."

"You're building those beam weapons!" Brigid said with sudden comprehension.

Billy nodded. "In part. They come in right handy, as you've seen. But mainly we've been lashing together the means of making tools to make better tools. Including neutron blasters that don't give the firer a lethal dose of radiation after just a few shots."

In the sudden deathly silence that filled the commissary, all heads turned to Nobby.

"Those nearby get far less exposure," Rita said softly. "But you might want to get checked out, when you have a spare moment."

"Wh-what?" Nobby stammered in response to the continued scrutiny from the three Cerberus people. "No worries about me."

He grinned shyly. "It's only this body, after all."

Chapter 14

"Are you sure you won't take mulled wine? I can heat you some right up," the wizened old man in the skullcap and indigo gown said in heavily accented English, bending over a little hearth inset in the sweating stone wall of the underground room.

Kane successfully struggled to control a reflex grimace. "No, thank you, Sri Goldshtayn," he said. "Cold water's fine for me."

"You got anything to eat?" Domi asked brightly.

The AKM that had been aimed at Kane's navel when the door opened had been held in the wood-brown and wood-hard hands of one Salah, a small, flat-faced man in a dark sarong and a fez. He was the owner-proprietor of a crack-in-the-wall shop selling herbs and powders and various equipment for use, as far as Kane could judge from a quick glance around in the dim orange light cast by a single brass lamp slung from the ceiling by chains, in rituals of various sorts. The narrow space—Kane could have spanned it by extending his arms to his sides—was dominated by a stuffed narrow-snouted crocodilian also hung from the roof beams.

Yet Salah had a partner, one normally invisible to the public, although as he was demonstrating now, definitely not silent. Ruven Goldshtayn was the aborigines' contact within Tanimbar City.

One of them, anyway, Kane thought. It was abundantly clear to him now that the vision Brigid and the rest had been vouchsafed by Yindi was incomplete. Perhaps not entirely false, but a far shout from the whole truth. Just as, for instance, it would have been obvious to a blind, drunk, blind-drunk grease monkey scraped off the floor of the lowest dive of the Tartarus Pit of your choice that commerce in goods and info—smuggling, espionage, call it what you will—had been ongoing between the aborigines and the islanders for years, if not right along since the nukecaust. And, specifically, contacts of a sort that just didn't seem to fit into the vision of the aborigines as happy organic people who did little but hunt and gather and dance around naked.

No more than the quartet of flesh-and-blood aborigines crammed into the low-ceilinged space beneath the creaky floorboards of Salah's shop fit that image.

"Of course, of course," the bent old man murmured in response to Domi's question. He tinkled a small brass bell. In response a little brown child in a blue sarong and fez appeared with a plate of fruit, which Domi, murmuring thanks, fell to devouring with her customary rapacity. The others declined.

Goldshtayn teetered over and sat on a three-legged stool at the table. "You may be wondering, my North American friends, at finding a Jew here in the east South Sea islands. The story is simple enough.

"Christianity came. Now it's gone, in these parts at least. Islam came and went. The dominant religion in the islands now is a blend of animism and vaguely Hindu-influenced polytheism. And us. God's chosen people. Suffering on."

The aborigines sat silent, their usual ebullience drained. Kane reckoned it was sheer fatigue.

"How come your people have stuck it out?" Kane asked.

The little man in the yarmulke shrugged. "Plenty of my people would argue with this—but then, that's the way we are. I think it's because of our essential pessimism."

"The power of negative thinking, huh?"

Old Goldshtayn nodded. Beaming. "Exactly! You see, Christianity and Islam made promises. Specifically, they predicted Armageddon, with redemption to follow."

He gestured around, a sweeping movement that implicitly took in all the world around them. "Armageddon we got, in trumps and spades. But redemption—" He shook his head. "That's been pretty thin on the ground, as you've no doubt noticed. We Jews, on the other hand, while we harbor notions of a messiah—where do you think the Christians got it from?— don't necessarily expect Him at any given moment. We should be so lucky that He should come while we walk the Earth.

"Whereas our God promised us plenteous suffering, and this God has always delivered. So when the battle of Armageddon was followed not by the rule of the righteous but the world basically turning into shit for two hundred years, the newcomers got disillusioned. For us Jews, it was more of the same."

"So how come speak English?" Domi asked, biting into an immense pear.

Goldshtayn beamed. "That, too, is simplicity itself, my dear young lady. Well before the nukecaust English had established itself as the language of international trade. Whereas non-Jews have remained obstinate about not learning Hebrew. Hereabouts you'll find that, while few of the common people understand English, the majority of merchants and traders do. Not to mention the functionaries of the god-king, inasmuch as English is the language of his court."

"Speaking of this god-king," Kane asked, getting impatient for the point, "how exactly does he fit in?"

"Exceedingly well. The people, you see, believe as they have for millennia that the gods are real. They believe the gods have loves and rivalries and even kill one another, even die. They believe mortals can be apotheosized into gods, and gods incarnated as mortals. Don't you think maybe the Christians cribbed a little something of that, eh? Never mind, never mind. When the god-king's silver disk appeared in the skies and burned up all those who would not bow down in worship to him with its ruby fire-flashes, sure, it was beyond the experience of most of the populace. But it was nothing out of line with their theological expectations."

"So he's been trying to suppress other religions."

Goldshtayn drank deeply from his battered tin tankard, clunked it down on the table before himself, wiped his beard with the back of his hand and sighed. "Mostly," he said, "no. This is where we, God's chosen people, get screwed again. As I said, my boy, to most of the pious pagans hereabouts, all gods are real. The Dewa Raja would not try to suppress belief in the others because that no one would sit still for. But he can make a go at forcing everybody to worship him as primary god, at least of the region—because, after all, the public sees that as natural. He's a god, he's also a king—why shouldn't he insist on being number one? It's what anybody would do, no?"

"But you won't worship him," Domi stated flatly, sitting back licking her fingers. The beaten-brass platter was bare save for a few stems and rinds. Not for the first time Kane marveled at the disconnect between her gamin slimness and horde-of-locusts appetite.

Goldshtayn's dark old eyes glittered at her. "And how did you know that, young lady?"

"We had Jews living in the ville for a while," she said.

"They traveled around a bunch. Everybody thought they were funny because nobody else had much use for religion. But nobody bothered them about that. Other stuff—" She shrugged expressively.

"Religious prejudice and race hatred aren't big in the nine baronies these days," Kane said. "People have basically found more pressing things to get excited about. Like muties."

"Ah, so," Goldshtayn said, nodding his big, mostly bald head. "Ah, so. I will not bow before the Dewa Raja. Therefore I find it expedient to take a partner, as in my excellent friend Salah, whom you met upstairs, to serve as front man. Plus I must add, he's very industrious."

He shrugged again. "This, too, will pass. Even as great world religions, like communism, enjoy their day in the sun and die, so must god-kings, too. Don't you think?"

Kane placed his big, scarred hands on the table and grinned through his beard. He didn't realize what a sign it was of the feeble little old man's courage that Goldshtayn didn't quail. With his already more than somewhat slightly sinister face underlit by the butter-colored flicker of a wick in a brass basin of oil, he looked altogether demonic.

"And that," he said, "is exactly what we want to talk about, old man."

"I DON'T LIKE this outfit," Domi complained as she and Kane strolled side-by-side through the morning crowds toward the great Slave Mart Plaza near the Tanimbar City waterfront. "Double hot in here."

"Quit bitching," Kane suggested. "It's hot in the Outlands where you come from, too."

"But it's a dry heat."

Kane rolled a wolf-gray eye at her in a don't-start-with-me

look. He couldn't see her answering expression for her veil, but he suspected it was a rebellious grin.

Despite her dissatisfaction with her Sea Dayak garb, which Kane had to acknowledge was no doubt less than comfortable, she was doing her best to fit in—at least when it came to walking with the almost exaggerated hip-swinging gait the local women displayed. Since even the ones who were far from fat possessed much more imposing hips than the slender albino girl, she was definitely playing catch-up. But then, as Kane had long known, vanadium steel was as custard to the will of Domi; he only feared she might cause herself serious lumbar-spinal injury with the extraordinary convolutions she was putting her pelvis through.

Tanimbar City was at once shabbier and more magnificent in the molten light of day. You could really see its extent, the big mansions and palaces and public structures with their whitewashed walls blinding in the sun, their gilded domes and minarets—which, their original function having been misplaced along with widespread observance of Islam, were still maintained as watchtowers and places from which alarm could be sounded with gongs and brass horns should the horizon suddenly sprout the mustard-and-blood-hued sails of a pirate fleet.

But you could also see the slums, precarious structures, some of which rose three and even four stories, despite the fact you could see where stucco had flaked away in so many places that they were nothing more than some lath-work frames jumbled together with thin lattices and daubed over with mud. It seemed to be mostly leaning against one another that held them up, and some leaned unnervingly out over streets that were mostly too narrow and shady already, while some bulged like plaster hernias. Kane refused even to contemplate what would happen when one of the region's inevitably earthquakes slammed into town for a visit, or someone inevitably got a little careless with one of the ubiquitous open fires or bowls of coals everybody used for cooking. Things'd go up as if they were drenched in high octane.

Then again Baptiste had told him Shizuka's people, a people long famed for cleverness and industry, had always chosen to live in houses of paper and wood, heated with their own charcoal pots despite dwelling on a cooler, northerly arc of this selfsame seismically unstable Ring of Fire. And more, many of them preferred to do so during the brief high-tech interregnum of the twentieth century, when they actually had alternatives.

Even though the streets were thronged with energy, noise and life and movement, faces and limbs of all shades, not excluding Domi's pigmentless pallor, and countless languages, including spindrift snatches of English, there was a quality here that Kane could feel and hear and see but not quite put a name to. Not hopelessness, which was so common in the scummy Outland villes or the Tartarus Pits or, he now recognized, in the gleaming Enclave towers in different form. But something not too far distant…fatalism, perhaps.

Then, of course, in the daylight you could better see the dirt. But his nose had brought him the bad news there in abundance last night. Fortunately his olfactory sense was giving up the unequal battle and growing numb to the stinks. He resolved to be careful to wash carefully anything he ate, keep an eye on Domi to make sure she did the same and be silently thankful that people who had survived the megacull tended to be highly disease resistant. He was also thankful that De-Fore had insisted on giving them both broad-spectrum antibiotic shots, product of another secret Totality Concept project, before allowing Mary Alice to whisk them off to Babar Island.

"Goldshtayn says the god-king's not so bad, even if he does want the Jews to worship abominations," Domi said. "He says he's suppressed piracy and encouraged trade."

Kane shrugged. He was dressed as a pirate himself again today. He was actually starting to like the getup; he assured himself it was only because of the freedom allowed his limbs by the loose blouse and trousers. Sure, that was it.

"Has a different feel from the Enclaves or the Pits," he admitted. "Lot looser. Easier. He doesn't seem to've tried to clamp the same iron restraints on behavior his cousins back in North America did. Mebbe because he lacked the resources."

"Or mebbe because people here wouldn't put up with it."

He grunted. "Mebbe so. Baptiste tells me Americans used to be known for their contrariness and independent ways. Don't see that much anymore."

"They were same back before the barons," Domi said with a heat that surprised Kane. "Back in the days of baron blasters. And some so now—what about Maureen Orion? Or me?"

Kane held up a hand. "Okay, peace. Point made. Although I can tell you from my experience that there's plenty of people, and not just sealed away in their nice clean climate-controlled Enclaves, who can't imagine any kind of life beyond meekly waiting to be told what to do and doing it. The point is, even if this baron has made the trains run on time around here, he's still on the other side from us."

Domi's shrouded head bobbed. "Sure."

Ahead of them the crowd abruptly parted. There was no change in the timbre of the polyglot babble, nor even any visible disturbance; the mob simply flowed left and right to let a pair of men swagger through.

A remarkable pair they were, too: big men, powerfully built, their already imposing heights exaggerated by turbans that had to have been a foot wide wound around their skulls. They wore silken tunics with double lines of gleaming gold buttons down the bibs, loose pantaloons, sturdy roll-topped leather boots. Silken veils hid all their faces except their restless, suspicious eyes. And every square inch of cloth was lustrous raven-wing black. The only items they displayed that weren't jet-black were the gold-chased silver scabbards and gold-pommeled ivory hilts of the sabers bouncing at their waists—and the kris strapped to each man's left forearm.

Their eyes, one pair brown, one pair blue, swept over Domi and Kane. They didn't so much as pause.

The instant the pair passed, Domi turned her head and made a spitting gesture that was unmistakable even through their veil. "Mags."

Kane's big shoulders shook with silent laughter. The crowd had already flowed back into one seamless stream about them, just like water. "Too right, as our Aboriginal friends would say." He shook his head. "I don't believe it. Son of a bitch has got himself a low-tech Magistrate Division."

"Triple shits," Domi hissed. "You right all 'long. This baron enemy of everything good."

Before them two- and three-story commercial buildings, of clearly more durable construction than the tenements—pink-washed brick and even stone—fell away to either side to reveal the Slave Mart Plaza: a hectare of smooth and gleaming concrete, near as Kane could figure it, bordered on three sides by splendid warehouses, countinghouses and assorted public structures. The fourth side lay open to the docks, and beyond it the harbor, water invisible beneath a dense encrustation of hull, and masts tugging at the fearfully blue sky above, and all dominated by the ormolu bulk of the *Varuna*. Vast as it was, the plaza was totally full of spectators packed bung to chinklepin.

The god-king hadn't suppressed slavery itself—according to Goldshtayn's matter-of-fact account, that would never have been accepted by the population. He had squatted on the slave trade, however; the court held a monopoly on slave ownership, although mercantile concerns and even individuals could lease slaves from the god-king. Citizens both rich and well disposed toward the divine monarchy, Kane guessed. Enslavement was primarily a leading form of criminal punishment—fines, floggings and, of course, public execution being the popular alternatives—and nongovernmental seizure and trafficking in slaves was prohibited on pain of decapitation. Which meant as far as Kane could see that the god-king's goons, his fleet, army and his Mags held a monopoly on slaving.

But no amount of enforcement, no matter how swift or atrocious the penalties exacted, could entirely end freelance slaving, any more than it could the prevalent piracy and smuggling. Kane didn't really understand the system, but when Goldshtayn got through telling them that part, Domi and the four aborigines were already asleep and Kane had learned more than he actually cared to know.

At the far end from the docks rose a set of viewing stands of some kind of smooth white stone. A better-dressed audience occupied these. The stands were dominated by a grand central pavilion, narrow but almost two stories tall, of some white material, possibly stone, as well, carved into a fine latticework, which had the effect of admitting air and allowing the occupants to see out, but making it impossible to see into the interior in any detail.

"Bastard's watching from in there," Domi said, nodding her head toward the peaked-roof structure. "Bet."

"No bet," Kane said.

Before the stands rose a broad dais. Wide marble steps mounted it to either side. It was the old auction block where the slaves had been sold. Kane was surprised at its magnificence, given there had probably been no practical way of keeping the slaves from crapping all over it, not to mention bleeding. Maybe marble was easy to clean, and anyway conspicuous consumption was apparently not considered a serious faux pas in this part of the world.

The crowd expelled a great geyser of noise. "What happened?" Kane asked. He had been scanning the gigantic buildings fronting upon the plaza, occupied with figuring fields of view and possible escape routes.

"I think one guy just gouged the other's eyes out," Domi reported.

The slave block now served as a battle platform. So many had flocked to Tanimbar City to join the god-king's holy expeditionary force to Australia as mercenaries that aspirants to officer rank had to prove their mettle in single combat against one another. If the loser survived more or less intact, as the one contestant had evidently just failed to do, he could stay in the ranks as a grunt. Winners got promoted. And if the winner stayed in, higher rank came with each additional round, with growing prizes to sweeten the pot.

Of course the longer a competitor stayed in, the greater his chances of death and dismemberment. That's what made it entertainment.

"Which guy gouged his eyes out?" Kane asked, not particularly interested.

"Dude with four arms," Domi said.

Kane's eyes snapped to the dais. A figure in a loincloth knelt on the marble top, weeping copious amounts of blood through cupped hands. Above him the victor, seven feet tall as near as Kane could make it and clad only in billowy white pantaloons now liberally sprayed with red, brandished his arms in triumph over his head, which was shaved bare except for a horsetail-length black topknot.

All four of them.

Kane swallowed.

"Kane," Domi asked, sidling in close and pitching her voice low and urgent, "are you sure you know what you're doing?"

"No."

Chapter 15

"How are you doing?" Brigid asked. Sally Wright looked up and around quickly, something like fear on her face. The tall redhead patted her shoulder reassuringly.

"Sorry," Brigid said. "I wouldn't have believed it when I had been…out…as short a time as you. But I guess I've forgotten what's it's like to spend my time dreading who might be reading what over my shoulder."

The new archivist gave her a shy grin. "You mean I don't have to feel bad about being jumpy?"

"I don't think you have to feel bad about anything. But maybe that's me."

Dotted throughout the expanse of redoubt Bravo, doing business as Cerberus redoubt, were small compartments and even large ones, subdivided into cubicles, containing desks with computer workstations. With its brutal devotion to the concept of order—and domination, of course—the Totality Concept would not be denied its little bureaucracy. Nor its disproportionately large and bloated bureaucracy, to judge by the amount of space dedicated to the task.

Since all the computers were tied into the same local-area network, it was only a matter of possessing the proper passwords to perform any task you desired. Although Brigid didn't know all the passwords—Lakesh was far too fond of playing his cards right up against his skinny ribs for that—she knew more than enough to get them to the relatively low-clearance collection of nukecaust records purloined from the baronies' databases.

Although sheer fortitude and the pressure of the mission had enabled them to suppress it during their brief, nearly disastrous foray into the basements of what had been University of Wisconsin, the Australians shared a mild claustrophobic streak. In particular they found the weight of the vanadium alloy and concrete of Cerberus, and the bulk of the peak beneath which it was buried, to be disconcerting. That wasn't odd in Brigid's eyes; after all, they had passed their whole lives to date beneath the unbounded starry skies of the island continent.

What was odd was that they seemed annoyed and impatient with their own unease at being cooped up beneath a mighty mass of metal and stone. As if that in itself were somehow unexpected, although to Brigid it seemed the most natural thing on Earth.

Unwelcome surprise or not, the psychic unease was real and present to some degree in all four. So Brigid had staked out a relatively open corner of the largest and most spacious area of Cerberus workstations.

"I haven't turned up anything beyond tantalizing hints yet," Sally said. "I only wish I could scan through the files as fast as they do."

Brigid's gaze followed Sally's nod to where the four aborigines sat, each at a monitor. Screens of data flickered past, none slower than one a second. Even Bush Baby Bob, his head turbaned in bandages, was taking his turn.

Brigid blew out a long exhalation. "We all do what we can, I guess."

She walked over to stand beside Billy Handsome. "Don't mean to intrude," Brigid said.

"Not a problem." The talker turned his red-dreadlocked head aside to flash a smile at her. The screens continued to flick past; obviously he was reading them with his peripheral vision.

"You're all—how should I say this?—prodigiously talented."

"This?" Billy stopped paging through his file, swiveled his chair to face the senior archivist. "Don't be too impressed. It's a trick, mostly."

"Could you teach it to me?"

For once Billy showed his teeth in an expression other than a smile; his full lips made a sort of oval around his teeth.

"Not so easy," he said. "You don't rightly have the referents, I'm afraid. But if we get a chance when we're done with this—when we've got the turtle back to Lilga—we'll teach you what we can."

The smile returned. "Fair enough?"

"I suppose so. But there's something that's been bothering me. When I went to Uluru before, what I saw struck me very strongly as, well, a nonliterate culture."

At mention of the word "Uluru" the other three stopped what they were doing and pivoted to look at her. Their relaxed affability never flickered, but something more had entered the mix. Reverence? Expectancy?

Rita laughed. "You mean you thought we couldn't read," she said.

"Well—"

It was Billy's turn to laugh. "No worries, Brigid," he said. "We couldn't."

Brigid stared at him.

Her thoughts resembled a school of small fish into which a shark had suddenly torpedoed. As she tried to head them back into something accessible to sense, Nobby exclaimed, "Sally!"

He lunged to the refugee archivist's side. The woman sat quivering-stiff in her chair, arms down and locked at full extension, hands knotted into fists so hard the bones threatened to tear through the skin on the backs of her hands. Her face was paper-white. Her lips, completely bloodless, writhed, but no sound came out.

"Seizure?" Billy Handsome asked.

"No," Rita said. She knelt at the stricken woman's other side. Nobby had already drawn back at her gently insistent air-pushing gesture, so as not to add the pressure of presence to whatever stress load was jamming the woman's system.

The talker looked up at her companions. "Vision."

Brigid froze with her finger a centimeter from punching the intercom button to scream for DeFore to come on the double. The dark blond far walker said something to her companions in their own language. Then she turned to Brigid.

"She'll take no harm," she said. "But if someone might bring a cup of cool water and a towel, that'd not go amiss."

Brigid complied instantly. Her long years of training in rigid self-control paid off now—as did several years' experience of real bone-busting, blood-spurting emergencies out in the big bad world. Moving precisely but without apparent hurry she brought the objects Rita requested. She took off Sally Wright's glasses and began to wipe her brow as Rita applied paper towels soaked in ice water to the insides of her wrists.

Then Rita took one still rock-hard fist in her own strong square hand, began to stroke the underside of the wrist while murmuring words unknown to Brigid. There was nothing evident in face, posture or action but concerned compassion yet the impression Brigid could not shake away was of a human worried about a beloved pet.

GET FREE BOOKS and a FREE GIFT
WHEN YOU PLAY THE...

Lucky 7

SLOT MACHINE GAME!

Just scratch off the silver box with a coin. Then check below to see the gifts you get!

YES! I have scratched off the silver box. Please send me the 2 free Gold Eagle® books and gift for which I qualify. I understand I am under no obligation to purchase any books, as explained on the back of this card.

366 ADL D34F

166 ADL D34E

FIRST NAME | LAST NAME

ADDRESS

APT.# | CITY

STATE/PROV. | ZIP/POSTAL CODE

7 7 7	Worth **TWO FREE BOOKS** plus a **BONUS** Mystery Gift!
🍒🍒🍒	Worth **TWO FREE BOOKS!**
♣♣♣	Worth **ONE FREE BOOK!**
🔔🔔🍒	**TRY AGAIN!**

(MB-04-R)

DETACH AND MAIL CARD TODAY!

The Gold Eagle Reader Service™ — Here's how it works:

Accepting your 2 free books and mystery gift places you under no obligation to buy anything. You may keep the books and gift and return the shipping statement marked "cancel." If you do not cancel, about a month later we'll send you 6 additional books and bill you just $29.94* — that's a saving of over 10% off the cover price of all 6 books! And there's no extra charge for shipping! You may cancel at any time, but if you choose to continue, every other month we'll send you 6 more books, which you may either purchase at the discount price or return to us and cancel your subscription.

*Terms and prices subject to change without notice. Sales tax applicable in N.Y. Canadian residents will be charged applicable provincial taxes and GST. Credit or debit balances in a customer's account(s) may be offset by any other outstanding balance owed by or to the customer.

Slowly, as if being cranked, Sally's fist began to open. It got about a quarter of the way, and then simply relaxed. Rita repeated the procedure with the other hand, with the same result.

Brigid had set a cup and wet cloth down on the thin carpet. "Why did that work?" she asked in wonder.

"I spoke the language of your soul," the far walker said. Lightly she began to massage the woman's temples, muttering again in the same language.

Slowly Sally's whole body relaxed; the spasm was broken. Rita held her hands about a centimeter to either side of Sally's head, then eased back and stood away from her.

"What did you say?" Brigid asked.

"Essentially I told her she was safe, and it was okay for her soul to come back home."

A terrific heaving sob ripped from Sally Wright's lips. She crossed her arms over her keyboard, dropped her head onto them and began to convulse with huge sobs.

"She knows you better than me," Rita told Brigid gently but pointedly. "Best you comfort her, if you will."

It occurred to Brigid that she and the Snakefishville fugitive knew each other hardly at all, although she knew better than to discount the soul bonding of having faced deadly peril together. But they hadn't faced it very long, nor had great exposure to one another since. But quibbling didn't seem a good response. She cradled Sally's close-cropped mouse-blond head against her bosom and caressed her head.

"There, there," she crooned, feeling totally ineffectual. "It's all right, Sally. You're safe. Everything's fine."

She looked up past Sally's crown at Rita. "I wish I could talk the language of the soul."

The sturdy blond woman could do no more than silently shake her head.

But skillful or not, Brigid's attempted ministrations seemed to be working. Sally latched on to her arm with a double-handed grip that Brigid feared would leave her ulna permanently grooved, but her horrible rib-cracking sobs dwindled to mere heartbroken crying, and finally a fishlike gasping for breath.

Wordlessly Rita handed Brigid the porcelain cup and a fresh damp hand towel. Brigid washed the woman's face again.

"Better now?" she asked, as Sally made a couple of snuffling hiccuping sounds and began to breathe more or less normally. The crushing pressure on Brigid's forearm eased.

Then it was back with interest, and Sally was staring into Brigid's green eyes with her own gray-blue ones huge as a frightened kitten's. "Kane," she gasped. "I…saw…Kane."

"Surely he's not *that* frightening."

"No—Kane's in danger! They're going to kill him—I saw it!"

A FIST WITH KNUCKLES like pebbles poking out through dense curling underbrush of black hairs slammed the side of Kane's jaw and snapped his head around on his neck. Red-and-bright-yellow lightnings flared behind his eyes.

Slowly he turned his face back toward his opponent: a man an inch or so taller than him and much heavier, although much of that was sagging around his pale waist. He was hairy enough for a balding mountain gorilla; the most prominent expanses of visible skin were his capacious gut, and his face from halfway up his cheekbones to almost the crown of his head. Like Kane he wore only a pair of trousers, these sun-faded blue cotton secured by a rope belt obscured from view beneath his gut. He was panting like a dog.

Kane smiled.

"Is that the best you've got?" he asked, wiping away a

trickle of bloody spittle from the corner of his mouth without deigning to look at his hand.

The man spread his arms—he had the span of a bull ape, too—and charged, roaring like a furious water buffalo.

Kane stood and waited, almost as if lost in thought. He actually heard the onlooking throng suck in its breath.

As the huge hairy arms began to curl in to encircle him in a spine-snapping bear hug, the former Magistrate moved.

He took a short step forward, using all his mass and a savage turn of his hips to power an uppercutting palm-heel strike that slammed right up under the multiple black-bearded chins.

The huge hairy man rose off the marble floor of the dais, polished to near-glass slickness by decades of miserably shuffling feet. His vast capacious belly actually bumped Kane and sent the smaller man staggering backward.

But it was the big man's own flight that was most impressive. The bald crown of his head rose eight full inches in the air. At the same time his body swung upward from his fur-topped feet as if hinged at the ears. He actually achieved the horizontal, at about the plane of Kane's eyes, before slamming back onto the dais like an overstuffed piece of furniture dropped from a passing blimp.

Groaning, he raised his head from the marble as if it were a globe of condensed matter. Then his head fell back with a whump of finality.

Kane licked his thumb and used it to police up any stray flecks of bloody saliva that might have collected in his beard.

"Next," he said.

"You crazy," Domi said as he sat beside her on the carved marble bench. Her arms were crossed beneath her breasts, which were surprisingly full for her slight build. Not that anyone could tell for the sack she was wearing.

"Yep," he said. He began to towel sweat from his shoulders and gray-shot chest hair with a cloth she had waiting. Contestants and their supporters got reserved seating on stone benches in front of the box seats, it turned out.

Wordlessly she handed him a corked gourd. He uncorked it and tossed in a mouthful, swishing it around. Then he froze. His eyes blinked, went wide. Then he spit it on the stone at his feet.

"What the hell's that?" he choked. "Tastes like paint thinner."

"Watered arrack. You just weren't ready for the taste."

"Pest, that's alcoholic, isn't it? That's the last thing I need right now."

She shrugged. "Water dilutes *arrack—arrack* kills the germs. Win-win!"

"If you say so."

"Not much alcohol. You can take it, you strong man. Or would you rather drink raw fruit juice? Then next match you can turn around, drop pants and hose your opponent down with runny shit."

He showed her a bewildered grin. "You're always a world of surprises, Domi. After all these years you can still say things that flat revolt even me."

She crossed her arms again even tighter than before. "No need to thank me. I'm just an Outlands gaudy slut. Mebbe I should try for a role in god-king's harem. Be appreciated there."

"You know better," Kane said with a laugh. "Barons're hung like mice—you know that. Your talents would just be wasted."

He looked at her. "And thanks, Domi. I really do appreciate it."

He wasn't much concerned their seditious—or was it sacrilegious?—banter might be overheard. For one thing the next match was already in full swing, a tall, bulky African-looking guy in olive silk pajamas fending off shin kicks from a bearded white dude in baggy shorts. Because they were close together Kane and Domi could hear each other, but farther than they sat apart their voices got swallowed up in the crowd's happy gore-anticipating roar.

Besides, while English was definitely understood in these parts, it wasn't widely so.

TO REGISTER APPLICANTS for the Grand Holy Fleet, as Sri Goldshtayn said it was being called, a line of clerks sat behind a long table festooned with gold, white and black bunting—the Dewa Raja's colors. When the bald teak-colored man with a hat like a felt trash can on his shaved head seated at one end of the table gave him the squinty eye and cocked his pen peremptorily, Kane had spoken right up. "I'm Hardin. I speak English. Anybody speak English here?"

The pen flicked down the line. Four seats along an albino dwarf waved a stubby hand at him from the shadow of a tattered yet tasteless red, purple and green silk parasol, which also boasted a fringe of little yellow tassels, about a third of which were MIA. "What is it with dwarfs this month?" Kane muttered beneath his breath as he made his way to the putatively English-speaking registrar.

"I speak Ingrezi perfect, you betcha," the dwarf chirped in a voice about the same pitch as Domi's. "What I can do you for?" He tittered in a glass-breaking key. Kane realized he was a eunuch, as well as a dwarf.

Cheer up, he told himself. You've finally found somebody it sucks worse to be than you.

The albino eunuch dwarf might have overestimated his

command of English, but it proved adequate to the task at hand. Kane recited the string of lies Goldshtayn and the aborigines had cooked up for him over *arrack*. He had, so he said, seen service as a captain in the Sultan's Own Rifles in Singapura, had slain so many bandits, rebels and, of course, Sea Dayaks. He had heard of the noble god-king's great crusade and traveled here at great personal expense and danger to offer his sword to the heroic Dewa Raja, blah, blah, blah. The albino eunuch dwarf wrote it dutifully all down, or wrote something down. Peering at it, Kane couldn't tell if he had indecipherable penmanship or was writing in a non-Roman character set. Or mebbe it was just trying to read it upside down.

Something in the dwarf's manner suggested very strongly that he knew Kane was reciting a string of lies, and whether he was writing them down faithfully or making up a whole new string of lies to amuse himself didn't mean shit to a tree sloth. All that mattered was that the requisite documents be duly written down.

Along with the flora and the natives, Kane noticed, bureaucracy had made quite the comeback after the nukecaust.

THE SUN WAS DROPPING toward the forested hills west of Tanimbar City. The referee, a round-shouldered and moon-faced middle-aged man who looked Japanese and wore a black *gi* with a red belt, stood smiling blankly at Kane's side as they awaited the announcement of Kane's next match. His third, it was the final bout of the day; the winner would get the choice of moving on to the competition's next stage or taking the rank and prizes he'd won and bagging it.

Kane was unsure what the matches needed a referee for. If there were any actual rules he hadn't seen them enforced. Domi had turned up a kid water-seller with a gap in his teeth and yet another fez whose scanty possessions included a few scattered fragments of English. He had confirmed that that big four-armed mutie bastard really had gouged out his opponent's eyes, both of them. It was considered unsporting to go for both at once, but the crowd loved it.

The announcer was a squat, self-important man in resplendent robes of gold and black who wore what appeared to be a double-decker trash can for a hat. Capacious as his own belly was he obviously didn't eat much: there was little room left for niceties such as a stomach by the size of the lungs he had to have possessed, and these of rhinoceros hide. He was able to shout the whole damn crowd down. As impressive a feat, in its way, as any combat feats Kane had witnessed today.

He finished bellowing in Malay, a language the day's other final competitor shared with the Tanimbar City mob. Then he set off roaring the whole spiel in almost comprehensible English, as a ritual courtesy to Kane. "Kiptin Hardin of Sultan of Singapura's Own Reefles…"

Kane tuned him out to concentrate on taking deep breaths to oxygenate himself. His fights had been tough, but he hadn't taken much damage. His hard-contact unarmed-combat training had served him well.

"And his opponent…give it up, everybody, for Tanimbar City's own favorite son, Bandu, Lord of Rakshasa!"

That doesn't sound good. Kane shook himself and focused his eyes.

Upon the four-armed monster mounting the platform and cracking all four sets of knuckles.

Chapter 16

Grant sat and watched the sun immolate itself in the flames that consumed the Darks' western peaks. A brisk breeze blew out into his face. Two swords rested on a rack before him, naked blades up to slice the sun's last rays. One long—*katana*—one short—*wakizashi. Dai-sho:* the long and short of it. The unique badge of the samurai, the noble warrior-in-service of old Japan. Shizuka had presented them to him as a token of his service to New Edo.

Knowing all they represented, he had accepted.

The fiery and beautiful woman warrior had made the same offer to his blood brother Kane.

Knowing all they represented, Kane had declined. Gracefully, for Kane.

Behind him, the barest breath of sound. The shadows made scarcely less noise racing toward infinity across the plateau that stretched forth from the entrance to Cerberus.

But he heard. And the *katana* with its yard-long blade was in his hand. But he did not rise, nor even turn.

A soft laugh from behind. "Well, I still might have shot you."

"I would have sensed your intent, Rita."

"I believe you would've done, at that. But if you knew I was here, why'd you lay hand to the blade?"

"I never take anything for granted where survival is on the line," he said. He still hadn't turned his head. The sun expired in a glory of purple and gold. It would have made a tasteless painting.

"Least of all when someone comes up behind me who hasn't exactly been generous with the truth."

The blond aborigine far walker sighed. "Will you bisect me if I sit beside you?"

"Not if you mind your manners."

"Tell me you didn't crack a smile when you said that," she said, settling down into a squat at his side.

He snorted. "It's beneath me to lie, under the circumstances."

She shook her mop of ropelike dreads. "We've not lied to you."

"Perhaps not directly. What about by omission?"

"Not even that. Or so I believe."

At last he looked at her. "Do you think I'm stupid, the way Philboyd and Neukirk do? You sure haven't told us everything."

"Have *you?* You haven't exactly gifted us with your life story, Grant, my friend." Her tone was light.

"I doubt it's near as interesting as yours."

She sighed and looked off at the pale green and blue draining slowly from the sky, leaving a curtain of dark. "What would you have of me?"

"How about the whole story."

She looked at him. Her heavy hair shadowed her strong-featured face. "Have you really got time to hear seventy-five thousand years of history?"

"Just the high points." He sighed, shifted, untied his legs, stretched them out before him. "What's with this seventy-thousand-year thing you people keep going on about? What exactly happened seventy-five thousand years ago, anyway?"

"We came to Earth," she said quietly.

ONE ON ONE Bandu didn't seem too overwhelmingly huge to Kane. No more imposing than say, a minor skyscraper from a preskydark ville. He loomed over the outlander, grinning out of his brick-red face.

His teeth appeared to have been filed to points. Or mebbe they grew that way.

Kane had assumed a modified boxer's stance, hands up and curved—his Sin Eater was back in Goldshtayn's basement in custody of Tyree—about chin level. He had his head ducked somewhat forward, hoping the monster would try to punch down into his face so Kane could bust his hand by tilting his head a little more and taking the blow on the thick cap of his skull. Of course, with that mass and those muscles, conceivably Bandu was one of those rare specimens who could implode a human skull with a single blow of the fist....

Bandu jabbed down with one of his left upper arms. Kane got his fists in the way and took a rocking uppercut to the pit of his stomach from the right lower arm. It missed the solar plexus, in part because Kane was standing slightly hunched forward with his rib cage partly in the way to begin with. But it still blew the air out of his lungs and lifted him off his feet.

He staggered back, just managing to stave off the reflex to drop his hands to clutch the world of hurt in his belly. Nonetheless Bandu might have gotten quite a meal had he chosen to press his advantage. Instead he went strutting around the platform's periphery, holding all four arms triumphantly aloft to invite the plaudits of the crowd. Which were forthcoming.

Kane promptly darted two steps forward and launched a savage sideways heel kick for the huge creature's right kidney with his left boot. Instantly Bandu wheeled with breathtaking speed, both right arms lashing out backhand to swat his attacker. Suspecting Bandu's leaving his back unguarded had been a setup, Kane had already checked his forward motion and the kick, dropped his boot to the marble and ducked. He felt the breeze of passage of those colossal arms over his head, then snapped up to deliver a right roundhouse kick aimed for the nerve center right below Bandu's navel.

The toe of his boot thunked home with satisfying impact, and Kane instantly danced back to avoid being grappled by the four arms that suddenly clutched for his rapidly retracted foot. He had either missed the nerve junction or the monster shrugged it off. Attacks like that affected standard humans in different ways, too.

And who knows how this puke is put together? he wondered. The operative phrase being "put together." Kane doubted the creature was a mutant. He suspected Bandu was a purpose-built biofact like the Baronial Guards.

Kane was on his bicycle, circling backward and counterclockwise. The monster circled warily with him, treating his smaller opponent now with at least token respect. Why not have a whole bodyguard of these things? Kane wondered, knowing the god-king's pavilion was surrounded by a phalanx of the normal human local ersatz Mags. Probably too expensive.

"Why run, little pale skin?" Bandu's voice was about what Kane expected: like a whale fart, vast and low and bubbling up from the depths. "You a coward?"

"Yep," Kane replied.

He beckoned with all four arms. "Come to me. You cannot flee forever. I promise I will not hurt you—long!" And he roared with laughter, highly appreciative of his own wit. Lots of the crowd joined in. Either laughter really was the universal language, or the anglophones in the crowd weren't pulling for Kane.

But Kane knew Bandu was right. Kane couldn't run forever. He had no doubt that if he tried the god-king would quickly come to the conclusion that he wasn't officer material after all, and order his black turbans to serve a termination warrant on him local style. He also knew he had little chance of dealing the giant any useful hurt with a straight-on attack.

Got to be treachery, then. Kane grinned a wolf's grin. He loved it when that answer came up.

"Yaah!" He put his head down and charged screaming at the monster. Lack of self-esteem was not a vice the four-armed man was showing much evidence of; playing his arrogance might lead him to open up and allow Kane to slip inside.

Bandu punched to meet him with his left-hand pair of arms. Huge and muscular as he was, he didn't omit to put his hips in it. Kane managed to take both shots on his forearms with his wrists crossed for bracing.

They still blasted him clean over backward and sent him skidding across the smooth marble on his ass.

One rule that did exist and was enforced: unlike sumo, you could touch the platform with any part of your body as often and hard as you liked and not lose—at least until something important caved in on unyielding marble. But like sumo, once you went out of bounds, that was it. And Kane was on a trajectory to stage dive right into the now howling mob.

Only by rolling on his belly and sprawling his limbs to maximize drag did he save himself from flying into space. He stopped hanging out from just below his clavicle north.

To his surprise he found himself looking down into the upturned white oval of Domi's face.

"Kane," she said softly, "you're sucking."

"Strategy," he assured her. "Got him just where I—"

Her ruby eyes focused past him and her mouth opened in a gasp. Suddenly her face was receding as if the earth had opened up and swallowed her.

Or as if Bandu, moving with speed and stealth utterly unexpected in such a behemoth, had grabbed Kane from behind and military-pressed him right over his head.

For a moment he held Kane aloft, his lower hands bracing his upper elbows as he turned in a circle, playing the mob. From here he could slam Kane onto an upraised knee to snap his spine—always a crowd pleaser—or just wham him down and let gravity and hard smooth stone do the work. Either would leave Kane firmly ensconced on the last train to the coast.

Kane never knew which option the four-armed biofact opted for. He just felt Bandu begin to power him down.

And reached down himself to grab the luxuriant black ponytail hanging from the back of the monster's scalp with both hands.

Bandu jackknifed violently as his very own strength and Kane's not-trivial mass yanked his head forward and down. Kane was slammed into redwood thighs. He clung to the hawser-thick hair for dear life, which was exactly at stake here.

Bandu toppled forward right on top of him. His forehead crunched into marble with a mountainous thud.

The monster had made an arch of himself and so all his weight had not come down upon Kane beneath him. It didn't prevent most of the air from being mashed out of the man's lungs.

Kane didn't let such a minor thing slow him down. Though blood was gushing everywhere from Bandu's head, that only proved what Kane could already feel: the monster wasn't chilled. His heart was still pumping it out. He was unquestionably stunned, which meant Kane had an opportunity that he had to seize.

He slammed a hammer-fist blow on the back of the unmoving giant's neck, mostly on principle. It produced no visible effect, and probably no actual one, either, but it helped Kane wriggle free of the enormous mass weighing him down. From there, his vision going black and his whole body feeling as if it had the vacuum of all space inside, he swarmed up to sit astride Bandu's barn-door upper shoulders.

Kane made himself grab the convenient handle the ponytail offered before he sucked in a huge breath. His head swam from the oxygen rush. He reared back, hauling hard, lifting Bandu's face from the scarlet pool on the marble.

Then Kane drove himself forward, slamming the monster's face back down.

He did that twice more. The huge body tensed once beneath him, filling him with terror that the beast was going to rear back and toss him like a bull.

Instead Bandu subsided with a sigh. Kane could still feel the monster's heart pounding through his own thighs, felt the bellows rise and fall beneath him. Bandu was still alive, but by now well and truly concussed. Out of it.

Kane sat upright and raised his arms in the air. After a heartbeat of unbelieving silence the crowd erupted in applause.

Kane felt his arm grabbed by the referee, who hauled him bodily to his feet with the arm above his head in the universal signal of victory. The referee came up alongside and began to bellow to the crowd.

The ref let Kane's arm go. Kane took three steps to the edge of the dais, dropped to his knees and puked.

GRANT DREW a foot up by his butt, cocking his knee. "Now you got my undivided attention. What are you people, anyway?"

"Humans, even as you and your friends are."

"Listen, Rita, you're a nice lady. Your friends are all so nice it's a damn wonder you don't sprain your faces smiling. But don't try to blow smoke up an old door-busting Magistrate's butt, all right? The hybrids say they're as human as we are, too."

"They say they're as terrestrial in origin as you, no? As us. We are humans, derived from planet Earth. But all of us were born in space."

He cocked an eyebrow. "Not Australia? If I hadn't seen you do some totally inexplicable things, I'd be sizing you up for a tinfoil hat shaped like the great pyramid long about now."

She laughed. "You are quite a clever man, Grant, although you choose to mask it behind rough-hewn ways. Our current bodies were born in Australia. *We* were born in space."

Before he could protest or question more, she wrapped her arms around her own knees and continued, "Our legends say that a giant red egg descended long ago from the heavens to the earth—to Australia. It broke open on impact. The survivors, white-skinned, emerged to eke out a life in the barren land. The egg decayed to form the red earth of the central desert."

She looked at him over her biceps. "That was us. The crew. Our ship was the last survivor of a mighty starfaring fleet. The rest had all been destroyed in a battle with an enemy too terrible to imagine."

She shook her head. "Too terrible to remember. I pray I never do."

The wind began to die. Its last remnants whistled among the rocks and rustled the dried grass.

"To survive, we had to adapt. We darked up, over time. We learned the hunter-gatherer ways to enable us to stay alive in a harsh land—one which, I grant, was alien to our individual experience, even if our kind did spring from this soil. And from that point, as legend says, the elders of our people decreed that things must never change."

"Why couldn't you use your technology to live? Or did you lose all your gear in the crash?" He shook his head. "Wouldn't you still have had the knowledge to rebuild, even from more or less ground zero?"

"Not exactly. Our ship was gravely damaged in the battle, and worse in the crash landing. But survival called for more than mere adaptation—we also had to hide. Because we had no way of knowing whether our enemy could track us here or not.

"Earth of that era was utterly primitive. To use any fragment of our technology would have amounted to broadcasting our presence, if the enemy had once come into Earth orbit. It would have stood out like what you'd call a sore thumb."

"But that knowledge is coming back, isn't it?"

She smiled and brushed hair from between her face and him. "I said you were far more perceptive than others generally give you credit for."

"How? Mebbe more important, why? Why now?"

"Our ship, you must understand, was itself a living thing—a created sentience, a self-aware being."

"Living steel?" The memories of ancient legends sent a shudder through his powerful frame. "An intelligent computer?"

"That's part of it, but more than that. He was the ship, and he lived, even as you or I live. And though he was grievously injured, he formed a desperate plan. And when he spoke of it to the survivors, all of us agreed to it. This process took ten years."

Grant shook his head. "You folks don't rush into much, do you?"

"In that day we had learned only the most insignificant trifle about patience. Are you familiar with the Internet, Grant?"

He stared at her, blinked, shook his head quickly as if clearing water droplets from his face. "What?"

"The Internet."

"Well, yeah, we were taught some of its history. And the baronies use something similar to communicate among themselves."

Rita nodded. "Good. You know that if, for example, you wished to send a message across the country, it was broken down into tiny pieces called packets, and it was then copied and all the copies sent by different routes to be reassembled at their destination?"

"Yeah. But shouldn't Nobby be telling me this?"

Her smile was crooked. "This is my province—the lore of the people. Strange as that seems. Nobby could tell you how to *build* an Internet. I know, in outline, how it works."

"Do you know why it was designed that way?"

He nodded slowly. "We were taught that, too. It was originally intended to allow communications to reliably go through even if a nuclear war zeroed out most of the commo infrastructure." He uttered a quiet bark of sardonic laughter. "Of course, they didn't exactly reckon on how much nuclear war they'd get."

"You have the concept cold. Redundancy, dispersion, reassembly upon command." She drew in a deep breath, let it go in a quick, voiceless whoosh. "And this was done to our souls. By the ship."

"To your *souls?*"

She nodded. Her face was toward the place the sun had

died, deresolving slowly as the darkness coalesced. "I was broken apart. All of us were. The pieces were scattered across a continent."

"How—?"

"The soul pieces were assembled into pseudopersonalities. Artificial souls—perhaps you see why we're not patronizing when we tell you there is much to our lore that your language cannot express—there is much *our* language can barely hint at. This was done through the medium of the Dreamtime."

Grant's customary scowl deepened, but from concentration, not annoyance. "So when one of you died—"

"The fragments were resorbed into Tjukurpa. Then in the fullness of time they were reassembled to form another temporary soul. The components of our real selves stayed separated for over seven hundred centuries. Now they are being gathered together. Reassembled into their original forms."

"You mean to tell me—"

"That I'm seventy-five thousand years old. Yes. As are all of us you've encountered so far. As will all of us be...who've survived. I am reborn. And yet I'm not. I'm different. The me I remember, shadowy as that memory is, is a different person."

She touched herself between her full breasts. "I carry the weight of three thousand generations. The parts that are now once again *me* have participated in literally thousands of lives—hundreds of thousands. For all that the eldest decreed that things must never change, for all that we were reshaped to insure that nothing would change—in seventy-five thousand years, things change. And things happened that were never anticipated—the European invasion. For the first time we received a substantial infusion of alien genetic material. New lives, new souls were brought within our ambit. At the same time, some of us wandered far and were lost.

"The eldest tried to account for such events as best they could, and they were very wise. Each packet into which my soul was split was copied several times over before being dispersed, and so the copies have been passed along. I'm sure some have been lost, some pieces of me, bits of information. Yet I feel whole. And alive, in a sense I—none of the men and women I have been—have not known for millennia."

For a time they sat side by side in silence as the night solidified. "What about your body?" Grant asked at length.

She gave him a grin of such frankness he looked quickly away. "I take it you don't mean *that,* then?"

"I mean—hell, you're right about our language. Damned if I know how to say this. How about the original occupant? From what the women told us, from what we've seen, from what you've told me, all this—this reassembling is a recent development. This body wasn't born with you inside, is what I'm trying to say. I think."

"I have to use a computer metaphor again, and it's not a good one, I'm first to admit. The packets that made up this body's birth personality were taken apart and redistributed to recreate the original personalities of the crew."

"But what about the person you—your body used to be?"

She shrugged.

"She's dead?"

"She no longer exists as such. It was her destiny."

He drew in a deep breath and let it slide out flared nostrils. "Seems damn cold."

Rita held her hands forth with palms outspread.

"So you just got zapped into somebody else's body—" he snapped his fingers "—like that?"

She shook her head, smiling ruefully. "It's not that simple. Part of what's different about me from the way I was when I was…disassembled…is the mingling of my essence with the residue of the soul that occupied the body. Memories. These transactions take place, ultimately, on a cell-by-cell basis. That's something Nobby could explain much better."

"I'll chill him if he tries," Grant said with apparent conviction. "I know there's plenty you're not telling me—hell, that's got to be the understatement of the last ten or twenty thousand years at least, huh? I know there's questions I should be asking, stuff it could be important to know."

He shook his head. "But if you tell me any more right now my brain'll explode and come squirting out my ears."

"We wouldn't want that." She sprang upright, reached a hand down to help him up.

He looked at her.

"I guess there's no point in my trying to seduce you tonight, is there?" she asked.

"No." He grasped her forearm to forearm. She drew him upright as if he were no more than a child.

"I don't even want to tell you what it would feel like right now."

Chapter 17

As the crowd's chants of blood lust began to crescendo, Baron Thulia-appointed emissary of the nine baronies, sneezed into a silk handkerchief. It was a juicily productive sneeze. The lower-grade hybrids packed in the pierced-ivory pavilion behind the god-king's portable throne tittered shrilly.

Daubing at his face, Thulia glanced over his shoulder in irritation—and something else. He personally had little contact with subbaron hybrids in North America, although of course he knew of their existence. He found these unnerving. For one thing they refused to speak or allow that they understood English, though Thulia was certain they did both; certainly the god-king was more than fluent. And anyway their gobbling, mewling, gibbering speech creeped him out.

"Is our sport not to your liking, then, my esteemed visitor?" the god-king asked in his odd fluting voice.

"It's not that—choo!—not that at all, Your Majesty," Thulia said. Even in the heat and humidity and the pain in his sinuses, not to mention total immersion in the indescribable reek of all the sweaty overagitated apekin jammed into the plaza, he felt a desperate desire not to give offense to his host. He had a terrifying image, which he could not altogether purge from his mind, that if he did he would be seized by the Dewa Raja's hybrid retainers, the hooded ones, and they, gibbering, would carry him off down the trapdoor-covered steps, which was the only means of access to the divine pavilion, and he would never be seen again. "It's more the climate which disagrees with me, I'm afraid."

The god-king smiled languidly. "I sorrow that we lack the means to modify things more to your liking, cousin."

The god-king seemed uncommonly solicitous today. Perhaps he was warming to Thulia. Since that appeared unlikely, the North American baron considered the possibilities: that he was either prone to spells, as so many of the barons appeared to be, or was trying to put him off his guard preparatory to doing something unspeakable to him.

They were, he understood glumly, in no way mutually exclusive.

THE WORLD MAY NOT LOVE an underdog—except, in Kane's experience, the way sharks love a wounded grouper—but everybody loves a winner. The crowd was cheering as a whole squad of attendants trotted off bearing the still semiconscious Bandu by his many limbs. Domi was up on the dais with Kane, managing to hop and hug him at once, as he finished mopping sweat and less pleasant substances from his face.

Gathering his wits along with his breath, he gave her an affectionate-appearing but stinging swat on her felt-clad fanny. "Security," he hissed to her. "Scoot."

Her ruby eyes were huge above her veil. "Sorry. Double stupe, me." She kissed his sweaty beard-crusted cheek through her veil and scampered down and into the churning mob.

A shadow fell across Kane's face. He turned his head to discover it had been cast by the extravagant black turban of one of the two local Mags who had come up onto the dais. The eyes staring at him above the scarlet-trimmed black silk of their veils glittered at him like jet cabochons.

One of them snapped something. It sounded like, "Turn away from us and put your hands behind your head." But Kane knew full well that anything a Mag said was supposed to come out sounding like that.

"He says you come with," the announcer said in an almost conversational voice. "You be presented to god-king now."

Kane nodded. It seemed the safest thing to do.

The two tall black-veiled sec men led Kane off the back of the platform and onto a path marked by a crimson carpet fringed in gold. It led to the pavilion, which Kane now saw to be made of sheets of ivory, carefully unrolled by artisans from great tusks, flattened, pierced and figured with exquisite skill. The pyramidal roof was some white stone, possibly alabaster, cut to thin sheets so that even from without Kane thought that they must be translucent. Above the gazebo towered a structure whose scale Kane—with certain other claims pressing upon his attention—had not really appreciated until now. The facade rose a good hundred feet above the plaza. It had a whole story of foundation and wide marble steps flanked by great gleaming blocks of stone before one even reached the shadowed portico of squat, slightly convex-sided pillars of what appeared to be rose granite.

The *talwar*-toting Magistrates stopped him a little over two yards shy of the pavilion. It was just far enough that his eyes wouldn't focus through the looped and scrolled piercings of the walls, especially since within was shadowed and dim.

"The God-King, Ruler over the Waters, Subduer of Pirates and Bringer of Plenty to the Devastation, salutes you for your performance, Captain Hardin," declared a voice from inside. The effect was only spoiled by a slight catch when the herald hesitated, obviously to read the victor's name off something.

Kane covered his right fist with his left the way he had seen some other contestants do and bowed from the waist, not low. He had to do something or blow the whole scam right here right now, although even an entirely pro forma bow to a baron made his guts, still sore from Bandu's punch, knot up inside him. He hoped he wouldn't be compelled to bend the knee to the creature.

He wasn't. He straightened. Faintly a liquid sibilant bubbling sounded from the other side of that ivory screen. The hair rose on Kane's nape. There was no mistaking its source. It was the gobbling, giggling speech of low-level hybrids.

He could see hints of them now, pallid faces and splayed hands pressed against the ivory screen.

BY DINT OF ENORMOUS effort Thulia restrained himself from swatting at the hybrids crowding around him with no respect for his person. Although he towered above them he knew it would have done him no good—especially not with the local baron, who after all chose to surround himself with the creatures. Not for the first time since beginning this dreadful exile to the hell of the South Seas he wondered at the concept, article of faith really, that hybrids were all significantly more intelligent than ape-men. These certainly didn't act it. But then, Baron Thulia had little direct experience of them except as mostly silent and ever so respectful technicians applying the periodic treatments beneath Archuleta Mesa. He got a little misty-eyed over those halcyon days, before the facility was laid waste by the monsters in apekin form who had gone rogue from Cobaltville.

Behind him the human herald looked up from the saucer of moist clay into which the victor's name had been scribbled with a stylus—paper got too soggy to readily take ink in this humidity, and the Dewa Raja was clearly unwilling to employ technology at the level of handheld computers this close to his sweaty public.

Thulia's eyes narrowed, focusing on the winner of the day's barbaric contest, who stood scant yards away sweating like a beast. His brief nostalgic excursion had brought a hint of awareness bubbling to the back of his conscious mind. Frustratingly it floated and danced just out of reach. *Can it be possible I've seen this man before?*

"YOU HAVE EARNED the rank of captain in the Grand Holy Fleet," the unseen herald's voice decreed. "You have thus confirmed the rank that you bore in the Sultan of Singapura's Own Rifles, and may at your discretion advance to the next level of the tournament to compete for higher rank and great, great prizes!"

A big guy with a shaved head and queue hanging down his wedge-shaped back, not too different from Bandu's do, stepped forward.

"Hail, Captain Hardin," he said in surprisingly clear English. "I am Tuan Parang, once privileged to serve as chief of the Dewa Raja's personal guard, now Vice-Raja of Tanimbar. It will be an honor and a pleasure to serve beside a man such as you have shown yourself to be." He was clearly a politician—had to be to have a job like this—and yet the deep and forthright way he spoke, and the way his dark brown eyes held Kane's gray ones as he spoke them, made the outlander suspect halfway he meant them.

The viceroy thrust out his right arm. After the briefest surprise-born hesitation, Kane reached out in return.

The crowd went crazy all over again as they gripped each other, brawny forearm to brawny forearm, dark against pale, even as Kane had often exchanged handclasps with his blood brother Grant. The renegade Mag felt a pang of honest regret he was on the other side from this one.

Smiling sternly, Tuan Parang bowed and stepped back. Kane's answering bow was deeper than the one he'd given the unseen god-king, as well as more sincere. The crowd quieted to let the herald do his final thing.

"You may now turn, honored Captain Hardin of the god-king's holy army of retribution, and accept the plaudits of the throng!"

Before he could do so, the sound of two hands clapping fell down on his head from above like acid rain. In his scrotum he knew something was badly, badly wrong.

Even before he looked up to see a single tall and heavyset figure in black step forward from the portico above and out to stand, slowly applauding, on the end of the great white gleaming pier of stone over Kane's head. His black garb was not the silk pajamas and outlandish head rag of the local sec men. It was the formfitting uniform of the Magistrate Division of a North American barony, with the flash of Cobaltville on the breast and a Sin Eater holstered on the left forearm.

The Mag had a pale, round face that seemed little more than a bent-down terminus to a thick column of neck. The supraorbital ridge was prominent, accented by a single eyebrow like a charcoal smudge arcing almost from temple to temple. The nose was a shapeless wad of scar tissue. Yet the face's overall impression was almost benign, thick lips set in a sardonic smile, and the dark eyes beneath those atavistic browridges glittered with both mocking humor and quick intelligence.

Quick, *evil* intelligence. Kane knew.

"You picked a strange place to get yourself caught, Kane," the Mag said in a mild, well-modulated deep baritone voice.

"I guess it figures, with all the humidity and decay around here, a maggot like you would coming crawling out into the sunlight, Vladek," Kane said.

One of the low-tech local Magistrates behind him buried a fist in Kane's left kidney. A fountain of scarlet pain seemed to blow out the top of Kane's spinal column into his brain and blast his consciousness to swarming fragments. He went to his knees, knotting about himself.

Tuan Parang raised his sculpted, handsome face to the foreigner. He frowned.

Vladek didn't so much as glance at him. "He had a companion," he said. "A woman. Find her and bring her, too."

Hands like steel claws grabbed Kane's triceps so cruelly that their pain penetrated the dim red haze of agony in which his consciousness still swam. He was raised halfway up. His legs would not support him still as he was dragged up the steps and into the deceptively inviting cool of the great hall beyond.

Chapter 18

"A remarkable story," Brigid said, sipping coffee. She was leaning back in her commissary chair as if it were actually comfortable, a position out of character for her. It was late at night, at least by her biological clock, which was all that mattered here in the changeless depths of Cerberus, which knew not day or night nor the changing of the seasons. But Sally, who was a keen, indefatigable researcher, had turned up some valuable leads from information culled by the astonishingly quick-reading aborigines. Brigid wanted to pursue those leads as far as she could before fatigue degraded her thinking processes too far to make the effort cost-effective.

Caffeine is a crutch, a puritanical voice nagged from the back of her skull, nasal and disapproving and packed tight with Enclave nanny-think. She moved ribs and shoulders in a soundless laugh.

If a crutch is what I need to keep hobbling toward the finish line, a crutch then I will use.

Grant was pacing. "You really should have a striped tail to swish," Brigid told him.

He stopped and looked at her, his customary scowl morphing into a frown of puzzlement. "Huh?"

She waved a hand at him. "Like a caged tiger. Sorry. I'm getting giddy. I wonder, though—"

"What? I mean, don't get me wrong. I know she wasn't telling me the whole truth and nothing but. I don't think she *lied* to me, not as such, although I have to admit my usual instincts for reading people are sometimes way off the mark with this bunch. But—"

"But even if she did not affirmatively lie to you in what she said, she may have lied most effectively in what she did not."

"Exactly."

Brigid frowned, sat forward, holding her cup in both hands as if to draw warmth from it. "I wonder if the ship didn't decay away. Maybe it's still buried there beneath the sand near Uluru. Maybe that's the prize they're so afraid of the barons getting their hands on."

She looked up at him. "There's ample evidence just that we've seen that the science the crew possessed before they…hid themselves…surpasses anything the hybrids have. At least as potent as that of the Annunaki and the Tuatha de Danaan. Maybe even more. If the barons were to get their hands on that—I can see why both the aborigines and we would find that outcome very, very bad."

"Then why do they have you and this Wright woman—and hell, their own selves—going twenty-seven hours out of every twenty-four looking for a goddamn magic turtle?"

Brigid shrugged. "I guess we won't know until they find it. I'm beginning to suspect that what looks to us like their patronizing of us may be right in some ways. I honestly am not sure whether we'd grasp what the turtle truly does if they told us about it."

"Are you going to find it?"

"I think so," she said in a measured pace. "We've found mention of it, know when and where it came into this country and some of the places it's been since."

She shook her head. "It seems to have been passed along

from collection to collection as if it were hot. I wonder if its mystery powers have something to do with that. Ah, well, given that it's in our records at all, that we've already picked up its chain of provenance, and given that record keeping grew steadily better and more comprehensive from when it entered America right up until the long night—yes, I think we'll find it. And soon."

"Why couldn't you all have just done a global search through the database for the key words, 'Mackenzie Turtle,' anyway?" Grant asked, drawing himself a mug of coffee. It was his pet mug, an oversize one holding as much as two conventional cups. On the side was enameled the gaudy red-gold-green shield and Cyrillic lettering that identified it as originating with the Soviet Border Troops Directorate of the KGB. He had found it on a shelf in a cupboard in Cerberus itself.

"Do I try to teach you how to kick down doors, Grant?" she asked, although she smiled as she did so. "That was the first thing we tried. It's what generated our first leads. The thing's not always referred to by that name, you see. Often as not there's only an item number and a description, of unpredictable length and accuracy."

Grant grunted and sipped black coffee.

"I wonder," Brigid said, almost dreamily, "how Kane is doing right now."

SHITTY.

The bucket of cold water hitting Kane in the face was like a bucket of cold water hitting him in the face. He stirred, moaned, raised his head from where it hung with chin resting on clavicle. His arms were winged out up and behind him in classic crucifixion-style, only fastened to a seeping chill stone wall with manacles, instead of to a big board with nails.

He was hardly aware of the pain in his wrists any longer. "Welcome back to the land of the living, Kane," Vladek said, his mild voice almost cheerful. "Enjoy it while you can."

Kane could see nothing at all from his right eye. Not that the vision in his left was great shakes. Without taking any great interest one way or another, he wondered if the eye was out. He had seen beatings hard enough to do it, even himself dealt out a few—and what he'd been getting at the ham-hock hands of Vladek and his burly-boy local torturers was up there with the all-time classics, no question of it.

Then with a ripping like an internal membrane giving way, the lid opened. Sort of. It had apparently been cemented shut with semidried blood. It wouldn't open far. It was probably puffed mostly shut, as well.

Now he could rejoice in the full if blurry glory of his old classmate Vladek. At least he had binocular vision back to triangulate the range for spitting. But his best effort fell pitifully short.

Vladek, of course, put back his head and laughed heartily. "You've still got the stones of a true Mag, Kane," he said. "I have to hand you that. Speaking of which, mebbe I *will* hand them to you—your stones, that is to say."

"Might be…better…than listening to your bullshit, Vladek. What's the fucking point here, anyway?"

The Mag laughed again. He was just one happy guy. "As the one-time golden boy of the Cobaltville Magistrate Division," he said, "you know pain-based interrogation is unreliable. Especially on a trained Mag. So you may be forgiven for wondering—"

He turned and drove a fist, clenched so that the first finger joint was braced by the thumb to form a hard spear tip, just beneath Kane's short ribs—already well-basted in blackish drying blood—on the left-hand side. Kane grunted and closed his eyes.

It was like having a spike driven through him.

"—why I'm doing this. And the answer is fun. Fun and payback—for the trouble you've caused your baron and for all the good Mags you chilled. Of course, this is just a down payment. Once you've told me everything you know about your whole treasonous operation—and what nasty business brings you skulking around this part of the world—you'll get payment in full. With interest."

He turned, grabbed up a rag from the bronze water pot to wipe away the blood he'd gotten on his hand. "Okay, boys. Take him down."

He held up a syringe. A crack-nailed thumb depressed the plunger. A droplet of clear fluid appeared at the needle tip, like venom on a viper's fang. "It's time he and me had a little talk."

THE GREAT AND MIGHTY Tuan Parang prepared himself for sleep.

The Dewa Raja had displaced him from the grandest quarters of the palace on its height. That meant nothing to him whatsoever: it was only to be expected, and in any event the only reason the Vice-Raja consented to occupy quarters of such grandiose luxury was that no less was expected of his station as ruler of the divine kingdom's southern march.

Besides, his current quarters were scarcely less ostentatious, or even smaller. This was, after all, a palace.

He had chased off the last of his body servants. As the most energetic and tireless—not to mention fearless—of the god-king's rising young officer corps, he had come eventually to appreciate the necessity of a good batman, as he had the need for a proper staff. He had more important services to render his god-king and people than tending to his own linen every day. Yet he had only so much tolerance for having them hovering about him incessantly. Like stinging flies, he thought.

Or the hooded ones the god-king drew about with him like a swarm everywhere he went these days. They had always been there, from the day of Tuan Parang's first, proud introduction to his god and monarch, after he had defeated a daunting number of *wa-ko* pirate ships from the Islands Where the Sun is Born off Sunda with but a single twelve-gun war junk and a plague-weakened crew. But then they had hung in the background, like shadows.

Now they followed the god-king as if they were his shadow.

He shrugged as he sat on the edge of his grand canopied extravagance of a bed to pull off his own right boot. He declined to wear sandals except when going to bathe, believing that whenever awake he should be always prepared to march straight out and onto campaign roads or the quarterdeck of a warship, and even after he got a batman, believed that any soldier ought be able to take off his own damn boots. Of course they were boots of the finest quality, for durability and also softness. Tuan Parang also believed that a soldier's feet no less than his sword were his most vital implements, and to neglect the care of one was as bad as another.

He smiled as he drew off his other high-topped yellow boot and cast it aside. Perhaps I should not have been so hasty running off all the servants, he thought, or anyway so thorough. There had been among them, as always, more than one fair maid whose flashing eye made it abundantly clear that it would be her pleasure to serve him. Nor indeed was that strictly because of his power and repute, nor even the hawk-like handsomeness of his face, nor yet the sinewy strength and grace of his body and limbs.

Famed throughout the land was Tuan Parang, for his prowess as a swordsman.

He stood to divest himself of his last garments, his loose trousers of scarlet silk. As his hands undid the silken cord that held them he froze. Automatically his spatial awareness reminded him of just where the plain but serviceable—and comfortable—hilt of the sheathed *talwar* he had hung by the head of the bed lay in relation to a right hand whose calluses had been shaped by years of intimate contact with it.

He could not have said which sense revealed the intruder: was it the tiniest sound betraying otherwise faultless stealth, a stirring in the heavy jasmine-scented air, a motion tug at the edge of vision, a tiny, vagrant wisp of odor like the scent of an unfamiliar blossom? He straightened slowly, right hand at ease, thumb and fingers lightly curved, ready. For like any master fighter, he knew relaxation was readier for swift decisive action than tension could ever be.

"You might as well come out," he said, his deep voice level. "I know you're there."

In the light cast by a single oil lamp upon its thin brass pedestal by the bed, most of the chamber lay lost in shadows. From behind one of the columns supporting the vaulted ceiling, itself scarcely visible, stepped a figure. Small, slim, yet upright, and swathed from head to foot in a dark hooded cloak.

Tuan Parang scowled. "A hooded one? Let me warn you, not even being one of the Dewa Raja's pet monkeys excuses you invading my bedchamber thus."

"I crave the great Lord Parang's pardon if I give offense by my intrusion," a voice said. It held two surprises: it was in English, and it was unmistakably the voice of a young woman.

The tall man couldn't restrain a smile. It was a thin smile, suggesting it might not stretch much farther before snapping.

"You do so offend, woman," he answered in the same language. "How do you propose to win my pardon?"

"I bring before you gifts."

Parang cocked a brow. "What gifts are these? You seem empty-handed."

"Rubies," the woman said, "and ivory."

The hooded cloak dropped free. Beneath lay a woman—and nothing more. Such a woman as he had never seen—and he thought, as master of a substantial swath of the South Sea, that he had seen all the world had to offer in that line.

She was clearly an albino; he was more than familiar with the concept, and with actual albinos, for that matter. But none like this: from the short, spiky crown of white hair on her head, down past cherry-tipped breasts, surprisingly full, flat stomach, narrow waist and flared hips—a figure surprisingly full for one so slender—to the snowy patch between her thighs, she seemed a figurine sculpted by an unparalleled master to represent a very *dewa* of allure.

A flawless idol of ivory. A beauty exquisite enough to stir the most jaded connoisseur. And the eyes fixed upon him with frankly challenging invitation were veritably ruby in hue.

"You did not lie, Ingrezi," he said. "Are such treasures offered only to please the eye?"

She smiled. It made him instantly hard. "Not at all, *tuan besar,*" she purred.

She walked forward, making no more noise than the shadow, trailing her cloak behind. As she came up to him and he smelled the clean femininity of her, he held up one great, scarred hand.

"I know you," he said, not ungently. "You must be the hooded companion of the champion today—Hardin. The man the foreigner had taken up, for whom he had his men search without result."

She reared her head up defiantly. "I am that woman."

"Is it not your man who was cast into the dungeon of this very palace, then? Do you not betray him, coming before me thus?"

Her eyes blazed red fire. "Even a warrior of such renown and honor, Lord Parang," she said haughtily, "yes, and all your power, too—I permit you or any man to accuse me of betrayal but once. That man who fought and won today is my friend, my lord, and I will not insult your intelligence by pretending I am not here to petition on his behalf. But he is my comrade, not my mate."

Parang frowned. But he stroked his chin with the strong fingers of his sword hand. "He has displeased the allies of my divine lord. I do not see how any intercession I can make can aid him, even should I grant it."

"Hear what I have to tell you, O Lord." The nude ivory woman smiled. "But first, permit me to *earn* a hearing...."

KANE'S WHOLE UNIVERSE, as he lay strapped to the table, was a red pulsation of pain.

He scarcely felt the jab into the inside of his left elbow.

Instantly warmth began to flow outward from the site of the injection. Soothing, relaxing.

A fragment of memory floated to the surface of Kane's disordered brain. He smiled and opened his eyes. They made a cracking sound.

Vladek loomed above him, a black colossus. "Lucky I brought my chem interrogation kit from Cobaltville," the Mag said, his voice seeming to echo down a long tunnel. "Now we'll find out just what brings a traitor like you to Tanimbar."

"Not a chance, Vladek."

Vladek's single brow knotted like a hairy black caterpillar stung by an opisthotonic. "What the fuck are you talking about?"

"You were…racked up during chem interrogation training. That…unfortunate accident."

The scar across Vladek's forehead flushed scarlet. "Don't talk about that!" he snapped, voice almost falsetto. Then, asserting control over himself with a visible spasm of will, continued in a deeper key, "I picked up what I need to know, have no fear, my friend."

"Bullshit. If you had you'd know about the…conditioning."

"What conditioning? What are you raving about?"

"We got a series of injections of standard Magistrate Division truth serum," Kane said, forcing his split lips to form the words precisely. "Built…built up…resistance."

The single eyebrow rose. "Oh, so? Well, we can take care of that."

He snapped his pale fingers. A little wizened cypress knot of torture tech, naked but for a grimy twist of loincloth, bobbed his shaved head and shuffled forward bearing a white plastic case marked with the nine-spoked-wheel-and-justice-scale emblem of the Magistrate Division. Vladek took forth a fresh injection unit, twisted the blue plastic sheath off the needle tip and smiled.

"We'll just give another dose to the one we hate most," he said.

Chapter 19

The bloody bearded lips spread into a wider smile. Then they relaxed. The puffed eyelids fluttered. The gray eyes rolled up until only whites showed.

"What is it?" Vladek demanded. "What's happening?"

The loincloth-clad chief torturer felt with splayed fingertips at the side of Kane's throat, then moistened a finger with a yellowish tongue and held it beneath Kane's nostrils. Then he looked up and spoke.

The words were gibberish to Vladek. "He says the prisoner sleeps," said the interpreter the god-king had provided, one of the local-style Mags who had removed his veil to reveal a cruel, lean and tanned but Caucasian face. His English was accented in a way Vladek did not recognize, but was perfectly clear.

Vladek dashed the emptied syringe in tinkling fragments on the well-worn stones of the torture chamber floor. "Get a bucket of water and wake the fucker up, then. What are you stupes standing around gawking for?"

The torturer looked up in alarm. Wagging his head, he babbled a string of agitated Malay syllables.

"What?" Vladek shouted, rounding on the interpreter. "What's he farting through the fucking mouth about now?"

Spittle sprayed the local Magistrate's face. His dark eyes slitted. But he was a Magistrate for all the difference in uniform and kit. His voice was level when he answered.

"He says the man is unconscious. Drugged out. If you rouse him, his heart will likely give out."

The torturer listened, nodding his old bald egg of a head as if he understood. Vladek would not have put it past the little bastard to savvy English perfectly well, and just put the visiting fireman through the whole silly rigamarole to yank his chain.

Vladek's disgust was complete. If you couldn't trust a torturer not to jack with you, whom could you trust?

The ancient torture tech spoke. His few teeth were brown stumps fallen like standing stones from a long-abandoned shrine. "He says," the interpreter said, not bothering to completely suppress his own grin, "that if you can get your answers from a dead man, truly your skill is the greatest ever known."

BACK PRESSED to the rough sweating stone wall of the underground passage Tuan Parang held up a hand. He didn't perform the oxymoronic act of calling aloud for silence. Domi understood fine. The viceroy was dressed in loose brown pantaloons, sandals, a loose white blouse and a dark blue sash holding the heavy-bladed chopping dagger or short sword that gave him his name on one side, and a *talwar* on the other. Domi had resumed her hooded cloak. She remained naked beneath.

As a one-time contract sex toy, Domi had well understood how to find the necessary bedchamber, even though few attendants spoke a language she could understand. Some things, again, were universal. To get to a place where she could show the Vice-Raja what she wanted to, however, required the cooperation of Parang himself. Who better to know the secret ways of the palace than its customary occupant?

Parang had readily agreed to act upon the words the pleasure Domi had given him had earned her the right to speak, and investigate her wild claims upon the instant. He didn't seem a real deliberative sort. Domi did feel trepidation that the god-king would have built into the palace places and passages he never revealed to his satrap, so cleverly concealed that even in years of occupation Parang would not find them. But the big and well-built man seemed to know full well where the hooded ones were generally to be found going about their mysterious business, even at this hour of the night.

He already fully mistrusted them, it seemed, although he had no inkling of their real nature. And he had been unwilling to accept at face value Domi's claim that they were "demons," as she called them, not trusting her ability to get the concept across to a man from such a predominantly low-tech culture. The viceroy was far from stupid, but his mind wasn't the sharpest weapon in his rack.

She had chosen to fly solo on this. The aborigines were nice. They were nice to her, which she was far from accustomed to, even in Cerberus. But mebbe too nice for the sort of work that needed done and fast, too prone to ask questions.

Besides, Kane was her friend. She'd lost him. She would get him back. Big time.

Ferret sharp, her ears picked up the shuffling of feet. A moment later, a pair of small figures passed, backs to the humans, cowled heads bent. A bubbling murmur came from them, distinctly inhuman. Domi actually saw the skin at the back of Parang's neck rumple as some of the human body's few skin muscles reacted to the eeriness of that sound.

Then they heard louder sounds, like giggling but no kind of laughter: the pair who had just passed greeting a newcomer going the other way. Domi shrank inside her cloak and a hand sought an interior pocket. *I hope he bought my descrip-*

tion of their infrasound wands, she thought. But even if he didn't he's got to know how screwed we are if an alarm gets raised—

The figure shuffling into view had its head down likewise, features obscured within the folds of its hood. Quite possibly it could not see them; in any event, taking for granted the sanctity of the dungeons beneath the palace, it was oblivious to the possibility of danger.

At least, until some unknown stimulus made it raise its bowed head. In time for a fist to obscure its whole field of vision like a falling moon.

Domi's first reaction to the thump of fist on face was concern that her companion might have killed the hybrid. Then it occurred to her she didn't really care; it would have to be restrained from raising the alarm one way or another. If it died now, well, that was life in the Outlands. Even ones as outlandish as these.

But Parang was a man well versed in all the nuances of mayhem. And he had, as Sri Goldshtayn had told of him during his briefing and as could be heard repeated in every souk in the city, a sense of justice as fine-tuned as his fighting skills. It was not his way to slay those whom he wasn't certain deserved it, any more than it was to hesitate putting the whack on those who did. The figure Parang dragged by a handful of its robe back down the hall and into a tiny storeroom that he opened with an apparent master key carried in his sash was clearly still breathing, only stunned. Whether it was in process of expiring from a subdural hematoma induced by the blow, Domi couldn't tell.

Closing the door softly, Parang laid the hybrid on the flagstones. Age-darkened barrels stood stacked around them. The storeroom smelled of must and mildew, but there were no clues, olfactory or visible, as to what the casks contained. Domi knelt quickly to pull the hood down from the unmoving creature's head.

Breath hissed sharply inward over Tuan Parang's teeth. He said something in rapid Malay, and then in English, "Veritably, it is so."

He looked at her with wonder in his eyes, and not a little fear—an expression Domi doubted very many others had ever seen there. "You have spoken truth, Perempuan Putih."

There was no room for skepticism, nor any need to display more of the unconscious creature. That outsized head with the elongate cranium; the small yet not unappealing features; the huge eyes, now half-lidded; the downy wisps of brown hair along the gleaming expanse of skull: humanoid they were, but inarguably not human.

"These are the evil creatures who have beclouded the godking's mind with their spells, for so great is their craft and guile that even a divinity might be taken in by them."

Whoa, listen to yourself, girl, she thought, and silently blessed Brigid Baptiste for encouraging her to read. She had recently discovered a particular taste for the writings of Robert E. Howard, and his legion of cronies, imitators and successors....

Parang scowled in thought. "It might not be seemly to take counsel of a mere woman, and a mere slip of an Ingrezi at that," he said ruminatively. "Yet I am a man who prizes results, and would never have gotten where I am had I spurned wisdom when I found it. So, O fair one who has led me thus far by my *talwar,* whither would you lead from here?"

BRIGID BAPTISTE'S green eyes bulged slightly at the image on the screen of the terminal in the commissary. Audiovisual feed from the command center was being patched through it. "Lakesh?" she asked, a tentative note in her voice.

The large-headed figure was naked but for a sort of diaper about the loins and his spectacles. He would have looked like Gandhi but for the startling blue eyes. And the swirls of red-and-yellow paint daubed on its chest, face and upper arms.

"Who else might I be?" the outlandish apparition demanded with asperity. Then the great blue eyes blinked. "Oh. Yes. I see. Forgive it, dearest Brigid—Old Man and Yindi are initiating me into some of the mysteries of Tjukurpa. Behind me—"

He nodded his head back toward where a number of mostly naked figures danced around a nocturnal bonfire. Brigid felt aftershocks of the vision Yindi had shown her, Domi and Shizuka months before, felt a loosening of her joints and unease in the pit of her stomach.

"—you see a *corroboree* in progress, which is to say—"

"A ritual to invoke the guidance of the elders," Brigid said, unable to contain her pedantry. Especially as far off balance as her mentor's bizarre appearance had put her.

Lakesh nodded. "To be sure, to be sure." He showed her a huge smile, indicating—fatuous old fart!—he still knew something she didn't. "Yet since there is none elder than Old Man, the ritual, like the Dreamtime itself, has taken on a new significance. Or, at the least, a new nuance. Let me expatiate—"

"None older than Old Man?" she broke in. "But the souls of the original crew are reinhabiting the bodies of the living, and they're all seventy-five thousand years old at the least!"

Lakesh's eyes blinked in a mixture of surprise and disappointment. "You know about that?" he asked.

She nodded.

"It appears some of my colleagues have been talkative," said Old Man himself, crowding into the picture with Lakesh.

Lakesh scowled, and for a moment Brigid thought a shoving match would ensue—not without hope that it would. But Old Man ignored the scientist, which no doubt rankled Lakesh most of all.

Old Man was grinning all over his round, weathered head, though, indicating he bore no rancor to whichever of the four working with Baptiste and Grant might have spilled the sacred beans. "They have," Brigid acknowledged, declining to be specific, just in case. She had lived too long under constant threat of informers in the Cobaltville Enclaves to rat off Rita.

"Well, it doesn't seem to have driven you mad," Old Man said with the same relentless cheeriness all the crewfolk seemed to display all the time. "No harm, no foul, as the saying goes."

"I'm...glad you feel that way," Brigid said. "Still, given that we are working together, not to mention facing danger together, don't you think a bit more candor might be appropriate?"

"Oh, no," Old Man said, laughing like an indulgent uncle. "We don't want to dole out too much too quickly. It's for your own good, of course. We have no desire to alarm you, nor yet to undermine your self-confidence."

"There's no need to be priggish about it, Brigid," Lakesh said. "We have decided upon the course we think best for all concerned."

The tall, flame-haired senior archivist felt a pang of deep desire to partake of the arcane skills of a far walker so that she could reach through the screen, grab the two old men by their scrawny wattled throats and give them both a good shake.

"Thank you so much for your confidence, Doctor," she said in words that tinkled like tiny icicles breaking, one by one.

Just as some people don't understand English when it doesn't suit them to, so Dr. Mohandas Lakesh Singh possessed a selective and convenient deafness to irony. "It is nothing, dear Brigid," he said, as if oblivious to the undertones of his own phraseology. "I have full faith in your abilities, as well as those of your new protégée, Sally Wright. Speaking of which, let me not forget the original purpose of my call—how goes the search for the turtle?"

He knew how to press her buttons, stifling her annoyance by invoking the ironbound discipline of the professional in her. Damn him anyway. "It goes," she said. "We can establish its location as late as the mid-1950s. However, a physical search revealed it is not still where it was then. We turned up some water-damaged records that some of the Moon base scientists believe they can restore sufficiently to derive at least some information from them, however. We are expecting results at any time."

Lakesh nodded. "Good, good. Press onward. It's absolutely vital that we recover the artifact as quickly as possible. Time is pressing: Kane's aborigine companions report that the god-king's preparations to invade Australia are quite advanced. Speaking of which, what do you hear from Kane?"

She hesitated. "Nothing. He's fallen off our scopes. We have lost all trace of his biolink transceiver." She had been at some pains to hide the fact from Grant, who would have insisted on haring off after Kane himself regardless, doing Kane and everybody else precisely no good. The Aboriginal team accompanying Kane and Domi acknowledged concern, in their perpetually cheerful way, but they were unwilling to take action until they heard something concrete from Domi, whose own transceiver showed she was still in Tanimbar City. In fact her biometrics had recently showed a most distinctive spike of intense physical activity….

Lakesh was as mellow as the aborigines: "Our friend Kane

can take care of himself, to understate the case grandly. I wouldn't count him out just yet, Brigid, my very dear."

A figure came up behind him and touched him lightly on the arm. It was a woman, and even in the poor nighttime light and beneath the paint Brigid could see that for all her characteristically marked aborigine features she was more than handsome—and her own loincloth did nothing to conceal the fact she possessed a body to die for.

Lakesh looked up, smiled when he saw her. She said something the audio pickups didn't convey. Lakesh climbed to his feet with alacrity, which almost suggested the faded rejuvenation Sam the imperator had bestowed upon him was kicking in again.

"I must return to the ceremony," he said. "Now, if you'll excuse me—"

The screen went blank.

Brigid's palm slammed down on the table next to the keyboard, making the mouse jump on its pad and causing Collins and several Moonies, taking their morning coffee break a discreet distance away, to stare at her. She ignored them.

"That randy old goat," Brigid declared. "Ceremony, my—"

"Doctor," a tentative voice said. "That is, Brigid?"

She turned. "Yes, Sally? What is it?" Her habit of self-control enabled her not to snap at the self-effacing new archivist.

"I hate to disturb you, but I—"

She glanced nervously at the others in the commissary, then stole up to Brigid's side as if hoping they wouldn't see her. For her part Brigid glared at the others, putting all the energy of her still-vigorous annoyance with Lakesh into green death eye beams. Collins and the Moonies looked hastily away.

Sally leaned low to speak softly toward Brigid's left ear. "I just thought of something most disturbing, Brigid. It's impossible for the aborigines to have come from Earth's past!"

"So," THE DEWA RAJA SAID in his eerie voice, drawing the sibilant out into a hiss that more than recalled the Annunaki heritage he shared with one of his two hearers. "My trusted viceroy has allowed his curiosity to get the better of his loyalty to me."

"I don't think it's his curiosity he's being led around by, God-King," Vladek said. He ignored Baron Thulia, who stood with them in an antechamber to the god-king's sleeping room, watching a monitor displaying images captured by one of the very few select—and hidden—video cams the god-king had secreted within the Tanimbar palace.

The Magistrate's voice was brusque, as if he was unaware of speaking to a superior being. Baron Thulia longed to see him slapped down for it. He'd do it himself, but his allergies were acting up again—and the creature was really quite intimidating, in his brutishly physical apekin way.

The Dewa Raja seemed not even to notice, which rankled Thulia even more, given how imperiously the local baron had insisted *he,* Thulia, render him due submission.

Vladek stabbed a blunt finger at the hooded figure that followed Parang as the tall man dragged the hybrid he had just stunned down the hallway. "That's a woman. It's got to be the one who was with Kane earlier today—yesterday. Who in turn is damn near certain to be a renegade outlander criminal named Domi. Albino bitch. Professionally speaking, she's a damn gaudy slut."

"Indeed," fluted the god-king.

"With your permission, God-King," Vladek said, "I'll jump back to Cobaltville with the renegade. We have proper interrogation facilities there."

"You do not have my permission, Magistrate. When the

ape-man awakens I will question him personally, to insure that no further errors are made."

Vladek's scar flared scarlet. "At least let me pull in the bitch and Parang," he said.

"My sensors indicate they have returned to Lord Parang's bedchambers," the Dewa Raja said. "I will see to their...disposition. You may withdraw, Magistrate."

"But—"

"I have acceded to your presence," the god-king said without apparent emotion. "It is even possible that you might still prove of use despite your mishandling of the chemical interrogation. But I will not be argued with. If you persist I will have you flayed alive."

For a moment Vladek hung there, his rage so quiveringly palpable that Thulia dared hope he'd go ahead and vent it and incur the promised punishment.

Instead the Magistrate spun and stamped from the chamber.

The god-king cocked a slender moon-pale finger. A hooded one appeared. "Summon Bandu," the god-king said. "It is time he redeemed himself."

TUAN PARANG SAT on his rumpled bed, turning the long, slender, silvery metallic object Domi had taken from the stunned hybrid. It was an infrasound wand.

"This is all very strange," he said in a wondering voice. Domi felt a certain sympathy for him. She understood how hard it was for such a man to admit to the slightest weakness, including—perhaps especially—that peculiarly unmanning variety, doubt.

She licked her lips. She lay beside him with her ass upturned like two scoops of French vanilla ice cream. It was Lord Parang's loss that he lacked the cultural referents to note the resemblance between the snow-white cheeks of her rump and two scoops of French vanilla ice cream. Watching the way he subconsciously ran his strong fingers up and down the wand was stirring her appetites....

Get a grip, girl, she told herself sternly. Duty calls. She would never feel the same intense bond to Kane as she did to his comrade Grant. But the dark-haired chiller with the wolf-gray eyes was still her comrade in arms, part of the only family she had in all the world.

"It is strange indeed, my lord," she said, her voice seductive enough to insure he'd listen, but not enough to get him distracted. "Is it any wonder that, possessing such potent magics, the demons have enchanted even the mighty god-king?"

She had demonstrated the potency of the infrasound wand by using it to blast the unconscious hybrid's head to jelly before Parang's eyes. Superstition not untinged with dread had overcome Parang's sense of honor toward a helpless captive. Where feral-girl Domi was concerned, meanwhile, it was getting good use from a bad enemy.

Parang nodded. His brow was furrowed. An uncomfortably unaccustomed mass of thought was weighing visibly upon him. "Yet where does my duty lie? I cannot act against the hooded ones without acting counter to the wishes of my liege."

She frowned, since he wasn't looking at her face. "But the Dewa Raja only wishes thus because he does not know the truth," she said, lying as seamlessly and fluidly as a stream of mercury. "Doesn't duty command that you strike down those who have so ensnared the god-king's mind?"

He shook his head. "If only I could be certain—"

A shadow fell across the bed. Domi and Tuan Parang looked around.

To see a seven-foot-tall apparition standing just inside the spill of orangish lamplight. With a sickle-bladed sword gleaming in each of its four black-nailed hands.

Chapter 20

The monster construct roared something in Malay. Domi hadn't picked up more than the merest wisp of the tongue, but she didn't need to know the words to catch the gist: "And now you die!"

Waving naked sword blades is another universal language.

Bandu charged, curved swords held wide to slice and dice. Domi lunged half off the bed, her bare rump poking up in the air. Her right hand dived into her hooded robe, which lay in a mound by the bed.

Meantime Tuan Parang was grabbing for his *talwar* hanging in its scabbard at the bed's head. It was painfully clear he wouldn't get it out in time. Roaring, Bandu closed for the kill.

Domi rolled back onto the bed with her arm held out straight. Bandu's eyes went wide.

Clutched in Domi's tiny white fist was a stubby semiautomatic pistol, her Detonics Combat Master. It took two and a half pounds' pressure to break the sensitive single-action trigger when she thumbed off the safety. She applied it early and often.

Big muzzle flashes underlit a very surprised expression on Bandu's rugged features in yellow as the naked albino woman dumped eight 180-grain beveled-ashcan hollowpoints into the biofact's naked chest. Launching the .45 ACP blockbusters from such a relatively light frame caused the handblaster to kick powerfully, and the rifling bite as the lands in the barrel imparted spin to the bullets torqued the grip ferociously in her hand. But even shooting one-handed she had little trouble keeping all her shots in the torso area, since she was firing at all but contact range, and the flame from the barrel added an angry red burn mark the size of one of Domi's hands with fingers outstretched to the collection of bruises left by the previous day's bout with Kane.

The pistol's slide locked back. The last two spent casings tinkled like fat brass cans onto the polished marble floor. "I triple hope that's you chilled," Domi said. "That's all there is and there ain't no more."

Still on his feet, Bandu uttered a groan that seemed to come straight up from his belly. The exhalation vented out several of the holes in his chest with bubbling little squeals and foamings of pink lung blood. He dropped to his knees with a thump, then toppled sideways. His swords clattered on the floor.

"You are a woman of many surprises," Parang said, standing now in his silk trousers with sword in hand.

"Unfortunately," Domi said, brandishing her slide-locked blaster, "I'm a woman of no more magazines. Best not be any more bad guys."

It was the wrong thing to say.

Shouting with macho fury four of the local-talent Mags, black-turbaned and veiled, rushed from the shadows of Tuan Parang's bedchamber. As they converged on the half-naked Vice-Raja with swords drawn he stooped, caught up the four-foot-tall bedside pedestal lamp near its base and swung it like a club at his leading attacker.

Reflexively the man threw up his *talwar* to block the blow of the improvised club. His sharp steel sliced the thin, soft brass stalk neatly through. The boat-shaped lamp itself tumbled, struck his cloth-wrapped head and burst open. Yellow fire cascaded down the whole left side of his body like a fast, hot flow of lava.

As the man commenced to thrash and scream, Parang side-stepped the overhand cut of the next black-clad stoneheart, then stepped past him, extending his left arm and turning it over so that the back of his wrist struck the onrushing man in the sternum as Parang pivoted his hips clockwise. It had the effect of clotheslining the swordsman. His black-slippered feet flew up and out from under him and he landed on his back on the rug with a coccyx-jarring thud.

The burning man was staggering about, arms extended, dripping flame and shrieking. Evidently the local Magistrate academy didn't teach stop, drop and roll. The two black-clad chillers still on their feet fanned out to take Tuan Parang in a pincers movement.

They were big men, little or not at all smaller than the vice-roy; their turbans made it hard to tell. They moved with panther confidence. They were two to his one, and wore armor beneath their loose black blouses.

Tuan Parang aimed a savage whistling backhand cut at eye level of the man approaching from his right. It had no chance of connecting; the swordsman was too far away. But instinctively the Mag rocked his balance back to pull his head out of harm's way, killing his forward momentum.

Parang meanwhile had rolled his right wrist and reversed direction with blinding speed. As the man to his left cocked his own sword arm for a cut the Vice-Raja's *talwar* described a sine wave, rising and then slashing transversely down. The curve of the blade concentrated all the stroke's force on a very small arc of blade: it sheared through the man's turban and the thin steel skullcap beneath to lop away his skull from the left side of his forehead to right temple. With one green-irised eyeball popping from the split-open orbit to whip at the end of its optic nerve stalk, he fell. When his head struck the stone floor his brain popped right out of his violated cranium and rolled two paces like a mass of dirty bread dough.

The speed of his own blade scarcely slowed, Parang brought it high and down to meet the right-hand attacker, who had resumed his charge. Steel rang on steel as the man's own cut turned into a desperate parry.

Too fast for the eye to follow, they exchanged three singing strokes. Then Parang's blade swept in a horizontal arc and the black-turbaned head popped free of its neck on a blood geyser.

And the man whom Parang had clotheslined was behind him, sword raised for the killing stroke. The viceroy spun, but without hope of preventing the blade from entering his own flesh.

The black cloth concealing the right side of the sec man's face shredded, as did skin, muscle and finally yellow bone. Half his face simply erupted then into a welter of blood, skull and clumps of brain. He fell.

"Wand," Domi said. She lay on her belly pointing the hybrid blaster with both hands. Then she pivoted and fired another invisible infrasound blast at the man whom Parang had set afire, who was turning in place in shrieking, blazing circles.

"Quiet, now," she said. "But still smells bad."

Jumping off the bed, she quickly rolled her empty Detonics in her robe. Tucking it under her left arm, wand in her right hand, she stood and looked at Parang.

"We go get Kane from dungeon now, yes?"

Even standing there with great chest heaving, face and torso splashed with blood and brains and gore dripping from his blade in clots, he ran an appreciative eye down her nakedness. Then he grinned.

"I think this means I am discharged from the Dewa Raja's service," he said.

"I take it that's a yes."

NEITHER THE DUNGEON keeper nor the two black-clad guards keeping watch over the prisoner who hung unconscious from the wall by his wrists thought anything when they heard the key turn in the lock of the heavy ironbound teakwood door. Then a great lean tiger of a man burst in, half-naked and smeared with blood, followed by an entirely nude woman whose skin was the color of the full moon at midnight.

The black-clad guardsmen were still gaping when Tuan Parang chopped them down.

The dungeon keeper, a squat brown shaved-headed man in a dusky orange robe, fell to his knees and beseeched Tuan Parang in Malay. Domi gathered that he was known personally to the viceroy and pleading for his life on that basis.

Domi looked around, found an iron bar resting on the rim of a brazier filled with coals burned down to gray ashes and cooled. She took it up, hefted it experimentally, then clouted the dungeon keeper across the bare pate with it from behind.

He fell over, curled into a fetal position, clutching at his split and blood-spurting scalp with both hands, mewling and kicking his sandaled feet in agony.

Parang frowned at the naked woman. "Why did you do that? He is a friend."

Domi nodded pertly. "Why I did—save his life. We chain up now, god-king doesn't blame him later for losing number-one prize prisoner."

Tuan Parang's brow rose. "You are a very clever young woman," he said slowly. "Too clever, perhaps."

"No second-thoughts time now," Domi said. She pulled the jailer's bloody hands away from his wounded head, yanked them behind his back and secured them with a set of manacles as deft as any Mag. Then she tossed him quickly and with equal professionalism and came up triumphantly brandishing a set of keys. These she took over to where Kane hung slumped with his head dangling to his chest. She undid first one wrist and then the other.

Tuan Parang was there to help her ease Kane's not inconsiderable weight to the floor. "Thank you, Lord," she said.

She fetched a half-full bucket from beside a nearby wall. "Hope this water, not slops," she said, and slammed the contents into Kane's face.

It was water. It ran pink down his face and into his beard and dripped onto his chest. Kane moaned, stirred.

"Back so…soon, Vladek?" he rasped. "You must've… missed me."

"No such luck," Domi said. "Only me. And Tuan Parang." The gray eyes snapped wide open. "Domi?"

"In the flesh."

"So I see."

"Crack mighty wise for a man look like he used blood for eyeliner, and it ran."

"I crack mighty wise for a man who feels like his head's been used for a piledriver." He sat up, rubbing at the back of his skull. "What the hell are you doing down here buck naked with the Vice-Raja?"

"Saving your ungrateful ass. You no like, we go 'way, leave you to male bond with big pig Vladek."

"You are a lucky man, friend," Tuan Parang said in his deep voice. "This one has done much and dared all for you, yet she says she is not even your mate."

"No, we're both spared that," Kane said. "Loyalty's a strong suit of hers, unlike modesty and tact."

Tuan Parang reached a hand down to Kane. "I don't know who you people are," the warrior said, hauling Kane effortlessly to his feet. "But if all your folk are like you, I do not know why you don't rule the world."

"Only two-three more of our people like us," Domi said.

"And we wouldn't rule the world if you gave it to us on a plate," Kane said. "We just don't want to let the hybrids keep it any longer."

"Hybrids?" Parang asked.

"Demons," Domi quickly supplied.

"Thanks, friend," Kane said to Parang. "And thank you, too, Domi, so you don't whine."

"We must get you out of the palace quickly," Tuan Parang said. "Soon the god-king will realize his assassins failed to take the Lord Chopper, and the alarm will be raised."

"Quick and easy," Domi said. "I'll call our friends."

"Not in here," Kane said. He swayed and put a hand to the wall for support. "Can't. Vladek bragged. Whole dungeon's surrounded with metal. Faraday cage. Blocks radio signals."

"C'mon, let's go out in the hall," Domi said. "Pretty Mary Alice can whisk us all right out of here."

She gave the infrasound wand to Kane. With an arm around the waist she guided the still unsteady man out the door through which she and the viceroy had entered. Tuan Parang accompanied them, *talwar* in hand. He had the air of a man whose comprehension events have well and truly escaped and who doesn't really anticipate it will catch them again anytime soon, but nonetheless remains gamely interested in what might happen next.

Domi unrolled her cloak carefully on the floor so as not to

spill the contents bundled inside and extracted her trans-comm. She spoke quickly into it. Then she rolled the communicator back up in the cloak and tucked it under her arm again.

"They're on their way," she said. "We'll have you out of here and back to Cerberus in two shakes of a lamb's tail, Kane."

"Negative. We still haven't learned what we came here to."

"More than you think, Kane. And anyway, remember that we can bounce back to the redoubt, get you patched and then be back in Tanimbar right away. Right here, if you feel nostalgic for this dungeon atmos—"

A smell of roses, and a ripple ran through the air. The four aborigines stood there. "You gave us some worries, mate," Jonny Corroboree said. "But it looks as if you pulled through just fine."

"I'm still alive and most of my parts seem to work," Kane said, "if that's what you define as 'fine.'"

"Well, just step right on up and join arms, and we'll be right off," the talker said. None of the aborigines gave the still stark-naked Domi more than a friendly nod of greeting. Jonny looked the extra member of the group up and down. "And this would be Tuan Parang, would it not? Are you coming with us, Your Lordship?"

Parang looked thoughtful. "Yes," he said after a moment's hesitation. "I—"

Mary Alice gasped and pitched forward onto her face. The back of her sweater was torn open in a circle, and a circular hole had been punched out of her rib cage and the left side of her spine, revealing one slowly pumping lung.

Behind the fallen woman the corridor had filled up with hooded ones and Vladek.

Chapter 21

Tyree pivoted and blasted back down the corridor with his Kalashnikov on full-auto. War Boom Ben fired his Makarov. Hooded figures flew back, trailing mists and pennons of blood. The cowl fell away from one as it bounced against a wall and toppled forward, revealing its characteristic huge-eyed hybrid face. The others ducked back around the corner.

"Your weapons are certainly loud," Tuan Parang remarked.

Jonny Corroboree knelt by the far walker. "Mary Alice! Bloody hell."

"Let's get back to the other side of the damn door," Kane said. "We're not getting out of here anytime soon."

Though his motions were stiff, not fluid as they customarily were, Kane leaned down, grabbed a handful of intact fabric on the back of Mary Alice's sweater and half carried, half dragged the stricken woman back into the dungeon.

The others were back in the torture chamber. Domi slammed and locked the door. Kane hoisted Mary Alice with Tyree's wordless help and laid her out on the table. She was conscious, her eyes half-open. Blood frothed from her nostrils and the sides of her mouth.

His knobby face a mask of concern, War Boom Ben came to examine Mary Alice and put his ear next to first her lips and then her chest to listen to her respiration. Then turning so she couldn't see, he shook his head slightly at Jonny Corroboree.

"No need to…hide," the far walker said in a thin, fraying voice. "I'm done for. Feel it."

Jonny stepped up and took a wrist in his hand. "Don't talk, Mary Alice."

She smiled. "Get…get the turtle to Lilga. Promise."

"That's not our bailiwick. It's Billy's lot."

"Promise."

He took her slim pale hand in both of his. "I promise. We'll find it and get it to her."

She shut her eyes, drew in a deep breath, let it out. It bubbled as she died.

Jonny squeezed his eyes tight shut.

The aborigines had brought both Kane's and Domi's packs, as well as Domi's enormous M-14 longblaster. Jonny moved quickly to Kane, made him sit on a stool while he checked him over. Domi quickly jammed a fresh magazine into the butt well of her Combat Master, then dragged on a blue long-sleeved shirt, a pair of khaki shorts, socks and her boots from her pack.

The door exploded inward.

A big chunk of it caught Tyree in the chest and sent him flying across the low-ceilinged stone chamber. War Boom Ben plunged a hand into Kane's pack, came up holding his Sin Eater in its power rig. He tossed it to Kane as hybrids, some with hoods slumped back, others still cowled, crowded in the door tittering and mewling fiendishly.

Kane caught the holster in his left hand, drew the blaster with his right. "All right," he said, clicking the selector past triburst to full rock and roll. "Now we dance to *my* music."

War Boom Ben dived to the side as Kane held back the guardless trigger and waved the Sin Eater. Flaming like a blowtorch, it filled the chamber with intolerable racket and shredded the small and fragile hooded ones.

His slide locked back. He yanked free the spare box attached to the power holster. Before he could drive it home, Vladek appeared in the door aiming his own Sin Eater for the center of Kane's chest, armored with nothing but congealed paths of his own blood. Vladek's thick pink lips parted in a smile.

From her knees Domi shot him with her handblaster.

The albino Outlands woman had been holding down at center-of-mass level for hybrids, in case Kane's blazing blaster spared any long enough to be a problem. As soon as Vladek appeared she squeezed off a pair of shots as fast as she could crank the light single-action trigger.

Vladek was good and Vladek was quick. Or maybe in her excitement Domi pulled off the second shot, easy enough to do under the circumstances. The first big scoop-nosed slug punched through the great muscle of his right thigh. The other gouged a divot of stone furred in green-black mildew out of the wall. Bellowing, Vladek dived back out of sight with his own Sin Eater still silent.

The three surviving aborigines were aiming blasters alertly at the entrance. Kane quickly started strapping the power holster to his right forearm.

"Perempuan Putih—White Girl! Captain Hardin, if that is your name."

It was Tuan Parang, calling from the chamber's far end. He was hunched over, indicating a round-topped hole in the wall: a secret passageway.

Black-turbaned guardsmen swarmed through the front door with blades in hand. They shouted hoarsely and danced in yellow stroboscopic muzzle flashes as the aborigines' blasters bellowed and burned them down.

The chamber stank worse of fear and blood and spilled guts

than it had before. Head reeling, Kane said to Parang, "What about you?"

"I stand. I shall hold these."

"You sure?"

For a moment the expression on his blade-lean face set. Then he laughed. It came from the depths of him. "You pursue some great end. All my ends have burned to ash within this hour. I shall fight here, in my palace, and either triumph or show the demons how to die!"

Kane eyed the opening dubiously. He had the impression it led down. "Where does that go?"

Parang grinned. "To a place I told White Girl about. A place where wonders are stored. Wonders I suspect may be helpful to you."

Domi tugged Kane's arm. "Let's haul. God-king can send coldhearts faster than we can chill. Meaning we are chilled big time if we stay."

"I couldn't put it better myself," Jonny said.

"What about her?" Kane nodded to Mary Alice, whom Tyree and War Boom Ben had carefully arranged on the stone table lying on her back with her hands crossed over her small breasts. Her expression was peaceful, as it had been when she died.

"She's returned to Tjukurpa," the bull boy said calmly, hefting his AK. "They cannot hurt her more. And her shell might yet help us achieve her dying wish." He showed Kane a grin that differed as greatly from the aborigines' usual indefatigable cheer as a shark's differed from a happy baby's.

Kane returned it in kind. "You are a true coldheart, my friend."

"Too bloody right, cobber."

The two quickly prepared the far walker's body for its final journey. Then Kane turned to Parang.

"Thanks," he said.

"Strength to your arm, friend." He stuck out his hand and they shook, gripping forearms.

"And yours, Lord Chopper."

Kane turned away. Domi took the tall and now erstwhile Vice-Raja at a sprint, jumping up to wrap her legs around his narrow waist and dragging his mouth to hers for a quick but deep kiss. "I won't forget you, Tuan Parang," she said, and Kane could have sworn her ivory cheeks were wet.

"Nor I you," the Vice-Raja rumbled. Domi disengaged and dived down the passageway.

The others followed, leaving Parang standing thoughtfully, sword in hand.

"ARE YOU SURE you know where we're going, Domi?" Kane asked, trudging along with his head bent sideways on his neck to avoid scraping his crown on the low, rounded stone ceiling.

"No," Domi said, marching stolidly in the lead with her M-14 slung and a Nighthawk clutched in her fist. "You want to go back and ask directions?"

"Only a little less than I want to march blindly down a tunnel into the earth."

Jonny walked in front of Kane, right behind the albino woman. War Boom Ben followed Kane. Last came Tyree, his AKM held ready.

Fogged though his brain was by his experiences of the past twenty-four hours, not to mention aftereffects of the "truth" drug Vladek had so inexpertly administered, Kane thought to perceive the rationale behind the aborigines' march order. Tyree was the most expendable; indeed his main task was to buffer the others from risk. So he took the most exposed position.

"How did you find out about this mystery spot you're guiding us to?" Kane asked. "Did this Parang dude give you a guided tour of the whole damn palace while I was out? And why did they build a secret passage straight from the dungeon to this place, anyway?"

"Too many questions," Domi said. "The tunnel from the dungeon joined another secret passage, remember? Or is your brain still all crapped up? Man your age got to take care of himself better than you do."

Kane growled.

"Tuan Parang told me about a mysterious part of the palace denied to even him. He said there was a metal monster which kept watch over the entryway…."

"Metal monster?" Tyree asked from the rear.

"Wizard!" War Boom Ben exclaimed in a tone of genuine delight. "A security robot, I'll wager!"

"But Parang said he had heard…rumors," Domi finished.

"And that's where we're going? Toward something rumored?"

Domi nodded.

"What, for instance?"

"Won't say. We just have to see."

Domi shucked her pack and dug briefly in an outside pocket. From a foam-padded rigid case she withdrew an item of high-tech reconnaissance: a dentist's mirror, about one inch across stuck on the end of a six-inch chrome rod. She crouched and poked it around the corner about a foot from the floor.

"Whoa," she breathed. "Check this out, Kane."

Kane let down his own pack, nodding gratefully as War Boom Ben helped him off with it. Skinny all-knees-and-elbow geek he might have been, but he displayed surprising physical strength. Which was fine by Kane, whose whole body felt as if it had been sculpted out of boiled pasta.

Kane used both hands on the wall to lower himself to his knees as Domi slipped aside to give him place. He took the dental mirror in fingers that felt and functioned like cold sausages and fumbled it out into the cross corridor.

The view wasn't good, even if both your eyes weren't still swollen halfway shut the way Kane's were. The image was small and distorted. But that was because the mirror was too small to show up at all well on most vid pickups unless you moved it too rapidly, and an autonomous security bot, if that's what lay down the hallway, would almost certainly filter it out as random input, like a rat scuttling by. They had, back in the so well-stocked armory within the redoubt, nifty little fiber-optic probes whose pickup ends showed a cam or other watcher no more than a hair, with little vid units that showed at least a somewhat less astigmatic view of what was to be seen. But they were bulkier—and far more likely to be detected by baronial electromagnetic-emissions sensors. The humble mirror was easy, relatively durable and used no power.

It took a moment of rolling the shiny fluted cool-metal handle between unresponsive fingers, another interval of effort to focus his eyes on the tiny reflection, and yet more time before Kane's still impaired brain would process what his eyes showed him: the figure of a man standing by a door at the far end of ten yards of corridor, clutching a hand-and-a-half sword with a straight flame-waved blade.

But not exactly a man. Or at least this was the first man Kane had ever seen with such weird distorted proportions: long arms, squat armored torso above bowed legs, big face with cheekbones, brows and chin prominent beyond the point of acromegaly, wearing a helmet like a minaret spire, with all kinds of weird little knobs and protrusions sticking off at odd angles.

It was also the first man Kane had ever seen who appeared to be made entirely from gleaming polished yellow brass.

"May I?" asked War Boom Ben, crouching excitedly at Kane's side. Kane drew back the mirror cautiously and handed it over, then let Domi and Jonny help him to his feet and back.

It seemed the tech boy did no more than poke the mirror head out past the wall and pull it right back. Then he was on his feet, practically vibrating. "I'll be dipped and sheared for a hogget," he murmured. "They've a security bot in the guise of a traditional temple-guardian demon!"

"Great," Kane said. His voice had more than a bit of rasp to it. Possibly one of this captors had punched him in the throat. It was hard to remember; they'd pummeled him pretty comprehensively, although Vladek yelled abuse and kicked people when they did something—such as punching his throat—that risked putting him permanently beyond interrogation. "So it combines all the best features of a demon and a warbot. Right?"

"Oh, no doubt, no doubt." Ben nodded excitedly.

"I'm happy." Kane looked at Domi. "Are you happy?"

"From what Tuan Parang said," the slim pale girl said, "it's programmed to warn intruders off. Zapping you to ash isn't its first option."

"Now, that's encouraging. But it probably is the second option, right? When we don't take the hint?"

Tyree slung his blaster. "Allow us," he told Kane and Domi, urging them back with gentle air-pushing motions of his big pink palm.

War Boom Ben placed his back to the wall just out of sight of the sec bot.

The big-shouldered bull boy walked right out into the corridor.

Chapter 22

The dungeon looked as if Jackson Pollock had been hired to decorate it. With a fire hose.

In blood.

What was left of Tuan Parang lay slumped against the carven stone torture table. Half a dozen armored human swordsmen had been able to inflict no more than minor slices on him before he butchered them like pigs.

But the hooded ones' infrasound wands had shattered and rent him from a distance. In the end neither his skill nor strength could save him.

Using a spear haft as a crutch, his right thigh wrapped in yards of white linen already mostly dyed red and black by blood and dungeon filth, Senior Magistrate Vladek of Cobaltville levered himself forward in a painful but relentless hobble. Cruel was Vladek, and a bully, but he was neither cowardly nor in any way weak. Like any good Mag—like the accursed traitor Kane himself, once the shining paragon of the whole Magistrate program—the only way to stop him was to incapacitate or kill him.

The man lying sprawled half on the floor like a mass of stirred-up red gelatin had been the same way, clearly.

Tuan Parang rolled his remaining brown eye at Vladek. "They have won beyond your reach," he said through half a mouth, slurred but intelligible. "I have beat you, Ingrezi."

"You were valorous to the end, Parang," Vladek husked. He raised his left arm. His Sin Eater snapped into his hand. As it struck it blasted once.

Parang's lone eye vanished. Blood and brain matter struck the stone behind his raised hand with a splat audible over the fearful head-crushing echoes of the single gunshot.

"Valorous," Vladek said. "But still an asshole."

Turbaned local Magistrates crowded the dungeon. A couple searched for keys to release the chief jailer, his round face bloody from bludgeoning, who had been shackled and locked in a holding cell subsidiary to the main chamber. Vladek reeled, staggered back a few steps to put his back to the wall. The bullet had missed his femoral artery, or he'd be bled-out on his back in the corridor, face even paler than usual and staring at the ceiling. But it had ripped a big chunk of muscle out the back of his thigh, and he had lost a lot of blood. Your average coldheart would have been gladly lying down waiting for dust-off. But Vladek was a stoneheart true.

Yet still human, still with limits he was dangerously crowding.

A woman lay on the torture table with her hands crossed over her breasts; from what Vladek could see they hadn't been anything to write home about. She didn't look much like most of the snooping Australian savages he'd seen pictures of. Her features were fine, her skin pale ivory no doubt even before the blood had drained out of them. She was unmistakably dead.

Damn shame, Vladek thought, moistening his lips with his thick tongue. Being a Magistrate entailed certain perquisites, but back home you had to be careful how you exercised them—your higher-ups in the Mag Division were always looking for large, heavy things to hold over your head, and the Trust could be surprisingly namby-pamby about what its servants, even lower-level initiates to the mysteries such as Vladek himself, got up to. Whereas the god-king didn't seem to give us a rat's ass, and the locals took an even more rough-and-ready approach to life.

Baron Thulia would probably wet himself if he knew what Vladek was thinking. Thulia was a weakling, sure proof that even hybrids—even *barons*—weren't invulnerable superhumans. That was a definitely interesting datum that Vladek had duly filed away in his mind. In the meantime, the other barons thought as little of the hypochondriacal ninny as Vladek himself did. Or they never would have stuck him in this humid shithole, doing a scut job that called for nothing more than the midlevel thug Vladek comfortably knew himself to be.

Comfortable for the present, anyway. When he caught up with the renegade Kane and then helped this weird local baron squash the savages in Australia, he was due for a rocket rise through the ranks. And if Erica van Sloan thought different, up her nicely turned ass with a white-hot poker; the barons did recognize ability in their human underlings, and with their vaunted intelligence would be quick to assess what more Vladek could do for them—and recompense him accordingly.

"Senior Magistrate!" a wavery tenor voice said from the door.

BRASS EYELIDS SNAPPED open as Tyree showed himself. Glares of actinic blue light blazed from the cruel brazen face.

A voice, appropriately metallic, blared out from the demon bot. Something peremptory in Malay: a warning, no doubt, quickly repeated in a tonal language Kane thought was Chinese and at last in English. "These are sacred precincts, protected by a curse! Go back or face the wrath of your god-king!"

Domi was crouched just in from the mouth of the low-ceilinged passageway, which had led here from the secret dungeon exit, just at the point where she could see in the dentist's mirror without being seen. Kane sat beside her trying to watch the minute image and hoping he was out of the sec bot's field of view. Both of necessity had their backs to the action. Kane had his Sin Eater in hand anyway.

Tyree was walking forward with his arms extended out from his sides. "I'm on an urgent mission from the Dewa Raja himself, Chief," he said in his mellifluous and deceptively mild voice. "You got to let me pass, there's a good demon."

The robot began to screech. Eventually it ran down its option menu to English. "Warning! Warning! You will be struck dead if you do not leave at once!"

It began to walk toward Tyree. Still holding the big sword upright before its hideous masklike face with its right hand, it let go with the left and began to extend it toward the aborigine. Who was now well down the naked corridor with no place whatever to hide.

More by an uneasy roil in his still-churning gut and the lifting of his nape hairs than by what his eyes could tell him of the tiny image in the mirror, Kane realized there was something wrong about that hand. Triple wrong.

Chilling wrong.

"Tyree, get down!" he shouted. "Infrasound wand—"

Tyree dived to the side. War Boom Ben pivoted into the corridor, bringing up both his hands before him. The passageway filled with blue light, shot with pulsating rings of yellow radiance, that somehow filled Kane's soul with atavistic fear. He wrapped an arm any which way around Domi's head to shield her ruby eyes, then threw himself backward, carrying them both to sprawl back up the way they had come.

The flash of blue-white penetrated Kane's eyelids. He heard a horrific crash. Then clattering and tinkling, metallic, as if chunks and bits were falling on the stone floor.

He opened his eyes. Through big orange balls of afterimage he saw Jonny Corroboree leaning over him, grinning ear to ear above an outstretched hand.

"No worries, Kane," he said. "Take a good five or ten shots' exposure at this range to do you any lasting harm, or so you'd notice, anyway. Bit rough on Ben, I fear, close as he is, which is one reason we're so eager to reclaim what we've lost."

Kane let the aborigine help him stand. Domi, all spring steel and hard rubber, had bounced right back to her feet and was already shrugging on her pack and the sling of her giant battle rifle.

"What about the door?" Kane asked. "Bound to be blast armored and require some kind of positive ID to pass—"

Another blue glow, flash and crash from the corridor. "Not anymore," Jonny said.

SPEAK OF THE DEVIL, Vladek thought. He turned. "How may I serve you, Baron Thulia?" he asked, hardly bothering to mute the irony in his voice. He wasn't sure the pallid little freak recognized it anyway.

"Is it true?" Thulia demanded. "Is it true you've let the captive slip out of your grasp?"

Vladek shrugged. "For the moment. He won't get far."

"But was he not Kane! Kane the renegade—?"

"Was. Still is. And this time when I catch up with him I'm hauling him back to C-ville."

"Such disrespect!" Thulia shrilled. "You really should show me more respect, Vladek. Really you should. And, ah, the god-king may have something to say about your plan to remove a prize captive—"

Rage flared up within Vladek. It was never that far beneath the surface as it smoldered. "A lot he's got to say about it! He's not even one of the nine—he shouldn't even exist. And after his own piece-of-shit sec boss turned the renegade loose himself—"

He spun back to point, outraged, at the massively violated corpse of Tuan Parang, erstwhile Vice-Raja of Tanimbar. What he saw made him forget Parang and his wrath at one and the same instant. His blood turned to liquid nitrogen in his veins.

Having made sure there weren't fugitives or would-be ambushers skulking in the shadows and side cells a pair of black-turbaned local Mags had turned their attention to the pretty chill on the table. One was just reaching as if to unfold her hands for a better gawk at her boobs.

"Don't, you triple-tainted stupes!" Vladek screamed. "Stand away from that whore!"

One Mag had already lifted Mary Alice's left hand by the wrist. A half-dozen little shiny globes, each about twenty-five millimeters through, spilled like marbles from her hands, cascaded down the side of the table and bounced upon the smooth-worn dungeon floor.

For all his injuries Vladek had almost made it to the door when the microgrens filled the dungeon with fire and blast.

As THEY PASSED through the ruins of the armored blast door, which had been partially melted and partially peeled back and out into a giant metallic blossom, Domi murmured, "Badges? We don't need no stinkin' badges."

"I worry about you sometimes," Kane said. "I really do."

Following almost immediately the discharge of the beam blaster, which had opened up the door like a birthday present, had come still another thunder crack as ionized air fled whatever awful destructive force the blue bolts unleashed, then a single sharp rifle shot, then the curt distinctive clatter, relatively slow but mighty authoritative, of one of the 7.62 mm branch of the Kalashnikov clan lighting off full-auto. Then Tyree's voice had drifted back through the breach. "Clear."

It was another artificial half-bubble cavern, with a glassy fused quality to the stone that suggested to Kane a whole lot of heat had gone into the shaping of it. It was spacious by comparison with the claustrophobic colon of a tunnel they had traversed for what Kane thought had to be the better part of a mile, but still fairly modest. Maybe ten yards in horizontal diameter, with the apex of the ceiling perhaps half that. A semicircular hole about three yards in diameter yawned in the far wall. Lines of faint overhead light strips marched down its apex along what was evidently a level tunnel. A single rail of what looked like some dirty-white matte synthetic led into it from a sort of concrete pier on which they stood. An elongated half egg with seats inside was parked where the rail met the platform. They had obviously entered a terminal for some kind of miniature rail line.

To Kane's right a booth was built into the curving wall, with big waist-up windows of what a slight distorted quality told Kane's practiced eye were untinted armaglass above firing ports: security hard point. To his left a door stood open revealing a lighted space beyond, with shop tables and machinery visible inside. A faint odor of machine oil was detectable over the harsh stink of burned propellant and lubricant, not to mention the richer reek of recent human death.

Two guards in pale blue-and-white uniforms and helmets lay cooling on the platform. The appearance of one's uniform had to be deduced by the fact his boots and the bottoms of his trousers legs matched his buddy's; he had been turned about inside out and largely cremated by the blue bolt. The other lay on his back, staring at the ceiling past the little blue hole in his forehead, with arms outflung and an AK-looking long-blaster lying beside him; the fried chill had a twisted lump of slag beside him that probably began the day as a similar blaster. Two obvious techs in canary-yellow jumpsuits stood shaking by with hands behind their heads. One had a dark stain spreading from his groin. It wasn't blood.

Kane let his Sin Eater snap back into its forearm holster and looked an inquiry at Tyree, who was holding down on the two terrified techs with his AKM. Ben the tech boy was inside the sec booth studying some kind of control console.

"The burst was to get these boys' minds right," Tyree said with a shrug. "Overkill, I'd say in retrospect."

He was about to add something when he suddenly went stiff and his eyes half-closed. Kane's Sin Eater whapped back into his hand, but it was immediately obvious the two techs had no intention of taking advantage of the break in his concentration, if in fact they even noticed. In their current state that seemed unlikely.

Kane glanced quickly around.

The other two aborigines were in the same trancelike state.

Chapter 23

"Kane, what—?" Domi began.

Tyree's gallows frame shuddered violently. Then he raised his head. His eyes opened, as yellow as a lion's.

He smiled. It did nothing to detract from his resemblance to a beast of prey.

"Good show, Mary Alice," Jonny murmured, opening his own eyes.

"What?" Kane asked.

"She took some right bastards with her," the talker explained, "with some dinkum help from the excellent Tyree and War Boom Ben."

"You mean—" Kane shook his head. His thoughts were trying to scatter like a shoal of fish among whom a barracuda has just darted. His Sin Eater was jumping back and forth between holster and hand with little servomechanism mosquito whines. "She— Wasn't she—?"

Jonny laid a gentle hand on his shoulder. "Her spirit hung about to make sure we were helped away, and she was avenged," he said. "Now she's well and truly home, back to—back to the ship."

Allowing the blaster to rest at last in its holster, Kane squeezed his eyes slowly shut. His sanity teetered like a fine china cup on the tip of a none-too-competent juggler's pole. Mary Alice had seemed a gentle and unassuming soul, although she had endured hardship and danger with neither complaint nor hesitation. He wasn't sure which unsettled him most: the notion of that sweet and lovely woman as her own avenging angel, or that her mates knew what her spirit had *seen,* and maybe even helped along.

The rational explanation was that the aborigines were simply imagining it. Except these simple "savages" claimed to be recovering memories from a time in which they were as far advanced technologically beyond Kane's folk as the baronies were beyond, well, the hunter-gatherer lifestyle the crew had assumed for 750 centuries of protective coloration—and survival. And as their almost casual destruction of a battle bot that would have shrugged off Sin Eater bullets and even microgrens proved their claims absolutely right.

Not for the first time, Kane realized his sense of what was rational was all out of fit with what was undeniably real.

"Fell for the booby-trapped-corpse gag, did they?" Domi asked brightly. "Stupes. But that'll only hold them so long. Shouldn't we jump in that funny little car and motivate out of here triple quick?"

"Dunno where it goes," Kane said.

"Better take it than the last train to the coast, no?" Domi asked sweetly.

"There you go being right again."

He turned to the two captive techs. "All right. Where does this thing go?"

They stared at him. For the first time he noticed they had pale brown skin—kind of greenish ivory, now, but he could interpolate—and Asian-looking eyes. "No, don't tell me—"

They both began to babble at once in a language Kane could not comprehend a syllable of. Again he had a vague sense it was Chinese. It could have been Old Martian for all he knew.

"They don't speak fucking English."

"Or even Malay," Domi added.

Jonny stepped up and spoke to them in the same language. They shut up. Then the one with the dry drawers spoke, eyes down, voice sullen.

"You savvy their lingo, too?" Kane demanded, disbelieving.

"Too right," Jonny said, all smiles. "It's my job."

He bobbed his head toward the sullen tech. "This one says they won't tell us anything."

"Fuckin' A," Kane said.

He stretched his right hand toward the defiant technician. His Sin Eater slammed his hand. His forefinger was curved.

So was his thumb, to hit the firing selector. He didn't give the man a mere triburst; that would not have conveyed the desired moral lesson. Instead he unzipped the man from nut sac to crown with a long loud special delivery of half a box of twenty 9 mm cartridges. The man did a little dance as the metal-jacketed bullets lanced through him, then fell right straight down into a pool of his own intestines.

"Stone chilling, even for you," Domi said through the echoes of the burst, not without an audible note of approval. The three aborigines stared at him with shocked expressions; the shooting had drawn Ben from the booth with his Makarov in hand.

"I'm not in a patient frame of mind." He swung the barrel of his Sin Eater in its perforated shroud to bear on the surviving tech. A thin wisp of bluish-green smoke drooled from its muzzle. "Now, spill your guts, pal, unless you want to do it the same way he spilled his. Get my drift?"

Rising-falling syllables began to flow from the man's fear-slackened mouth, along with a string of bile. Jonny gave a final frown to Kane and then listened.

"He says—rather a lot, really, as you no doubt gather. But what's pertinent is, this monoline leads to the underground hangar."

Kane's eyebrows rose. "Hangar."

"Where the mother ship is kept." Jonny frowned again slightly, this time in obvious perplexity instead of disapproval for Kane's coldheart interrogation technique.

"Except he keeps throwing in the word for 'blimp.' Airship, anyway. Now what on Earth d'you think he means by that?"

IT WAS A GIANT DELTA, matte black, was what he meant. Giant as in its rounded wings were as easily broad as an old-style American football field from wingtip to blunt wingtip. Although it didn't possess discrete wings so much as it seemed to *be* a wing. A vast, fat, bloated wing, mounding to impressive height in the center before tapering away both sides. It rested in a cradle like the keel and spars for Noah's own ark done up in gleaming alloy, held in place by what appeared to be hinged clamps.

"Holy shit!" Domi said. "What's that?"

"It's a *mother* ship," Tyree said. "That's for dinkum sure."

MOVING BRISKLY, perhaps to forestall Kane applying another of his drastic solutions, Tyree had trussed up the tech with wire and synthetic tape from the repair shop. It made no nevermind to Kane: once the bad guys got here, they'd know their little maglev car was gone, and it wasn't as if there could be much doubt either where it had gone or who had taken it there. All he cared about was that the guy not raise the alarm himself. Once the bull boy and the tech boy had gone into action, he didn't spare it another thought. A curious mixture of coldhearted and squeamish themselves, one thing the aborigines undoubtedly were was competent.

Not bad for folk who had been…disassembled…for seventy-five thousand years. And they more than hinted they were far from back to their old selves. Not that that surprised Kane, but he found it slightly scary to think about what the aborigines were like when they were all the way on-line.

They didn't need the Chinese tech to operate the little levitating car for them. The controls looked simple enough, but War Boom Ben had jumped right behind and pronounced himself ready to go as if he'd had a personal hand in designing them. He seemed, quite candidly, to understand the function of machines and circuitry automatically—even as the glib and cheerful talker Jonny appeared to speak every human language.

Domi had shared the rear seat with Kane on the trip, which took a good ten minutes at a brisk clip—maybe thirty miles per hour, although it would have been tricky to estimate under the conditions even if Kane hadn't recently had his skull pounded out of round and pumped full of narcotics. The three aborigines were clustered up front talking low in their own tongue. Domi's trend of thought clearly paralleled Kane's.

"Spooky people," she murmured. "Help us kick baron butt big time—unless they take over, mebbe."

"Mebbe," Kane said quietly. "But they seem to have other plans, not that I can read them for shit." He shook his head. "Might be worse things could happen than if they did take over."

Domi shrugged. Anybody "taking over" had little appeal to her. She was a true wild child, an ultimate free spirit. She would take direction from her Cerberus comrades, at least if she thought they had better ideas than she did, but she never let anybody boss her. After years of knowing the albino, Kane still had little clear concept of what motivated her to aid in their fight—except for the fierce, uncompromising love she bore them all, as her sole family and tribe.

"Thing's definitely not an Aurora," Kane said out the side of his mouth as they approached the craft's stern. He nodded at what appeared to be huge oblong ports to either side of a central bubble. "Those are two-dimensional vectoring nozzles. Looks as if it may have maneuvering ducts covered by those louvers, too. Whatever it is, it doesn't rely on anything like gravitic pulses for motive power."

"Got an aft-firing laser, though," said War Boom Ben. "Mounted inside the blister. Looks like a stubby telescope."

"I see what you're talking about," Kane said. "Have to take your word for what it is—"

A Klaxon began to wail.

Chapter 24

"Shit!" Kane said over the raucous rising-falling tone. "We're blown. Run for the ladder by the nose!"

He could hear alarmed shouts echoing across the hangar floor during the valleys of the Klaxon's sine-wave blare, as well as barked commands, unmistakable across language barriers. Small arms opened up. Their sound was a reassuring pop-pop like harmless pyrotechnics; the expanse of concrete floor was even wider than it looked, and the range was extreme for handblasters, especially machine pistols fired full-auto, so they'd be hit only by accident.

Which did damn little to reassure Kane. One thing hard experience had taught him was accidents happened. And he still basically had ripped and stained silk trousers and a nice coating of congealed blood for body armor. Not that his companions had any better protection.

When they had almost reached the after section of the gleaming alloy cradle in which the craft rested, a pencil of eye-searing pink light flashed between him and Jonny, who was running right in front of him. As thunder cracked from air rushing back to fill the void the laser's ionization path had left, Kane yelped and backpedaled reflexively, even though his conscious mind, coming late to the party and no damn wonder, understood it was precisely the wrong thing to do.

Worse was Jonny Corroboree, sensing somehow, putting

on the brakes, too, and turning to extend a hand back to Kane. "Need help, cobber?"

"Don't be double stupe!" Kane screamed back, waving and trying to will his body back into action. It suddenly felt as if his legs were made of lead. "Go! Fucking *go!*"

Behind Kane Domi wheeled and dropped to one knee, expertly twining her left arm through the loop of the M-14's shooting sling. She settled into a classic kneeling rifleman's pose, right elbow high, left directly beneath the heavy longblaster's forestock and propped on her bare alabaster knee. She welded a pallid cheek to dark hard wood, let out half a breath and squeezed. The big longblaster bucked and boomed, driving her back perilously far but not over.

Two hundred yards away a pink cloud puffed out behind a blue-and-white uniformed sec man who was aiming a strange device their way. He fell backward, arms flying out to the sides. The laser rifle bounced on the floor.

"Dinkum shooting, girl," Tyree shouted, running up behind her firing his AKM with left hand alone. With his right he caught her left biceps and towed her right after him as she reeled and tried to gather her balance.

A burst of better aimed gunfire splattered the pavement where she had knelt as the bull boy and she vanished into the cradle's ballistic shadow, sending up little spouts of concrete dust and chips.

There was fire coming from their right now too, all projectiles. The handblaster bullets made weird pocking noises as they struck the mystery craft's black flanks—then whined as they tumbled away.

"Shit!" Kane yelled as a ricochet laid open his cheek.

"Closer under the hull!" Tyree called. "Ricochets less likely to hit."

Running like a starving man to a buffet table, War Boom Ben had almost reached the ladder near the flying machine's blunt nose. It led up to a port open in the curved black underbelly. The ladder itself seemed a permanent component of the support cradle.

A hybrid technician in a tinfoil-looking jumpsuit emerged from the port. For a moment it stood in a posture of cartoon shock, blinking its huge half-human eyes at the onrushing aborigine. Then it unsnapped an infrasound wand from its belt with alarming alacrity and pointed it at the oncoming youth.

"Damn!" Kane exclaimed. Still at the dead run—it had taken way too much to build up that momentum, and he wasn't going to give up any now—he stretched out his right hand at the full extent of his arm. His Sin Eater smacked his fist with a gratifyingly familiar impact. The blaster was still set to full rock and roll, and he didn't dream of changing it. He just blazed the mag in the hybrid's general direction.

Bullet jackets sparked off the cradle's alloy. Kane used them to walk his fire right into the hybrid tech. The slender death-dealing wand had just come to bear on War Boom Ben as he slowed to make his turn up the steps to the port. Then blood squirted from the hybrid's skinny side and back, and the left side of his bulging skull popped off as if built to. The near miss by infrasound bolt made the tech boy's shaggy hair literally stand on end.

He drew his Makarov and ran up the steps. "Wait!" Jonny called, then said something in his own language.

At the head of the ramp the tech boy paused, looked back. His expression was rebellious. But then he gripped the handblaster's butt in both hands, pointed the muzzle ceilingward and stepped to one side of the open hatch.

Tyree had released Domi and slung his Kalashnikov. The

albino girl more or less had her balance back, although she proceeded more at a high-speed forward fall than a run. She clutched her own longblaster to her like a militant teddy bear.

Tyree's right hand came up with a black Jericho .40-caliber handblaster, compact and wicked. He extended his left to Domi. "Handgun!"

"What?"

"Handgun! Give me yours, please!" Domi managed to stop without falling over on the concrete, drew her Detonics and held it out. Tyree snagged it without slowing.

He passed Kane, who was also slowing down, because for some reason it felt as if no air at all were coming into his lungs however hard he tried to pump them. Nevertheless he reached the foot of the ramp only a few steps after the racing bull boy, having successfully fumbled a fresh magazine into his own blaster.

Jonny Corroboree stopped him with an upraised palm. "Let him take this dance, mate."

"I'm a professional," Kane wheezed.

Jonny grinned immensely. "So is he."

What is wrong with you? a voice raged from the depths of Kane's skull. *When did you get triple stupe enough to be eager to go through a door?*

"Right," he said. He stopped. The Sin Eater popped back in its holster. He hunched over with hands on knees and sucked air hard. He knew damn well that was a poor way to do it, but so what.

Tyree charged up the ramp and past War Boom Ben without slowing. From the corner of his eye the panting Kane thought he saw him extend his arms to both sides like wings as he went through.

He heard a double pop, and the bull boy was briefly silhouetted by yellow flashes in stereo. Then a volley of shots came too fast to count, the muzzle flares a steady strobing like an old-time movie projector.

The shots and flashes receded into the belly of the beast. Jonny went up the ramp to pose across the hatchway from Ben. Domi came up to Kane and helped him hobble to the ramp and up the steps as if he were ten years older than Lakesh's chronological age.

Which he felt.

A sort of hash-smoke haze of peppery burned propellant and oils hung around the entryway. From somewhere Tyree's voice called back in the fleet tongue.

"All clear," Jonny said with a nod. "After you."

But fevered nerd enthusiasm overcame War Boom Ben's manners and he rabbited in next. Kane didn't mind. He wasn't going anywhere quickly himself even though people were still shooting at him from a distance.

Then a new voice joined the chorus of small-arms chatter, a deeper resonant snarl. Machine gun! Kane whipped inside faster than he thought he could, Domi still hanging on and keeping right up. Jonny stepped in behind and sealed the hatch with a swipe at a wall panel as if he'd crewed this boat his whole career.

Then again, Kane realized vaguely, the current inhabitant of the trim desert dweller's body had been born and spent his whole life crewing a starship. A creepy sensation tingled down his back and along the hairs of his arms.

"Big mess," Domi said approvingly. Two of the Chinese guards and another hybrid tech lay in the three-yard-wide space just inside the hatch in various attitudes of sudden death. A perforated synthetic mat beneath Kane's bare feet meant the drying blood was tacky instead of slick.

"Come ahead on, folks." A cramped passageway extended into the vessel; Tyree's voice floated back down as if from some distance. Which it was, as Kane, Domi and the talker made their way along to a stairway that led up and up. Although it could have served no purpose to employ visual stealth-tech internally the claustrophobic walls seemed to blot up most of the photons from the little amber safety lights placed at intervals along them.

They passed several more bodies en route. Kane spared them not a glance. He took it for granted that if Tyree left them behind, they were chills for sure.

The control room was a spacious half dome way up at the central hump's apex. Several seats, solid and well cushioned, apparently against acceleration, faced both a large curved expanse of canopy and an array of big-screen displays.

"If it looks familiar, folks," War Boom Ben said, "that's because the design was inspired by the old original *Star Trek* series. Your late-twentieth-century designers doted on the show."

He was sitting in one of the seats and playing a keypad built into the arm without looking. Numbers, diagrams and menus flickered on and off the monitors too fast for Kane's eye to have followed even if he hadn't been half-stoned and altogether spent.

He shrugged. It didn't look familiar to him. He plopped himself down in the seat next to the tech boy's. "How the hell does he know about twentieth-century TV anyway?" he demanded, mainly of the air.

"They know everything any of their people ever experienced, more or less," Domi said quietly. "Dreamtime, Kane."

"Not exactly," Jonny said softly. "No one of us knows everything. Except perhaps Old Man."

Kane shook his head, mystified.

"Thanks, lass, you're a lifesaver." Tyree handed the Detonics back to Domi. The slide wasn't even locked back, meaning he hadn't even burned up the eight shots it carried.

"Show-off," she murmured as she accepted the wep back. The bull boy just grinned clean across his ugly but compelling badlands of a face.

"Can we save the gosh-wow and the mutual admiration till we get the fuck outta Dodge?" Kane demanded.

War Boom Ben was wagging his head in delight. "This is really elegant, even if it is right prim—I mean, even if it is, ah…"

"Okay, it's stone knives and bearskins compared to what you had in the fleet," Kane growled. "Now, what the fuck, over?"

The tech boy glanced back at Jonny, apparently wondering how badly he'd assed up. The talker gave him an encouraging nod. "It's all menu driven. Even one of y—that is, even a child could operate this machine!"

He poked at the keypad. An image of a cartoon penguin appeared briefly on an individual display before the central seat, peering at them with big eyes as if surprised. The big screens produced four displays of feeds from vidcams dotted around the craft.

"Here they come," Domi murmured as a party of sec men in blue helmets trotted toward the ramp with machine pistols at port arms. The blasters were a design unfamiliar to Kane, although they seemed derived from the old Karl Gustav—not that different in profile from his own Sin Eater, but bigger and bulkier.

"Can you lock the damn door?" he demanded. He didn't relish the thought of a firefight in here, even though yet another sec man and a hybrid had clearly lost an earlier brief encounter and been rolled to the side of the compartment, out of the way. Kane didn't think even Tyree could swat bad-guy bullets out of the air, and neither could Kane.

"Better!" Ben announced. He moved a cursor bar flashing down a menu on his screen, stabbed a button.

Multiple muted thunks echoed through the craft below and behind them. Kane jerked in his chair and craned left and right, as if he could actually see anything that way. "What? What's going on?"

Seat and deck rose beneath him with a gentle, insistent pressure. It seemed to Kane the vast craft wobbled ever so slightly. War Boom Ben did something else, and the craft rose again briefly, then stopped. Again it swayed just a touch.

On the monitor showing the view from the starboard cam the sec men had stopped and were staring upward with their mouths black ovals in the wheat-colored ovals of their faces.

"Art," Ben murmured. "Just art. They use compressor-driven air jets for fine maneuvering and attitude control. Oh, that's brilliant."

"What the hell?" Kane demanded. "Is this thing antigravity?"

Ben turned him an only moderately condescending grin. "Oh, not at all, cobber, not at all. It's the low-tech answer—lighter than air."

Kane blinked and tried furiously to hammer the words into sensible shape on the anvil of his mind. Which seemed to have turned to cottage cheese. "You mean—" he began, not as if he actually had a clue what the tech boy might mean.

Ben nodded. "The tech told the truth—it's the blimp, Kane, it's the blimp! Or dirigible, I suppose, since it's hard-shelled and you can clearly steer it, after all."

"Don't worry," Jonny said, bending over Kane's shoulder from behind. "He's that way with everybody when the fit's upon him. Seething. Techno-shamans are like that, don't you know?"

Kane twisted in his chair and stared at the talker. The desire to ask what a techno-shaman might happen to be, or whether Jonny was pulling his leg, warred within him with a deep, deep desire never, ever to know.

Something thumped like hail on the windscreen. Kane jumped in his chair. "They're shooting at us again," Domi said. She had laid her rifle down and was fishing in her backpack, whose bottom she rested on the synthetic-covered floor. "Ah. Here we go. Want a fig?"

"Jesus! No."

"No worries," Tyree said. He walked up to the front of the compartment and rapped the windscreen with knobbly knuckles. "Polycarbonate. Whole bird's sheathed in it. Their small arms can go whistle, even if they bring up a fifty."

"What if they bring up something bigger?" Kane demanded. The bull boy shrugged and chuckled briefly.

"How about their hand lasers?" Domi asked.

"Doubt they'll do much to her," said the distracted tech boy. "Still, best not to tarry."

"All right, let's make like seagulls and get the flock out of here," Kane said. "I don't believe I said that."

He turned to Ben, starting out of his seat. "All right, Junior, jolly good show and all like that. Now hit the highway and let the pros handle it."

"I'm more than capable, Mr. Kane!"

"You a combat pilot, Sparky?" The boy's big-eyed blink told the tale. "All righty, then. Clear."

Domi tugged at his arm. "No, Kane. You're in no shape."

"Blow that. This kid's a wizard techno-whatever, but he's not a combat jock." Neither, strictly speaking, was Kane, whose customary role was to point and shoot while Grant the master Deathbird pilot drove. But Kane *could* pilot a bird. A chopper, anyway. And this thing had to be easier to fly than a chopper, since just about everything was.

Domi nodded. "Right. *I'll* drive."

Kane made fish motions with his mouth. War Boom Ben looked rebellious. Probably not out of prejudice against Domi's gender, but rather prejudice against letting the bone-in-nose savages fly the advanced air vehicle.

Jonny slapped him jovially on the shoulder. "Things're hotting up nicely, lad. We need you and Tyree to nip back smartly now and see if you can make play with the sting in our tail, right?"

Ben nodded and jumped out of his seat, probably inspired by the hot blood of pursuing new nerd prey rather than out of deference to his more-or-less nominal chief of mission. Domi was in the seat before he was fully upright.

Just to be sure Tyree urged Ben back out the hatch at the aft of the control cabin. "Weapons—" the tech boy called over his shoulder as he vanished.

"Got 'em now!" Domi called. "Menu driven, just like he said. Woo-hoo!"

"Mebbe you better figure what makes this sucker go, first? Anything this broad in the butt has *got* to be designed for flight over fight." He wondered how fast they could actually go. Although the craft had a fairly streamlined shape, it was so huge he'd be surprised if it topped out over a hundred-fifty klicks per hour. Two hundred max.

The big vessel began to pirouette. It reminded Kane of a scene in a cartoon he'd watched over Domi's shoulder in Cerberus a year or so ago—she ate that stuff up. It featured big unlikely looking cartoon hippos got up as ballerinas, dancing to some limp-wrist music.

"Actually, what I figure we need to get straight first," she said as the giant stressed-concrete clamshells swung into view, "is how to open the door."

A giant fist struck the side of the ship, jolting it sideways through the air.

Chapter 25

"What the hell was that?" Kane yelled. Padded as it was, his seat's port arm had added another bruise to the marvelous Technicolor collection over his ribs.

Jonny, who had stayed on his feet by grabbing the back of Kane's chair, pointed at one of the external-vid pickup displays. "Believe those blokes just fired a rocket of some sort."

Kane's eyes bulged. "Shit! An RPG. This thing can't be armored to stand up to shaped charges. Domi, open the door and get us clear!"

She shook her close-cropped head. Her brief white hair was spiky with sweat. "I can't, Kane. Nothing anywhere gives a clue how to do it."

He moaned loudly and slapped himself in the forehead. "Of course not! What am I thinking? We can't open the door. Flight control has to do it."

"I'll call and ask if you think it might do some good," Jonny said, "although not even I think quite that highly of my persuasive gifts."

"No, no," Domi said, frowning in concentration. More menu pages flashed by on the system display. Not as fast as for Ben, but respectably. "I got our key to every door, right—" she poked a button with a triumphant forefinger "—here!" A finned sausage shape appeared on a display.

"What the glowing nuke shit's a Maverick?" Kane demanded, squinting at the legend beneath it.

"Air-to-surface missile," Domi said. "AGM-65G Maverick, if you read the rest of it. Electro-optical and infrared real-time operator guidance and a three-hundred-pound delayed-fuse penetrator warhead."

"Sounds delightful. So what?"

"So this." Domi mouse-clicked. Another display lit up with a black-and-white image of giant concrete clamshell doors. They looked familiar somehow. Except they had a big white crosshair glowing over them.

Kane felt some kind of vibration beneath his feet as if mechanical things were going on inside the giant aircraft. The picture of the missile suddenly lit up with a red border. The words "Missile Armed" flashed on the screen.

His hair stood on end. "You're not—"

A line of white smoke spurted out in front of the giant black delta and struck right in the middle of the clamshell door. A beat, and then white smoke erupted back at them with a yellow-white sun glaring through the midst of it.

"See?" Domi said brightly. "Nothing to it—"

The shock wave hit them. The monster ship's nose was pushed up and the craft wallowed backward. Kane cringed as the cavern roof approached the control cabin's clear top. The craft's wide flat tail struck the wall with an impact that jolted Kane back against his seat. The nose pitched up farther and the top of the craft struck the cavern roof. Light fixtures shattered, drooling white sparks across the canopy.

"Bloody hell," a voice spilled aggrievedly from the intercom speakers. "Warn a body before you do tricks next time!"

"Sorry," Domi said.

The craft settled back to level, still wallowing. Kane felt

his stomach rebel. This was more like being on a boat on water than in an aircraft.

"You won't mind if I take a seat?" Jonny Corroboree asked, slipping into the last free command chair.

"Knock yourself out," Domi said distractedly.

"What I'm hoping to avoid, really."

Ahead of them the smoke had begun to clear. The great clamshell doors were visible again.

"Still there, dammit," Kane said. He checked the displays. Nothing was lit red, which had to mean nothing major was broken. In the external hull views no sec men were to be seen. Apparently the explosion and the ensuing crash, low-speed as it was, had convinced everybody to seek cover for the moment.

"Can't last," Kane said aloud. "Domi, get us out of here. But try not to do it by bashing us ass-backward all the way back to the palace."

"I'm on it like evil on a Magistrate, Kane." Her hands worked the keyboard. Joysticks popped up out of the arms of the magic command chair. Domi grasped one, did something. Another slight vibration thrilled through the frame of the giant ship, and a thin whine came to Kane's ears. The big craft moved slowly forward and down with only a bit of hair-raising screeching as it ground against things getting clear of the cavern wall and ceiling.

"Computer holds her pretty steady if nothing too radical happens," Domi said. She was leaning forward, frowning in concentration, eyes flicking among displays. Kane had to admit she really did seem to be in control of the huge aircraft, more so with every second.

The whole inside of the cavern lit a hellish green. Thunder crashed, barely muted by the hull. Kane jumped. "Christ! Now what?"

Horrid screams came from the intercom. Then Kane realized they were whoops of triumph. "We have achieved a teal-green death beam!" Tyree crowed.

"Yeah!" Ben crowed.

Another screen lit up with the two aborigines' faces crowding into frame. They seemed slightly distorted, as by a fisheye lens. "We can fire the laser from back here," the bull boy said. "Vaporized a squad fixing to shoot some manner of manpack missile at us."

"You can control it from up there, too, actually," Ben said.

"So you can give us all the breathing room we need while we figure out how to blow this joint?" Kane asked.

The two men's expressions changed. "Not exactly," Tyree said.

"The power system's rudimentary," War Boom Ben declared. "Takes time for the capacitors to recharge."

"Capacitors?" Kane asked Jonny.

"Batteries."

An alarm went off. Kane looked around wildly and then realized it was another missile-armed alert; he'd heard nothing at all the first time. Probably sensory overload.

Domi launched. This time she kept the craft moving at a walking pace against the back blast. Kane wasn't thrilled when chunks of debris bounced off the canopy right before their faces. But it held without apparent damage.

"Bloody hell!" Jonny exclaimed when the white swirling smoke cleared enough to reveal the blast doors still there. He looked sheepishly around at the other two.

"Sorry," he said.

"Cracked!" Domi sang out. "Okay, hang on. Third time's the charm."

She launched a third Maverick. The bunker-buster missile

exploded in another white-and-orange fireball and instant billow of smoke. The big delta craft plunged right on in.

Kane felt his fingers digging into the arms of his seat as he waited for the crunching impact. Instead there were many impacts, thumping, grinding. The huge craft shook, and for a terrible instant stuck.

The engines' whine rose to a squeal as Domi throttled up. The craft shook again and then pushed through, with an even louder squealing of the polymer fuselage against jagged concrete. A vast section of the door gave way and fell away around them as they pushed through into a green-and-pink-and-orange dawn sky.

Kane and Jonny whooped and pounded the arms of their chairs as the craft seemed to leap free of the last restraining grip of the shattered doors.

"What?" Domi demanded. "Don't tell me you're surprised?"

A few red indicator lights blinked or glowed. Domi gave them a quick glance, then did something else with an on-screen menu, quickly skimmed the resulting page. "Lost some outside sensors," she said. "Nothing that's going to make us explode."

Kane glanced at the hull pickups, all of which seemed to be functioning. He did a double take. "Domi, can you bank this thing right?"

"Hang on," she said. The big craft rolled. Kane realized it was deliberate enough in its maneuvers it would be hard to overcontrol. And not having to worry about keeping the wings—or a spinning rotor, just another kind of wing—providing lift took a lot of stress out of flying, even down here in the weeds. Then again, the delta ship was slow, logy and made a great big black blotch in the sky for something that was supposed to be stealthy. So there were clearly trade-offs here.

But bank Domi did. The planet rolled beneath them. The craft began to turn right, as well as roll, confirming Kane's surmise that the ship was a lifting body—one giant wing.

"Bloody hell," Jonny breathed.

Below them ranks and ranks of boxy vehicles were parked beneath camou nets. In the dawn twilight they were dark and indistinct. But Kane recognized them instantly.

"Sandcats!" he exclaimed. "Dozens of the suckers!"

"How'd they get here?" Domi demanded.

"This bastard sure isn't a fighter plane, and I don't think it's a bomber, either," Kane said. "Even though it's armed, I'm betting it's a cargo bird."

He frowned. "But wouldn't it take months to haul all these wags over here from North America—or wherever they came from?"

"Dunno," Domi said. "What say we burn up some more missiles and see how many these things we can smoke, huh, Kane?"

"Sounds fine to me—"

A green flash reflected off the dull upper surfaces of the baronial-service APCs. "We just destroyed some kind of missile launched from the hill we just exited," Tyree reported.

"Crap!" Domi said. "Forgot to turn on threat sensors!" She flipped through on-screen menus again, made hurried choices.

A variety of tones, beeps and flashing displays commenced to produce a cacophony of bad news. "We're illuminated by radar," she said, reading a helpful display.

"We're supposed to be stealthy, dammit!"

"Know triple nothing 'bout radar. Guess being close and big has something to do with," Domi said imperturbably. "The computer also seems to think various rocket electronics are warming up. And, um—"

Suddenly the craft skidded left and bounced high into the air. A brilliant red line bisected the sky at an angle, out the window to starboard.

"Energy-beam weps. Double good this baby's got strong maneuvering thrusters, huh?"

"What's with all the air defenses?" Kane demanded. "Who's going to attack from the sky, Sea Dayaks?"

"From Sri Goldshtayn's narrative it seems the god-king or his predecessors had a falling-out with your North American barons," Jonny said.

"They not the only ones," Domi said.

"Perhaps the Dewa Raja feared attack from the nine baronies?"

"Could be," Kane said. "Forget strafing, Domi, and start herding this pig along as fast as you can. We'll just have to hope they can keep missing somehow till we mosey out of range."

She flashed him a quick red glance. "What makes you say that, 'mosey'?"

"Look, this is a blimp, a dirigible, a gasbag, right? Stands to reason it's slow as—"

She moved the left-hand throttle forward. Way forward. And the back of Kane's seat began to press against his back. The engine sounds got louder and louder.

"Good show," Tyree said from the aft bubble. "Spoiled the tracking solution for that laser cannon of theirs."

Domi had the aircraft level. Even the distant hills visible out the canopy, turned buttery orange by the red eye of the sun peering between slats of slate-hued clouds out over the sea, seemed to be rushing by awfully fast. And acceleration was still driving Kane back into his seat.

"Domi, what's our airspeed?"

"Five hundred knots and rising, it says. Whatever knots are."

"Miles per hour on steroids." He blinked. "Shit! How is this possible?"

She shook her head. "Didn't build. Just drive."

A moment later War Boom Ben burst into the cockpit, although that didn't seem the right term for such spacious accommodations. His eyes were wild and his ball cap was jammed on his head backward.

"Jonny! May I?" He gestured at the seat the talker occupied. His manner suggested a schoolboy needing to pee.

"If Domi won't do any loops or barrel rolls for a while?"

"Not up to me. Nobody else shoots at us, then no."

Jonny got up. The tech boy slid into his seat and began punching keys.

"Who's going to shoot at us," Kane asked, "the Tanimbar air force?"

"They've obviously got one, mate," Jonny observed. "We're riding in part of it."

Kane grunted.

"Wizard!" Ben exclaimed. "You people aren't as ignor— I mean, they've got it figured out."

"Had," Kane said, a bit grimly. "This bird probably dates back before skydark. Figured out what?"

"How to eliminate boundary-layer turbulence! The whole ship's surrounded by an electromagnetic field, you see. Keeps the airflow from breaking up and creating drag. Cuts friction down to practically nil."

"Which means…?"

"We can go supersonic! We'll be back at Uluru in an hour or two."

"If we can just figure out where Australia is—all due respect and everything," Kane said.

Domi and Ben looked at each other and grinned. Ben played his keypad.

A map appeared on one of the screens up front. It showed a sickle-shaped mass helpfully labeled Tanimbar Island. Below it was a complex curve labeled Australia. A little yellow flashing arrow was pointing northeast into the ocean from the vicinity of where Kane judged Tanimbar City to lie.

"I should've known it could do that," he muttered.

"This is so cool," Domi commented. She banked the craft gently to head them in the proper direction to reach their goal without circumnavigating Earth. Kane let the air sigh out of him and subsided into his chair. He felt a vast expanse of weariness open like a chasm beneath him.

But he wasn't ready to give in yet. There were questions to ask. The trickiest was which one to ask first?

"What holds us up?"

"Beg pardon?" War Boom Ben asked. He was surfing the help menus again. At the rate he was going, give him another five minutes and he'd know more about the damn airplane than the men who built it.

"In the air. Why do we fly? Lifting body shape doesn't make us float."

"Oh. Helium, Mr. Kane. Most of this bird's empty space, you see. All filled with helium. Divided up into many small compartments, though, so it won't all go whooshing out when there's a leak."

"Helium."

"Oh, yes. Clearly your designers were trying to emulate the hybrids' antigravity devices on the cheap. So they created a whacking great lighter-than-air craft. A lifting-body zeppelin."

"But blimps, dirigibles, they're slow. We studied some about them in flight training. Why can we go fast?"

The tech boy rapped the side of his seat with his knuckles. "Lightweight synthetics," he said. "Bones and skin of the aircraft. She's like a bird, Mr. Kane—mostly air. Or, as I said, in this case helium. Because she's rigid and hard-skinned—and because the EM field cuts out air friction—she can move along at quite a pretty clip."

"I see. One thing?"

"Yes, Mr. Kane?"

"Don't call me Mr. Kane."

He looked at Jonny. "Something's not right here. They must've been using this craft to shuttle Sandcats here for the invasion. How much can this thing carry, Ben?"

The tech boy keyed in a query. "One hundred tonnes, the specs claim. Don't know if that might not be a hair optimistic, but one never knows."

"Whoa. So they wouldn't even need many trips to bring the war wags here. Nor get them to Australia, comes to that."

He brightened. "But we've put a crimp in that plan, anyway."

"I hate to be the vulture at the feast, mate," Jonny said from behind Kane's chair. "But they might have another craft like this one. And there's the *Varuna*."

"The god-king's giant-ass gilded barge," Kane said. "What about it?"

"As we indicated when we passed it in the harbor, she's not what she seems," the talker said. "She is in fact a hydrofoil cargo ship. She could carry a number of those vehicles and crews for them across to northern Oz in a matter of hours herself."

Kane sank down in his seat. "This just keeps getting better and better. Well, we have something concrete to report now, anyway. Looks like the god-king's big recruitment drive is just a scam to cover up the real invasion."

"Mebbe not," Domi said. Kane cocked a brow at her.

"They want to conquer and hold a foothold in Australia, I bet. So they need bodies. Ones with swords and spears do fine for most purposes. Come to that, why not use bowmen and swordsmen and all like that for the actual attack? Pack 'em in the Cats for cannon fodder, back 'em up with some bad boys with blasters, and the heavy blasters on the wags themselves. Plus, hey, they can train up some of the locals to shoot auto-blasters. Not that hard—point and click, bang-bang-bang."

Kane blew a long breath out between pursed lips. His beard was getting bushy and he felt as if it should have turned white by now. "So instead of a nice leisurely sailing voyage to invade Australia with a bunch of infantry waving garden tools, the god-king is getting ready to hit the beach with a mechanized battalion. Can your people resist?"

Jonny and Ben exchanged looks. "We will," the talker said, and his smile was conspicuous by its absence. "But it'll do small good. We have few firearms. Most of our weapons are war booms and spears and the like, frankly not as effective as theirs."

"What about your beam weps?" Domi asked.

"Don't have enough to do much good yet," Ben said. "Can't turn 'em out too quick. Even though we borrowed enough parts from North America and elsewhere to put together a few machine shops of our own. And part of the knowledge we've lost consists of how to make better ones quicker. Ones that don't take so much out of the man who shoots them, for one thing."

A moment of silence ensued, pierced only by the muted engine sounds. The antiturbulence field apparently eliminated or greatly reduced wind noise, as well.

"No help for it," Jonny said, shaking his head. "Our mates in North America have to find the turtle soon and return it to Lilga. Or it's a long dark night ahead for us all."

"Look on the bright side," Kane said. "We have their super-high-speed low-drag stealth cargo blimp. It's got weps if nothing else. We're almost home free, and once we link back up with your Old Man and Lakesh, we can work out some scheme to slow the invaders down a bit."

The craft shuddered once. "The aircraft has just entered supersonic regime," a feminine voice announced from the air.

"Cool," Domi said. "It talks."

"When should we raise Uluru?" Jonny asked.

"The craft seems to like a cruising speed around a thousand knots," Domi said, consulting her screens. "That makes it—"

She looked up as an oblong cursor appeared on a big screen, white with crosshairs and emulating the display on her individual monitor, then moved down and left to the middle of the mass of Australia. Landmark names glowed alive in yellow as the cursor came near them, predark villes such as Darwin and Katherine. Alice Springs appeared near the center, then the McConnell Ranges; Domi shifted the cursor down and left until Ayers Rock sprang up. She centered the cursor on that and clicked. It disappeared, and the legend "Ayers Rock" turned white and commenced to blink.

"How'd you know where Uluru was?" Kane asked.

"I made Brigid show me on a map after we got back."

"Cruising speed attained, one thousand knots," the recorded computer voice said. Domi clicked more buttons. "Initiating autopilot. Destination, Ayers Rock. Estimated time of arrival, fifty-eight minutes and twenty-three seconds."

"Outstanding," Jonny said.

"Yeah." Kane let himself sprawl in the seat and laced his fingers behind his head. "As for me, I intend to celebrate the success of our hair-raising escape by taking a nice nap."

Though he was so fatigued he was sick to his stomach and

his head felt like a lead balloon, he found himself unable to do more than doze fitfully for ten or fifteen minutes. Domi, on the other hand, had curled up in her chair and conked right out; she now lay on her right side, snoring softly and drooling onto the back of her hand. She looked adorable, even to the hardened Kane.

"Beg pardon, gents, lady," Tyree's voice said from the cockpit speaker. "But we seem to be being pursued by a flying saucer."

Chapter 26

The sea below was giving way to yellow beach fringing sere brown land. They had reached the Australian coast.

Kane kicked the side of Domi's chair. "Wake the rad-blast up, Domi. Damn scout disk is chasing us!"

Domi snapped upright, clutching for her hands-on throttle and stick controls. The great black skycraft seemed to bounce left and upward. A ruby lance sliced across the sky to starboard of them.

"What made you dodge?" Kane asked Domi.

"Instinct." She adjusted the angle of the aft-mounted vidcam. In a moment its display showed a characteristic silver disk, apparently hanging in space behind them.

"Tyree," Kane said urgently, "mebbe you could shoot back?"

"Have done," the Bull Boy said tersely. "Dead-centered the bastard, too. No joy."

"Is it time to start figuring out where they stow stuff like parachutes and inflatable life rafts in this thing?" Kane asked. "Presuming they do, of course."

"Might not be necessary, Kane," Tyree said.

"If you've got good news, don't keep it to yourself."

"We can jerry-rig Ben's neutron-beam weapon to draw upon the laser's power supply. That might put the disk out of commission."

"You can do that with a hand wep? Won't it overload?"

"After one shot," the bull boy said. "So we'll need to make it count."

Kane became aware of someone standing beside his chair. He jumped in his seat and his head spun around. His Sin Eater slapped his hand.

It was an old aborigine man with short white hair and beard. A very old seeming man. Indeed, it was—

"Old Man!" Jonny Corroboree exclaimed. He and War Boom Ben gushed forth greetings in their ancient tongue.

After a polite nod in the direction of the four staring eyes possessed by Kane and Domi, the ancient spoke quickly and quietly to his compatriots.

"You drive," Kane reminded Domi.

"Thing's just hanging back," she said, turning her attention to the screen. She began to make the giant craft swerve and juke across the sky.

Ben the tech boy took off down the passageway at a gangling run. Old Man turned back to Kane, who had let his hand-blaster go back in its holster, smiled politely, nodded and disappeared.

"What the hell?" Kane demanded.

"We draw near Old Man," Jonny the talker said. "His power here is great enough to project his likeness."

Another line of coherent ruby brilliance split the sky directly overhead.

"How can they miss us?" Kane wanted to know. "We're Earth's fattest target." He observed on the display that they were also rapidly bleeding airspeed as Domi maneuvered—a necessary concomitant. Indeed, even the huge airship would become remarkably more maneuverable as it dropped below supersonic, and after all it wasn't as if they had a prayer of outrunning the disk craft.

"Probably not trying to hit us, Kane," Domi said. "Want to force us down."

"Oh." Kane turned to Jonny. "Are we close enough so Old Man can use his mystic juju to flash-blast the saucer?"

Jonny shrugged.

The huge aircraft began dancing all over the sky: left, right, up, down, porpoising, wallowing around the central axis. "How the hell are you doing that, Domi?" Kane demanded, hanging on to the padded arms of his seat.

"Not," she said succinctly. "Found preprogrammed evasive routine for computer pilot. File name 'Last Ditch.'"

"That's encouraging," Kane gritted.

He was used to going into aerial battle with his destiny—his own personal black-clad Magistrate ass—in another's hands. He couldn't help but grin at what Grant would make of putting it that way. But it was true: over the years and many missions into the very heart of darkness, Outlands style, Grant had flown the Deathbird and Kane had been a passenger. Aircraft commander, granted—able to shoot at the bad guys, sure. But all that stood between Kane and a grease fire smoldering down in the weeds was Grant's wizard skill and intuition as a Deathbird jock.

As avid a driver as she was, Domi was not in Grant's class piloting a fat delta airship. But then, who alive would be? There would be only so much Grant could do if they had him here.

We could, you know, a voice said in his skull. If we could just sweet-talk the aborigines into having the far walker with his bunch bring him here to take over…

He dismissed the thought. Not even Grant aided by the flight-control computer would have an appreciably better chance of pulling them through a dogfight with a scout saucer than Domi's inspired madness—inspired by her well-honed instinct for survival. The aborigines, moreover, had made it abundantly clear they could, or anyway would, risk no more far walkers on this endeavor. Looking at it with brutal door-busting Mag objectivity, Kane knew perfectly well that as far as this group's mission went, it was accomplished; their continued survival, from a mission standpoint, was purely optional.

Besides, no point both Grant and I going up in a column of black smoke in the middle of the Aussie desert.

The canopy lit again with ruby reflection, with that weird distinctive clarity and keenness that denoted coherent light. A warning buzzer began to rasp like an amplified cicada.

"We got problems?" Kane demanded.

Domi was flashing through the screens again, almost as fast as one of their Australian companions. "Yes and no."

"What the hell kind of answer's that?"

"Thermal sensors show they just scorched some polycarb skin off the port wing upper surface, 'bout midway between tip and centerline. No real harm, not even much increased drag."

"Then what's with the 'yes, problem' bit?"

Domi gritted her teeth. "Shut *up,* Kane, and let me fly!"

"Perhaps the young lady means," Jonny said with his diplomacy potted to the max, "they didn't miss."

Kane rounded on him. He was getting furious now—could feel himself about to snap into rage. Fatigue and sustained abuse had sapped his self-control. He hated the fact, which didn't make it any easier to keep from teeing off on the smiling aborigine. Most of what held him back was the necessity of climbing over Domi to get at him.

Jonny plucked a button from his bush jacket and flicked it at Kane. It bounced off Kane's ribs, still bare but for streaks of dried blood. Kane froze, looked down at himself, then back at the talker with utter astonishment.

"Easy, my friend," he said.

Kane drew in a deep, shuddering breath. The spasm was broken, the rage had evaporated. "You're good," he said.

"I am that, mate."

Another flash. The big craft moved sideways. It seemed in response to the hit, not the evasion routine. But lasers have no impact.

"Uh-oh," Domi said.

"What 'uh-oh'?" Kane demanded. "What does 'uh-oh' mean?"

"They holed one of our helium cells on the starboard wing. We're venting gas."

"They trying to destroy us or just force us down?"

"Mebbe don't care. Shut *up*."

This time Kane felt no anger at all. The pixie-ish albino woman was furiously busy despite the fact the computer was doing most of the flying and no doubt damage control. She was obviously going full-throttle herself, trying to find any edge she could to keep them going a little longer, a little closer to their goal. That they were still alive hinted loudly she was doing as well as humanly possible. Kane left her alone.

"Tyree, Ben, how are you coming back there?"

"We haven't forgotten our friends following behind," Tyree said, almost casually.

Flash. The seat fell away beneath Kane. His stomach seemed to jump into his throat.

"Shit!" Domi said. "Bad one. Put big gash in starboard wing, upper."

"We going down?" Kane asked with a calmness that surprised him. But the dirigible had already ceased its elevator-with-snapped-cable downward thrill ride.

"Not yet. But we've lost top-end speed and are losing buoyancy. They getting serious!"

Another flash. Another. The great vessel rocked as huge glowing holes were burned in its nonreflective black hide. It possessed, Kane guessed, self-sealing mechanisms in the gas cells, possibly even means to generate more gas, more lift. But he knew with cold surety that whatever means it had of repairing itself and keeping skyborne, Domi and the flight computer were already maxing them out.

Kane glanced at the ground down the vast black slope of the starboard wing. He could see one tear, wrenched his eyes away. The desert looked conspicuously closer.

He looked at the altimeter. They had been cruising at an altitude of ten miles, into the stratosphere—where the big ship just trucked along, since unlike a conventional aircraft, which relied on its wings for lift, there was no downside to the thinning air, and hence lessening resistance to their forward flight. But they had already lost half that. They were little more than sixteen thousand feet up now, and the altimeter readout was flickering too fast to read, all in distinctly the wrong direction.

"How much can she take?" he demanded. He was trying to ignore the brilliant red flashes now, even if he felt each one like a Shockstick to his scrotum.

"Triple buttload," Domi answered. "She triple big, triple strong. Problem is, they can dish that out—and more!"

Ruby glare filled the cockpit—

And instantly dimmed. The canopy's clear synthetic had darkened automatically to prevent laser blinding of the aircrew—a possibility for a beam that incredibly potent, even as reflected, scattered coherent light. The streak of darkness on the canopy faded; long before it was gone Kane could see the raw wound the laser had left in the fuselage right next to the control compartment, edges glowing yellow-hot like lava.

But the red glare seemed to have awakened a persistent echo within the cockpit. There were red lights flashing or shining everywhere across the displays, it seemed, and Kane became aware of a demonic chorus of audio alarms he had been tuning out.

"We losing it big time," Domi muttered through clenched teeth. "Ben, Tyree—"

"Almost got it, Domi!" Ben sang out in triumph. "Hold her up just a moment longer."

"Do what I can." The violence of the airship's maneuvering had steadily decreased since the silvery saucer started firing for effect against the fleeing dirigible. Now it was doing little more than a queasy wallow. "Lemme know when you ready, then haul ass. I give you five seconds to get clear, then boom, she goes!"

"Ahh…" Tyree drew out the syllable. "Right, lass."

Domi didn't react. But Kane looked sharply at the speaker.

"They're closing!" Ben hollered.

Kane's eyes flashed to the display showing the feed from the rear vid pickup. The scout disk looked twice as big as it did before.

"Going for the kill shot," he said in a voice whose calmness astonished him.

"Uluru!" a voice yelled from the intercom.

The screen washed out in a blaze of light. Kane flinched instinctively. But the little display could never pass enough power to emit sight-damaging light levels, even if it had been CRT rather than a plasma display. And of course there were cutouts in the system to prevent an energy overload burning the screen itself out.

The vast delta craft gave him plenty to flinch about. It was as if the devil's own iron-shod hoof had booted the mother ship right in her flat wide ass. The impact whiplashed the three in the cockpit. The immense craft bucked and skidded like a Sandcat on ice.

Domi squealed like a frightened horse as she fought the controls.

Fortunately, the airship still had positive buoyancy. Otherwise they would have died and that was that. It still wanted to stay up more than it wanted to plow a giant furrow in the red-brown dirt of Australia.

Barely.

The image returned to the screen as Domi restored a semblance of control to the airship's flight. The angle seemed slightly different. Kane guessed the first pickup had been knocked out and slack taken up automatically by another cam.

The silver disk had dwindled again, to almost the size it had been during most of the one-sided dogfight. But that wasn't all. It wobbled, like a wood chip on a windblown pond, and a great incandescent wound in its silver skin bled black-and-purple smoke.

A flash. Blue-white beams shot from the saucer ship's interior. Mirror shards peeled off the top of the disk and glittered away. The scout disk was yawing madly now, erupting smoke and jets of dazzling fire. It began a mad plunging, up and down, then reared abruptly back as three fresh explosions flashed from inside.

Then a white fireball simply consumed the craft. It turned into a comet of smoke and debris, the smoke first black, then white as it followed them a moment longer, then slowed.

Debris began to rain on the gray-green scrublands below.

Kane and Domi were leaning toward each other, hugging and pounding each other's backs, laughing and hollering like fools. Kane's cheeks were wet, and he didn't know for a fact all the tears came from Domi's ruby eyes.

"What about Tyree and Ben?" Jonny's gentle inquiry snapped them back to reality.

Domi didn't even have to touch her keyboard. The answer glowed on the displays.

"Gone," she said in a voice suddenly desolate.

"You mean radiation from the overload?" Jonny asked.

"I mean *gone*." She pressed more keys. A new graphic appeared, a three-dimensional schematic of the craft. A dozen breaches showed on the wide delta shape like strokes of a pen with luminous scarlet ink. But what snapped up the eye was a great red cup-shaped depression in the center of the airship's stern, like a bite taken out from between the driving ducts.

"Bastards in the saucer must've spotted Ben and Tyree aiming the sting wep at them," Kane rasped. His throat felt sandblasted. "They were closing to flash-blast the weapon bubble."

"They and our boys must have fired simultaneously," Jonny said in a wan, lost voice.

Domi gasped. "They never had a chance!"

Kane reached out to clasp her chalk-white hand gently in his big, sun-darkened, scarred one.

"They never meant to," he said quietly. "All along they intended to shoot the overload beam the microsecond it was ready."

He looked out at the landscape, now seemingly about to climb into the cabin with them. "Thank God they did."

She came half out of her seat to cling to him and sob.

DOMI RECOVERED rapidly enough to resume the nerve-grinding task of trying to shepherd the big craft to Uluru. Inexorably it lost both altitude and airspeed. Yet there were tiny advantages to be seen and seized: Domi found out the craft's sensors could somehow detect thermals ahead, and the warm-air upwellings fountaining invisibly against the vast matte-black underside of the craft actually pushed it back up into the sky, a few hundred feet's grace gained each time.

But it was a fight she and the valiant ship were bound to lose. The real question was whether they could keep from hitting the planet too far from Uluru to survive a trek across the desert. Jonny Corroboree still retained the desert-survival skills of the personality born into his current body—indeed, attuned to Tjukurpa as he was, all seventy-five thousand years of skills, with some gaps, or so Kane guessed. But he knew *he* wasn't up for a long hot wilderness hike in his present condition. And who knew what shape they'd be in after what he strove optimistically to think of as their landing?

When the McConnells rose before them they were clearly below the tops of the peaks. The mountains loomed like a blue-gray stone wall as they grew closer, seemingly impenetrable.

The flight computer, it seemed, had terrain-following skills, and Domi had a few of her own, if born mostly of sheer desperation. She quickly discovered that the altitude jets could be used to counteract the Gs of lift that tried to push them into a turn in even a vertical bank between cliffs, so that she could whip the thing on edge to pass through a space that would have shattered it otherwise, without veering into one of the very unyielding stone masses she sought to avoid. The mother ship's positive buoyancy, dwindling though it still steadily was, kept them from dropping as precipitously as a conventional craft does when banked ninety degrees, with no lift opposing gravity's steady pull.

So Domi and the flight computer together threw the giant machine through maneuvers that threatened to turn Kane's stomach inside out at the same time they threatened his very sanity. The lighter-than-air craft, huge and mortally injured though she was, could perform stunts that would have meant instant blazing death in a heavier-than-air machine, fixed or rotary wing. And so, seesawing left and right and somehow even squeezing a few extra inches of altitude from rising air masses near obstacles that rose in their path, they came safely through the mountains.

Sitting—if that was the word; only his safety harness kept Kane from oozing into a puddle on the deck—in his seat, utterly spent, Kane became aware that the white on-screen circle that was their destination was bigger and brighter and pulsing more insistently.

Jonny snapped forward in his seat. "There!" he said, flinging out his arm to point ahead. "Uluru!"

Kane saw it, just a hump rising from the desert floor. "I see it," Domi said in a weary voice. She was slumped in the pilot's seat. The tension of the running fight and then the heart-stopping passage through the mountains had sucked the energy, practically the life from her slight body. She seemed barely more substantial than a ghost.

She adjusted the magnification on the display showing the view from ahead. The great rock halfway filled the screen. Its angled oblong mass had gone gray with the onset of early afternoon.

"My people," Jonny said, with almost tearful gratitude. There were structures of some sort visible near the base of the huge boulder.

"I'm going for it," Domi said, sitting up with renewed energy. "I think I can put us down almost at the foot of the damn rock—sorry, Jonny."

His smile was a shadow of its former self. "No worries, Domi."

"You think you can make it?" Kane asked. "If there's a tall goat in our path we'll knock him on his ass as it is."

"No goats, Kane. Australia, remember?"

"Kangaroo, then. Oh, and don't plow through the camp if you can help it."

She turned a wicked grin at him. "If I see Lakesh, can I steer for him?"

"That's affirmative."

IT SEEMED like forever before they actually reached Uluru. As with a helicopter, the mother ship depended little on airspeed to stay airborne. All the same, Kane felt the speed trickling away as if it were his own lifeblood leaking from his veins.

What *was* their lifeblood leaking away was altitude. Uluru was clearly visible out the windscreen now, getting visibly bigger. But even as it did the ground got nearer and nearer.

Kane kept waiting to feel the scrape of rock on the bottom of the hull. He tried not to tense in anticipation. It didn't help, and in a crash might get him hurt worse. Of course, there was no telling in this case whether relaxation on impact would make the stellar difference between triple chilled and merely double chilled....

"We're gonna make it. Yes!" Domi exulted.

"Steer away to port, Domi," he directed. "We're too close to the camp."

With an obedient hiss the attitude jets turned the airship's nose. But it took time for the drive jets pushing them in a new direction to overcome the inertia driving their substantial mass straight on the way they had been going. Kane actually forgot to worry about hitting the ground out of concern they would wipe out Jonny's people. The talker himself tactfully refrained from comment, but his rigid posture told the whole tale.

Then their true course shifted, at last, to clear the tents and stone structures. There was a good-sized ville, far more structures than Brigid, Domi and Shizuka had recounted seeing.

And then their broad black belly did kiss the desert.

A grinding scrape, just what Kane had been dreading to hear, thrilled right up his spine. Still slightly buoyant, the mother ship skipped off the earth like a stone.

"Oh, shit," Domi said almost matter-of-factly. She clearly hadn't been expecting that particular trick. The big swollen delta was nose up and soaring back into the sky, with both lifting-body shape and helium conspiring against their safe return to Earth.

Domi pressed buttons. The attitude blowers began to drive the big rounded nose back toward the planet. Then the hissing stopped.

"Damn," Domi said. "Compressors gone. Try angling the drive nozzles."

At her command the two-dimensional ducts vectored thrust downward, to drive the tail up and the nose down. Unfortunately, the dirigible, after trying for the last few hours to fall out of the sky, now stubbornly resisted returning to Earth.

"Puppy-fuck!" Domi exclaimed. "Dumping helium, dammit."

"Are you sure that's a good idea?" Kane and Jonny demanded in unison.

A great hissing filled the cockpit. "No," Domi said.

The airship began to descend. No—it began to fall.

"We land now," Domi said with a certain grim triumph, "one way or other."

Jonny turned to them. "Kane, Domi," he said, flashing his biggest, brightest smile, "it's been a pleasure."

"Likewise," Kane said.

"Me, too," Domi said.

They hit.

Chapter 27

The impact filled not just their ears but their bones and their being with a colossal grinding crunch. The craft rebounded yet again, but this time it did not glide far. The three occupants were thrown about like rag dolls in their seats, but their safety straps held. The mother ship's nose dropped right back down and it plowed once more into the ground.

Literally plowed: a great bow wave of tan soil was thrown up to either side. The friction braked them so quickly that they were thrown forward against their harness. So quickly that Kane dared hope.

"Looks like we're through the worst of it," he said to Jonny through a taut grin.

Then the underside of the dirigible's nose struck a buried sandstone shoal.

For a moment it seemed the titanic hurtling mass would stop dead. The breath was blasted out of Kane as he was shot against his harness like a bullet from a blaster. He felt metal straining and trying to shear in the clamps holding his padded seat in place.

With a glass-breaking shriek of tortured metal Jonny's couch broke free. At the same instant the dirigible's nose rode up and over the obstruction and the craft slid onward, grinding across the desert amid a cacophony of destruction.

Kane saw Jonny's seat slam into the windscreen. The whole view forward vanished behind a curtain of dark, dark red.

Then Kane's world went black.

HE OPENED his eyes to a sky that seemed to be half green, half purple. It was illuminated by a wan yellowish glare.

"Hell needs a new interior decorator," he croaked.

"My hopes for your full and prompt recovery soar," said a familiar voice from somewhere to the left of the pounding mass of ache that was his head. As differentiated from the giant insistent throb of pain that was his whole body. "That my excellent friend Kane greets his return to consciousness with a witticism."

It seemed as if Kane could feel every one of his prior incarnations. They all hurt, too.

"Lakesh," he croaked. "That settles it. If I'm chilled, this is Hell. But Domi missed the ville. So I must be alive."

He cranked his eyeballs left. It seemed that they actually ratcheted in their sockets.

Dr. Mohandas Lakesh Singh sat beside the pallet on which Kane lay in a folding wood-and-synthetic chair. The glow of the kerosene lantern danced yellow on his head. He held a tall glass of dark fluid in one hand, with ice in it no less, and a fur of condensation wrapping it. Beside him sat a familiar white-bearded form, grinning all over its seamed aborigine face.

"Where is Domi?" Kane asked.

"Here," a voice said on the other side of him. He turned his face that way, although his neck vertebrae all seemed to have spikes. Domi, clad in a man's blue chambray shirt faded nearly as white as her skin and, if Kane was any judge, nothing else, sat cross-legged on another thin mattress or pallet beside him. She cupped her own tall glass of iced beverage in both her tiny pale hands.

"Glad you made it." He became aware of chanting outside the tent. Aware that it was night. He forced his head back to the old men in their lawn chairs. "What about Jonny?"

Old Man's smile faded. He shook his white head slowly.

"Fuck." Kane turned his face back up toward the joining of unlikely colored panels directly overhead. His eyes stung. No doubt it was smoke drifting in from the fires outside.

"What the plague," he asked eventually, "is that you're drinking?"

"Iced tea," Old Man said. "A most delightful beverage of your world. Would you like some?"

"Ice? Where do hunter-gatherers get ice? In the middle of the desert?"

"As I suspect you've gathered, Kane," Lakesh said, "these people are not simple hunter-gatherers. Or at least, are no longer."

"Yeah. And the old dude sitting next to you seems to have 'em dancing like puppets on a string." He turned his head to glare at the two elders. "Just like us—ever since he snatched you."

Lakesh sighed theatrically. "My good friend Old Man has been forced to expedients he finds most distasteful," he said. "As we ourselves so frequently do—"

"'Distasteful'?" Kane echoed in outrage. "That's just not good enough. Son of a bitch has a lot to answer for."

He sprang. From somewhere—the raging depths of his anger—his abused body and limbs found strength to snap him upright. In a panther bound he was behind Old Man, wrapping a bare arm around his neck.

Around nothing.

Old Man still sat there, beaming beatifically. Kane's arm had clenched through his neck and against his own triceps.

"Oh, dear," Lakesh said as Kane tottered, fighting to find the balance that had abruptly deserted him, "have you not realized all we see of Old Man is a holographic projection?"

Kane toppled forward. Through the Old Man, over his chair and back into black.

"So you call to seek my assistance, Mother?"

Erica van Sloan sucked in her breath. The sibilance from the screen—which was white with a single, simple Chinese ideogram glowing upon it in red—was almost foreign to her. Yet somehow she recognized the voice of her son.

"Yes, Sam," she said measuredly.

"You admit to failure, yet again."

He is on the other side of the world, she told herself, forcing herself to aspirate slowly and evenly. I am here, in the midst of my stronghold, surrounded by fighters loyal to me. She knew that the possibility existed that none of that might matter in the slightest, yet she certainly had reason to believe her son's powers to be severely curtailed.

At least his more mystic powers. She was hoping, on the basis of something slightly more substantial than sheer wishfulness, that his temporal power might be greater than he had let on for a time.

"Please don't play games with me, Sam," she said, forcing a note of weary patience into her voice. "This is not properly my task. It isn't taking place in North America. Why won't you let me see you?"

"Because I choose not to," the voice said languidly. "You look well, Mother. It appears age has not caught up with you…as yet."

"You've played that card too often, Sam."

"Perhaps I have. Perhaps I have. The multiverse weighs heavily on my mind these days. I find it difficult sometimes to concentrate on the merely mundane. Not to mention tedious."

"The matter at hand is not precisely *mundane*," she snapped.

"Of course not. Why else would I consent to receive your call, Mother dearest? Do you know what the hour is here?"

"A little after ten in the morning. It's night here."

"Ah, so it is. I but toyed with you: in fact I had no notion of the hour, nor whether the sun stands in the sky above or not." A pause. "It is days since I have seen the sun."

"I need your help," she said flatly.

"Indeed you do. And I am to share in the prize?"

"You always were."

"I believe, should I decide to help you, my direct participation entitles me to a larger share. We shall speak of this later. Now, tell me, did you expect better from the ludicrous Thulia?"

"I expect nothing at all from that one. I sent him as a sop to the other barons, who'd prefer him dead. They think he's a fool. They're right, of course."

She ran a hand through her long, heavy, midnight-black hair. "I expected more from the strange baron-class hybrid who calls himself the god-king." And more, she would not admit, from Vladek. Although if the god-king's own sec chief and viceroy had betrayed them, perhaps in truth there was little her hand-picked Magistrate could have done. Which was why she had refrained from sending more Mags to haul him back in manacles.

And then again, she admitted to herself, if I destroy my Magistrates whenever the bastard Kane gets the better of them, I'll soon run out.

"His faction came off second-best in the civil war after unification," Sam said. "Yet the losers of that conflict have not done too badly for themselves…all things taken with all things. What is it you would have of me, Mother?"

She hesitated. "We lost the HAUL," she said.

"The Heavy Advanced Utility Lifter, yes," the unseen Sam said. "And something else, as well."

"The god-king's scout disk. As you obviously know. Somehow Kane and his savage friends pulled off the impossible again—the HAUL carried no weapons capable of bringing down a saucer."

"But your heavy lifter has served its purpose, has it not? Surely it transferred sufficient Sandcat AVFs from the North American baronies to disperse the primitives and seize the technological treasure they have stolen?"

"It transferred them to Tanimbar. The god-king wanted them all assembled there before staging to Australia. He feared if he tried transporting them piecemeal from North America to Australia directly the savages would find some way to interfere."

"He has gathered a mighty surface fleet."

"Junks and praus. One in one hundred, perhaps, with a working engine. *Varuna* cannot carry all the Sandcats at once, much less with crews and modern weapons for our shock troops. Meanwhile the savages must be getting closer to that which they seek. We dare not endure the delay of sailing the lot across to north Australia."

"And you think I can help you?" Amusement tinkled in the words. "If I could simply wave my hand and teleport them all to Australia, would I be rusticating here in the charming company of Qin Shihuang Di's jade-enshrouded mummy?"

"No," Erica said, quailing inside at the acid trip his tone had taken. At least her will had iron enough left in it to keep it from showing in her features or voice. She thought. "But I think you have…assets. Material assets. Which might be of great assistance."

"Why, Mother, dear," he said, in apparently genuine delight, "so you know about my Ekranoplans?"

FROM A SECRET subterranean base near Vladivostok, two craft set forth south across the Sea of Japan. As ungainly as they were unlikely in appearance, they would have been the largest conventional aircraft ever built, surpassing even Howard Hughes's infamous Spruce Goose in size and carrying capacity.

Had they been aircraft. But they could never fly. Their wings were stubs, ludicrously out of proportion to their vast-bellied bulk. Never large enough to lift them into the sky.

But enough to lift them twenty yards or so above the water's surface, riding in the dense ground-effect: like hovercraft, they were GEVs. More boat than airplane, capable of the speed of a four-engine cargo plane for a fraction of the fuel consumption. They had a great distance to travel, past the ruins of the Korean Peninsula and the Japanese Home Islands to the far South Seas. But most of their immense lifting capacity was currently devoted to fuel, ample fuel to carry them and their crews to their destination in a flight lasting nearly twenty-four hours.

From Tanimbar they would help *Varuna* shuttle the Dewa Raja's blitzkrieg battalion to northern Australia in the matter of another day or two. The bulk of his forces, some twenty thousand men armed with their more primitive weaponry, would follow at their leisure in the ragged surface fleet. Those troops would be sufficient to occupy the country and hunt down the remnants of the savages after the specially trained and armed shock troops and their Magistrate cadres, Sandcatborne, had scattered them and seized the secret of Uluru. Which had dared defy Erica van Sloan once, and would never be permitted to do so a second time.

Four of the bizarre not-quite-flying machines had been built. Two had survived somehow, and fallen into the possession of servants of Sam the imperator by secret, doubtful means.

They were the last of the Caspian Sea Monsters.

They were Ekranoplans.

Chapter 28

The Armbrust shuddered once, hard, on Domi's shoulder as it ejected the plastic reaction-mass out its fat flared rear. As plastic petals deployed from the countermass and eased it to earth, the antitank rocket's engine kicked in. The rocket accelerated noiselessly, flashlessly and almost smokelessly toward the rear of the Sandcat.

The Army of Retribution armored carrier exploded with a giant roar and gouts of yellow fire. The rear ramp of the armored wag fell open. Blazing figures staggered out, their waving arms like wings with flames for feathers.

The lead Sandcat, which had rolled on in advance of the little convoy to reconnoiter an obvious ambush point where the dry wash they followed passed between two outcrops of big green boulders, pivoted adroitly by reversing one set of tracks while rolling the other forward. It started to trundle back. The USMG-73 heavy machine gun set in its cupola, protected by the armaglass bubble, stuttered and flamed, seeking Domi's life.

Bullets whanged and keened off the gray-green rock below her position. As she turned to leap down to safety behind the ridge she saw a gusher of dust erupt from the mound of boulders to the Cat's right. Whether the tons of rock and rubble displaced by the blast, command-detonated by members of the aborigine ambush unit Domi led, crushed the wag or merely dropped in its path she didn't know. But the machine gun's deep-throated snarl ceased.

She heard blasterfire popping as she ran down the back slope, slipping on scree, snagged up a second Armbrust launcher by its strap. There was still a good deal of screaming going on, from the burning rifle squad from the wag she'd blasted or the freshly hurt.

She reached level ground, raced toward the ridge's abrupt trailing end. She hoped the half-repressed birth personalities of the small band she led currently dominated the recovered crew personae: the hunter-gatherer aborigines were masters of stealth and surprise. The crewfolk, space born, were not.

There was nothing wrong with their valor. That, so far as Domi was concerned, was their problem. She herself, with her true feral child's utter lack of a sense of fair play toward enemies, was a born guerrilla. And the first precept of every successful guerrilla throughout history was to run away. Guerrilla warfare, as she knew instinctively, was the recourse of the weak. Cowardice was the guerrilla's cardinal virtue.

She came around the butt of the rise from whose top she had blasted the rear-guard fighting wag. It still blazed enthusiastically. The men who had emerged from it now lay in smoldering heaps.

Men with blasters had leaped from the three remaining wags and begun to fire back from the ground. As Domi watched, several of her warriors stood along the top of the far ridge firing longblasters from the hip, of all things trying to get a better angle at the prone invaders. From an improvised hard point atop the long silver squashed-cylinder tank of the fuel wag a machine gun opened up. The three raiders were knocked down like bottles from a fence.

The god-king's goons had learned from the previous raids

she had planned and frequently led, Domi reflected. Or maybe they just watched an old *Road Warrior* vid.

She prepped the rocket launcher, knelt, shouldered it and aimed at the rear of the big bloated metal maggot glistening in the desert sun. It was late afternoon, so the convoy's sec men would have had all day to bake in the enervating north Australian early-summer heat and get tired and cranky and slow.

Although tens of thousands of aborigines were streaming toward Uluru from all over the landmass, many having recovered their crew identities or in process of doing so, they had pitifully few modern arms, and fewer still of the neutron-beam handblasters. Which the Sandcats were proof against anyway. Their traditional weps would chill a man as sure as a bullet or a blue bolt, sure, but range and firepower matter. The brutal fact was that for all that they greatly outnumbered the invaders, the aborigines stood no chance of contesting their advance.

Not in fair fights. Nor even by attacking their leading elements, although booby traps and ambushes did what they could to make them cautious and slow them. But the ambushes were proving as deadly to the teams who sprang them as to their ostensible victims. Which hadn't dented the aborigines' willingness to volunteer for them. To try and die.

Domi admired that. But wild child that she was she reserved her deepest regard for those who kicked the enemy where it hurt and got away clean to hurt them again.

Anyway, the invasion's armored spearhead was its least vulnerable part. Their weakness was their endlessly increasing supply train, dragging food, water, ammunition and most of all fuel across hundreds of desert klicks. That was their jugular.

Even with the aid of the painfully few far walkers Domi had no realistic hope of cutting it for any protracted period.

But she and her too-brave raiders could squeeze it. Slow the relentless, remorseless, resistless advance—for a time.

Whether that was worth the sacrifice depended on one thing only: did it buy enough time for Brigid and Grant's team to track down the elusive turtle and get it back to Lilga?

Domi got the big bright bug in the crosshairs of her simple optic sight. Its dorsal MG raked the slopes, sheer reconnaissance by fire; she knew none of her people hid there.

She pressed the trigger.

Motion caught the corner of her eye as a man in a black turban rose from the scrub not seven yards away, aiming a Kalashnikov at her. His beard split in a snag-toothed smile.

THE BALL ROLLED to bump to a stop against the toe of Kane's right boot. He stooped and picked it up. "Hi, Lilga," he said to the little girl in the gunnysack frock who was following it. "Hinting, are we?"

"I wondered if you might want to play with me today, Mr. Kane," she said with her bright, crisp kid enunciation. She was not at all shy.

He laughed and tossed her the ball. She caught it deftly, cupping her small toast-brown hands. "Yes, I would," he said, "later."

He strode on toward the command tent, where as always Old Man and Lakesh could be found, plotting and trying to one-up each other. Part of Kane looked forward to the coming interview: he had never encountered or even imagined someone who could get over on Lakesh as consistently as the aborigines' Eldest could. It drove Lakesh crazy to come out second in the omniscience derby—and, of course, he could never let on that he had. It was pure joy to watch.

One of the few in Kane's increasingly frustrated existence.

Passing Lilga, who now stood smiling cheerfully up at him, he paused to ruffle her mop of pale brown curls. She laughed. These were the happiest people he'd ever encountered—not that there'd been much competition where he'd grown up in the Enclaves of Cobaltville—and it was manifestly genuine; they maintained it, as he had seen, in the face of certain death. And Lilga seemed to have the sunniest disposition of all.

All the others who came in contact with her deferred to her. At least adults—children don't do deference well, even when sternly instructed to at least try to show respect. But even the other aborigine kids treated Lilga as if she were special. Yet she never acted as if she expected it; Kane had never seen her anything but friendly and happy.

It made him feel old and encrusted in scars thick as rhinoceros hide.

He ducked down and pushed aside the tent flap. A chill air blast caught him in the face. Old Man had some means of climate-controlling the interior, although Kane neither saw nor heard traces of a fan or compressor or anything else to account for it. For his part he refused to accord Old Man the satisfaction of asking, a habit he'd learned well dealing with Lakesh.

"Greetings, friend Kane," he heard as he straightened, allowing the flap to fall behind him and cut off the furnace blast of the late day outside. Only by the phantom Old Man's voice could Kane tell him and Lakesh apart. They talked pretty much alike. "I trust we find you well."

"My wounds have all healed up, yeah."

Pretending to sit in a chair, Old Man turned to Lakesh, who sat beside him at the folding camp table. "He chafes at what he perceives as his captivity. A mettlesome young man, Lakesh."

"He is indeed. Yet do not be tempted to underestimate him. He is at least occasionally capable of tempering his brashness and impetuous nature with keen insight."

"You sent for me," Kane said flatly. "Was there anything beyond watching you two polish up your comedy routine? Because if that's all, I can go back to doing something vital, like kicking over rocks around camp to see if any god-king's elite chill squads're hiding under them."

"It is not from caprice that we have urgently desired you to remain here," Old Man said. "We must remain alive to the possibility of a strike by our foes."

"Bullshit," Kane said. He was in truth intimidated by Old Man, a little scared of him—given what just the rank and file aborigines seemed capable of. It was no reason for Kane to defer to him: quite the opposite, in his mind. "Your tech boy geeks and girl far walkers have balls bigger than most coldhearts' heads. Your bull boys are more than capable of flashblasting any raid the Dewa Raja's likely to mount. Unless they hit us with an air strike, and so far we've seen no sign they even have Deathbirds, much less any more saucers."

"The logistics of maintaining helicopters in the desert, at the end of a supply chain half the circumference of Earth in length, likely prohibit our enemies' deploying them," lectured Lakesh. "They find sufficient difficulty keeping their surface transport mobile—thanks especially to the inspired efforts of our dear Domi."

"Yeah. She's white death and no mistake. I just don't see why I'm not out there lending a hand."

"Well, in truth, it was Dr. Lakesh who insisted on keeping you close—"

Lakesh's purloined blue eyes shot a quick dagger his colleague's way from behind the thick lenses of his spectacles.

But his mouth and voice smiled indefatigably as he said, "Your time for action may have come, friend Kane."

Kane arched a skeptical brow and crossed arms over his chest. He wore whipcord pants and an off-white linen shirt, with the sleeves rolled up and his Sin Eater strapped to his arm. "Oh, so?"

"Despite your friend Domi's truly impressive skills," Old Man said, "and despite the efforts of our fighters to slow them, the invaders draw near Uluru. They have almost won through the Tanami Desert. We now must move the bulk of our people south to the shelter of the Musgrave Ranges."

Kane grunted. The camp population had swelled enormously in just the week or so he and Domi had been here. Over a hundred thousand aborigines, he guessed, had to be gathered in the shadow of the great rock that was the symbolic heart of their people—and apparently more, from what Brigid and the other women had experienced, and from the invaders' stone determination to seize it.

To say they traveled light was an understatement. They came naked or nearly so, bearing nothing personal but a few spears and knives and blasters. Mostly they carried food and water. As Kane understood it, the aborigines had little attachment to physical possessions. And whatever they had possessed before now belonged to a life they were leaving behind.

One way or another, he thought grimly.

"Won't be easy, moving that many people."

Old Man chuckled. "They moved here readily enough, despite hardship. We are hardy folk, well adjusted to our environment."

"I know. You've had long enough to adapt. What about Grant and Baptiste, their team?"

Lakesh and the elder exchanged glances. "Dear Brigid believes they are closing in upon the turtle."

"With all due respect, Baptiste's felt that way before."

"Just so. But Rita, their far walker, believes they have adjusted their thought patterns properly so that the turtle will now seek to be found, instead of seeking to remain concealed."

"It's got in the habit of hiding," Old Man said, "just like the rest of us. Amazing how set one gets in one's ways after just a few hundred centuries."

IN ONE FLASH Domi resigned herself to death. She triggered the antitank rocket launcher. It spit its counterweight out the back, and its deadly missile whispered away toward its target.

A whirling darkness struck the back of the blaster's turbaned head. His eyes rolled up in his dark face. He fell forward, discharging a burst not into Domi's unprotected flesh but into the ground at his feet.

The tanker truck turned into a miniature yellow sun. Domi dived back around the curve of the ridge as flame ballooned toward her.

An instant later a wiry aborigine youth tumbled down next to her. The flames didn't reach so far, but dragon's breath eddied around the rock to caress them, reeking of burning petroleum, and their ears popped as the dynamic overpressure rolled past them.

The young warrior, dressed in a camou shirt and loincloth, grinned at her in triumph. The name he used was a crew name, with rising-falling tones like Chinese and phonemes Domi couldn't even fit her mind around, much less try to pronounce. He answered to Rig, an abbreviation of sorts.

"So much for them," he declared. For some unknowable reason he spoke with an American accent—which was to say, no accent Domi could detect.

She grinned and they exchanged high fives.

"C'mon," she said. "Help me hunt up our survivors and far walk our fannies out of here. It's time for the 'run away and live to fight again another day' part."

KANE'S GRAY EYES, narrowed, flicked from one to the other. "What really scares me," he said, "is that I don't think you old guys are trying to be funny."

He sighed and let his arms drop. "What do you want me to do?"

"Keep the invaders from Uluru as long as possible," Old Man said. He wasn't smiling now. "The rest of our people will go to a hidden camp in the mountains, where Yindi awaits."

Although Kane had rested up from his traumatic time in Tanimbar—he'd had little else to do, other than rest and fret, with both Old Man and Lakesh insisting he stick close to camp—he suddenly felt infinite weariness flood into him.

"What do I have to fight with?"

"You will have ten thousand fighters to assist you."

"How many blasters?"

"Not quite two thousand. Our ammunition stocks are ample."

"Blue bolters?"

"Fewer than a hundred."

Kane shook his head.

"Understand, please, we do not expect you to win," Lakesh said.

"We won't."

"You must delay them as long as you can, Kane," Lakesh said. "All hangs upon it. More than, I daresay, you can imagine."

Old Man leaned forward. His seamed face seemed contoured into a very stylized mask of caring and concern. Kane figured it was a shuck.

"Mr. Kane, please allow me to level with you."

"If I can stand the novelty."

"By now your *anam-chara*—your soul friend—Brigid Baptiste has told you that our people do not spring from this Earth's past, but from its far distant future."

Kane nodded warily. "Yeah. Another little detail you forgot to mention up front."

"Kane, please understand," Lakesh said earnestly, "our friends felt grave concern about loading us down with too much detail—"

Kane silenced him with a wave of his hand. "Yeah, I know all about their worry that if they told us too much truth, it'd make our savage little heads explode. Go on, Old Man."

"You have heard how our fleet was destroyed in a great space battle against a potent force—a force that we can only call evil. A great, grave evil. We fled seventy-five thousand years into your past—and hundreds of thousands of years into our own—to escape, and then concealed ourselves in such a way as to leave all but no trace of our once and future existence because nothing less had a chance to succeed."

"And here you let us think it was the Annunaki who whipped you."

Old Man nodded. "We did. But remember the legend which Yindi, whom you have yet to meet, showed your friends. Some of the serpent folk were friendly to us, some unfriendly. Like all that was revealed to Brigid Baptiste and Domi and Shizuka, that was true, even if not the totality of the truth. Which, of course, would take far more than a single human lifetime to convey, in fairness to us and our selectivity with it."

His smile returned. But briefly. "The Annunaki are not the evil we fled, nor are the Tuatha de Danaan, nor the Formori, nor any of the alien races who have visited Earth in your past. Nor yet the Archons, who sprang of the union of Annunaki and Danaan, nor the hybrids they engendered with you humans. With *us,* I should say."

"You're not human," Kane snapped. "I'd have to be triple stupe not to be aware of that."

Old Man smiled. "But I am Old Man, the eldest of my people. You may believe, friend Kane, that the entirety of my existence has been devoted single-mindedly—and joyously, permit me to add—to serving and preserving them.

"Our primary concern has been to keep ourselves from the awareness of these races. Our deepest desire has been to slip away unnoticed. But the earlier invasion of our sacred mountain by Erica van Sloan and Baron Beausoleil and their men rendered that impossible—made it imperative we get away as quickly as possible, without further regard for stealth. Yet as I say, none of them is the evil that defeated us—will defeat us, our younger incarnations. Which destroyed our fleet and dispersed our folk. Yet there is some connection, which not even I can fully ascertain. And there is a force abroad in this world today that may indeed bear some more intimate relation to that evil."

"Those Chinese sec men, in the underground hangar in Tanimbar," Kane said quickly, his head snapping up on his neck. "Sam. The imperator."

Old Man nodded slowly.

Kane squinted. "You mean *he* evolved—evolves—into this cosmic evil? A hundred thousand years in the future?"

"I do not know what role Sam may play in the evil's coming into being and ripening to maturity," Old Man said. "It may indeed be none. He may simply partake of similar evil, be touched and tainted with it. I tell you honestly, I do not know."

Kane sighed. "I don't have much reason to believe you. But I can't see it matters one way or another at this point."

"You do not lack wisdom, as my esteemed friend Dr. La-kesh has divined. But one thing to keep in mind is that we crewfolk are not the only ones who can move backward and forward through time. As well through the various alternate realities you have characterized as casements."

"Thanks for sharing that information with me," Kane said, "since there's nothing on Earth or in Hell I can do about it."

"Ah, but there is—win time for your friends to bring back the turtle."

"And that's going to help? What is it, some kind of dou-ble-super-wonder-wep to chill all the bad guys?"

"Much more than that." Old Man's face split into a vast beaming smile. "Oh, much more. If we get it back, all will at once be made well, Kane, my dear young friend."

Kane's eyes went pale and narrowed to slits. "That doesn't mean it's going to enable you to just cruise away from Earth in this mystery starship of yours and leave us to eat lots of death?"

"I assure you it does not," Old Man said.

"Believe him, Kane," Lakesh said.

"Yeah. You're both so trustworthy." He sighed. "Oh, well. Not like I've got anything better to do."

He wheeled, started to walk out.

"It's a suicide mission, you know," he said from the tent flap.

Lakesh met his gaze squarely. "Yes, Kane my beloved friend," he said, "it is a suicide mission. Yet if our friends do not return the Mackenzie Turtle to us before the god-king and his minions enter Uluru, believe me if you believe nothing else I ever say—those who fall quickly in battle, futile as their deaths may be, will be the lucky ones. Lucky beyond imagining."

Chapter 29

The *Varuna* and the strange stub-winged flying craft had shut-tled the North American Sandcats and their crews, mostly lo-cals crash-trained by Magistrate cadre, to Australia in a matter of a day or so. Then they had continued their trips: old soft-skinned wags, all of which surviving in the islands belonged to the god-king by proclamation; supplies; sword-and-spear cannon fodder. Eventually both Ekranoplans had been at-tacked by suicide-commandos far walked into them, one crip-pled, the other destroyed crossing the Arafura Sea between Tanimbar and Oz.

There had never been many far walkers among the crew. And while self-teleporting saboteurs and assassins were un-stoppable, they simply could not do enough damage to jus-tify the loss of their wild talents. Even if they eliminated the god-king—and incidentally Thulia, whom the Dewa Raja kept always near him, not that any players in the game ap-peared to consider him anything but incidental—it would not stop the invasion. Erica van Sloan and the remaining barons in North America would press the attack with redoubled fury.

Indeed even the far walkers might not be unstoppable. Passing by the rear of their tent one day, Kane had overheard Lakesh and Old Man muttering together. Details escaped him, but he caught the distinct impression a small team sent to blow up Erica van Sloan in her chambers in the Cobaltville Monolith had simply vanished tracelessly. Sam's powers had been sharply circumscribed since his failure to seize control of North America and the world, but apparently still enabled him to take particular care of his mother.

In turn Kane had wondered why, if Sam could interfere with *that* jump, he hadn't done more to actively counter the aborigines? Kane decided that he had too little evidence and less understanding. Old Man was obviously a major hoodoo in his own right, with abilities to dwarf the scary powers Yindi let Baptiste and the other women see. Who knew what esoteric battles might be being waged beyond human perception?

Whoever did, Kane reckoned, he'd be the last man on Earth to join them.

He never doubted Old Man and his people were doing everything in their power to resist. But Domi's far walking logistics raids were no more than pinpricks, and the invaders butchered out of hand any aborigines they encountered.

Whether they fought back or not was immaterial.

"BIT OF A BOTHER, what?" said Billy Handsome in a mild voice. It sounded muffled emerging from within his helmet.

It was nighttime in what had been the American Southwest. The stars gleamed bright and seemed close in the high desert air. The six of them, four aborigines plus Grant and Brigid, stood in their bulky rad suits on a concrete-bordered island of sere dead soil with a buckled blacktop parking lot before them and a wide, much-buckled street behind them, gazing at the mostly collapsed Maxwell Museum of Anthropology in Albuquerque.

The talker glanced down at the rad counter in his hand and shook his head. "Not a place to tarry, even in these suits."

"At least we are not likely to need to fight our way in or out," Brigid said.

"Don't count on it," Grant said.

The museum looked as if, none too recently, some large and intensely heavy object had landed on it from great height. At one point it had been a long low box in the usual Southwestern Pueblo-emulating style, rising to two stories back away and to the left of the six. Now it was sort of dented in, just north of center along its long axis. Whatever had done the damage—presumably during the nukecaust—had vanished.

Leaving aside the lethal levels of gamma and neutron emissions, it was a pleasant autumn evening. From the brush that had reclaimed the rubble of houses to the west a pack of coyotes yipped to each other as the moon rose above Sandia Peak.

The explorers' own breathing echoed inside their polycarb rad-suit helmets. Grant and Brigid wore shadow suits beneath; the aborigines had declined them. Supposedly shadow armor was proof against radiation. Neither North American was inclined to trust that to any great extent, and both were unashamedly glad when they saw the actual rad levels here. Evidently core fissiles from a fusion bomb, targeted probably against a main warhead storage facility in what had been the northern extremity of the city, now a vast green-glass crater, had condensed out of vapor and drifted seriously right across this patch of the planet.

I'm just happy to have the shadow armor, as well as the rad suit, Brigid thought.

The ground beneath their sealed boots, which though tan soil, appeared to have the consistency of concrete, vibrated. "Tremor," Grant said, more in disgust in alarm. "All we fucking need."

"The earth-shakers awakened a great deal of latent seismic activity in this part of the continent," Brigid said. She was aware, painfully so, that she spoke just to be saying something.

"Nothing for it," Billy said. "Let's go on in."

"Not all of us," Grant said. "Leave Brigid out. And Rita. Come to that, mebbe just Nobby and I should go in."

The talker shook his head, still smiling, but sadly. "Sorry, mate, we can't quite do that. Rita's best to find where the turtle's actually hiding, since she can sense it."

The walker nodded her helmet. "I feel it now," she said. "It's eager to awaken. Just trembling on the edge now. But it can't cross over by itself."

Grant looked at her. "If you say so," he said without irony.

"Nobby's not necessary at all—items like the turtle aren't his pidgin, so to speak. As for Bush Baby Bob—"

"I go," the few-spoken bull boy said mulishly. "I'm expendable."

"Now, that's no way to talk, cobber."

Brigid sighed and set her shoulders. "Kane and your people are in grave danger. Immediate danger. None of us is going to stay outside while our friends face death. Let's just quit debating and all go in."

Grant looked even grimmer than usual but said no more. The entrance on the building's south end had been blocked by the collapse of a multistory concrete structure across the narrow walkway. Whatever had fallen on the Maxwell had left a gaping rent in the side nearest the party. Grant and Bush Baby Bob led the way to it and stooped to peer inside.

Grant carried a large plastic hand lantern that gave wider illumination than the Nighthawk microlights. He carried a Copperhead in his other gauntleted hand. It wasn't a personal blaster the way a Sin Eater was, just a blaster from the armory. He wouldn't mind parting with it if it got contaminated with radioactive—and intensely toxic—heavy metal particles.

He poked the blaster's muzzle brake into the building in

advance of his head and shone in the light. Inside appeared to be an office, with a desk and a skeletal swivel chair lying on its side, half turned to rust on the floor. Its cushion padding had desiccated and crumbled to dust.

Bush Baby Bob pushed inside. He held a lantern of his own and a Franchi SPAS riot gun, each one-handed. Frowning unhappily, Grant followed. Stooping and high-stepping, the rest followed.

Half the room and the hallway beyond stood open to the sky above. Grant and Bob moved on into the corridor. The second floor had fallen into the ground floor at an angle, blocking the hall to their right.

"Whoa," Grant said. "What a mess."

"This way." Rita nodded her head left. "I feel it." Her eyes shone behind her faceplate. "Don't you?"

She moved out in front and went that way. With misgivings—for she was their ticket out of here, but more importantly, she was the key to the whole mission, saving the earth and, just maybe, Kane—they let her lead, and followed warily, casting their eyes and their light beams from side to side.

The corridor turned right. With unspeaking unity of mind Grant and Bush Baby Bob shoved forward to make sure it was safe to go around, then let Rita resume the lead.

The walls shook around them. Dust drifted down from the ceiling, which was here intact and even sported a weird random almost-checkerboard of acoustic tiles and gaps. They heard the creaks and cracks of structural shifts—structural failures. Small. For now.

"Damn," Grant said softly.

"It is as if there is something that does not want us to find the turtle," Brigid said. "Something very powerful."

Grant turned his head to squint at her. "You're joking, right?"

"You feel it, too?" Rita asked without turning her head.

She came to a gape on their right where the door had been. She gestured inside. "*Here.* It is here."

Brigid shouldered past Grant and the bull boy to stare into the room. It was mostly blocked by collapsed ceiling. And more—the second floor had partly come down here. Looking up, she could see stars, and a crazy-angled block of structure that seemed to be bouncing up and down as if still in motion from the earlier tremblers.

"Must have sucked a handful of plutonium dust down right into here," Grant said. "Rad meter's going bugfuck. Even in these suits, anybody in there longer than five minutes might as well just stay with the rest of the exhibits. 'Cause they're history!"

The earth commenced to spasm like a giant in convulsions. The straining beams that held the remnant of the second floor from obliterating the turtle's resting place began to crack with gunshot sounds.

THE BATTLE WAS OVER. At least eight thousand aborigine warriors lay in the desert staring up at the first stars to appear in a sky befouled with smoke and dust. An ashy pallor had fallen over Uluru, at whose base their slayers had encamped. Behind it the day died in fire and blood: just another casualty of the charnel house.

A pavilion had been erected in the midst of camp, a great gaudy tent of some synthetic that was silk to the eye but that repelled soil and stain. Within the god-king toasted victory with Vladek and Thulia in air-conditioned comfort and pale wine.

The Dewa Raja's beautiful but immobile face reflected only serenity. Not so his guests'. A dozen hooded ones tittered to one another with heads together. Vladek, the coarse black hair gone from the back of his head to show a rough ellipse of scalp scorched angry pink, stood in a fresh black uniform, almost vibrating from the thrill of spilling blood. He was too exalted to sit—which was good, since sitting was none too comfortable for him, and wouldn't be for a while yet. His quick action had preserved himself and Thulia from the full effects of the frag and incen grens the intruders had left on the witch woman's corpse. But not all—the fireball that consumed the sec men in the torture chamber had caught him from behind.

"I still don't see, Your Majesty," Thulia said, interrupting himself to sneeze, "why we don't send a party to secure the caverns at once."

He had barely wet his pointy pale tongue in the wine. He couldn't taste anything. The tent's refrigerated air aggravated the sinus condition brought on by the abominable dryness of this abominable land.

"Is our victory then not sufficient for your pleasure, cousin?" asked the god-king in his strange compound voice.

"He just wants out of this wasteland as quick as possible," Vladek said. "I don't blame him."

"Cultivate patience," the god-king commanded airily. "The secrets that lie within have waited millennia. They will wait until the morning. Our troops are tired. It might render them clumsy. We can afford to have nothing damaged."

"That accursed apekin bitch van Sloan and Baron Beausoleil thought they had the rock secured," Thulia pointed out. Too late he realized he might have spoken a little too candidly with one of Erica van Sloan's sworn minions in his presence. Vladek was a frighteningly powerful and thrustful man, whose streak of violence ran wide and near the surface even for an ape-man. Yet he only snorted and quaffed wine. Thul-

ia felt a fresh stab of grievance like an ice pick in the belly—
how little regard he has for me, an over-being, a baron!

"Yet they were repulsed, driven out in the end," he forced
himself to finish.

"Let them bring their flesh-eating bats," Vladek said, sneering. "Our radar-aimed machine cannon will rip them in pieces
the way we did the savages themselves."

"Their magic has failed in the face of superior force and
will," the god-king said. "The matter is as simple as that."

Outside a shot cracked. Harsh cries of alarm followed,
then a hailstorm of blasterfire. Thulia cringed in terror as an
explosion thundered right outside the god-king's pavilion.
Blue light flashed, a lancelike line so bright it was clearly visible through the fabric of the tent.

"What's this?" Baron Thulia screamed. "What's going on?"

Vladek formed a fist of his left hand. His Sin Eater purred
into it. "Bastards committing suicide," he said. "Simple as that."

Chapter 30

With victors' arrogance—if not baronial arrogance—the invaders had made a small oversight selecting the location of their command pavilion. A narrow gully snaked through the encampment. It passed within thirty yards of the tent's left rear corner.

From the arroyo's nearest approach rose eleven men: ten surviving aborigines, two of them tech boys armed with the rare neutron handblasters, and Kane. Through the treacherous late twilight they stole toward the back of the tent. It was a good time for a sneak attack: the human eye had not yet fully adjusted to the absence of sunlight, and in the dimness the human body naturally tended toward a relaxed, less than wholly attentive state.

But hundreds of men were awake and moving all around, and the tent was well guarded by the god-king's sec men, armed with both swords and blasters, who knew well the price of anything less than total vigilance when guarding their master's person. A black-turbaned Mag loomed up abruptly from the gloom, walking toward the gully—probably for a quick leak—too far from any raider to be quickly silenced. Kane shot him once through the center of the forehead with his Sin Eater, then lobbed a gren toward the tent.

It struck a sec man hurrying around the corner in the face and exploded, obliterating the upper half of him in a searing yellow-white flash. The night awoke around them with answering flashes like fireflies on jolt, the muzzle flames of dozens of blasters firing on the infiltrators at once.

The firing was exuberant, the more so since the bulk of it was done by men who had never handled an actual blaster until weeks or days before. What was really happening was that the startled soldiers were shooting in all directions from the midst of their own camp. Far more bullets smacked home in the flesh of their own fellows than found intruders.

Inevitably some struck the pavilion, as well. Kane loosed a triburst from his own Sin Eater as he slogged toward the big tent at the greatest speed his full-body armor permitted, just as a blue-bolt flared and crashed from behind him. A wag blew up in an orange flash followed by shrieks as occupants spilled out as torches.

Kane himself felt a nut-shot of despair as he watched the tent-side flex in response to his triburst, then clearly shed the bullets without holes appearing: bullet-resistant fabric. Well, this way I'll know the fuckers're dead, he told himself.

A bull boy matching him stride for stride, firing an M-16 from either hand, grunted and tumbled into a rolling confusion of dust and rag-doll limbs as a machine-gun burst raked them. The bullets clattered against Kane's polycarbonate hard-contact suit, staggering him but failing to penetrate.

Shedding bullets, Kane reached the tent, ran around to the front, replacing the box in his Sin Eater's magazine well. One of the Dewa Raja's guards met him coming out the flap. The sec man hacked at Kane's head. Kane blocked the cut with an upflung forearm. Steel clacked on polycarbonate.

As he jammed the sword cut, Kane let his handblaster snap back into his forearm holster; he'd need all the bullets in the mag and more in just a moment, with little prospect of a chance to reload. Then he drove his right fist into the black-clad man's gut.

The turbaned god-king sec man bent slightly at the middle as breath oofed out of him. Then he straightened. The inertia of his undercoat of mail had absorbed Kane's punch.

He grinned triumphantly until Kane imploded his face for him with a forward smash of his polycarbonate-clad elbow.

Kane threw the faceless man from his path. From a wallaby-hide pouch slung around his waist he grabbed a handful of microgrens, armed them quickly. His suicide squad's few survivors were fighting to keep the invaders converging on the god-king's tent off his back. They couldn't possibly buy him more than a fistful of seconds.

Hopefully that's all I'll need.

He stuck his arm into the tent flap and scattered four of the little gleaming globes of death.

He turned, then, Sin Eater slapping his hand and blazing instantly into life. Charging enemies were bowled over howling as bullets stormed through their vitals and smashed their limbs.

Behind him he heard a ripple of thuds. Prepping another tiny gren with his left hand, keeping the Sin Eater in his right, he pushed inside the command tent.

Right away he saw the god-king standing at the pavilion's rear. His inhumanly beautiful face was as immobile as an ice sculpture, set in a look of amused disdain. Before him a phalanx of hooded ones pointed infrasound wands at Kane. Between him and them were a gaggle of the black-uniformed coldhearts, some standing, some writhing from absorbing the brunt of the microgren blasts—and some not moving at all. Vladek and Baron Thulia stood beside the god-king.

Vladek raised his Sin Eater and fired a triburst over the hooded ones' hoods and right between ranks of sec men up front, showing how much he cared about risk to his comrades. All three metal-jacketed bullets slammed the breastplate right over Kane's heart. The impacts clacked his teeth together and drove him back a step. He had no clear shot at the Dewa Raja, so he lobbed his ready microgren at the perfect golden head.

Vladek reached up and batted it down. It bounced off the back of a hybrid's cowl and dropped right between Vladek's feet and the god-king's, bringing them both inside its radius of lethal effect.

Vladek grabbed Baron Thulia by a shoulder and pitched him facedown on top of the gleaming sphere.

"Nooo!" the baron shrilled.

The gren went off. Its blast was muffled in flesh. The baron's frail body rose a foot into the air on a cushion of silver-white glare.

His right arm flew away trailing scarlet strings to bounce off the tent wall.

Kane blasted his Sin Eater full-auto at the god-king. Vladek, unarmored for the victory celebration, ducked behind the sec men and hybrids standing before him, drawing the foreign baron down with him.

The hooded ones opened fire with their wands. Caught between invisible beams and equally invisible bullets, the human guards could only scream, dance and die.

Kane's Sin Eater ran dry. He smashed it across the bearded face of a still standing sec man. The Mag roared and fell back a step. Then the right side of his body seemed to quiver, and compound balloons of blood and shreds of flesh erupted out of him as several infrasound beams struck him at once.

An infrasound beam brushed the side of Kane's helmet. It felt like fabric ripping in his brain; his tooth roots stung, and fat yellow spots danced behind his eyes. He lunged forward, smashing a hard-shelled fist down on a hooded head, feeling the thin, outsized hybrid skull pop like a great egg. With a whistling scream of despair the hybrid died.

More beams struck him. The armor prevented them from taking direct effect on his body. But the vibrations they passed punished him like spiked fists. He staggered, the wind driven from his lungs, vision swimming in red, as chunks of tough synthetic began to be blasted from his armor. He drove himself forward by the sheer force of his hate: One more step, another after that, and I'll feel the god-king's windpipe collapse beneath my fingers.

After that he didn't care.

A black shape hurtled toward him. Before Kane could react, the bull-rushing Vladek tackled him around the middle and slammed him onto his back.

"ENOUGH!"

His voice all but drowning the rising thunder of the earthquake and the building coming down about their ears, Bush Baby Bob tossed Grant from his path as if the big ex-Mag were a child and charged into the room. Rita screamed at him to stop. He ignored her.

Brigid tried to control her terror as fist-sized shards of ossified acoustic tile clattered down on the top of her rad-suit helmet. The fear of the silent, hideous death of rad exposure warred with fear of being entombed alive. She managed to hold on—barely.

An overstressed wooden beam broke. A section of the upper story fell with it, perhaps a ton driving it like a jagged-tipped lance against the bull boy's side. Brigid heard ribs shatter even above the grinding tumult.

Bob half spun. The huge mass drove down and past him.

The raw end tore open the whole side of his rad suit, exposing a shirt already sodden black with blood.

Rita tried to lunge in to the bull boy's aid. Grant picked himself up in time to seize her arm in an iron grip. "If you get chilled, he dies in vain!" he roared.

The walker glared fury at him, then melted weeping into his arms. Nobby pushed past them, into the still clear part of the room right by the door.

"Watch yourself, mate!" Billy Handsome called. Behind his faceplate was a mask of agony; there was nothing he could do right now for his friends, for his people, but watch and wait.

"Got it!" Bush Baby Bob bellowed in triumph. "I've got it—got the turtle."

He reappeared, staggering, through a swirl of dust. He stretched out his left hand, pressed something into Nobby's gloved palm.

With a rending squeal the whole upper floor fell in.

HALF-MAD WITH PAIN, half-blind, half-deaf, Kane lashed out with armored forearms that were still lethal weapons. But Vladek had him in the classic mount position, thighs around hips, pinned. It was a simple matter for the big Cobaltville Mag to get his palms on Kane's biceps and use his full weight to drive his arms down.

Not all of the human guards had been taken out. Three jumped forward in response to the god-king's shrilled command to secure the now helpless Kane. Leering down in triumph beneath his one black brow, his scar pulsating crimson against his pale face, Vladek swung off Kane and stood, dusting his hands off against each other.

Kane's Mag helmet with its slightly concave red visor was wrenched cruelly from his head. A strap cut his left ear across.

He was lifted half-upright, then dragged before the Dewa Raja with his armored toes scraping the exquisite Bokhara carpet.

"Kneel before the majesty of the god-king, dog!" snarled a sec man in thickly accented English. Kane was rammed down on his knees.

Blood-matted hair hung in his eyes. Although his head weighed a ton he made it swing side to side to shift the hair away. He blinked; his vision cleared somewhat. Then he raised his face to stare at the Dewa Raja.

The hybrid stood gazing down on him with huge blue eyes. He appeared as much some exotic bird as human, and the wispy crest of bright yellow hair crowning his high pale scalp only reinforced the effect.

"Mr. Kane," he said, his voice eerie music, "you have caused much trouble to my kind. I admit I have small reason to love my North American cousins, who drove me forth decades ago. Yet the natural order must be preserved, as even you must certainly admit. Animals who rise against their masters must be destroyed. And the survivors of the nine might find the supremacy my seizing Uluru and its secrets confers upon me an easier pill to swallow if I send them your head as a sweetener."

The fatigue of failure was overcoming even Kane's vanadium-steel will. His head slumped. A big hand, hairs like coarse black threads stark against its pallid skin, grabbed his chin and forced his face back up, nails gouging jaw and cheek.

"Manners, Kane," Vladek said in ripe, gloating tones. "Have you degenerated so far that you've forgotten a Magistrate always shows respect to his betters?"

"Show me one," Kane slurred, "and I'll respect the fuck out of him. But not this bug-eyed taint!"

He barely felt the backhand blow that torqued his head around on his neck so savagely his cervical vertebrae squealed against each other and red sparks shot up through the back of his skull. He let his head roll over and around and cocked an eye at Vladek, who had struck him.

"And I'm not a Magistrate any longer, you worthless piece of shit."

"Enough!" piped the Dewa Raja. "If your object is to annoy me sufficiently to spare you a lingering death, Mr. Kane, you have succeeded. Senior Magistrate Vladek, blow out this renegade's brains!"

"It's way too good for him," Vladek said, holding up his left hand and forming it into a half-open fist. "But it'll be my pleasure, God-King."

His Sin Eater appeared in his hand. He lowered it deliberately toward Kane's face, running his swollen pallid maggot of a tongue over his fleshy lips in anticipation.

Then to Kane it was as if everything shimmered: him, the air, the world. Then his eyes were dazzled by intolerably bright flashes of light, and reports drove like ice picks through his eardrums into his brain, and he went blind and deaf and out.

Chapter 31

Air. Cool, sweet air, caressing his face like a lover's fingers.

"I'm alive," he said in a hoarse whisper. The words went like razors up his throat. "Shit."

"You're welcome, Kane."

He made his eyes open, although his eyelids were puffed and glazed with drying blood as if he'd just gone fifteen rounds with a champion heavyweight boxer and lost every one. The rest of him felt that way, too. Except the parts that felt worse.

A wide dark shadow rose against a starry sky. By the flickering glow of a nearby campfire he made out a familiar longjawed face, mouth framed by long mustache and set into a permanent-seeming scowl. "Grant?"

"Last time I checked."

"Water," Kane croaked. "I'm dry as rad bones."

The fall of a soft bare foot on soft earth, the sense of a small presence. Kane looked around to see Lilga hunkering beside him, proffering a pottery jug. Without ceremony she tipped it and sloshed cool, clean water into his open mouth.

He heard fizzing inside his skull as the cells of his dehydrated tongue absorbed water. Nodding the girl thanks, he took the jug, shoved himself into a seated position. He turned his head and spit the remnants of the first mouthful of water into the dirt, then glugged greedily from the wide mouth of the earthenware vessel.

He coughed, shook his head, then held up the jug and poured water over his face. Shaking his head again and blowing, he became aware of the sound of chanting. The cool, astringent smells of conifers and the sweetness of moist earth.

"Mountains," he said. "We're in the mountains. The camp?"

Grant nodded slowly. "All together again."

Kane was struck from two sides simultaneously, forcing the air from his chest like a bellows. He made a croaking noise at the agony in his ribs.

He became aware of women in stereo. "Domi?" he said wonderingly. "Baptiste?"

The latter detached herself and stood back from him briskly. "Good to have you back alive, Kane."

"Doesn't feel that way." He gently detached Domi, who was pressing too tight upon his ribs, which seemed to have been replaced with scythe blades.

"Thanks to the heroism of friend Grant and the lovely and gifted Rita, you might just survive to see another dawn, my dear boy," said an all too familiar voice. "Thanks to the sacrifice of Bush Baby Bob, we all might get to."

"Lakesh," Kane said. He turned his head to see an unearthly figure. The somewhat spindly doctor was naked but for a loincloth, body and face daubed with swirls of coarse red-and-yellow paint. Beside him stood a sturdy middle-aged man and the inevitable Old Man, each similarly decorated.

"You must be Yindi," he said to the middle-aged man.

The other nodded. "Welcome, Mr. Kane."

Kane tried to stand, couldn't. Grant reached down and hauled him to his feet. He swayed. Instantly Domi and Brigid were back at his sides, holding him up.

"Easy," he said briskly. "I think I'm broken." He realized

he was wearing only a pair of sweatpants. The cool mountain breeze soothed his tortured skin.

"Nothing serious," Grant said. "Your hard-contact suit sucked up most of what the wands dealt out. You look like you been used to hammer railroad spikes, though."

"Petechiae," Lakesh said. "Capillaries ruptured just below your skin. Blooming bruises, akin to the symptoms of low-level irradiation. They will fade in a few days."

Kane looked at him again. "You're naked and covered in paint," he said. "Why?"

"Not precisely naked, my boy, as you can plainly see. Old Man and the excellent Yindi are allowing me to take part in the grand corroboree in progress."

"Funeral rites for the human race, huh?" Kane said. Bitterness welled up within him with such force his vision literally blackened for a moment.

"You're fused," Domi said from under his left armpit. "Talking crazy. We *won*."

"Bullshit. We were slaughtered." He shook his head. "Why aren't I dead, by the way? Didn't Vladek blow my brains out, just like the god-king told him to?"

"Rita far-walked in with Grant just as Vladek was about to pull the trigger on you," Brigid said. Her voice had an edge to it, a sign of emotion that even her tungsten self-control couldn't entirely suppress. "Grant dropped flash-bang stun grenades, then grabbed you and they jumped right back out."

"So that's what the sound-and-light show was. Not Vladek evacuating my skull. I don't suppose you got a chance to drop off a few handfuls of microgrens on your way out?"

Grant shook his head. "Negative. Weren't going to use real bombs going in so we wouldn't chill ourselves, not to mention you. And we had to get you out as close to instantly as possible or die a lot, which would've obviated the whole damn exercise. Place was full of coldhearts."

Evidently more invaders had rushed to the god-king's aid. But Grant's words confirmed Kane's worst fears: the god-king still lived, as for that matter did Vladek. Not that Vladek meant shit, but it rankled Kane's ass that the maggot would live to celebrate victory. Except—

"Domi said we won," Kane said. He pushed the two women aside so he could stand alone, as gently as he could, which wasn't very. Neither took exception. "What did she mean?"

Yindi held out a broad hand. Its palm was covered by a smooth rounded shape that seemed to gleam green and gold in the firelight.

"The Mackenzie Turtle," he said in his deep sonorous voice. "Our friends recovered it from the heart of a cataclysm. One of ours was lost."

Kane felt his knees start to buckle, caught himself, held out his hands to forestall a fresh attempt to support him. "I'm sorry," he said. "I'm sorry for Mary Alice and Tyree and War Boom Ben. I'm sorry for the ten thousand good men who got butchered like animals today." Tears ran freely down his bearded cheeks. He made no attempt to check them.

"As are we all," Yindi said. "It is why we dance—we dance their spirits back into the Dreamtime."

"You got the turtle." Kane accepted the artifact from the shaman. It was cool, hard and as smooth as glass. Strangely pleasing to the touch, and after a moment he became aware it seemed to be pulsing gently in his palm. Or maybe that was his heartbeat he felt.

"This is it?" he demanded. "All this suffering and dying over a chunk of carved—what is it?"

"Malachite," Brigid said. "A basic carbonate of copper."

"That's still a rock, right?"

Baptiste's green eyes flicked to Lakesh. "A mineral. But, yes."

"It is not what it is made of," Old Man said with a gleam in his eye, "but how what it is made of is *arranged.* The information encoded in its very crystalline structure. And the power."

"The power?" Kane asked stupidly. "Is it a weapon?"

"Oh, no, Mr. Kane."

Kane tossed it rudely back to Yindi. "Then begging your three wise men's pardons," he said, "I don't see it means glowing nukeshit. Because the god-king is camped all around Uluru with a fucking mechanized army, and without some kind of hellacious damn superwep there they will stay until they have done whatever it is you were all so hot and bothered for fear they would do."

Old Man smiled. "Just because the Mackenzie Turtle is not a weapon," he said, "does not mean it is not the instrumentality that will undo our enemies. Now, if you please, my friends, come along. The ceremony is about to begin."

IT WAS A GREAT BOWL amid tree-clad peaks, shadow-shapes against the stars. In the very middle of it a space perhaps thirty yards across lay clear, and in the midst of that two fires blazed high. Otherwise, the valley was full of people, tens of thousands of them, sitting and chanting softly.

A great knee of rock jutted from a mountainside into the cleared space. Upon its bald end perched the folk from Cerberus. With them sat Billy Handsome, Nobby the tech boy and Rita, the sole survivors of the teams who had accompanied them on their quests.

Grant was looking around with something like unease.

"Lot of people here," he commented sotto voce. "And I see campfires all down the valleys that run away from this place."

Sitting cross-legged between him and a silent Brigid, Kane nodded. "There's got to be hundreds of thousands of them. More have been arriving all the time—but most were waiting for us when we hiked in from Uluru, and they looked to have been here for a while."

Brigid raised her head and looked at them. "Why, that would mean—"

"This is the main camp. The people around Uluru were bait. The aborigines *wanted* the invaders to go there."

Billy the talker turned a smiling, handsome face toward him. "Most perceptive, mate. Our ways aren't yours, and our agenda isn't, either, and we're right sorry for any worries that's caused. But we told you straight—our aims and yours are in harmony. So just wait and watch. And whatever you do, please don't try to interfere in what goes on. For your sake, and ours, and the future of humanity."

"That's an encouraging build-up," Grant said.

Into the circle stepped Lilga. She looked tiny in her ragged smock, very much the young child she was, yet she strode confidently as any queen, to stand with her head held high and her heavy locks spilling down her shoulders, waiting.

A flat-topped hump of rock perhaps half a yard high rose from the ground before her, which had been tamped down hard by tens of thousands of dancing bare feet. From the murmuring human ocean emerged Yindi, with the projection that was Old Man walking beside him. They approached the rock. Yindi held forth the turtle to Lilga. She took it, turned it over in her hands, smiling delightedly as if it were the greatest toy ever. Then, solemnly but unable to completely suppress a smile, she handed it back to him.

The shaman crouched and laid the carved malachite turtle on the anvil-rock. Then he picked up a head-sized stone, raised it high and brought it down violently, smashing the Mackenzie Turtle to powder.

"What!" Brigid Baptiste exclaimed, half rising. From behind Rita touched her lightly on the arm. Brigid sat back down, looking troubled and confused.

As Old Man looked on, his smile grave now, Yindi painstakingly scooped the green powder from the top of the rock into a clay bowl with his hand, brushing carefully to transfer as much as possible into the receptacle. The bowl obviously contained some sort of fluid, and into this he stirred the powder from the smashed figurine with what appeared to be a piece of polished bone.

He stood, then, went to Lilga and held the bowl to her.

"My God," Brigid gasped. "Lilga—she's just a little girl!"

"What do you mean?" Grant asked in a low voice.

"She's not—she hasn't been taken over by one of the crew, has she? And this, this will cause her to be possessed, won't it? Her personality will be subsumed into someone else's. She'll die!"

She and Domi looked at each other and then started to stand, reaching for their holstered handblasters.

"Dear Brigid," Lakesh began. The tall redhead ignored him.

"*Please,*" Rita said urgently.

"She knows," Billy said with quiet fervor. "It's been her destiny right along, and it must be, for she bears the genes of the navigators."

There was no way Lilga could have heard any of their words over the vast low susurration of sound, as loud as a great wind yet as soft as the play of water in a fountain. Yet she looked up even as she reached for the bowl, caught Brigid's eye and then Domi's, and Kane's each in turn, and smiled and waved with pure child's joy.

Then she took the bowl in both hands and drank.

Her body convulsed. She flung the bowl away in a spasm that brought her head back and down so far her long locks brushed her heels.

"Damn you, what have you done to her?" Brigid shouted. She was on her feet now, eyes flashing, Domi at her side. They looked ready to take on all quarter million aborigines, or however many were assembled around the two campfires and the stricken little girl.

Lakesh was babbling, trying to calm the women. No one paid him any mind. Kane locked his hand on Brigid's wrist.

"Whatever they did, it's done now," he said firmly. "We can't put that bullet back in the blaster. Nothing can. Do you hear me, Baptiste?"

Grant was similarly restraining Domi from launching unilateral war. Brigid looked at Kane with stricken eyes, then nodded. But she did not sit down.

Down between the campfires Lilga lay thrashing in the dust. Kane felt the skin on his own cheeks tauten until it threatened to split. "I don't like this one damn scrap better than you do, Baptiste," he gritted. "We played ball together, the girl and I."

Lilga stretched out full length on her back, kicked once, lay still. The watching multitude gasped. A thin, lost keening escaped from Domi's throat. Her cheeks ran with tears.

The little girl's body began to glow. It was as if every cell began to emit a gentle golden radiance. She opened her eyes. Then she rose, not through any apparent agency of her muscles, but rather as if she lay on some sort of invisible hinged panel that swung her slowly upright.

Overhead, Kane realized with a shock, the stars had been blotted as black clouds rushed together, seemingly from every point of the compass, to converge above the twin fires. Now they roiled as if about to birth a tornado.

"Do they get twisters down here?" Grant rumbled. "Because if they do, they're fixing to have one."

Instead the girl slowly raised her arms from her sides until they pointed up toward the ominous seethe of darkness. Her body shone so brightly they couldn't look at it. Golden light shot from her, a pillar of light that pierced the heart of the darkness, and dispersed it.

The column of golden light vanished. The glow from the child's body faded until it no longer hurt to look at her.

"I have no idea what I just saw," Grant said as hundreds of thousands of throats released pent-up breaths in unison, "but whatever it was, I have to say it was impressive."

Yindi and Old Man had stepped back from Lilga when she accepted the bowl containing the drink made from the powdered turtle. Now Old Man approached her with deliberation.

He knelt. "You are Uluru-the-Ship," the girl's body said, in the voices of a hundred thousand.

"I am," Old Man said. "Command me."

"You are healed completely?"

"I am, O Navigator."

"Then restore yourself to your original state."

"It shall be done."

She closed her eyes as if in extreme concentration and raised her hands again.

Suddenly Old Man was standing on the promontory beside the onlookers from Cerberus. "It's done," he said in a voice loose with relief. "I am free."

"Uluru-the-Ship?" Lakesh demanded, obviously trying

hard not to sound querulous and failing. "Old Man, whatever did the child mean by that?"

"What she said, of course, Dr. Lakesh. The powdered turtle has awakened the ability coded within Lilga's genes, of the navigators, the most skilled adepts of all the crew. I must apologize for the traumatic side effects as memories and knowledge crashed in upon her. There is, sadly, no gentler way to effect a transformation of such magnitude—and no one else currently incarnated among the people was able to undergo it. Now she has the power to draw and direct energy from the very fabric of space—and to fully awaken, and command, the great vessel that brought our people here millennia ago."

He touched his painted breast and bowed. "Your humble servant."

"You're the *ship?*" Domi asked. "How can you be a ship?"

"I am a sentient computer," Old Man said. "I am the ship's mind and heart."

"But if the ship is…awakening," Kane said, "how come you're standing here conversing so casually with us?"

Old Man shrugged a bare brown shoulder. "It's an autonomous subroutine. Only the navigator can invoke it, and now she's channeling virtual energy—what you might describe as zero-point energy, Dr. Lakesh—into the actual physical vessel to fuel the transformation. It all requires no conscious effort or attention on my part. Ah, this will be young Corumjerri with a message for us."

A young man came running down the spine of the rockthrust with his long hair flopping like tentacles about his shoulders. "Old Man, you asked that we tell you when the ABCs called again, after the Transformation ceremony."

"ABCs?" Kane asked.

"The invaders," the messenger said.

"Lad Corumjerri's mislaid his manners," Billy Handsome said sternly. "It means 'Aboriginal Bum Cleaners.' We used it to get the whites spewing, once upon a time."

"Sorry," Corumjerri said, although his grin indicated he wasn't very.

"How'd they get our frequency?" Kane demanded.

"I gave it to them," Old Man said. "They have done my people—the people whom I have done my poor best to safeguard for 750 centuries—terrible hurt. And I am not without malice. I was built and programmed as a ship of war, as well as peace."

Kane looked around at Grant, who shrugged, Brigid, Domi and Lakesh. Not even the director of Cerberus could find anything to say,

"Come," Old Man said cheerily. "We mustn't keep the god-king waiting."

"SO YOU'RE HOLED UP in the mountains with the rest of the savages, Kane," Vladek's image said from the communicator screen. The comm unit had been set up in a little tent off in the woods near where the rock-knee jutted from the slope. "It's a good place for you. I don't know if your little pals had anything to do with the weird pyrotechnic display over the mountains a few minutes ago, but it's going to take more than that bullshit to keep us from hunting you down like mad animals and exterminating you. Especially once we get hold of Uluru's secrets."

The Cobaltville Magistrate was outdoors, with the starry sky for a backdrop and the dark mass of Uluru itself vaguely visible over his right shoulder. Past his left shoulder could be seen the god-king, sitting on a very ordinary camp stool looking on with his usual expression of frosty disdain.

"Why aren't they calling from the tent?" Grant asked quietly out of the side of his mouth.

"Probably doesn't smell too good right now," Domi said with a snicker.

"Ah," Old Man said, addressing the screen and Vladek, "the secret of Uluru. You and the god-king—all of your expeditionary force, in fact—are about to experience the ultimate secret of Uluru firsthand, rather before you anticipated."

Vladek's single brow compressed, like a caterpillar in motion. "Who's this old fuck in the war paint?"

Behind him, Uluru began to glow, as Lilga's body had.

"It's the ship," Kane burst out. "Uluru-the-Ship. They meant it. It *is* the damn ship."

"Impossible," Brigid said. "Uluru is a single huge boulder, a solid object. It has caves and passageways inside it—I was in them—but nothing that could possibly constitute the living quarters of a ship, much less propulsion or life support."

"It is the ship," Old Man said, beaming. "Not just a spaceship, but a dimensional ship. And it is also…me."

"What the fuck are you people raving about?" Vladek was demanding. The god-king had risen and approached a few steps toward the unit.

"Why are you telling the enemy all this stuff, Old Man?" Kane demanded.

"Because he is dead," Old Man said.

The great boulder was glowing more brightly. Behind Vladek and the god-king Kane could see motion as the invaders' encampment stirred awake, heard querulous voices raised, turning to surprise, awe—and fear.

"Under the guidance of the navigator's will, my friends," Old Man said, "what you perceive as Uluru-the-Rock is itself beginning to change. The molecular bonds within are shifting, breaking. Its crystalline-lattice structure alters, forming its interior back into the passages and compartments that once held our fugitive race, into life-support systems, propulsion—weapons."

"And the radiance is caused by—" Lakesh began excitedly.

Old Man bulldozed over him. "The simultaneous breaking of quadrillions of molecular bonds. It releases energy. Lots of it. Specifically high-frequency radiation—invisible emanations from X rays roaring up through gamma."

The god-king's face was floating beside Vladek now like a strange moon, its perfection marred by something akin to fear. "What is the creature saying?" he fluted. "What is happening? Vladek, I demand answers this instant!"

"Lethal radiation," Grant said.

Old Man smiled. "Enormous quantities."

Unlike Lilga during her transfiguration, Uluru was shifting wavelength visibly, getting whiter as it brightened. Already Vladek and the Dewa Raja seemed to be standing in the day's full light.

"What's happening," Kane said, "is that you're fucked, Vladek. You, that freak next to you, your whole gang of stonehearts. And to prove I'm a bad winner, I just wanted to mention before you die that I always thought your face looked like something tattooed on the end of a blunt dick."

In the background Uluru now blazed unbearably white. A horrified look came over Vladek's face. He and the god-king half turned toward the rock.

Their faces softened like wax, began to melt. They seemed to turn insubstantial—

The screen went black.

Into the sudden silence, Old Man said, "An annular pulse of extremely hard radiation has destroyed the sending set, my friends. It has radiated out from Uluru itself—which is to say, from me, from my substance—and instantly killed every living thing within a twenty-mile radius."

Kane swallowed. "What about us?"

"Distance and the mountains' mass protect you. Recall your inverse-square law. And now, it is done. The war is over. The evil ones are destroyed."

Kane stood at the blank screen and felt relief wash over him. There would be more battles—the barons were relentless—but for the moment the Cerberus exiles had prevailed.

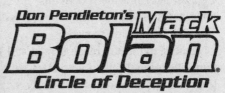

TAKE 'EM FREE

2 action-packed novels plus a mystery bonus

NO RISK

NO OBLIGATION TO BUY